Flowers for Her Grave

Books by Judy Clemens

The Stella Crown Series
Till the Cows Come Home
Three Can Keep a Secret
To Thine Own Self Be True
The Day Will Come
Different Paths

The Grim Reaper Series
Embrace the Grim Reaper
The Grim Reaper's Dance
Flowers for Her Grave

Flowers for Her Grave

A Grim Reaper Mystery

Judy Clemens

Poisoned Pen Press

Poisoned
Pen
Press

Copyright © 2011 by Judy Clemens

First Edition 2011

10 9 8 7 6 5 4 3 2 1

Library of Congress Catalog Card Number: 2011920315

ISBN: 9781590589182   Hardcover
      9781590589205   Trade Paperback

Poisoned Pen Press
6962 E. First Ave., Ste. 103
Scottsdale, AZ 85251
www.poisonedpenpress.com
info@poisonedpenpress.com

Printed in the United States of America

For my pal
Jennifer L. Baumgartner

Because it's never too late to find
someone who really "gets you"

Acknowledgments

Thanks once again to those people who help make Casey and her world come alive:

Master Doug Custer and Jennifer L. Baumgartner, for teaching me everything I know about hapkido and the martial arts.

My cousin Jean-Paul Clemens, for help with the Spanish. Hope I got it right.

Barbara Peters, my editor, for her invaluable eye and feel for plot. This book would be very different without her patient and constructive criticism.

The rest of the staff at Poisoned Pen Press, who make the entire production process a joy.

The (late) Stately Raven Bookstore and its staff for offering me a welcoming home while you could. I am going to miss you more than I can say.

And, of course, my nearest and dearest, for providing an atmosphere of encouragement and affirmation in which I can write—Steve, Tristan, Sophia, and my mom, Nancy. You're the best.

Chapter One

"Sixty-three bottles of beer on the wall, sixty-three bottles of beeeecr…"

Casey pushed her hands over her ears. "I can't take it. I can't. Not one more minute. I swear, I'm going to kill him. Or kill myself."

Death sighed. "More work for me. No one *ever* considers how these things are going to affect *me*."

"*Sixty-two bottles of beer on the wall…*"

Casey groaned. "Take me, L'Ankou. I'm begging you."

"Quite an offer. Better than the one he's giving me. Can't say *anyone* would want to pass a bottle around with *him*."

The man in question was drunk, obviously, and hadn't had a shower in days, if not weeks. His clothes were a conglomeration of things he'd scavenged, and his beard was a filthy rat's nest of graying hair and dried grass and who knew what else. The odor of alcohol, stale smoke, and B.O. filled the boxcar, where Casey had taken refuge during the night. It was getting on toward noon of the following day, and the sun had heated the car to an almost unbearable temperature. Casey didn't know where the train had traveled during the last several hours, but she didn't care. When it stopped, she was getting off.

Death peered out through a crack in the car. "Where do you think we are?"

"No idea."

"Yeah, me neither. Hang on a minute." Death was suddenly gone.

Casey rolled onto her side, turning her back to the drunk. The floor of the empty boxcar was so hard, she felt like she was one big bruise. At least the rhythm of the wheels on the tracks was steady—better than a bumpy ride in the back of a truck.

"You'll never guess." Death was back.

Casey grunted.

"No guess? How 'bout if I hummed a little Carrie Underwood? Or that guy who sings about checking for ticks?"

Casey didn't move.

"Okay, if you give up. We're almost in Nashville. We should be stopping within minutes."

So. The heart of country. Casey felt a pang in her own heart. Her late husband Reuben, Mexican immigrant that he was, had somehow formed a love of the genre, and had practically insisted they visit the city on their honeymoon. Thank God she'd been able to talk him out of it. The last thing she'd wanted to do their first week of married life was visit Dollyworld. They'd gone later, of course, but for their honeymoon she'd wanted somewhere quiet, where she didn't have to wear a cowboy hat or see Reuben modeling an oversized belt buckle.

She sat up, stretching, trying to ease the kinks from her muscles. The bum on the other side of the car had fizzled out somewhere in the fifty bottle range, and lay on his back, snoring loudly. He'd be going farther than Nashville.

The train whistle drifted through the air. So they were arriving in the city, or the suburbs, anyway. Intersections. She made sure she had all of her possessions and hadn't left any trash behind. Her quick exit from Kansas had been accompanied by gifts from her friend Bailey, a teenager who'd seen Casey at her worst, beaten and battered. She'd helped Casey escape from the hospital, and had offered a duffel bag of necessities: clothes, shampoo, washcloth and towel, even a pre-paid phone. Added to that was the make-up Casey had used a few days earlier. If she could just find a bathroom she might actually be able to make herself presentable. The bruises and cuts on her face could use a good, thick layer of cover-up.

She thought about the final article in the bag—a card signed by all of the kids, all of her new young friends from Kansas, telling her to *Get well soon!* With lots of hearts and exclamation points. Bailey had told her to wait to open the bag until she was "on the road." Probably because she was afraid one or both of them would start bawling. Casey was tired enough now she felt tears pricking her eyes, so she concentrated on making them disappear.

The train let out a long whistle blast, and the boxcar shuddered and slowed. Within minutes they came to a complete stop. Casey slid the door open and took a deep breath of fresh air.

"*Eww*," Death said. "Nothing like the smell of smoke and oil."

"Better than what's in here." Casey took one last look at her sleeping companion and jumped down from the car, wincing as her sore body jarred against the ground. "Let's get going before someone sees us. Or we die of B.O. inhalation."

Wending her way through the train yard, Casey peered around boxcars and engines, wanting to avoid confrontations with anyone who would question her presence. At one point she couldn't help but pass two men unloading boxes, but they didn't give her a second glance, so intent were they on finishing their job. Casey kept moving, and soon stood on the sidewalk in front the station. People crowded everywhere, rushing to make a train, carrying packages, headed out into the city.

"We did it," Death said. "Now, how 'bout a show? I wouldn't mind a little *twang*."

"Forget the music. How 'bout a *shower?*"

Death sniffed. "Yeah, that tramp on the train isn't the only one who's smelling a little ripe."

Casey slung her bag over her shoulder and began to walk. As during her earlier visit with Reuben, she was surprised at what she saw in Nashville. Most of her pre-conceptions had been wrong. Sure, there were people wearing shirts with leather fringes, and pointy cowboy boots, and she spied a restaurant called the Wildhorse Saloon, but mostly it was the same as any other city. Chain restaurants like Ruby Tuesday and The Melting Pot you come to expect anywhere, just like the hotels—Drury Inn, Doubletree, and the lot.

"How 'bout that one?" Death pointed out a Sheraton just down the road. "Looks nice."

"Too nice for present company," Casey said. "Can't see me showing up in the lobby looking like this without the nicely-groomed desk clerk getting a little too curious."

"Then we keep walking?"

"You got it."

Death let out a sigh and trailed behind her. "You're never any fun. Walk, hitch a ride, beat up a bad guy…can't we do anything normal people do?"

"You're not a person. And you're certainly not normal."

"Right. I keep forgetting that."

They walked in silence for a few minutes, and Casey's headache began to dissipate. Until Death started to whistle. And then hum. And then sing right out loud.

Casey stopped dead on the sidewalk, causing Death to stumble through her. She shivered.

"Don't you *dare* blame me for that," Death said. "You're the one who changed course."

"But you're the one who's annoying. Can you not shut up for one second?"

"I'm trying to enter into the spirit of the town."

"Well, don't."

Casey began walking again, and when she looked around, Death was gone. Thank God.

The hustle of the city's streets slowed as Casey passed into the outskirts of town. An empty building here. A vacant, weedy lot there. Groups of people huddled on sidewalks, or in front of shady mini-marts. Finally, she spotted a motel that looked about like her own condition. The Rest E-Z. A one-story building, each room with an external door and parking spot. The sign promised cable and an outdoor pool. Too bad the pool was covered with algae, and had ducks swimming in it.

Casey sat on a bench across the street and pulled out the cell phone Bailey had given her. She centered herself, focusing on relaxing her neck and shoulders, then called her lawyer's private line.

"Don Westbrook."

"Hello, Don."

He gave a quick intake of breath. "Oh, thank God. You're all right."

"This line clean?"

"Of course. Where have you been?"

"Around."

"I know one little town in Ohio where you've been spending some time. You do realize you're wanted by the police?"

"Yes."

Don was silent.

"I didn't mean to do it, Don." To kill the slimy mobster who had attacked her a week earlier in Ohio, she meant, but she didn't want to put it into words, in case the line wasn't as clean as Don thought. "It was an accident."

"I'm sure it was. But are you positive your present course of action is the correct one?"

She let out a sharp laugh. "Are you kidding? What in my life has happened the *correct* way?"

"Casey—"

"I need money, Don."

He exhaled so heavily she could almost feel the breeze. "You know I can't send you money. I'd be aiding and abetting a fugitive. I could get disbarred."

Casey rubbed her forehead. "Then what am I supposed to do?"

"Come home."

"Where the police would find me and send me away? I don't think so." She sagged against the bench. It had been a mistake to call. "Good-bye, Don. I'm sorry."

"Wait! Just wait. Listen. I have some things that belong to you."

"What things?"

"Things you left behind about a week or so ago. They were hidden in a garage, among the rakes and shovels and pink bicycles."

It hit her so hard she gasped. "My backpack?"

"With everything in it. Your wedding rings, your clothes—not that *they're* worth anything—your *Dobak*—"

"Omar's hat?" She pressed the receiver against her ear. "You have my baby's hat?"

"It's here. Nice young man named Eric showed up at Ricky's house the other day, claiming to be a friend of yours."

Eric. Sadness washed over Casey. "He is…was…he's from Ohio."

"So he said. Told Ricky all about it. Backs up your story of the mobster, by the way."

He would. He'd been there when she'd stabbed the thug and watched him bleed to death on the street.

"Ricky brought the bag to me," Don said. "And made me promise I'd get it to you. He also wants me to tell him where you are when you contact me."

"Please, Don," Casey whispered. "Please send me my things."

He was quiet for so long she thought he'd hung up.

"Okay, I'll arrange it. Where should I send them?"

She almost sobbed with relief. "Do you remember where Reuben wanted to go on our honeymoon? Before I convinced him otherwise?"

He hesitated, then gave a little chuckle. "Yes."

"There's a cheap hotel on the edge of town. The Rest E-Z. Send it there under the name of my maid of honor."

"I don't…oh, right. The girl with the freckles on her shoulders. She was a cutie. Ricky tried his best with her, didn't he, poor schmuck? Someday he'll find the right girl. So are you staying at this hotel?"

"I will be once you call and tell them your wife is coming, who got mugged at the train station and lost her ID and everything else she owns. They'll need a credit card number or something."

He went quiet again.

"*Please*, Don. I know I'm asking a lot, but I need…I need…" She choked up, unable to speak.

"Okay. Okay, Casey. It's all right. Don't cry."

Casey sniffled. "I'm sorry. It's just, I haven't slept in a bed for a week. I'm tired, I'm dirty. I'm just so…so tired."

"I'll work it out, okay? I'll make the call and you can be in the motel within minutes. All right?"

She took a deep, shuddering breath. "All right."

"I'll overnight your pack to you. You'll have it by tomorrow."

"Thank you, Don. Thank you so much. I don't know what I'd do without you."

"I know. I wish…when you're ready to come home, I'll be here. We'll take care of things. You do realize the longer you wait to show your face, the deeper you're in trouble with the law? And with this young man Eric you have a witness on your side?"

"I'm sorry. I don't mean to make things hard for you."

"I know you don't."

Didn't mean she wasn't doing it, anyway.

"Casey, about Pegasus…"

Not them. Pegasus. The car company responsible for her husband and baby's deaths. Their faulty product had ended Casey's life as she knew it, in a huge fireball of pain and heartache. "Don, I know they want to find me So, me staying lost is better for everybody."

"I got a call from them a few days ago."

Casey waited, breathing through her mouth.

"They aren't looking for you anymore. They're letting it go."

Not possible. "But that other car accident. The more recent one. Aren't they worried about that?" While in Ohio, Casey had discovered evidence of a second crash, in which a man lost his life. Another death Pegasus wouldn't claim as their own.

"They are worried," Don said. "Petrified. But they won't be able to get out of it this time. There's no doubt it was because of the car itself. They've got bigger problems than you now, honey."

A huge weight lifted from Casey's shoulders. "I don't have to hide from them anymore? The man with the face and the woman with the hair? Or Dottie Spears?" The CEO, who had made Casey's life hell for months, at first acting like her friend, and then as her enemy. Casey had hated her like she'd never hated anyone before.

"No more hiding from Pegasus, Casey. You're free of them."

Free. "Now it's just the cops, who want me for murder."

"Casey, sweetheart, if you'd just come home, we'd work it out. We have this Eric guy's testimony, as well as yours. Please—"

"Don."

"Yes, Casey?" She could hear the resignation in his voice.

"Tell Ricky and my mom I love them, okay?"

"I'll tell them."

"But don't tell them where I am. I can't...I can't see them yet."

Casey hung up the phone and rested her forehead on her hand. Free of Pegasus. She couldn't believe it. Now, if only she were free from the law, which technically was a lot more dangerous as far as her real freedom went.

"Come on, hon. Let's get you over to the hotel." Death was suddenly so close beside her on the bench Casey felt chilled to the bone.

She shivered. "Don's calling the motel."

"Well, come on, then. By the time we get over there they should have talked to him."

Casey slung Bailey's bag over her shoulder and trudged toward the Rest E-Z.

Death paused on the sidewalk in front of the door that said, "Office." "Not the nicest establishment we've ever stayed in. I hope there aren't fleas."

"It's a little skanky, I know. But a *bed*, L'Ankou. I hardly remember what one feels like."

The lobby was tiny and worn, but mostly clean, with a clerk to match. The little man behind the counter was of an indeterminate age. His wrinkles and missing teeth made Casey's guess lean toward the older end of the scale, but the twinkle in his eye belied the rest of his body. He wore a checked cotton shirt, and a nametag made with a Labelmaker. *Hi! Please call me Claude.*

"Kimberly Tifton," Casey said. "My husband was going to call and—"

"Just got off the phone with him," Claude said. "Sorry to hear about your troubles. You okay? Should I call the police?" He examined her face and its multiple abrasions and swelling, leftovers from her time in Kansas.

"Please don't. It's already taken care of, and I'm fine. I just need some sleep."

"Sure thing. We'll get you right set up in a room." With friendly efficiency, Claude checked her in and handed her an electronic key. "Out the front door and to the right, missus. There's an ice machine at the end of the row, if you want some for…you know." He gestured at her face.

"Did my husband tell you about my bags?"

"Said they should be delivered tomorrow morning. We'll give you a buzz as soon as they're here."

"Thank you."

"Glad to help out. You get some rest now."

Casey found the room with no problem. Again, small but clean. She set Bailey's bag on the little table, kicked off her shoes, and fell across the bed.

She was asleep before Death could ask her to turn on the TV.

Chapter Two

The phone woke Casey at nine-twenty-five the next morning. Casey had somehow managed to sleep all afternoon *and* all night. "Mrs. Tifton? This is Maude at the front desk."

Maude? Really? The motel was run by Claude and Maude?

"I have a package for you."

Casey sat up. "I'll be right there."

Hi! Please call me Maude was the female version of the night clerk. Small and ageless. Only this half of the pair smelled of smoke and didn't have the same twinkle in her eye as she examined Casey from head to toe, squinting at her beat-up face. "You Kimberly Tifton?"

"That's me."

"Then I guess this is yours." She kicked at something on the floor, making no move to pick it up.

Casey rounded the desk, and her heart lightened at the sight of the large box. "It is. Thank you."

"Strange shaped luggage for a woman to be carrying." Maude pushed out her lips, her arms crossed.

Casey didn't feel like explaining. She picked up the box, trying not to appear overly enthusiastic.

Maude tipped her head toward the other end of the room. "Breakfast is only out five more minutes. Better grab it if you want any."

Food. Casey's stomach growled in response, and she carried her package to the meager selection of pastries and canned orange juice. She hesitated. Inside the box should be some money. And with that money she could go somewhere and buy a *real* breakfast. Much more appealing than dried out danishes and overly-ripe bananas.

With a last nod at Maude, Casey lugged her box back to her room, where she set it on the bed and gazed at it. Her things. *Her* things. Stifling a cry, she ripped open the tape, not sparing the cardboard. Her heart gave an extra beat at the sight of her bag's familiar canvas. She yanked down the zipper, plunging her hands into the depths of the pack, toward the pocket holding her treasures. Carefully, hands shaking, she pulled the items out and released them from their wrappings. Holding Omar's hat to her face, she took a deep whiff. She didn't know what she'd expected. Even back in Ohio it hadn't smelled like baby shampoo. After all it had been through the past couple of weeks it smelled even more like the backpack itself. But it was still soft.

She set it down and picked up the other little bundle. Jewelry. Reuben's wedding ring, and the necklace he'd given her so long ago. She ran her finger along the curve of the gold band and imagined it on her husband's finger. But that just made her think of what his finger had looked like after the accident, like nothing she'd ever seen before, or wanted to see again. Unfortunately, that image of his charred body was still the one that came first, like a black shadow over the man he had been.

Hastily, she wrapped the items back up and set them to the side. She closed her eyes, trying to even out her breathing. They were just *things*. Things she'd done without for the past week. Things she was so glad to have back.

"Still no shower?" Death leaned against the pillows, legs outstretched on the bed's cover, and wore a Labelmaker nametag just like Maude and Claude's that said, *Hi! Please call me the Fourth Horseman of the Apocalypse.* "Oh. You got distracted. Anything good in there that your brother or that nice lawyer sent along? Or your friend Eric?"

Casey hadn't thought about that—the fact that Ricky had probably looked through the bag. That Eric *certainly* had, because he'd known exactly where to take it. Casey went hot at the memory of what had almost happened between the two of them, scared and passionate, in the depths of the old theater. There had been some hard kissing, and clothes flying, before Reuben's ghost had interrupted them. She pushed the image away, turning her attention back to the contents of the bag.

"So what's there?" Death would've been digging through the bag that second, if it were a possibility. As it was, Death just had to wait.

A little more tentatively now, Casey began taking things out. Her jeans, shirts, underwear, socks…all freshly laundered. Had Ricky done that? Or Eric? She put her *Dobak* aside, and laid her hand on it.

"Oh, no," Death said. "Does that mean it will be even longer until you bathe?"

She smiled. "No point in taking a shower and then getting all sweaty."

Death's nose wrinkled. "You and your workouts. Like missing a few days is going to send you back to fat land."

"Not fat land. Just to a place where I'm not so fit. I do need to keep up my strength, you know."

"For all of those bad guys we keep coming across. How about this for an idea? We move in nicer circles, and avoid fistfights and nasty people? Ever thought of that?"

Casey continued through the bag, taking out her bathroom supplies—some of them brand new, thanks to Ricky, probably—a couple paperback novels, and her wallet. She flipped it open, studying her face in the driver's license. So much had happened since that photo had been taken. The print still said Casey Kaufmann, her name before she'd become a Maldonado, and her address was from the house where she'd grown up. The house where Ricky still lived. She and Reuben hadn't been married long enough that her license renewal had come up, so the ID served as a reminder of what had come before. In the picture she looked happy, healthy, and completely unaware of the tragedy her life would hold.

She riffled through the cash pocket of the wallet. Lots of money there. More of it than she'd had before, which most likely meant Don had gone against his better judgment and added what he could. He'd thrust himself into the "aiding and abetting" category by sending her bag—he probably figured he might as well send the money, too. Someday she'd thank him for all of the risks he'd taken.

At the bottom of the bag, Casey found a folder. It hadn't been there before. She took it out and looked at the plain manila cardstock.

"Anything good?" Death asked.

Casey opened it. On top of the stack of papers was a letter, in Ricky's handwriting. She set it aside, waiting to read it until she'd seen what else was there. Underneath the stationary lay a photo. In it, she and Reuben smiled into the camera, a newborn Omar between them on the hospital bed. She looked sweaty and pale and exhausted…and happy. Reuben's dark hair was mussed, and bags underscored his eyes, but again there was unmasked joy. Omar, as usual during those first days, was asleep, his entire face scrunched, as if he'd had to close it all down in order to get any rest.

"Ah, photos," Death said. "Haven't I always told you to carry some with you?"

Casey turned the picture face down and looked at the next one. There she was, with Ricky and her mother, the summer before the accident. Casey was giving Ricky a noogie, her arm around his throat and her knuckle rubbing his head. His face was scrunched up—just like Omar's—and he was laughing. Their mother sat on a lawn chair to the side, her hand over her mouth, her eyes dancing. Reuben had taken the picture one Sunday afternoon when they'd all had dinner together.

That photo, also, got flipped over.

"That's it?" Death said, for after that photo there were just papers. "Great. More boring stuff, just like you."

"I never said you had to stay."

"How about turning on the TV? Maybe that wrestling channel, if they have it."

Casey pretended not to hear, and looked through the papers. Don had sent her all the information she could possibly need about where her money was stored. Banks, stocks, mutual funds…

Death gave a sharp clap. "Are we rich?"

"*I* am."

"Thank God. Maybe now we can stay somewhere with a little *class*."

Casey picked up the letter from Ricky, and tried to ignore the tears that welled in her eyes. How long since she'd seen him? How long since she'd even heard his voice? A little over a week ago, when she was back in Ohio and she'd talked to him on the phone. It felt like much longer. He'd begged her to come home. To take her house off the market. To get her life back.

Impossible, now, even if she didn't have to worry about Pegasus tracking her down to silence her. Now she was a fugitive. Wanted by the law. A killer.

Dear Sis, the letter said. *Here's your stuff. Interesting how it came to me. I'd like to hear that story some time, about you and this guy Eric. From the way he talked about you, I don't think he views you as just a friend.*

How could he? Besides their moment of passion, he'd seen her kill a man, and together they'd witnessed another violent death. Those kinds of things tended to be bonding experiences. So however Eric viewed her, it was definitely not as a friend. Not anymore.

So here's your stuff. I hope Don can get it to you. I'm sure you miss it. I washed everything, so at least that should save you one trip to the Laundromat, wherever you are. You know, your own washer and dryer are sitting in your house, waiting to be used. As are your stove, and your fridge, and your stereo.

Casey noticed he didn't mention her bed. He would know she wouldn't ever want to use that again. Not without Reuben.

I'm trying to keep up with your lawn, but the flowerbeds are getting so overgrown I'm afraid of what I might find in there. Mowing two yards and keeping the weeds away from both could be a full-time thing, if I let it, which I can't, since I do have an actual job, you know. Your house still hasn't sold. Not that you'll see me crying over that, even if I am whining about the landscaping.

If it were up to Ricky, he'd take the house off the market altogether, and wait for her to come home. She kept telling him that wasn't going to happen. And he kept ignoring her.

Mom misses you. I miss you.

Oh, God, she missed them, too.

She rubbed her eyes. Maybe Don was right. Maybe she *should* go home. Give herself up. Tell the truth. Hope the word of Eric, added to her own, would keep her out of jail. Get her life back on track.

Not that *that* was possible. Her life had been knocked far, far off track, and she couldn't ever see it going straight again. If she did head home, even with Eric's testimony, she'd be lucky if she were out on parole in fifteen years.

Casey glanced at the clock. Almost ten. Check-out was at eleven. Hardly time to get in a workout *and* a shower. She pulled the chair out from the little table and sank into it, considering her options. She couldn't stay at the Rest E-Z. Don knew where she was. Not that she expected him to send the cavalry after her, or even come himself, but it wasn't fair to him to have to hide what he knew. She needed to go somewhere else, far away, so he could honestly claim ignorance. The problem was, she couldn't use her own ID to get a decent hotel room, or the cops would find her.

With a regretful glance at her *Dobak*, Casey picked out some clean clothes and headed for the shower.

Chapter Three

"You have *got* to be kidding me," Death said. "Is this the step up I've been requesting?"

The Drive-In Motel sagged along the road in northern Georgia. Casey had hitched a ride just that far, and found this grungy hotel with no problem. "A step up would ask for ID. You know that."

"A step up would also have a room you don't have to rent by the hour."

"Try to be patient. We'll be out of here soon."

She didn't like the motel any better than Death, but it was a necessity. Where else could she crash for a few days and not leave a paper trail? She left her bag, zipped tightly shut, on the room's spindly table, and pocketed the key.

"Where are you going now?" Death was right on her heels.

"To start the process to get us out of here."

Death was so eager to leave the room Casey had to step out of the way to avoid being walked through. She didn't need that chill, even though it had to be in the nineties and the room's AC was anything but efficient.

A Holiday Inn took up a corner lot a mile from the Drive-In, and Casey walked in the front door. She smiled at the desk clerk, and continued through the hallway toward the back, to the outdoor pool. The swelling in her face had gone down over the past twenty-four hours, so the sight of her wasn't an automatic shock. No one raced after her, asking if she'd been mugged. She waited by the pool's inside door for almost twenty minutes until someone came in from the outside, and she went through with a, "Hi, how's it going?"

There was an empty chair under one of the trees surrounding the water, so she took a seat and pulled out the paperback she'd brought along. This pool, as opposed to the one in Nashville, had sparkling blue water and no ducks.

"What are we *doing*?" Death asked, sinking onto another chair.

"Waiting long enough the desk clerk forgets me coming in. Then, when it seems an adequate time I could have spent in my room, I will go back over and use the computer they have for guests."

Death nodded. "Sneaky."

"That's my middle name."

After a half hour of sweating and pretending to read, Casey went back to the hotel lobby. The computer was not in use. She exchanged nods with the desk clerk, sat down, and typed "buy fake ID on-line."

The search came back with over two hundred million results. She clicked the very first one. Buyfakeidonline.com. The web site offered several "Qualified and Reliable" sources, as well as some red flags to be aware of.

Like anyone buying a fake ID wasn't a red flag on her own.

Casey clicked on one of the "reliable" sites and was shown the list of states they would be able to give her. She checked for the scam clues the other site had given her, and saw good signs: they weren't promising to have it ready in a day (apparently there was no way to make a good one in that amount of time); they accepted cashier's checks ("please don't write 'fake ID' in the subject line!"); and they had an actual physical address to use for sending the order, rather than just a P.O. box.

Because of Casey's situation, she couldn't exactly print out the order form on the desk clerk's machine, so she copied all of the necessary information onto the back of a hotel brochure. The money would have been prohibitive for a lot of people, but she had more cash than she knew what to do with, and it was worth it to start a new life.

She clicked out of all of her search windows, cleared the cache, and walked back through the hotel to an exit out of sight of the desk clerk. From there, she went to the Rite Aid, where they took passport photos. Fifteen minutes later she was on her way back to the Drive-In Motel with a mug shot. Not the most attractive picture she'd ever taken, but it would do.

Back in her lovely room, she tore a sheet with one blank side from the outdated phone book in the nightstand and made her own order form, filling in a new name, the address of the Drive-In, and the request for Express Service, which was to take only five days. She had registered at the hotel under the name Molly Meade, and made certain the package would come addressed to that name. She didn't need the icky desk clerk knowing her new identity.

"Daisy Gray?" Death snickered, peering over her shoulder at the order form.

"It's a lesson I learned from John D. MacDonald."

"The author?"

"He said when you pretend to have a different name you should make it sound as much like your real name as possible, so when people call you by the new name you react naturally to it."

"I get it. Casey. Daisy. I guess they're a lot the same, although the 's' sound is different, isn't it? *Casey* has the hissing sound, while *Daisy* sounds more like a z, which could be confusing—"

"L'Ankou?"

"Yes?"

"Shut up."

"Okay, so they're pretty close. I see that. But Gray?"

"It doesn't matter how that sounds. People won't call me by that. Besides, I hardly know what my real last name is anymore."

"At least this is better than Smith or Jones."

"At least."

She finished up the order form and got her wallet.

"Now what?"

"Now I go get a money order and mail it. We should just be able to get to the post office before it closes."

"And then we wait."

"Yes."

"Here? At the Drive-In?"

"That's right. You don't like it, you can *go away*."

Death frowned. "Are you doing this to get rid of me?"

"Think what you like."

Death disappeared in a blue fog, leaving Casey alone to run her errands, which was a nice change. She got the order sent off, ate a large, delicious dinner at a local diner, and went back to her room, where she took a nap. When she woke up she worked out, performing one of her hapkido *kata*, and took a long shower, which wasn't necessarily as hot as she would have liked, but at least got her clean.

Interspersed between these various activities, she looked at the cell phone Bailey had given her. She longed to call someone—anyone—to hear a friendly voice. Her brother, her lawyer, Bailey herself. Eric. Finally, she took the phone and shoved it deep in her bag, where it wasn't a constant temptation. She couldn't afford to get found. Not now. Not before she had her new papers.

Casey's stomach soon began protesting her big dinner, unused to having such rich food. That night was a long one, with cramps and other symptoms of system overload. The only bright spot was that Death wasn't there to gloat.

By morning, Casey had sworn off rich food forever, and roused herself with a double workout. She barely made it through, but felt much better afterward. That was the beginning of a long several days, during which Casey just tried to keep herself occupied.

The first day, she bought her own cleaning supplies and scrubbed the room from top to bottom. She pulled the mattress and box springs apart and doused them with Lysol, leaving them to dry for several hours. Once the bed was ready, she put on a new mattress pad, new sheets, and a new blanket, leaving the others in a heap outside her door. The pillows, such as they were, went out with the sheets, and she replaced them with two new ones. She covered the carpet with shake-on sanitizer and swiped one of the vacuums and a brand new sweeper bag from the "Maintenance Closet"—not that she ever saw anybody *maintaining* anything. She moved the furniture to sweep every square inch. She purchased her own set of towels, and sent the old ones out with the rest of the linens, hopefully to be burned. For the rest of her stay she left the "Do Not Disturb" sign on the doorknob, and on the inside, she installed a brand new slide lock, which kept her feeling marginally safer.

After that, she had to find other things to do.

She did her laundry twice in the crappy Laundromat down the street. It was a novelty to have to guard her clothes while they were in the dryer.

She bought food at the closest Whole Foods store—many blocks away—and found delis for lunch where she could get soup, or sandwiches on whole wheat bread.

She worked out twice a day, once performing differing *kata*, once doing the more routine sit-ups and push-ups.

She studied her face in the mirror, amazed at how fast faces heal when one has a regular diet and enough sleep.

And she watched lots and lots of bad TV. Since the motel had no cable—their usual tenants not requiring the additional entertainment—she was stuck with whatever the networks were offering. Death always joined her for the evenings, getting a kick out of the various reality shows and offering advice to both the Big Losers and the nannies. The most memorable moment was when Death hovered inches from the screen, yelling at the mother of an out-of-control five-year-old that she should "shut the bugger up in the closet for a day with no food or water and see how he liked *that*." Somehow Casey didn't think Death would make the greatest parent.

It was a very long week later that Casey's query at the front desk brought a positive response.

"Oh, yeah," the icky clerk said, sucking on her cigarette. "Package came for you yesterday, *Miss Meade*." She said the name with a sneer.

"*Yesterday?*"

"I hid it under the counter so no one would take it. Guess I forgot about it." She inhaled again, her cheeks caving and her eyes regarding Casey with smug satisfaction.

"Thank you for taking care of it so well." Casey wanted to knock the woman out with a quick punch to the nose, but she restrained herself.

It didn't look like the old hag had tampered with the envelope, but Casey gave it a good once-over, to be sure. The seal seemed unbroken, and the postmark was the right one, so Casey would have to believe the best. The woman's eyes flicked from Casey's face to the package, and Casey could see the desire there. She wanted desperately to know what was in there. She'd probably studied it up and down to find ways to open it without Casey knowing.

She'd have to live with the disappointment.

Casey gave her a bright smile and took the plain brown package back to her room.

Daisy Gray had a Florida driver's license with a Tallahassee address, a motorcycle endorsement, and a birth date thirty-two years earlier. She had dark hair—still dyed from Casey's time in Kansas—and brown eyes. The heavily layered make-up made Casey's messed-up face from a week ago look surprisingly normal. The license would expire in two years.

Casey took a deep breath, closing her eyes. This driver's license was the beginning of a new life. When the cops came looking for Casey Kaufmann Maldonado or Smith or Jones they would find only air. Casey was about to disappear.

"So, can we finally blow this repulsive joint?" Death said, standing in the middle of the room, not touching anything. "Although I have to say you did at least make it livable."

Casey packed her bags, leaving the cleaning supplies, the new linens, and the extra lock she was sure the motel's usual clientele would appreciate. "Let's go. And let's never think about this place again." She smiled, and for the first time in months, she meant it.

Chapter Four

Florida was hot. Hot and muggy and miserable.

"Why did we come here again?" Death waved a fan made of feathers, which did nothing but move the sultry air from one place to another.

"I've always wanted to live in Florida."

"Why? It's hotter than hell down here."

Casey laughed, and Death preened at her response to the semi-witty joke.

"I'll find someplace nice," Casey said. "With air-conditioning."

"Well, thank goodness for that. Where are we, anyway?"

"Tallahassee."

Casey and Death had walked away from the rental car shop and headed into town. "I need a newspaper. Or a library." Casey brightened. "I can use a library again. Ms. Daisy Gray, library patron."

Death made a face. "Do I have to call you Daisy?"

"Only around people who can see you."

"And how are we supposed to know who they are?"

"How do you think? They'll look at you. People who can't see you look only at me, remember?"

Casey had discovered a couple weeks earlier that only those who aren't afraid of death could see the physical embodiment of it. Those who were afraid—and those people far outweighed their opposite—had no idea Death was anywhere in the vicinity.

So far those who had the ability to see Casey's companion had been limited to very young children, a man with Down's Syndrome, a deeply religious woman, and a woman who had lost her husband in a tragic accident. Sort of like Casey.

Casey glared at Death.

"What? Why look at me like that?"

"We've met other people who see you. Why can't you go bother them for a while?"

"I've told you. You're far more interesting than anyone else I've come across."

"I have a hard time believing that. What about Queen Elizabeth? John Dillinger? *Jesus?*"

Death winced and looked around like someone might hear. "Now don't go joking about *him.*"

"Fine. But there have to be others who would be more interesting, like…" She thought. "Like William Shakespeare?"

"Okay. Fine. You're more interesting than anyone I've come across in the *last two hundred years*. That make you feel better?"

"Tons." Casey stopped at a drug store and asked for directions to the library. It would be another two miles of walking. No matter. She could use the exercise.

Death, however, moaned and groaned about the extra work, asking why they couldn't just take a taxi. It wasn't like they didn't have the money.

"Look." Casey was trying to keep her temper in check. "If you don't want to walk, it's pretty simple. Don't do it. Fly, or float, or just transport yourself, whatever you people do. Or even better—go harass someone else."

"*You people*? Is that a racist remark? Should I be offended?"

Casey shook her head and walked faster. By the time she got to the library, she was sweating. She burst into the building, loving the rush of the air conditioning on her damp skin.

"May I help you?" The librarian—*Mrs. Elaine Simms, Branch Manager*—looked at Casey and her bags with some surprise.

"Yes, please. I'd like to use a computer."

"Do you have a library card?"

"No, but I'd love to get one."

"Oh, *gag* me," Death said. "Since when did you become so *chipper*?"

Casey handed over her driver's license.

"Do you have another form of identification?" the librarian asked. "Something with your current address?"

"I'm just moving here, so I don't have anything."

"But your license says Tallahassee."

"Oh, um, right. I've been gone for a while. Service assignment. Overseas. I sold my house before I left."

"Way to go," Death said. "You didn't sound like an idiot at *all* just then."

"All right," the librarian said. "No problem." She returned Casey's license. "You may use a terminal today, and when you have your new address you can come back. But you will need to leave your bags with me."

Casey clutched them. "I don't think I can—"

"It's a secure room. They'll be fine."

Casey backed toward the door.

"Casey," Death said calmly. "She's a *librarian*. She's not going to steal your pathetic little collection of clothes and toiletries. Or even your treasures."

Death was right. Of course.

"Fine," Casey said. She handed her bags to *Mrs. Elaine Simms, Branch Manager*, who scooted them across the floor into a room behind the counter.

"Terminal two, please," the librarian said when she was back. "Right there." She pointed Casey toward a computer.

Casey thanked her and got settled in the hard chair.

"So what are we looking for?" Death sat on the desk cross-legged, with a nametag reading, *Grey Walker, Life and Death Manager*.

Casey waved her hand. "Will you move? I can't see when you're hunched over the screen."

The man at terminal three gave Casey a startled look.

"Sorry," Casey said. "I'll stop talking to myself."

He gave her a wavery smile and returned to his work.

Casey went to monster.com and typed, "Martial Arts, Tallahassee, Florida," in the job search box.

sorry there are 0 martial arts jobs

She frowned, and typed in "Martial Arts, Florida."

The negative findings were repeated.

"Something else, perhaps?" Death said. "Crabby lady, Anywhere with AC?"

Casey shook her head and typed "Fitness instructor, Talla-hassee, Florida."

sorry there are 0 fitness instructor jobs

"How about your theater background? You could get back onto the stage."

"Not without giving myself away," Casey whispered. "My union card has my real name on it, remember?"

"Would you have to show it to be a fight instructor?"

"No worthwhile director would hire me without knowing my training, and how am I going to tell them that without advertising who I really am?"

"Just trying to help, Miss Negativity."

She typed in "fitness instructor" again, taking out 'Tallahassee.'

there is 1 fitness instructor job in Florida

Casey clicked on it.

"Well?" Death said. "Where is it?"

"Raceda."

"Nice. They've got great beaches."

"I don't know..."

"What? Too many fat people?"

She read the description:

Wanted: fitness instructor for enclosed community. Hours flexible. Must have personal training certification, as well as aerobics, swimming, and yoga. Must provide references. Previous experience necessary.

Casey hadn't thought about the reference problem. Seeing how Daisy Gray had just been born that week, she didn't have anyone to call.

"I say go for it," Death said. "You really don't want to be flipping burgers, not with your abs."

"What? I just show up and say, 'Sorry, you'll have to take my word I'm the right person for the job?'"

"No." Death was using a patient, soothing voice, as if dealing with a difficult child. "You go there, offer to lead some classes for free, and they can determine your suitability."

"But that doesn't tell them I'm not some psycho. They'll want to be careful, since it's an enclosed community. Those kinds of people are always paranoid."

"Fine." Death hopped off the desk. "Look for something else. A desk job. Construction. I don't care."

Casey looked at Death, who stood beside the desk, arms crossed. She sighed. Death was right. Again. That was getting old.

She caught the eye of the man at the next terminal—he was staring at her some more, and she wondered just how soon he'd be calling security. Casey quickly wrote down the information for the job, gave the man a way-too-brilliant smile, and went back to the front desk.

"Done already?" the librarian asked.

"Just needed one thing."

"Let me get your bags."

A minute later Casey was on the street.

"Now what?" Death squinted into the bright afternoon.

Casey headed back the way they'd come. "Now we find a way to Raceda. Guess we should've kept that rental car."

"If we do the rental car thing again, make sure it's not a compact this time. You've got cash, you should be riding in *style*."

So Casey picked a hybrid, with even less room for passengers than a compact.

"You know," Death said, squished between Casey's two bags in the front—and only—seat, "you *could* use the *trunk* for your baggage."

"Okay," Casey said. "Go on back."

"Ha, *ha*." Death wiggled around, trying to get comfortable, but couldn't find a position that allowed a line of sight over knees or feet. "Oh, *fine*. I'll see you there."

And Death was gone in a puff of irritated mist.

Casey turned on the radio. It was playing Pink's, "So What." She turned it up as loud as she could bear it, and sang along.

Chapter Five

The Flamingo Apartments lived up to their namesake. Tall, skinny, and pink, with white and lime green highlights, and palm trees surrounding the parking lot. Behind the building Casey could see the ocean, sparkling and blue, lined with white sand. A pelican perched on the dock, and seagulls flitted about, calling to each other. Sailboats floated past, their sails taut, probably headed toward the marina Casey had passed on her way in. The docks there had been lined with more boats than Casey could count, from the smallest sailboat to the huge kind you could live on for a year. Casey was rested, and had eaten a good breakfast after staying overnight in a hotel.

"I'm glad I dressed appropriately."

Casey glanced at her companion, who wore all white, and held a walking stick with a brass handle. "Who are you trying to be?"

"The cool, southern citizen."

"You can do cool?"

Death glared at her. "I am the *epitome* of cool."

"Whatever." Casey looked up at the building through the windshield of the car. "I guess we go in the front. I wonder how tight security is?"

"Doesn't matter. You could take 'em."

"I don't want to *take them*. I want to act like a normal human being."

Death snorted. "Good luck with that."

Casey got out of the car and slammed the door.

"No need to get huffy," Death said, appearing suddenly on the sidewalk.

A guard in typical guard-style clothes met them just inside the entrance. He sat behind a large desk and smiled, his teeth shiny in his dark face. "Good morning. How may I help you today?"

"I'm here to see Mrs. Williams, please. I have an appointment."

"Oh," Death said. "*That* kind of normal human being. You have manners, and everything."

The guard looked at his appointment book. "Ms. Gray? Ten-o'clock?"

"Yes, sir."

"*Sir?*" Death choked out a laugh.

Casey took a deep calming breath, knowing it would look very bad if she tried to slug someone the guard couldn't see.

The guard picked up a phone and spoke into it. "Ms. Mendez? A Ms. Gray is here to see Mrs. Williams."

"Ms...Mrs..." Death said. "It looks like we may have joined polite society, at last."

The guard set down the phone and gestured toward the second set of double doors. "Mrs. Williams is expecting you. Right through there, please."

Casey gripped her purse—which still felt very strange. How long since she'd carried one of *those?*—and went into the main building. She was greeted by the smell of tropical flowers. Live palm trees reached toward the glass ceiling. Sunlight shone through the panes, lighting up the large room, and Casey almost pulled out her sunglasses. A bar took up the entire right side of the space, and a lounge with a dozen comfortable chairs and sofas were scattered—in a planned, casual sort of way—throughout the area. The bar was closed, but a little coffee shop on the left side of the hall was open, and a few people sat at small tables in front of it, one man with a newspaper, and one woman, about Casey's age, working on her laptop, with a cup of coffee and a half-eaten bagel at her elbow. She looked up, and a thrill ran from Casey's head to her toes.

The woman, even sitting, was tall, and her coffee-colored skin shone with health and fitness. A jacket hung over the back of her chair, which meant her muscular arms were revealed from under her tank top. She sat with a posture of confidence and no-nonsense, and her kinky hair sprayed out in a shining mass of curls, like a dark halo. But it was much more than her appearance that got to Casey. It was the look in her eye. Casey recognized it. It spoke of battles fought and won, of challenge, and of a desire to control her surroundings. Casey hesitated, wanting to speak to her, knowing that just as much was being broadcast about herself as about the other woman.

"Ms. Gray?" A small Hispanic woman approached Casey.

Casey tore her eyes from the table. "Yes."

"I'm Maria Mendez. Welcome to the Flamingo."

Maria had a pleasant accent, and was about as opposite in appearance from the woman at the table as could be, but her eyes also revealed something familiar. Not the sense that she had total command of her environment, but that she'd been through a lot to get where she was, and wasn't going to take any crap. She was probably in her thirties, and was dressed to a T in a dark business suit and heels. Her hair had been twisted into a perfect bun, with not one hair daring to fly free. Casey felt like she should salute.

"Please," Maria said. "Come this way."

Casey followed her toward the back corner, where they went through a door marked, "Office."

"Mrs. Williams is ready for you." She knocked on another door, and opened it. "Mrs. Williams, Ms. Gray is here."

"Come in, come in." Mrs. Williams got up from her chair to shake Casey's hand, and Casey choked back a laugh.

Death didn't bother holding it in.

The Flamingo Community Director, "Call me Sissy," was in her fifties, with bright orange hair. She wore a lime-green track suit, with a lemon-yellow headband, and bright white sneakers.

Her lipstick was an alarming shade of orange, matching her hair and her perfectly manicured fingernails. She looked like an upright, slightly pudgy, fruit basket. Casey wasn't sure if she was supposed to eat her or drink her.

"Thank you, Maria," the fruit basket said. "That will be all."

The receptionist backed out of the room, closing the door quietly behind her.

"Have a seat, please, Ms. Gray."

"Please, call me Daisy."

"*Please, call me Daisy,*" Death said, and giggled.

Casey, ignoring Death's rudeness, took one of the pink chairs. Death sat in the other.

"I received the e-mail with your vita, Ms. Gray, and it is quite impressive. It looks like you have experience with all areas of our program."

"I've been in the fitness field a long time."

"The problem comes, however, with your lack of references. We really do need to talk with some of the people you have worked for."

"I'm sorry," Casey said. "That's just not possible. All of the people I've worked for have either moved on or closed their doors. That's why I'm searching for work."

Sissy frowned. "Then even with your experience I'm afraid we can't—"

"Could I at least offer some free classes? Perhaps one of each kind. You could see whether or not you like what I do."

"But that still doesn't answer the *other* questions."

"Which are?"

"Whether or not you'd be a good fit for our community *personally.*"

"Which means she is worried you're here to scam the residents, empty out their bank accounts, and disappear into the ether," Death said. "Or else kill them all. You need to convince her you're not only a good teacher, but a good *person.*"

Casey thought she looked the part of a reliable citizen. She'd taken the time to not only clip her nails and get a haircut, but to buy some respectable khakis and a blouse, leave her bags in a hotel room—this time at a very nice Four Seasons—and actually put on some make-up. She couldn't *look* more respectable. There wasn't a whole lot she could do about her blank history.

"You're losing her," Death said. "Make something up."

She wasn't sure what that meant.

"A sob story," Death said. "Something to make her feel sorry for you."

"I'm…trying to start fresh," Casey said. "I'm coming from a…a bad situation."

Sissy sucked in a breath. "Were you in *jail?*"

"What? *No!*" Casey glared at Death.

Death's eyes rolled up toward the ceiling. "It's not my fault you're a bad liar."

"How about a trial run?" Casey said, trying to reassure Miss Citrus. "I'll give you a week of free classes. After that, we can re-evaluate. You can talk to your residents, see what they think."

"It's hard to trust their instincts," Sissy said. "After the last two instructors."

"What happened with them?"

Sissy looked like she had just sucked on the lime she resembled. "I can't talk about that. Let's just say neither of them was as good with people as I'd hoped."

"I'm good with people," Casey said.

Death about died laughing.

"Really." Casey did her best to sound convincing. And good with people. "I can work with all types. Old, young, in shape, out of shape, men, women. I love working out, and getting other people to exercise. I can improve their fitness and…and their lives." She made herself stop talking to just smile, and tried not to look desperate.

Sissy was wavering, Casey could tell.

"I'll even throw in a self-defense course."

Sissy brightened. "Oh, our ladies would like that." She'd made up her mind. "You can start your trial tomorrow. Pilates at six AM."

Death groaned.

"Perfect," Casey said. "What kind of schedule were you thinking for the rest of the day?"

They went over the times the residents were used to exercising, which would take Casey from early morning to evening, with a break in the middle of the day.

"We do have a resident who leads classes part-time, as well, so if we decide you're right for us, you can plan out a schedule that works for both of you. Since the full-time position is live-in, commuting shouldn't be an issue. We've never had a problem before with the classes spanning the day." She looked defiantly at Casey, as if waiting for her to challenge this statement.

"I'm sure it would be fine," Casey said, because what else was she planning on doing with her time? She'd be happy if classes took her from dawn to dark, with short breaks only for eating. That way she wouldn't have to think.

"Super. We'll see you tomorrow morning, bright and early." Sissy hesitated. "Unless you'd like a tour of the facility right now."

"That would be great."

Sissy punched a button on her phone. "Maria!"

The receptionist came into the room. "Yes, Mrs. Williams?"

"This is a prospective fitness instructor. Give her a tour of the community, please."

"Yes, ma'am."

"Thank you, Sissy," Casey said. "I'll see you tomorrow morning."

"At step aerobics," Sissy said. "Eight-thirty. I don't do Pilates."

Casey smiled. "It's not for everyone."

"And neither are the hours before dawn."

Casey shook Sissy's hand and followed Maria out into the reception area. Casey immediately looked for the woman at the table, but she was gone. Casey wondered when she would see her again, and hoped it would be under favorable circumstances and not when the woman needed somebody to beat up.

"So what did Mrs. Williams tell you about the community?" Maria asked.

"Not a lot."

Maria snatched a colorful brochure from her desk and handed it to Casey. "We're an enclosed community for singles and young professional couples. Age ranges from twenty-one to past retirement age."

"No kids?"

"Our residents prefer an adult atmosphere."

Casey gave the receptionist a quick glance. Maria's voice was professional, but Casey thought she heard some judgment in that last statement.

"So this, of course, is our administrative area." Maria gestured to the large office. "Out here—" she led Casey into the large front lobby "—is the last thing our residents see every day before leaving, and the first thing they see upon their return."

Casey could appreciate that. She wouldn't mind seeing those palm trees and smelling those flowers on a daily basis.

"And of course we have the coffee bar in the morning and the…*other* bar at night."

"Nice," Death said. "Nothing like a little partying and hooking up to make a happy home. With the coffee in the morning to help with the hangovers. Think they supply Advil?"

The bar itself wasn't open, since it was still just morning, but a man stood behind the counter, rag in hand as he dusted bottles and checked their levels.

Maria waved her hand toward him. "That's Jack Sandoval, the bartender."

He must have heard his name, or felt them watching, because he turned around. His bright blue eyes were piercing, even from across the room, and a slight, amused grin pulled up one side of his mouth.

Casey liked the look of him, and smiled back. He gave off the aura of being very solid and mature, his hair just thinning on top, his body lean under his white button-down shirt with its rolled-up sleeves. Probably in his forties. Not tall. But…solid. Yes. That word fit him very well.

He nodded to her, and turned back to his work.

"How many residents live in the building?" Casey asked Maria.

"There are one hundred-fifteen apartments in this main building, about two-thirds filled with singles, plus we have two more buildings toward the ocean, one on either side of the Flamingo, which each have fifty units. So at any given time we house close to three hundred people. This building tends to serve the younger residents, while the smaller two are more attractive to those who are closer to retirement, or who already have retired. They have their own gathering places in their lobbies, so the generations tend not to mix too much, except in the exercise arena or the outside pool. We have a few empty condos right now in this building. I'll show you one when we're done with our tour, if you're interested. After all, if Mrs. Williams hires you, you'll be living here, too." She led Casey up a flight of stairs, which opened into a wide hallway.

Casey made a note of the cameras mounted along their route. It looked like the Flamingo took its security at least semiseriously. "Do you live here?"

There was just enough hesitation before Maria's answer for Casey to realize she'd struck a nerve.

"I live off-property," Maria said. "On the other side of town. Most of the staff does, except for those who have housing as part of their salary."

"And Sissy?"

"Building Two. The Palm. Fitness instructors are usually younger, so they stay in The Flamingo. Besides, it's where the job takes place."

"Question about that," Casey said. "Or really more about the previous instructor. Can you tell me why she left?"

"He. *He* left. And no, I can't talk about it."

"Or the one before him?"

"That was another he. And that's not my story to tell, either. Suffice it to say they didn't work out and he left two weeks ago. Perhaps you'll have better luck." She slid a key card into a slot on a door, and it opened automatically. "As you can see, we're on our fitness floor, and this is our weight room."

Casey stepped in and was pleased to see a water cooler, which sat just inside the door beside a shelf of clean towels and a bowl of apples and oranges. The fruit wasn't enough to mask the usual smell of weight rooms—sweat. But this room also had a tinge of chlorine mixed into the odor, probably from the pool Casey could see through the glass wall on the far side of the room. It looked Olympic size, and was presently in use.

One man, a few years older than Casey, paced around the free weights area, shaking his arms. It wasn't his first day lifting, from the size of him. He had a full head of hair, not yet gone gray, and his legs were tree trunks. A weight belt encircled his narrow waist, and there was no sign of steroid acne on his back or shoulders. Casey approved.

Another man and two women, all older, used the weight machines. Casey was impressed at the quality of the facilities. She'd never been a huge fan of weight training, but she'd done some in the past, and could see herself using these.

At the far end of the room, overlooking the pool, stood a line of cardio equipment—treadmills, stationary bikes, and ellipticals. Only a few were in use now, again with an older contingent. Some of the exercisers were glued to little TVs on their machines, but others watched the water aerobics class in the next room. Casey walked over to see how many participants were in the pool.

"That's Laurie Kilmer, the resident who helps out with classes," Maria said, indicating the woman at the front of the group of swimmers. She was probably in her forties, with dark hair and overly-tanned skin. Her teeth were so white they practically blinded Casey with the reflection from the water. She looked fit, and from what Casey could see, was working the residents hard, but safely.

"Maria." It was one of the women on a treadmill, and she gestured for Maria to come closer.

Maria excused herself and went over to her.

"You the new fitness instructor?" The man from the free weights had drifted over and looked Casey up and down, not in a creepy way, but more like he was deciding if she would qualify for the position.

"Not yet. I'll be doing some classes this week, on a trial basis."

"That's good. Sissy can't seem to pick decent people."

That was funny. Sissy had blamed the *residents* for liking the previous ones.

The man gave a little grin. "You look a little more normal than the last couple."

If only he knew. "The last instructor wasn't normal?"

"Normal in that all he cared about was money. And getting in the women's pants. You know the story."

"Sure." It wasn't like it was a new one. "And the one before?"

"He wasn't so bad, as a person. Actually, he was a pretty nice guy. He just didn't have any idea what he was doing, job-wise. Injured more people than he helped, probably. One day he just stopped coming. Never showed up again, and good riddance. Guess he realized he was about to get fired and took things into his own hands." He shook his head. "There was a while Sissy was having such bad luck she wasn't sure if we should even keep the fitness center open, or should at least stop offering classes led by 'qualified' instructors. But then, she'd lose a lot of residents if she took that away."

"The last guy—what happened with him? Did he just stop showing up, too?"

He glanced toward Maria, then stepped a little closer to Casey. "Sissy found out one of the older women had changed her will to include him and about blew the roof. He was gone the next day. He may have known what he was doing as far as fitness, but he was an idiot people-wise." He crossed his arms, which were just as muscular as his legs. "You're qualified?"

"People-wise or fitness-wise?"

He smiled, revealing a gap between his front teeth that took several years off of him. "Either."

"Don't answer him," Death advised. "At least about the people part."

"I'm licensed as a personal trainer. You want to arm wrestle me, just to be sure?"

The man laughed. "I'll take your word for it. Wouldn't want to hurt you."

"Thanks. I appreciate it."

"Oh, come on." Death was suddenly behind the man, throwing air punches. "Give him what for. Show him who's boss."

"Del?" Maria was back.

"Hey, Maria. Just meeting the new instructor."

She looked uncomfortable. "Actually—"

"I don't have the job yet, remember." Casey smiled. "Del."

He shrugged, and grinned. "You'll get it."

"You're sure?"

"I can tell about these things."

"Well, I hope you're right. Nice to meet you, anyway."

He moved back toward the weight area, then stopped and turned around. "So you know my name. What's yours?"

"Daisy. Daisy Gray."

Death held a hand around Del's biceps, but looked at Casey. "Sounds *almost* like you mean it when you say that name. But you should practice some more in front of a mirror."

Del shivered and glanced toward the air conditioning vent in the ceiling. "So, anyway, Daisy, see you around."

Maria watched him go. "I hope he was..."

Casey could see the word choice going on in Maria's head— Discreet? Welcoming? Appropriate?

"He was very nice. Seems to like this place."

Maria led Casey across the room. "He's a good guy. A good resident. He's been here five years, or so, which is longer than most."

"So the turnover's fast?"

"Depends. Here in the Flamingo you've got some long-term folks, who come in their early twenties and stay a while, but you've also got people who show up for a year or two, and then are off to other places. The Palm and Pelican buildings are different, filled mostly with people who want to move somewhere warm in their older years. There's also a good portion that comes only during the winter months, and their condos sit empty half the year." She looked like she didn't think this was the best policy.

They walked past a counter, where a young Hispanic woman was folding towels.

Maria waved. "*Hola*, Rosa!"

Rosa looked up shyly, her eyes darting to Casey and back to Maria.

Maria rattled off something in Spanish, then turned to Casey. "I'm telling her you're applying for the fitness instructor job."

Casey smiled at Rosa, reaching deep inside for the bit of Spanish she'd learned from Reuben. "*Hola, un placer conocerte.*"

Rosa's shyness turned to pleasure at Casey's attempt to say it was nice to meet her, and she stood up straighter, her face growing serious with concentration. "Hello. It is a nice day."

"Yes," Casey said. "It is."

"*Adios*, Rosa!" Maria flipped her a wave. "See you later!"

Casey waved, too, and followed Maria through a door into a large, airy room. "Is Rosa new to the States?"

Maria frowned. "Why?"

"Just wondered."

"She's been a citizen for almost a year now. Came over from Cuba a long time ago. Completely legal. You have a problem with people immigrating?"

Casey held up her hands, wishing she'd kept her mouth shut. "Just making conversation."

Maria looked at her for a few seconds before saying, "This is our aerobics room," although it needed no explanation.

The room was large, one entire side filled with mirrors. The other walls had been painted a faint yellow. The floor was blond wood, and the lighting was recessed, spread throughout the ceiling at even intervals. Mats stood in neat stacks in one corner along with racks of exercise balls; hand weights and resistance bands lay in individual cubbies. As in the weight room, a full water cooler sat in the corner, minus the fruit bowl.

"There's a sound system," Maria said, pointing to speakers in each corner, "with portable mics for the instructors. And a wide selection of music, unless you have your own."

"May I look?"

"Of course."

Maria was right. There was anything she could want, from Golden Oldies to classic rock to hip hop to Top Forty. She flipped through and selected a CD for Pilates the next morning. Six AM would come awfully early—she might as well know what she was going to use before she got there.

"You're finished?" Maria said. "I'll show you the locker rooms yet."

"What?" Casey said. "No spinning class?"

"You'd think so, wouldn't you? But that's the one thing left to do. They've run out of space. It would mean either major renovation to change the two condos on this floor into a cycling room, or taking up room in the aerobics and weight areas. Nobody wants to do that, and the two residents on this floor don't want to give up their spacious suites." She pushed open the door marked, "Women," and Casey shook her head with disbelief.

These were way more than locker rooms. Roomy lockers, benches and comfortable chairs, multiple individual showers, and a sauna.

Death gave the sauna a pass. "Why people want to sit and sweat is beyond me. You may be boring with all your workouts, but at least you're *doing* something."

Casey agreed, but wasn't about to tell Death that.

"This is the training room, which separates the men's and women's locker rooms." Maria unlocked the door. An examination table sat against the wall, along with a whirlpool, a sink, and cupboards, filled with first aid supplies. A large metal desk was wedged into the corner with a new iMac, and a rack of hand weights rested on the floor beside it. As Maria had mentioned, there was a door on the opposite wall leading to the men's locker room, which apparently opened into the hallway across from the weight room.

"This would also be your office," Maria said.

Office? Computer? Casey's head spun.

"So, do you think you could work here?" Maria's voice was dry.

"I think I could manage."

It was nicer than any place she'd ever dreamed of working. Her old *dojang*, back home, was a tiny little room on the third floor of an old warehouse. It was hot, and cramped, and they were lucky if they had enough mats for everybody to use on a given day. But it worked. Casey had learned what she'd needed.

"Come on, then," Maria said. "I'll show you an apartment."

She took Casey up one flight, and opened a vacant condo. It was a furnished two-room space, with hotel-type furniture, and a few generic paintings above the bed and sofa. Apart from the bedroom and living room, there was a small kitchen, a full bath, and a good-sized closet.

"Nice," Death said. "If a little small. And it smells like mothballs."

"It's perfect," Casey said.

The sliding glass door opened onto a little balcony, which overlooked the outdoor pool. Several people floated on mats, or lay beside the pool on lounge chairs. A lifeguard perched in a tall chair, and a hot tub sat close below him, with one person in it.

"The higher-priced condos are further up, where you can actually see the ocean beyond the trees," Maria said. "Those, of course, are for the paying residents."

"Of course." Casey looked around the room. She could see herself being...well, not *happy*, exactly...but comfortable there. Yes, she could be comfortable.

Maria walked back to the door. "Would you like a walk around the grounds?"

"Sure."

The tour took them past the bar, where Jack the bartender gave Casey another amused wave, and included a peek into the mailroom and kitchen, the lobby of the Palm building, and a glance at the maintenance shed. Well, it wasn't a *shed*, exactly, being a full garage and storage area for the lawnmowers and a Gator, besides two pick-ups with the Flamingo emblem on the side.

They ended up on the private beach, where Casey breathed in the salty air and looked down the shoreline toward the marina on one side, complete with a restaurant over the water, and a line of condos down the other. The water was clear, the sand was white, and Casey didn't know what she did to deserve this opportunity.

"Job's not yours yet," Death reminded her. Death now wore a bright blue bathing suit with Hawaiian flowers, a visor, and shades, and sat on a lounge chair under an umbrella.

Casey held her hand over her eyes and looked toward the horizon, watching as two sailboats moved smoothly toward each other. "What a beautiful place."

Maria sighed heavily. "It is. Most of the time."

Casey was going to ask what she meant, but when she turned to say the words, Maria was already on her way back to the Flamingo.

Chapter Six

Casey spent the evening in her over-priced hotel room going over plans for classes. The schedule for the next few days would include a dizzying array of sessions, including Pilates, step, low and high impact aerobics, abs, body sculpting, BODYPUMP, Zumba, circuit training, yoga, boot camp, and senior exercise. Sissy had decided to wait on any individual personal training until Casey actually had the position. There had been a day in the past Casey could have taught every one of the classes in her sleep, but with all that had happened the last year and a half, it was like returning to another very foggy world.

Casey also went shopping, and invested in some workout ensembles. From what she'd seen at the Flamingo, her usual shorts and T-shirt wouldn't cut it, and her *Dobak* wasn't conducive to all-day exercise. Casey avoided the skin-tight Spandex, opting for gym shorts and tank tops, which were a bit colorful, but would do the job. If Sissy actually hired her, she would find something more her own style. She did, however, get a new pair of cross-trainers, which she could use no matter what happened.

"So, what do you think?" Death asked.

Casey was in one of Reuben's old, over-sized T-shirts, and lay in the very comfortable, very cozy bed. Her eyes had just begun to close when Death jerked her back awake. "About what?"

"The Flamingo. The job. Sissy's clothes." Death lay on the far side of the king-size bed in a nightshirt like the one Scrooge would've worn. All that was missing was the cap.

"The Flamingo itself isn't quite my thing, but the job would be great, for a while, anyway."

"And Sissy's clothes?"

"She seems nice. And professional."

"But the *clothes*, Casey, the *clothes* are *hideous*."

"Personal choice, L'Ankou."

"Right. I need to remember who I'm talking to. You're not exactly Fashion Central."

"I never asked you."

"But what about the last two instructors? Aren't you curious?"

"About their clothes?"

"About what *happened* to them. What exactly they did. Who the woman was who put the last guy in her will. And what if there were others?"

"They're gone, okay? That's all I care about. The residents have a clean slate, as far as I'm concerned."

"But the last two guys were scoundrels. At least the one was. The one before him was just unqualified."

"Good*night*."

"Okay, fine. But can you at least turn on the TV?"

Casey pulled the covers over her head, and Death gave up.

Five-thirty rolled around awfully early, but Casey was ready. She wasn't surprised to find herself alone as she drove to the Flamingo. Death wasn't exactly a morning person. Or spirit. Or whatever.

She signed in with the Flamingo's guard and walked across the empty lobby. The bar was closed, of course, with no sign of Jack. The shop on the other side of the room looked just ready to open, and the smell of coffee and muffins wafted across the air, making Casey's stomach rumble.

Casey arrived in the aerobics room fifteen minutes early, but already a group was forming. All women, and all of the age they would be heading out to work before eight. They eyed Casey with a look of half appraisal, half defiance, so Casey smiled and behaved in as non-threatening a manner as she could. According to Death, women weren't always excited to be around her, either because of her low body fat percentage, or because she could beat the crap out of them.

Casey thought perhaps the woman she'd seen in the lobby that first day would show, but no one who entered came even close to her stature and presence. Casey was disappointed, but not surprised. A woman like that probably had a *dojang* or *dojo* she attended. She was obviously much more than someone who wanted a tight butt, or a reason to dress in Spandex. Casey hoped she would at least see the woman in the lobby again sometime, so she could start up a conversation. She would like to have an ally—although with women like that there was no telling if she would be an ally or an enemy. Casey would simply expect the better of the two choices, but be prepared for the worst as well.

She found the CD of ocean sounds and slow music she'd chosen the day before and got the sound system set up, including the mic pack, which she clipped to the back of her shorts. She was hooking the mic over her ear when someone thrust a hand in her face.

"Andrea." The woman's light hair was pulled back in a messy ponytail, her eyes still puffy from sleep. "Welcome to the Land of the Dead."

Casey shook her hand. "Excuse me?"

"That's what we call ourselves. The six-o'clock crew. We don't exactly *want* to be here at this ungodly hour, but it makes the most sense in our schedules."

Casey laughed. "Gotcha. I'll try to make the session enjoyable."

"Enjoyable? I'll take bearable." The woman grinned and found a spot on the floor, between two others who looked just as asleep as she.

When the clock read six, Casey turned on her mic. "Good morning. My name is Daisy Gray. I'll be doing your classes the next few days as kind of a try-out for the job, so if you have comments, you can direct them to Mrs. Williams. Are you ready?"

There was a collective groan, and Casey started the music. By the time the hour passed and the women had stretched, sweated, and held positions most normal people couldn't halfway manage, they were finally starting to wake up. When Casey turned off her mic, Andrea and another woman came to the front.

"That was great," Andrea said. "Better than the last instructor, for sure. You'll be back tomorrow morning for aerobics?"

"I'll be here. Anything in particular you like to do?"

"*Like* to do? Not exactly. Whatever gets our blood pumping, I guess."

"She's not bringing *men*, Andrea. At least no one's tried that yet." The other woman slung her towel around her neck and gave Casey a slow smile. "I'd be up for it, though. Give me a good man in the morning, and I'm ready to go for the day."

"Krystal!" Andrea laughed. "You're awful."

"What? It's true."

Casey didn't doubt it. Krystal, with her curvy body and bleached blonde hair, looked like she spent a good bit of the time attracting the opposite sex. Even Casey could feel her magnetic pull. It was amazing that while Andrea, the first woman, had the same coloring as her hottie friend, she definitely had the girl-next-door appeal, while Krystal was undoubtedly the *femme fatale*.

Casey looked around the all-female class. "Do men ever show up for this?"

Andrea giggled. "Never. But there are some over in the weight room right now, praying for a glimpse of Krystal as she leaves."

Krystal shrugged. "It's my gift to them."

Andrea swatted her, but smiled at Casey. "The last two instructors were guys, but they don't really count, as far as attendees."

"You didn't like them?"

Krystal *harrumpfed*, and looked at her fingernails, like she had more important things to think about.

"They were all right," Andrea said. "Richie is a total sweetheart and Brandon was super buff, but neither one really fit here. I sometimes think people here didn't give Richie enough of a chance, but it wasn't up to me."

Krystal took a step away and pulled at Andrea's arm. "Enough about him. Come *on*."

Andrea gave Casey one last smile. "I guess we're off then. Thanks."

"My pleasure."

There were no more classes until eight-thirty, the empty hour and a half being time that would be filled with personal training, should Casey get the job. But once it got close to eight-thirty, people began to trickle in for step class, much more lively than the group at six. This was more of a mixed bag, age-wise, but again it was all women. Casey had a feeling any interaction she might have with men would take place in the weight room.

Sissy bounced in, this time in a raspberry-colored warm-up suit, with lipstick to match. The contrast with her orange hair was enough to make Casey go a little cross-eyed. Sissy came right up front. "Pilates go okay?"

"Great. Nice group of women."

"They are." Sissy hesitated. "I suppose you met some of them? Maybe one named Krystal?" An unreadable expression flitted across her face.

"Yes. And her friend Andrea."

"Andrea's a nice girl. I'm glad she's here."

Not Krystal, though, apparently.

"Ah, here's Laurie. Laurie! Over here!" It was the woman from the pool the day before who'd been leading the water aerobics. She approached slowly, as if unsure what was going to happen once she got there. Casey decided her original assessment held— Laurie was a fit forty-something, her dark hair obviously helped along by a bit of color, and her skin beginning to show signs of age around the eyes and mouth. It probably didn't help that she was tanner than what would be natural, and probably had been most of her life. Right now the fine lines were accentuated by her obvious anxiety.

"Laurie," Sissy said, "this is Daisy Gray. If she gets the job, you'll need to work with her on a schedule. We can't have her working every hour of the day."

"Of course. I'll do whatever I can."

Casey smiled at her. "I watched a bit of your water aerobics class yesterday. I liked the way you led it."

Laurie relaxed visibly, her shoulders dropping and her eyebrows traveling upward. "Really?"

"It's been a while since I've taught in the water. Perhaps you could give me some pointers? Get me up to speed?"

Laurie smiled, taking several years off her appearance, just like Del's smile had the day before in the weight room. "Well, sure, I'd be happy to. Do you have time before your class at one?"

"I've got Zumba at eleven, and then I need to grab something to eat."

"We can eat together."

"Sounds good."

Laurie smiled again, and found a place in the middle of the group.

"Okay, ladies!" Sissy clapped her hands, and the chattering ceased. "This is Daisy. She's doing our classes the next few days, and may be staying on. So give me feedback, to help me know whether to hire her, or not."

Great, Casey thought wryly. *At least there's no pressure.*

"All yours," Sissy said, and took her place in the middle of the front row.

Casey started the CD, turned on her mic…and froze. Death stood in the back row of the class, waving and smiling and wearing an outfit that would have fit in *Flashdance*. Leg warmers, headband, the whole works. Casey closed her eyes, but when she opened them, Death was still there.

She would just have to deal.

"Good morning, ladies, my name is Daisy Gray. Let's start with some slow up and downs."

She took them through an easy, low-impact session, so she could study them and see where they rated in the proficiency scale. She suggested extra platforms for some, fewer for others, and always gave an alternative exercise for those who might have bad knees. Death had a great time in the back, spinning and jumping and generally being a distraction. By the time class was over, Casey was ready to wring Death's neck.

Sissy trotted up and grabbed Casey's hand. "*Wonderful* class. Thank you *so* much."

"You're welcome. Glad you enjoyed it. Was it what you were hoping for?"

"Even better." Sissy clasped her hands. "I think I'll come back this afternoon for BODYPUMP."

"Great."

The women filed out, sweaty but happy, thanking Casey and saying they looked forward to the next day.

When they were all gone, Casey rounded on Death, who was still stretching. "Thanks a *whole lot.*"

Death paused, halfway in a squat. "What? That was a great class."

"Could you have been any more distracting? And what is that get-up? Are you auditioning for *Fame?*"

"Well, I *am* gonna live forever."

Casey groaned and drained her water bottle. "From now on, you can*not* take my classes."

"Why not?" It wasn't Death asking. It was Laurie, who'd apparently been in the locker room.

"Oh. Not you," Casey said. "Of course you're welcome to take whatever classes you want."

Laurie looked around the empty room. "Then who were you talking to?"

Casey waved toward the door. "Someone who just left."

"Oh. It wasn't Krystal, was it?"

Oh, boy. Another woman worrying about the bombshell from six AM.

"Nope. So, I'll see you at noon?"

"I'll come by to get you."

"All right. See you then."

Again time was built in for personal training, so Casey meandered over to the weight room, where several people sweated on the cardio equipment. She walked through the maze of machines, familiarizing herself with what was there so she would be able to put together programs. When she got to the free weights she tried them out to find where she stood—it had been months since she'd touched a barbell. She did better than she'd hoped, and stopped pumping when she realized she was gathering an audience. She set the weights down, waved to the onlookers, and meandered over to the weight machines, trying her luck at those.

Time passed quickly, and before she knew it, she was back in the aerobics room, picking out music for Zumba, which was basically a dance class. The class consisted of all new faces this time, except for Death, who now wore skintight Spandex and a smile. Casey ignored the back corner, and led the again all-female class through the exercises.

The class sped by, and the women seemed happy with their workout, clustering around Casey and introducing themselves afterward. Not that she would remember any of their names after one session. Laurie came in as the last of the residents trickled out, Death studying their clothes as they passed.

Casey smiled. "So, where can we get some lunch around here?"

"Don't you want to change first?"

Casey looked down at her sweaty outfit. "You're right. Give me a sec."

Casey hated leaving Laurie alone with Death, but there was no alternative. She couldn't exactly tell Death to beat it with Laurie there listening.

Fifteen minutes later, after a speed shower, Casey and Laurie sat in a little café across the street.

"The Flamingo has breakfast and dinner—if you like bar food—but you've got to go out for lunch, unless you want to make your own." Laurie made this sound like it was the least appealing of any other option. "Most of the residents eat somewhere close to work, except for the retirees, who hang out at the neighborhood restaurants. You've got your variety just on this road—Italian, Amish, Chinese, you name it. There's more exotic stuff on the other side of town—Japanese, Cuban,

Ethiopian. Not all of the closer ones are great, but it doesn't get boring, at least."

It was no wonder the residents needed so many exercise classes. If they ate out every meal they would be complete blimps, otherwise.

"So how have you enjoyed the morning?" Laurie said. "Do you like the variety? What do you think of the facility? Has Sissy said whether or not you'll get the job?"

"No, she hasn't. Yes, I enjoyed it. And the facilities are great."

"The senior ladies are especially appreciative. They like the attention, and it keeps them from growing too restless during the day when their husbands are out sailing or playing golf. Not that the older men don't use the fitness facilities, because they do, but usually the weight room, and swimming laps. They don't do classes." She giggled. "Could you see it? Old, saggy guys trying to kickbox? They'd throw their backs out for sure."

"I don't know," Casey said. "I've seen older men who have done a great job—"

"And some of the younger women. Can you believe them? They show up in their tight little outfits, with the perfect make-up. It's like they think they're going to land a man at aerobics."

"Maybe they're just more comfortable going out in public afterwar—"

"At least with water aerobics the old ladies wear one-pieces instead of skimpier ones. I certainly wouldn't want to see *that* first thing in the morning, or even in the afternoon."

"Good lord, this woman never shuts up, does she?" Death stood beside the table, tablet in hand, chomping on chewing gum, and wearing the typical server outfit of a striped shirt, khaki pants, and an apron. The nametag on the shirt's breast pocket said *El Muerte*. "Do you think she's ever going to order, or is this merely a 'working lunch?'"

"If you'll excuse me," Laurie said suddenly, shivering and casting a glance around at the other tables. "I'm going to use the little girls' room. We can talk water aerobics when I get back."

"Of course." Casey breathed a sigh of relief when she was gone.

Death took Laurie's seat across the table. "What's her problem all of a sudden?"

"You mean other than somehow feeling that you're in the room?"

Death shrugged. "Not my fault she's a head case."

"No, she's not. She's just nervous."

"About what?"

"I don't know. Me taking the job. What I think of the place, and of the people. I'm not sure. Maybe she's worried I'll take her spot."

"Has she said anything about the last guy?"

"Not a peep."

"Bet you could find out some good stuff if you asked. It would all come gushing out, the way she goes on."

"Oh! Daisy! You've found our little café." Sissy came waltzing in, blinding Casey with her fruity brilliance, and plunked down right in Death's lap. She ran her hands over her arms and glanced at the ceiling. "They keep it *so* cold in here."

Death made a face and squeezed out from under Sissy, pointing at her in a threatening manner. "Some people are just too giddy to live."

Casey waved, as if swatting away a fly, and Death's image wavered. Casey's hand went numb, so she tucked it under her arm. "Laurie brought me over."

"Laurie? Is she here?"

"In the restroom."

"I see." She hesitated, then said, "Laurie does a very good job as a sub for our main classes. I told you before she'll help manage your schedule when you start full time." She clapped a hand over her mouth. "I wasn't supposed to say that yet."

"Say what?"

Sissy took her hand away and leaned forward. "That we're going to offer you the job."

"Really? Already?"

"I've had a dozen women stop by my office this morning to say how much they loved your class. They about went nuts when I told them we were also adding a self-defense course. I'm afraid if I don't give you the job right this minute the residents will have my head!" She beamed at Casey.

"But what about my references? What about checking me out for a week?"

Death laughed. "Are you *trying* to sabotage yourself?"

"I know," Sissy said, "I've picked some doozies in the past. But I have a good feeling about you."

No wonder the last two guys had been trouble. Sissy was the head case, not Laurie.

"So will you take it?" Sissy said.

"Well, yes. I'd love to."

"Wonderful! I can't wait to tell them."

"Tell who what?" Laurie was back.

"That we're hiring Daisy. She'll be moving in today!"

"Already? Today?"

"Of course. People are ready for some stability again, and I don't want to let Daisy slip through our fingers. She'll be perfect, don't you think? Completely opposite from our last instructor. You should be able to work with her very well, don't you think?"

What was that that flitted across Laurie's face? Embarrassment? Fear? Disappointment? "I'm sure we'll do fine."

"Good. I've told Daisy you teach several classes, and will do your best to help her out with her full schedule."

"Of course I will. You know that. I've already *said* that." She gave a faltering smile. "The residents will be very happy."

"Yes, they will!" Sissy jumped up. "I have to go tell everyone!" She practically sprinted to the front door, then came running back. "I forgot my lunch!" She grabbed a take-out bag and zoomed out the door.

Laurie eased into the chair Sissy had vacated. She picked up the menu and studied it with more concentration than Casey thought necessary.

"Hmm," Death said. "Suddenly she's not so chatty."

Laurie looked up. "So, did you order yet?"

The real waitress, whose nametag said *Vanessa,* came over just then, looking much more professional than Death had. She neither chewed gum nor regarded Casey and Laurie with disdain.

Casey and Laurie gave their orders, and the waitress smiled and left.

Death watched her go, head cocked. "What ever happened to good old diner waitresses? Food's no good without that touch of grumpiness."

"Is everything okay?" Casey said to Laurie.

Laurie gave her a quick smile that wasn't quite convincing. "Sure, it's just…don't take this wrong, but I thought she was going to see how things went for a week before actually hiring you."

"Wow," Death said. "Rather blunt, isn't she?"

"I thought the same thing," Casey said. "She surprised me. I'm sorry if it makes you uncomfortable."

"Oh, no, I'll be okay." But Laurie's focus had obviously gone elsewhere. "It's just…I was kind of hoping she'd consider me for the position. But I guess that's too much to ask." Her mouth drooped. "You'd think she'd be happy to have someone from in-house instead of hiring a stranger again. No offense."

"No offense taken," Casey said.

Laurie waved a hand. "There's really no point in me getting all upset. Sissy probably never even thought about hiring me, anyway."

Laurie looked like she was done talking so Casey said, "I was wondering what went on with the last couple of instructors."

Laurie almost knocked her water glass over, then wiped up the drops with her napkin. "Nothing. Nothing went on with them."

Death laughed. "Which obviously means something did. With *her.*"

"I mean," Casey said as gently as she could, "why did they leave? You're obviously worried about what harm I could do. Is there anything I need to look out for? Or avoid?"

Death snorted. "You mean other than scamming old ladies and getting yourself written into their wills?"

"Oh," Laurie said. "I…" She took a deep breath, composing herself. "Richie, Richie Miller—he wasn't the last one, but the one before that?—he was having some trouble keeping up."

"He was old? Out of shape?"

"No, not at all. He was young. And cute. What I meant was he wasn't up-to-date with fitness. He still thought we should do Richard Simmons tapes, and sit-ups the old-fashioned way. A sweetheart, really, everybody loved him, but…" She shook her head. "He had no idea what he was doing."

"Why did Sissy hire him?"

"I can't imagine. Except he was adorable. And friendly. Everybody liked him. The problem was that people kept getting injured, and he didn't know how to deal with it. He eventually had to go."

But Sissy hadn't fired him, from what Del, the guy in the weight room, had said. "What happened?"

"Well, everybody thinks he took off, because one day he just didn't show up for classes. What the residents don't realize—and this is confidential, of course—is that Sissy gave him an ultimatum. He had to leave immediately or she'd sue him for every person who'd gotten hurt. She said she'd better never see his face again or he'd be sorry. So he left. No one's heard from him since. It's too bad, really."

"Was it really all his fault people were getting hurt?"

"Of course not. But Sissy—well, *people*—needed to have someone to blame. Like I said, he wasn't really qualified for the position, but he wasn't a bad guy. Most of the people who got hurt were doing too much, and he wasn't firm enough to rein them in. I wish…" She shook her head.

"What?"

"I wish I could have taught him a few things, but I wasn't actually on staff until later. And even then…" She looked away. "Sissy makes it very clear I'm second best."

Casey grimaced. She'd noticed Sissy was a little short with Laurie, but she'd hoped it was just the stress of hiring a new person. "So what about the next guy? Did he know what he was doing?"

Laurie went pink, and picked at her napkin. "Yes, he was… more equipped for dealing with the job."

"Ooo," Death said. "*Equipped*. I can guess what she means by *that*."

Casey glared at Death, and turned a sympathetic eye toward Laurie. She'd obviously been burned by him one way or another.

Before Casey could ask anything else, the waitress set their plates in front of them and filled their water glasses. "Anything else you ladies need right now?"

Casey smiled up at her. "I think we're good. Thank you."

The waitress left, and Casey dug into her BLT, hoping she hadn't set back her relationship with Laurie by asking too many questions.

Laurie picked up her sandwich, but held it above her plate without eating. "The last guy, his name was Brandon. Brandon Greer. He was…a lot more qualified than Richie. He had an actual personal training certificate, and an amazing résumé. He certainly knew what he was doing."

In more ways than one, apparently.

"So what happened with him?"

Laurie set her sandwich down and rubbed her hands on her napkin. "He got a little too close to some of the women. Older ones. Widows. Turns out he was just a…just a con artist in disguise."

"So Sissy fired him?"

Laurie nodded. "I—We never saw him again. Sissy told him to leave, and it was like he just vanished. He completely disappeared after he walked out the door. I mean, he's *nowhere*."

"Which means," Death said, "that our dear Laurie here has looked for him."

"I'm sorry," Casey said. "It sounds like you miss him."

Laurie's head shot up. "I don't. I don't miss him. He was— I'm sorry, I have to go."

"But—"

"Congratulations on the job. We'll talk about water aerobics later, okay?" She grabbed her purse, threw a twenty onto the table, and hustled out the door.

"Well, *that* went well." Death sat in Laurie's chair and peered at her uneaten sandwich. "Wish I could eat this. You going to?"

"No, but I'll take it back for her. She can eat it later, once she regains her appetite." She took another bite of her own sandwich and chewed it slowly.

"Uh-oh," Death said. "I see thinking going on."

"I'm just wondering. You haven't seen either of those guys, have you? Richie or Brandon?"

"You mean, like, are they dead? Not that I remember. And I would. Although Florida is one of my most frequent destinations. All the old people, you know. But my mind is like an especially efficient steel trap, and they're not in it."

"Efficient? More like annoying. Your mind is an *annoying* steel trap."

"Don't mock me. I remember everybody who goes to the other side. Tons of people go from down here in the glorious Sunshine State, and they're each up here in the old brain trust. Forty-seven people from Raceda last month, and none of them was named Richie Miller or Brandon Greer. The last person to go from the Flamingo complex was five weeks ago and that was absolutely an age thing. Nothing suspicious at all."

Casey finished up her fruit plate. "So that means these guys fell off the map on their own."

"Or they were *told* to fall off the map." Death shrugged. "But what does it matter? They're gone, you're in. Why and how they left isn't your concern."

"You're right. It's just…weird. And I'm especially curious, seeing how I've just made *myself* fall off the map."

"Then it seems to me you're in the right place."

"Yeah," Casey said, feeling suddenly content. "I guess I am."

Chapter Seven

"So would you like furnished, or unfurnished?" Maria held a key in either hand.

"Furnished, definitely," Casey said.

"Seriously?" Death said. "This is your chance to have really nice stuff. Make a statement. Have an actual *style*."

It was mid-afternoon, after Casey's BODYPUMP and water aerobics classes. Sissy had shown up for BODYPUMP, giving up halfway through, but Casey saw no one else she knew. She had enjoyed the older ladies in the pool, and they'd seemed to like the workout, even though she hadn't had a chance to benefit from Laurie's expertise. Several men had been in the water, as well, doing their own independent laps at the other end of the pool, along with a couple of women. A lifeguard watched from an elevated chair with an air of boredom.

Casey's next class was at eight, when she would teach kick-boxing, and following that would be an abs class. She was glad she'd kept up her fitness as well as she had while on the road, or she would have been dying.

Maria typed "Daisy Gray" into the computer and printed out some papers for Casey to sign. Maria's desk was impeccably neat, filled only with office items, papers, and her computer. A small photo of two children was taped to the corner of the computer monitor.

"Your kids?" Casey asked.

Maria didn't look up. "Yes."

"How old are they?"

"Six and four." Maria held out the papers and a pen. "Okay. It's all yours. The apartment you saw yesterday. You're responsible for phone hook-up, whether you want a landline, or a cell, or both. Utilities are taken care of, and trash goes in the chute at the end of the hall. No pets, no smoking, and no painting or holes in the walls without permission."

"Got it."

Maria glanced toward Sissy's closed office door, then leaned forward. "I'm sure you'll find it, and you're not really supposed to use it, but the previous tenants found that the service stairs, which are next to the apartment, are the quickest route to the fitness floor. If you prefer an elevator, the service one is across the hall. Just don't tell Mrs. Williams I mentioned it."

"The previous tenants? Were they the fitness instructors before me?"

"Yes." Maria straightened some papers on her desk and raised her voice back to its usual volume. "Mrs. Williams put up a sign saying personal training would resume tomorrow, and that there are some slots for new clients. Here's the schedule so far." She added it to the stack of papers Casey had already accumulated, along with her contract, her rental agreement, and her benefits package. "So you've got a few hours, if you want to move in."

"I'll do that."

"You need help with a truck, or carrying anything?"

Death laughed. "Yes, please, can you carry one of her two bags?"

"I'll be fine," Casey said. "Thanks."

Casey went back to her hotel to grab her things. After she'd checked out, Death was waiting at the rental car, wearing the uniform of a moving professional. The logo on the back said *Dead Lift. We Move More Than Boxes.* "So Maria the Receptionist didn't seem too thrilled about your getting the job."

"Why should she be? I'm the third instructor in a string of losers. She probably expects me to be gone by Christmas."

"Christmas? Are we getting close? I haven't even begun shopping."

Casey stashed her bags in the trunk and got in the car, where Death was already in the passenger seat. "What kind of Christmas list can you possibly have?"

"It's mostly the biggies. Moses. Elvis. Cleopatra. You can't *imagine* how picky that woman is."

"I don't suppose you get God anything?"

"You know the old saying—what do you give someone who's got everything?"

Casey didn't want to think about Christmas. Not yet. It would be her second without Reuben and Omar. Not nearly long enough to get through the holidays without trauma and a good bout of depression.

She changed the subject. "So now that I'm going to be staying in one place I won't be nearly so interesting, right? You can go on your way?"

"You're kidding. You think I'm going to leave without seeing how this turns out?"

"It was just a thought…"

They traveled in silence the rest of the way back to the Flamingo. Casey parked the car and used the phone on Maria's desk to call the rental company to pick it up. She waited until they arrived, saw them off, and watched as a shiny black Harley-Davidson pulled into a parking space in the nearest row. The rider pulled off his helmet, and Casey saw that it was Del, the man she'd met in the weight room the day before. He eased off the bike, took a briefcase out of the saddlebag, and walked toward her.

"Hey. You're still here?" He smiled, softening his words.

"Got the job."

"Wow, that was fast. But then, Sissy doesn't exactly—" He stopped.

Casey laughed. "I know. She's not the most cautious employer."

"I'm not worried. I'm sure you'll do a great job. I told you I had a feeling about you." He opened the door, and Casey went inside, lugging her bags.

Del took the biggest duffel and slung it over his shoulder like it weighed nothing.

"I don't suppose you need me, though, do you?" Casey said. "I didn't see your name on the personal training schedule."

"I'm always happy to learn new things, if you've got 'em."

They walked together through the lobby, toward the stairs. This time she opened the door for him.

Del started up the flight. "So what apartment did they give you?"

"Second floor. Same as the last guy." She led him to her door, and opened it.

He set her bag on the empty table. "Nice room." He meandered over to the balcony door. "Nice view."

"Yeah, I like it." Together they looked down at the pool, where she saw Laurie talking with a group of seniors. It looked like she was giving them swimming pointers. Also in the pool, swimming strong laps from end to end, was the woman Casey had seen in the lobby. Her dark skin made it easy to pick her out from the other swimmers, but even more noticeable than that was her efficiency and strength in the water. She pulled up at the end of a lap and shook the water from her hair. Her head swung up, and her eyes landed on Casey. They looked at each other for several seconds before the woman turned and dove back under.

Casey was ready to ask Del who she was when he shifted on his feet. Casey followed his eyes to a couple of women walking out to the pool. It was the two most memorable members of the early class. The nice woman and the hottie.

"I suppose you met them this morning," Del said. "Andrea and Krystal."

"The Land of the Dead."

"What?" Del gave a little laugh.

"That's what they call themselves. That early class. Because they're basically sleepwalking."

"Right. Brandon especially liked that class."

"Brandon, the last instructor?"

"Yeah. But he liked the senior classes, too. Gullible widows, and all."

"He was a real piece of work, wasn't he?"

"You're telling me. Made it hard for the rest of us guys." He grinned, and again Casey noticed the gap between his front teeth that gave him such a youthful look.

"Do you know who the women were that Brandon took advantage of?"

"In what way? Cleaning out their bank accounts, or breaking their hearts?"

"Or both?"

"In some cases, yeah." He shook his head. "He played things pretty closely, but he tended to go for the women who needed attention."

"So not Krystal."

He laughed. "I think even Brandon was a little afraid of her. Well, I'd better get going. I've got a dinner date tonight, and I don't want to be late."

"Going someplace special?"

"The best food around."

"And where would that be?"

"My apartment."

Casey smiled. "Really? You're a cook?"

"Trained at the Orlando Culinary Academy for two years."

"But you don't work as a chef?"

"Nope. I got sucked into corporate life, and now I know what the money's like, it's hard to back out. I've been working on details to start my own restaurant, but you need more money than I've got to dump into something like that. I'm not quite there yet. Until then, I just entertain my friends and co-workers." He brightened. "How 'bout I cook for you?"

"I'd love that."

"Tomorrow night. My place. Six-o'clock. You can do that, right?"

"I have class at eight, so I can't stuff myself."

He pretended to be offended. "You do not *stuff* yourself with gourmet cooking."

"Oh," Casey said. "*So* sorry."

"You should be."

He left, and Casey regarded her bags, suddenly weary.

"So." Death sat on the sofa, wearing black Adidas warm-ups and sneakers, which rested on the coffee table. "Time to make yourself at home. If you can, with this musty smell in here."

"It smells fine." Casey shook herself out of her stupor and took another tour of the apartment. There wasn't a lot to see. The bedroom was just big enough for the bed, a dresser, and a fairly large closet. The one window was a decent size, but too small for a quick exit, especially with its double panes and heavy-duty screen. The bathroom had a tub and shower, and no window. The locks on both the bedroom and bathroom doors were flimsy, doorknob buttons, easy to bust with a sharp kick. Not reassuring.

The living room held the most possibilities of escape, with two possible exits. The regular door, of course, with a deadbolt and the doorknob lock, and the sliding glass door that led onto the little balcony. There was an okay lock on that, plus a thick wooden dowel in the track at ground level. Casey took up the dowel and stepped outside to look around. Being on the third floor, the jump to the ground would be impossible without fracturing bones. But there was another balcony beside her, within jumping distance, and one on the floor below she could probably reach if she dangled from her own and swung over.

But then, she'd never have to do that, right? She was Daisy Gray, who had no police record of any kind, and absolutely no enemies.

The pool had only two people in it now, who seemed more interested in each other than in actually swimming. Casey looked away, not wanting to spy. And not wanting to think about what it would feel like to have a man's hands on her wet skin as she floated in the pool on a hot day...

She went back into her condo and unpacked her bags, able to fill only two dresser drawers. She kept her backpack stuffed with essentials for a quick escape, should one be necessary—money and paperwork, her old ID, her treasures, and some toiletries and clothes—and stashed it on the far side of the couch in the air-conditioning vent. It might mean her living room would get hot, but it was better than having someone discover her real name.

The kitchen was her final stop, and while there were dishes and pots and pans, there was nothing to actually eat.

"Shopping trip," she said.

Death waved a hand. "But you sent the car away."

"There's a supermarket within walking distance. I'm going. Why don't you go, too?"

"I'd love to!"

"I mean, go somewhere that's not with me. Food shopping isn't very exciting. Especially if I go to the Whole Foods store."

Death made a face. "You're right. See you." Death disappeared in a cloud of vanilla-scented smoke, which did help to dampen the smell of mothballs.

Casey trotted down the stairs to the lobby, where the bar was now open. Already a few people, still in work clothes, stood beside high tables, or sat on tall stools. Jack, the bartender, was wiping the counter with a cloth, at least ten feet away from the closest customers.

Casey angled toward him, and he looked up as she approached, his lips twitching into that same amused grin she'd seen when she'd first noticed him. "Get you something?"

"No, thanks. Just wanted to introduce myself. I'm Daisy. New fitness instructor."

He smiled bigger, actually showing a few teeth this time. "Prettier than the last two. But then, that's not saying much."

Casey laughed. "Thanks, I guess."

"I'm Jack, but then, you probably know that already."

"I've heard."

"Yeah." He wiped another non-existent smudge off the counter. "The Flamingo's like a small town. News travels fast, and it's impossible to keep a secret."

"Jack!" Somebody down the line rapped a knuckle on the counter. "Get me a refill?"

Jack pointed at Casey. "Be right back."

She watched him receive the order from the man and fill two glasses before inputting something in the cash register. He topped off the pretzel bowl and sauntered back her way. "Sure I can't get you anything? House wine? Club soda?"

"No, really, I'm just headed out to the grocery store."

"Moving in day, huh? Always nice to get a fresh start in a new place."

Casey wasn't sure what to say. Was he referring to her job, or something more? What exactly had Sissy and Maria told him? Would they share her personal information with the rest of the staff? But he wasn't looking at her anymore. Now he was wiping off the water spritzer. Not that it needed any more shining.

"Well, I guess I'll be off," she said. "Nice to meet you."

"Stop by any time. Bar's open till midnight, and I'm pretty much always around." He gave her one last grin before moving back down the counter to respond to another called order.

Casey found the grocery store just down the block, and spent the rest of the time before her next class filling her fridge and cupboards with the basics and making herself a quick vegetable stir-fry. She was soon trotting back down to the aerobics floor for kickboxing. She harbored a slim hope that the woman from the lobby and swimming pool would show up for this class—it would be the kind of class most in line with the look Casey recognized in her eyes—but didn't really expect to see her.

Death, however, wasn't about to miss something like this, and showed up with all-black workout clothes, ready to *kick some ass*. Casey was getting very good at ignoring it all, and smiled when Andrea and Krystal came in. They strode right up and took places in the front row. Again, Casey was interested by how two women with all of the same basic features and coloring could have such different auras.

She went over to them. "Somehow I'm not surprised to see you two here."

Andrea laughed. "We need to get the stress of the day out somehow, don't we?"

"And let out all our pent-up aggression from pandering to the all-male management at work," Krystal grumbled.

"That's right," Andrea said. "We can't exactly beat up our boss, can we?"

Casey agreed. "So you work together?"

"Bank down the street. You'd think in this day and age there would be more women in leadership positions, but at our place it's still all men at the top."

"I usually like men on top," Krystal said.

Andrea groaned. "You're going to make Daisy think we're complete sluts."

"Not you," Krystal said, winking at Casey. "Just me."

Casey laughed and held up her hands. "I'm not here to judge."

Andrea slid on her workout gloves and secured the Velcro straps. "Have you moved in already?"

"Yup. I got the usual apartment instructors use. What was the last guy's name?"

"Brandon." Krystal practically growled the name. "He was a horse's a—"

"Laurie! Have you met Daisy?" Andrea's smile was strained as she greeted the part-time aerobics instructor.

"We had lunch together."

"Great! We were just welcoming her to the Flamingo. She's moved in already."

"Into Brandon's old apartment." Again, Krystal said the name with disdain.

"Yes," Laurie said. "It's a nice one."

"Been there a lot?" Krystal said coolly.

"A few times. How about you?"

"Oh, that *is* a nice condo," Andrea said cheerily. "Great view of the pool, right, Daisy?"

Laurie's jaw tightened. "Know the apartment well, do you, Andrea?"

"Oh, not that well, I mean I've been in it once or twice, but—"

"Of course she doesn't *know it well*," Krystal said. "*I* told her. *I've* been in the condo, and the view is *fantastic*."

"Okay, everyone, are we ready?" Sissy danced into the room, this time in a lemon yellow velour tracksuit.

"Did you know?" Krystal said to Sissy. "Daisy's moved into Brandon's old apartment. We're having a contest as to who's been in it more. Laurie says it was her. I say it was me. Andrea thinks she's even been there a few times, but I think she's just remembering what I told her. What do you say?"

"*You?* Why would you—"

"Unless you want to join the fun. How well do *you* know that apartment?"

"I'm the condo manager. Of course I know that apartment. I can't imagine what you're implying."

"I'm sure you can't. You don't have that kind of imagination. But I *was* wondering, have you heard from Brandon lately? If anybody knows where he's been since he left, I would think that would be you. You know, being the *condo manager*, and all."

Sissy went bright red, and raised a manicured nail to point at Krystal. "You watch what you're saying, you little sl—"

"*Okaaaay!*" said Andrea, clapping her hands. "Time to get started with class!" She gave a high laugh and gestured to the clock. "Ready, Daisy?"

Casey blinked, both at Sissy's blinding outfit and the tension she felt among the four women in front of her. She was more than glad to cut that conversation short. "I'm ready."

The class leapt right into it, punching and kicking and shuffling as Casey instructed, and when Casey told them to imagine an attacker's face, they actually yelled out names. She thought she heard at least one person mention Brandon, but it went by too quickly, and there were too many voices for her to be sure. He had apparently made quite an impression on this bunch.

Most of the women stayed for the half-hour abs class at nine, and when that was over they begged for a preview of self-defense, which Sissy had planned for the next day.

"She's exhausted, ladies," Sissy said. "Give her until tomorrow."

The women moaned, disappointed, so Casey gave in. "I don't mind."

Sissy frowned. "You have to be tired."

"I am, but it's nothing sleep won't cure."

"If you're sure."

The ladies cheered, and Casey took a position in the front of the class. "So what are the three most important things when it comes to self-defense? Anyone know?"

"Strength!" someone yelled out.

"Pointy fingernails!"

"A good right hook!"

"Confidence." That was from Krystal, who seemed to have more than her share of it.

Casey nodded. "All good stuff. Especially the fingernails." She grinned. "But there are three you haven't mentioned that should be at the top of your list." She held up a finger. "Number one—speed."

Some of the women sniggered.

"Don't laugh, ladies. Your best chance of surviving an attack is to run away. Let's face it, a self-defense class can give you some good skills, but as a woman being assaulted by a man, your chances are less than good. Surprise, and getting the hell out of there, are your best friends. Got it? You have a chance to take off, you do it. No questions asked. Number two." She held two fingers up. "Any guesses?"

"Don't be stupid?" Andrea said.

Casey pointed at her. "Exactly. Don't be stupid. Do everything you can to *prevent* an assault. Don't walk to your car alone in a dark parking lot. Take a friend if you go shopping at night.

Make your own drinks at a party where you don't know anyone. Lots of you younger women–" she pointed out several, including Andrea and Krystal "—think nothing can happen to you. Let me be the first to tell you…it's not true."

Krystal cocked her hip. "So tell us your story. If you know stuff can happen, you must have firsthand experience."

"Another time." Wouldn't that be great? She could tell the whole group how she'd killed a man just two weeks earlier. That would go over well. And the cops would be on the doorstep by the time class was over. Casey held up three fingers. "So what is the final, and most important thing you can do to take care of yourself? What do you need to do to keep yourself safe?"

Sissy giggled. "Carry a gun?"

Several other women laughed.

Casey shook her head. "So a man can take it from you and put it to your head?"

Sissy reddened. "I was just joking."

"A lot of women see self-defense as a joke. It goes back to what I said about people thinking it can't happen to them."

"So what is it?" Andrea asked. "The most important thing?"

"Awareness," Casey said. "You have to pay attention to what's going on around you. If you think someone's following you, you're probably right. Take actions to get to a safe place. Notice where the shadows are. Where people could hide. If a man's looking at you funny, get out of his sightlines. Find a public place. Hold your car keys between your fingers. Never underestimate your opponent. And never, ever turn your back on someone you don't trust."

The women stared at her, some with their mouths hanging open.

"I thought this was a self-defense class," Death said from the back row. "Not a 'scare them shitless' class. You got a little intense just then."

Casey cleared her throat. "Sorry, folks. I just…this stuff is so important. I want you all to be prepared."

"So," Krystal drawled, "are you going to teach us any moves, or are we just going to leave here scared to death of getting raped and murdered on the way back to our condos?"

"Of course," Casey said. "You want to be my first volunteer?"

Krystal gave her that sultry smile and sauntered to the front. Casey could see Laurie wasn't the only woman in class who would like to see that smile erased. Casey herself felt no animosity toward the woman, but it didn't take a great stretch of her imagination to see why others would.

"Okay, so we'll talk about two things," she said. "The first is what you do with your hands."

"Hit 'em in the face!" someone shouted.

Casey laughed. "Good guess, but what might be the problem with that?"

It was silent for a few moments until Andrea said, "You can't reach it?"

"Exactly. There will be exceptions, but for the most part, a man is going to be larger than you. If he's got you—" she trotted to the wall, grabbed a step, set it behind Krystal, then stood on top of it and grabbed Krystal around the shoulders. "—there's not much chance to reach his nose or eyes. Try it, Krystal."

Krystal twisted around, trying to hit Casey's face, or any part of her head. She couldn't get close.

"So where *can* she reach?" Casey asked.

"Stomach!" someone said.

"Right." She reached forward and grabbed Krystal's elbow, bringing it slowly toward her diaphragm. "She's got me right here, in the solar plexus. The gut. That's going to knock my breath out, and it's going to hurt, giving her a chance to run away when my grip loosens. Where else can she reach?"

"Balls."

"Right. Curl your hand into a fist, Krystal."

She did.

"Now take the side of your fist and swing it up behind." She guided Krystal's hand toward her crotch. "That's called a hammer fist. It protects your fingers, and gets that solid mass of your hand hitting him where it hurts." She let go of Krystal and spun her around. "Now, if you're facing him?"

Krystal tried to reach Casey's face with her fingers, but Casey dodged the strike and grabbed Krystal's arm, twisting it behind her. "Not gonna work. Try again." She let Krystal go. Krystal balled her hand into a fist and aimed for Casey's nose. Again, Casey grabbed her arm and spun her. "Even if Krystal did connect, she's going to run the chance of breaking her fingers, or her thumb. Try this instead." Casey cocked her wrist, fingers and thumb spread back. "Hit him with the heel of your hand." She guided Krystal's hand first toward her throat, and then her stomach. "Either place would work."

"That's not really going to hurt him," Krystal said.

"But it's going to stun him. Remember what I said? You want to surprise him enough that you can *run away*."

Andrea was studying the situation. "Could she kick you?"

Casey let go of Krystal and pushed her gently back to her spot in the front row. "Come here, Andrea. Now, you've all just done a kickboxing class. Remember how you strike forward with your heel, your toes pulled back? You feel it in your calf, and your hamstrings? That's exactly what you're going to do here. Get him in the groin. Get him in the knee. The ankle." She pointed at herself, and Andrea aimed slow kicks toward those spots. "Anything to give you that jump on him. Anything to get away. To get help."

"What about screaming?" Sissy asked.

Casey smiled. "Scream as much as you can. Anything to get someone else's attention, or to distract your aggressor. The louder, then better." Although she couldn't remember making any noise when she fought that thug in Ohio. She was too busy trying to stay alive. "Okay, everyone partner up. Let's practice what we just talked about. Grab a step if you want, to simulate a height difference."

The women paired off, and Casey walked around the room, correcting mistakes and helping them to focus. While most could manage the moves, Casey could see their hearts weren't really in it. They were tired, or unfocused, or simply sure they would never have to use the skills to actually defend themselves. Casey wasn't sure how to deal with that. How do you make women attentive enough, without putting the fear of God in them?

After each woman had a chance to be both aggressor and defender, Casey stood on the step and raised her voice. "Okay! Good work, women. Can I have your attention one more time?" They quieted, and turned toward her. "We'll have a more formal class tomorrow evening. We'll practice these skills again, and add on a few more. Until then, what are the three most important things to remember?"

"Be smart!" someone yelled.

"Right. Common sense. Prevention. Don't put yourself in a dangerous situation. Another one?"

"Stay alert," Sissy said, clapping her hands like a schoolgirl.

"Yes. Be aware of what's going on around you. And last?"

"Hit 'em where it hurts," Krystal said.

Casey smiled. "Okay. That's a good one. Let's say that's number four. Hit 'em hard, somewhere soft. But what's the last one? If you find yourself in danger, what is the *best* thing you can do to save yourself?"

The class was so quiet Casey could hear herself breathing.

"You run," Andrea finally said.

"Exactly. Someone comes after you, you *run*. You run as fast as you can, and you don't stop until you're in a safe place. You got that?" She looked around the class, meeting each woman's eye.

"We run," Andrea said again, more confidently.

Casey nodded, and pounded her fist in her hand. "You *run*."

Chapter Eight

The Flamingo, Palm, and Pelican were surprisingly quiet in the late hours. It was close to midnight, and Casey sat on her balcony, drinking unsweetened hot mint tea. There was a chill in the air, but not enough to send her back in for a sweatshirt. The pool was still, its surface like unbroken, bluish glass, but several people lounged in the hot tub. Their occasional laughter was the only thing Casey heard, other than the ocean lapping against the shore beyond the palm trees.

"You gotta admit," Death said. "This is pretty darn nice." Death now wore a dark red housecoat and black slippers, and was holding a glass of red wine.

"It is." Casey took a deep breath of the sea air. "But I suppose I should go to bed. I have to get up in less than six hours for my Land of the Dead class."

"You know," Death said, "that's really not very PC."

Casey cocked an eyebrow. "Excuse me?"

"I mean, you wouldn't let someone call a class the Land of the Japs, or the Land of the Spinsters."

"That's because those names would offend people. Who is the Land of the Dead going to offend? Dead people?"

Death sniffed. "I know you like to pretend I don't exist, but *really*, Casey. Do you not see how that could bother me?"

"Do you not see how I don't care?"

Death sat up suddenly. "Uh-oh."

"What?"

"I gotta go." And Death disappeared without a trace.

Casey swallowed. It wasn't like Death to vanish like that, without an explanation. There must have been an emergency. A quick death somewhere. Casey didn't want to think about it.

Yawning and stretching, she stood up and went inside, where she got ready for bed. She dressed in her workout clothes so she would be ready when her alarm went off. No reason to dirty pjs, when she would barely be in them. She brushed her teeth, washed her face, and lay down on her bed.

And couldn't sleep.

She tossed and turned, wondering what her brother Ricky was doing. Was he still dating that woman she didn't like? Was the catering business going well? Perhaps she should get him and Del together—but no, she couldn't. What about Eric? Was he recovering from those events in Ohio? Did he ever think about their brief encounter in the back of the theater? Did he get as hot as she did, when he thought about it? And her lawyer, Don? Had he gotten in trouble for helping her?

Just how many lives had she screwed up?

She perched on the edge of her bed. Her brain was too busy for sleep. Her body was exhausted from leading so many classes that day. She needed something to occupy her mind. Someone to talk to. She couldn't call Ricky. She couldn't call Don. Or Eric. Not if she didn't want to mess them up even more. She wasn't about to call upon Death for conversation—she got more of that than she ever wanted. She looked at the clock. Twelve-thirty. Would Jack still be down in the bar? He'd said the bar closed at midnight, but she didn't really want to mix with whatever drinkers were still hanging around after last call.

Finally, she decided to just take a look. If there were lots of people there, or Jack was gone, she'd find something else to do. Simple as that. She slid on the soccer slides she'd bought at the shoe store, and went down the service stairs toward the first level.

Down in the lobby, she peered around the corner. Only two people remained in the bar area, a man and a woman, sitting very close together at a corner table. Behind the counter, Jack was doing his usual cleaning—at least, all the times Casey had seen him, that's what he'd been up to. She walked across the lobby and perched at a stool.

"Bar's closed," Jack said without looking up.

"But you said I could stop by any time."

He glanced up, smiling. "Ah, I wondered if I'd see you tonight. Thought it might be a little earlier, but this'll do." He grabbed a glass, filled it with club soda, and handed it to her.

"I really don't—"

"On the house," he said. "Just don't tell anyone."

"Wouldn't dream of it."

He slung his cloth over his shoulder and leaned on the bar. "So, what do you think of our little community so far?"

Casey looked up at the palm trees, the flowers, and the gleaming glass and countertop. "It's nice."

He gave a short laugh. "That would be one word for it."

"I thought it would be…busier." She gestured at the lounge.

"It was, up until twelve. Week night, you know. These folks like their partying, but they also have regular jobs. Wait till the weekend, then you'll see people out late."

"Young people hooking up?"

He grinned. "Not just young people."

"I thought the other buildings had their own lounges."

"They do, but that's the retirement crowd. The middle-aged crowd tends to hang here." He leaned even closer. "Sometimes they forget just how old they are."

"Age isn't a bad thing."

He rocked back. "Didn't say it was. Look at me. I'm not exactly a spring chicken." He smiled widely and spread his arms. "Prime of life, even with my thinning hair."

Casey smiled. He seemed to really mean it. He looked just like he should—no comb-over. No hair dye or teeth whitener. Just a fit, forty-something with confidence. And a very, very short buzz cut.

"The problem," he said, screwing a lid on a bottle, "is getting other folks to see it that way."

Casey thought of Sissy, with her bright orange hair, and Laurie, with her snow white teeth. They obviously hadn't bought into Jack's philosophy. But at least they worked at their health, promoting—and in Laurie's case, teaching—exercise.

Jack took a last look at the bar and came out from behind the counter. "Now, Daisy, I am off for my sleep, the one beauty aid I believe in, other than a good run in the morning."

"No aerobics for you?"

He laughed. "No, thanks. I see enough of those women at night. I don't need to see them during the day, too."

"Regular Casanova, huh?"

He looked surprised, then smiled. "Here at the *bar*, Daisy, not in my *personal* life. Most of these women, they're…not my type."

"Uh-huh."

He shook his head. "I'm outta here. You going up?" He gestured to the elevator.

She considered her plans. She was exhausted. Her body was tired. But she hadn't done her own workout. Her *kata*. And she was missing it. She glanced at the clock. Almost one. It was reckless. Stupid, even. But that huge, pristine aerobics room waited up one flight, silent and secluded.

"Just to the second floor, I think."

"Checking out your new domain?"

"Something like that."

"Well, goodnight then." He gave her a two-fingered salute and headed for the elevator.

Casey took the stairs to the fitness level. Everything was quiet. The floor was dark, lit with only security lights, and the window at the end of the hallway looked out onto the black sky.

Casey slid her magnetic key through the lock of the aerobics room, and the door clicked open. Not wanting to disturb the silence, she eased the door shut. The only sound was the quiet *snick* of the lock, which echoed throughout the room. Light filtered through the windows on the far end of the room, casting long shadows across the wooden floor. The steps and exercise balls huddled in dark lumps in the corners, and light reflected dimly off the wall-length mirror. The room smelled of sweat, and rubber equipment, and faintly of something fruity. Perfume, probably. Or the air freshener from the locker room.

Casey took off her slides and closed her eyes, then filled her lungs with air and raised her arms to the ceiling. She held the breath as long as she could before letting it out slowly, allowing her arms to drift downward. She repeated the process several times, then opened her eyes and began a simple routine.

Squat, swivel, extend, strike, turn, kick, jump, spin...

Her feet smacked lightly on the floor, adding their own rhythm to the night. Now it was just her breathing, and the tap of her skin against the slats.

Stretch, duck, strike, leap, step, hold, breathe...

She froze.

What was that sound? Another *snick*, like she'd made with the door as she'd come in. But the door to the aerobics room hadn't opened.

Casey straightened, and silently checked out every corner of the room. Her eyes had adjusted to the darkness, and she could see that no one hid in the shadows.

But she *had* heard that sound.

She padded over to the locker room and pressed her ear against the door. Nothing. No sound at all. She pushed open the door, ready to strike should someone be waiting on the other side. No one.

She backed out, and went to the aerobics room door. She stood to the side of the window and peered out. No one in her sightlines. She opened the door and looked up and down the hallway. Nothing. No indication that anyone had been there. She glanced up at the security camera mounted in the corner of the hallway. Had it caught anything just now? Had there been movement?

She stepped back into the aerobics room and eased the door shut. She had heard something. She knew she had. She couldn't just ignore it. If there had been someone in the locker room, why hadn't she been making any other sounds? Why hadn't she announced her presence? Was she breaking into Casey's office? Or was it a *he*?

Casey grabbed an eight-pound balance bar and went back to the locker room. Again, she prepared for an attack as she opened the door, this time with the bar in her right hand. No one came at her. She reached in with her left hand and flicked on the light. The brightness assaulted her, and she squinted at the bright tile and white walls.

"Hello?" Her voice pierced the silence.

No response.

She stood completely still, listening so hard it was almost painful. And then she heard it. A breath. No, a *gasp*.

Casey flexed her fingers and walked further into the room, swiveling her head from side to side as she passed the areas of lockers, and the sauna. Nothing. No one.

The area with the toilets and sinks was also empty, the clean shine almost blinding.

Which left only the showers.

Casey stepped carefully toward the row of individual showers. The curtains were all closed. Holding the bar firmly in her right hand, she swept open the first curtain to reveal the dressing area and shower stall. Empty. She did the same with the second, and the third. Finally, she stood before the fourth. She tightened her fingers around the bar, and yanked the curtain open.

A woman lay face down on the ground, halfway in the shower, halfway in the dressing area. She was soaking wet, but the shower had been turned off. Was it Krystal? Her blond hair spilled onto the tile floor of the shower, blood mingling with the messy strands, and her shirt lay bunched and torn around her shoulders, deep, bloody bruises dotting her back. Her arm rested in an unnatural position above her head, and her legs sprawled limply over the shower barrier and into the dressing area. A bloody iron hand weight, a ten-pounder, lay on the floor at her feet.

For a brief moment, Casey thought maybe this was where Death had rushed off to, but then the woman took a shuddering breath. Casey knelt beside her. She brushed aside the hair on the woman's cheek, and gave an involuntary gasp. It wasn't Krystal, as she had imagined, the victim of some jealous wife or boyfriend. It was Andrea.

Casey bent to look into Andrea's unfocused eyes. "I'm here, Andrea. I'm going to help you." She jumped up and raced to the training room. The door was locked. Uttering an oath, she ran back into the aerobics room, got her key, and rushed back to the training room, sliding the key through the lock. She lunged at the phone on the desk and dialed 911. A man answered, saying "Flamingo security."

"Security? I dialed 911."

"It comes right to us. What do you need?"

"An ambulance. Women's locker room."

"Who is this?"

"Ca—Daisy Gray, the new fitness instructor. Call 911! *Now!*"

She slammed down the phone and ran back to Andrea. "Help is coming."

Andrea took another shuddery breath, blowing a bubble laced with blood.

Casey stroked her cheek. "What happened, Andrea?"

Andrea swallowed forcefully, and attempted a smile. "I couldn't...do it."

"Couldn't do what?"

Andrea closed her eyes. "I couldn't run."

Chapter Nine

Casey sat in the waiting room at the hospital, shaking her knee up and down. She had blood on her clothes, her muscles had stiffened, and she kept dozing off and waking up abruptly, scaring herself. She hadn't been allowed to ride in the ambulance with Andrea, but the security guard had wakened Sissy. Sissy was too shaken to drive, so Casey got behind the wheel, something she usually avoided. Now, Sissy was at the hospital's registration desk, answering what questions she could about Andrea's insurance and family.

Two police officers stood on the other side of the room. One of them had already taken Casey's statement, and now they were waiting for a detective, who was checking out the crime scene back at the Flamingo. Casey was to stay put until she talked with her. Casey hoped the cops were there just to keep tabs on the situation, and not because they considered Casey a suspect in Andrea's attack.

Death sat beside Casey, pouting. "I hate waiting rooms."

Casey didn't respond.

"They're so…boring. I say, get it done, and move on. Why prolong the suffering?"

"Because sometimes people aren't *ready* to move on," Casey said. "Do you really still not get that? They're willing to live through the suffering to have more time *living*."

One of the cops glanced over, and Casey shut up. That would be just *super* to have the cops thinking she was a mental case.

"I wasn't talking about *their* suffering," Death said. "I was talking about *mine*, being put on hold like this. I think I'm coming to take someone away, and get stopped at the gates."

Sissy returned and sat on the other side of Casey. Her bright purple slacks and shirt were obscene in the sterile white and gray atmosphere. She kneaded her hands in her lap. "I just don't understand. Do you know how someone could get into the locker room like that? How could our security system not *catch* him?"

Casey really didn't want to list the ways, which included professional criminals, corrupt security guards, or, most troubling, violent residents.

"Did she *say* anything to you? Could she tell you who *did* this to her?" Sissy had already asked numerous times, but Casey's insistence that Andrea had said nothing didn't seem to sink in. Sissy acted as scared as ever that someone was lurking in the Flamingo, ready to kill the next person to cross his path.

"Does Krystal know?" Casey asked, changing the subject for what she hoped was the last time.

"I didn't call her. I wasn't sure if I should or not. We aren't exactly…friends."

"Maybe not, but Krystal and Andrea seem to be good ones. Andrea might want Krystal here when she wakes up."

"If…" Sissy hiccupped. "*If* she wakes up."

Casey wanted to reassure her, to say that of *course* Andrea would wake up. But she knew from very personal experience that many emergency patients never did. "Why don't you go ahead and call her?"

"Pointless," Death muttered. "This whole thing is pointless."

Sissy pulled out her cell phone and scrolled through her contacts. When she found Krystal's number, she got up and walked out of the room. She was back in under a minute, sniffling. "She's on her way. She was shocked. Completely shocked."

The double doors swung open and a man in scrubs looked around the room. Casey stiffened.

"You know she's alive," Death said grumpily. "Otherwise, why would I be in here and not there?"

Sissy popped up and hustled over to the surgeon. Casey followed.

"Family?" the surgeon said. His nametag read *Dr. Remon Neem*.

"We've called them," Sissy said. "But they live in Oregon. We're friends, from where she lives. I'm the manager of the condos."

Dr. Neem took in Casey's appearance, pausing when he reached the blood on her clothes, which she'd gotten from kneeling beside Andrea. "She was awake when you found her?"

"Yes."

"She is unconscious now. She is in very bad shape, and I cannot say what will happen. It depends how she progresses in the next twelve hours."

"What *happened* to her?" Sissy's eyes shone with tears.

"She was beaten very badly. There was a lot of internal bleeding, and the injury to the back of her head was quite severe. We will not know until morning if we were able to help her in time."

Sissy leaned against Casey, and Casey put her arm around the woman's shoulders, holding her up. "I'll take you home," Casey said. "Then I'll come back, okay? So someone's here when she wakes up."

"Krystal's coming. We can wait until then. And you can't leave until…until the detective gets here."

Right. Detective. Police. Everything Casey needed to avoid.

But she wasn't Casey Maldonado anymore. She was Daisy Gray. Fitness Instructor. Recent transplant from Tallahassee. Daisy had definitely not been in Kansas or Ohio recently, and she had *certainly* not killed anyone.

The surgeon took Sissy's hand. "We will let you know if she awakens, or if anything changes, all right?"

Sissy's sniffled some more, and tears leaked out from under her squeezed-shut eyes.

"Thank you, Doctor," Casey said.

He gave a little bow and went back through the doors.

"Come on, Sissy, let's get you back in a chair." Casey led her to her seat, and Sissy balled her hands into fists. "Oh, I should *never* have—" She stopped and pressed her hand over her mouth.

"What?" Casey didn't like the sound of whatever it was.

Sissy shook her head. "I can't…I'm *liable*."

"For what?"

Sissy hiccupped, and glanced at the cops. She lowered her voice. "The fitness floor hours are five AM to midnight. Andrea called me a couple weeks ago to ask if she could use the aerobics room during the night. She hadn't been sleeping well, and found yoga and meditation helpful. Krystal had been joining her lately, too. I wouldn't have allowed Krystal to use it on her own, of course, but the two of them seemed to enjoy doing that together. I didn't see the…the harm in it. Andrea has *never* caused a problem. Oh, what have I *done*?"

The cops looked over as Sissy wailed, and Casey held up her hand to say she had it under control.

"Sensitive, isn't she?" Death wore a surgeon's scrubs now, and was filing a fingernail. The nametag on the breast pocket said *Dr. Kevorkian*. "So the two of them were in a restricted area, after hours. Hadn't you just told their entire class not to put themselves in dangerous situations?"

"But they were together," Casey said. "Not alone. And within the building it shouldn't have been dangerous. Even if it *had* been only one of them."

"On the phone just now Krystal said she went up to bed ahead of Andrea," Sissy said. "Andrea wanted to do a little more of her yoga before going up."

Casey glanced at Death. "So she *didn't* take my advice."

Sissy wailed again, and squeezed Casey's thigh, her fingernails poking through Casey's warm-ups.

Krystal burst into the waiting room, and the cops immediately stood at attention. The male one for obvious man reasons, and the female for even more obvious woman ones. Her hand crept to her baton, and Casey hoped she'd get her jealousy under control before something bad happened.

Death whistled. "Ain't she something?"

Even this late at night, having been dragged out of bed, Krystal looked good. She wore a tank top and shorts, no make-up, and flip-flops. Her hair was mussed, and her face still had sleep lines, but that just gave her the seductive bedroom look her kind of woman can get away with.

"Where is she?" Krystal said.

"Oh, Krystal!" Sissy pulled herself from Casey's arm and flung herself at Krystal. "It's so awful. She just got out of surgery, but she's still asleep, and they think she might *die*."

Krystal looked at Casey over Sissy's shoulder, her eyes wide, arms stiff at her sides.

"The doctor said they'll know more by morning," Casey said.

Krystal's eyes closed briefly, then focused on Casey again. "How did you get here? Sissy's car? Can you take her home?"

"I'd be glad to, except I can't leave until I speak to the detective who's checking out the fitness floor."

Krystal paled. "So it really was there. I should *never* have left her." She pushed Sissy away and turned to the cops. "Can one of you take Sissy home?"

"I'm fine," Sissy said. "Really." And then she burst into a fresh round of tears.

The cops looked at each other, and the female one shrugged. "I'll take her. It'll make things easier. Come on, ma'am. Let's go." She took Sissy's elbow and guided her out of the waiting room, Sissy calling over her shoulder to "take care of Andrea," and to "let her know when anything happened."

Krystal stood in the middle of the room, arms hanging limply by her sides, her face haggard. "What happened?"

"We don't know."

"But you...you *found* her?"

"I went down to exercise. I couldn't sleep."

Krystal's face crumpled, but she quickly got it under control. "Andrea couldn't, either."

"That's what Sissy told me. Any idea why Andrea couldn't sleep for the last couple weeks?"

Krystal shook her head, but didn't say anything.

"She's not going to tell you," Death said. "She's known you, what? Twenty hours?"

Death was right, of course. Krystal had no reason to trust her.

"Do you know…" Krystal said. "Was she assaulted? I mean, sexually?"

Casey thought back. Neither she nor Sissy had asked. "The doctor didn't say anything. I'm hoping that means she wasn't."

Krystal let out a breath. "At least there's that."

At least.

Now Andrea just had to live to appreciate it.

Chapter Ten

"Ms. Gray?"

Casey blinked up at the woman standing by her chair. She cleared her throat. "That's me." Casey had fallen asleep, and she shook her head to wake herself up.

"I'm Detective Binns. Okay if we go somewhere more private to talk?"

"Sure." Casey glanced at Krystal, who had curled up on a couch, and was sleeping. Someone had covered her with a blanket. No one had bothered to cover Casey. She would choose to assume it was because Krystal was wearing shorts and had looked cold, while Casey had on warm-ups, and not that Krystal somehow inspired acts of chivalry while Casey was ignored.

Casey followed the detective to a small room off of the waiting room. Another officer followed, and shut the door behind them, but Casey barely registered him. She was still in a daze. Binns gestured to a chair, and Casey sat, trying to will herself awake. Binns pulled a chair in front of her. She was small and dark-haired, and she regarded Casey with compassion. "I'm sorry for what you've been through tonight. It had to shake you up."

Casey rubbed the sleep out of her eyes. "It did. I'll feel better once we know she makes it through the night."

"Before I talk anymore, I'd like you to run me through the events of the past several hours, please. Officer Gomez will take notes."

"Of course." Casey took a look at the other officer now, and immediately wished she hadn't.

Gomez was tall and dark, looking way more like Reuben than was good for anybody. He introduced himself with a distinct Spanish accent, which set Casey's heart hammering. She closed her eyes and took a deep breath to get her thoughts in order. *He is not Reuben. He is not Reuben.* When she'd recovered at least a little, she opened her eyes and focused on the detective, telling her about the extra self-defense class, how she couldn't sleep afterward, and how she'd decided to head down to the aerobics room. She got a little shaky as she talked about the sound she'd heard, and about finding Andrea and seeing the bloody hand weight, and calling security.

"Why didn't you call 911?"

"I did, but the phone must be set up to go directly to the on-site guards."

"Anything else?"

"Not that I can think of."

Binns sat back, studying Casey. "You're new in town."

"Just came yesterday, for the job. I got officially hired today."

"You didn't know anyone here in Raceda previously?"

"No. I found the job on monster.com."

Binns gazed at her some more. Casey knew she looked uncomfortable, but she figured most people would be uncomfortable in that situation.

"I want you to know right off," Binns said, "that we're not considering you a suspect in the attack."

"What? Why?" Casey checked herself. "I mean, thank you."

"Don't thank me. Thank Andrea."

"Andrea? Is she awake?"

"No. She roused just enough to say a few words to the paramedics when they arrived at the scene. She said your name, and that you had saved her."

"Did she name the person who attacked her?"

"No. Those few words about you were all she managed before she blacked out. So you're in the clear."

"But I could've hurt her and then called—"

Binns held up her hand. "It wouldn't be the first time an attacker contacted law enforcement, so if it weren't for back-up evidence, I would probably discount her statement."

"What evidence?"

"The security camera mounted in the service stairway caught you going up to the second floor at twelve fifty-four. Where had you been?"

"Bar. Talking to Jack, the bartender, not drinking. You can ask him."

"Oh, we will. Anyway, the camera on the fitness floor got you going into the aerobics room, and looking out several minutes later. Your clothes are not bloody in either of those films. Furthermore—"

"It wouldn't have taken long for me to go into the locker room after you saw me on the tape, beat up Andrea, and call the cops."

Binns' eyebrows went up. "Are you *trying* to put yourself back on the suspect list?"

"No, I'm just…looking at all the angles."

"We are, too, Ms. Gray. Believe me." She looked down at her notes, holding them at arm's length and squinting. "*Furthermore*, there was another key used to get into the training room before you were even on the floor."

"Another…from which direction?"

"The men's locker room."

Casey considered this. "Do you know whose card it was?"

"The access number belonged to Maria Mendez."

"The receptionist?"

"Administrative assistant. Who is, at this moment, in her home. We had a unit go directly there, and she was tucked up in bed, asleep. Her car was cold, and there was no record of her returning to the building after she left at five."

Casey tried to take it all in. "What about the camera in the other hallway? The one on the men's locker room door?"

"Sabotaged. It looks like someone used Vaseline to smear it. We get only the up close view of a gloved finger over the lens about two minutes before someone enters the men's locker room at twelve twenty-two. Then we get another blurred image of a person leaving the same locker room fourteen minutes later."

"That early? Are you sure? I heard someone when *I* was there, around one. That's why I went into the locker room in the first place."

"We're sure."

"And you couldn't tell who it was? Nothing about size? Tall? Short? Fat? Whether it was a man or a woman?"

Binns shook her head. "Or even if it's the same person both times. It's like a fun house mirror. The Vaseline created a lens that couldn't properly register correctly what it was seeing. Plus, the picture is black and white, and the only lights in the hallway were the nighttime security bulbs, which didn't offer a lot of illumination. We have our technicians working on it, of course, but I don't hold out a lot of hope."

Casey smacked the arms of her chair. "If only I'd been a few minutes earlier I would've heard something happening. I could've stopped it."

"You can't be sure of that." Binns' voice was gentle.

Casey sat back and exhaled. "So now what? Do you have anything to go on?"

"Frankly," Binns said, "you would be my number one suspect, if it weren't for the technology."

"And Andrea's statement."

Binns' lip twitched upward. "Right. New girl in town, known by no one, I'd almost think you came to town for just this reason. Although if that were so, you'd be across the border into Georgia by now."

"I didn't do it."

"I know." She sighed loudly and put her notebook away. "It would've made it a lot easier if you had."

A knock came on the door, and the male cop from the waiting room stuck his head in. He looked very somber.

"What is it?" Binns said.

"Andrea Parker." He paused. "She's dead."

Chapter Eleven

Casey's head spun, and she grabbed her chair. No. *No!*

"I'm sorry, sweetie." Death stood just inside the room, cradling Andrea's soul. "All that stuff I said about wanting it to be over…I didn't mean it."

Casey launched from the chair toward the door, toward Death. "You don't care! All you care about is yourself, and your *job*." She made quotation marks in the air. "You don't even think about the people themselves. Who they leave behind. Who they were."

The officer in the doorway paled. "I…I do. I think about them all the time."

"What?" Casey blinked, her eyes focusing on the man in blue. "No. Not *you*."

Gomez held her arm, and Binns got between Casey and the officer in the doorway, looking straight into Casey's face. "Ms. Gray, I know this has been a shock to you. This whole night has. Maybe you should sit down." Gomez tried to guide Casey to a chair, but Casey pulled away, her hands on her face.

"Officer," Binns said to the man in the doorway. "Why don't you leave us for a bit?"

"But I didn't—it's not true what she—"

"Not your fault. She's obviously not well. Gomez and I have it under control."

The officer backed out and shut the door.

"I'm sorry," Casey said from under her hands. "I know it's not his fault. I didn't mean to take it out on him."

"He'll be all right."

Casey leaned her forehead against the wall and took several deep breaths. When she'd calmed herself, she turned around, avoiding Gomez' eyes and backing away from him. "I'm okay. I'm sorry."

"I need to talk with the doctor," Binns said. "And you need to go home."

"There's nothing else I can do?"

Binns gave a little smile. "The best thing you can do for anybody is rest, and get your head together. I'll have Officer Gomez here take you back to your place."

Gomez. Not him. Casey couldn't take a Reuben look-alike right then. But it wasn't like they were giving her a choice. Casey averted her eyes from him and walked through the door Binns held open. They went down the little hall to the waiting room, where Krystal perched on the end of the couch, a pillow clutched to her stomach. She sat completely still, except for the tears that ran down her cheeks.

Casey nodded toward her. "Should we take her home, too?"

Binns shook her head. "I need to get her statement. I'll have an officer bring her home later."

"Can I talk to her?"

"Sure."

Binns followed Casey to the sofa, obviously wanting to hear the conversation.

"Krystal?" Casey sat next to her. Krystal didn't move. "Krystal, I'm so sorry."

Another tear trickled from Krystal's eye, but still she didn't blink.

"The detective wants to talk with you, and then she'll bring you home, okay?" Casey set her hand on Krystal's arm, and Krystal started.

She looked at Casey without recognition for a moment, before her eyes widened. "You! You were supposed to *save* her!

All that talk about self defense and being alert and all that crap. Where were *you* when she was being attacked?"

"I'm sorry, I—"

Krystal slapped Casey's face. Casey jerked backward, and Binns caught her as she fell off the couch. Officer Gomez placed himself between Krystal and Casey, just as Binns had protected the other officer from Casey.

"Whoa, Ms…" Binns looked at Casey, a question in her eyes.

Casey shook her head. She didn't know Krystal's last name.

"It's her fault!" Krystal shrieked, pointing around Gomez at Casey. "She should've saved her! She should've been there! Should've taught her better…" She dissolved into sobs.

Binns patted Casey's shoulder, then squeezed past Gomez to take Casey's place next to Krystal, putting her arm around her shoulders and murmuring something Casey couldn't hear.

Casey held a hand to her cheek. It stung, but there was no blood. It was a good thing her injuries from the week before had healed, so there was nothing to burst open.

"Are you all right?" Gomez was looking at her with concern, which was the *last* thing Casey needed.

"Gomez," Binns said. "Get Ms. Gray out of here."

Gomez snapped to attention. "Yes, ma'am. This way please, Ms. Gray."

Casey wanted to say something to Krystal to calm her down, to apologize again, but she would probably only make things worse. She followed Gomez out the emergency room exit and slid into the back seat of the cruiser.

"The Flamingo?" Gomez looked at her in the rearview mirror.

Casey nodded, and let her head fall back against the seat.

"I wouldn't rest my head there, if I were you." Death now wore a police outfit, complete with gun and baton. This time the nametag said *Officer Azrael.* "You don't know how many people—*criminals*—have laid their greasy heads there."

Casey closed her eyes and rolled her head the opposite direction.

"Fine. But don't blame me when you end up with lice. Or dandruff. Or dreadlocks." Death sighed. "Look, sweetie, I know you're tired, but you can't let people like Krystal make you feel bad. She's tired, too. And completely freaked out."

"I know."

"Pardon?" Gomez said.

"Nothing. Sorry." She glared at Death.

"Not my fault." Death gave her a look of innocence. "Anyhow, as I was saying, I know Binns isn't putting you on the suspect list, but you have to realize that most people will, once they think about it. You're brand new, you're teaching self-defense, they don't know you from Eve—who, by the way, looks an awful lot like Krystal. Except darker-skinned, with longer hair."

Casey opened her eyes to watch the lights go by. Already the sky was brightening. Dawn was coming, and it would soon be time for the six-o'clock class. The Land of the Dead. Suddenly, that name wasn't nearly so cute. There was no way they'd be exercising that day. The cops would have the area cordoned off, for sure. And Casey was in no shape to be leading it.

Gomez parked the car at the front of the Flamingo. He got out and came around to Casey's door, opening it and offering her his hand.

She climbed out on her own, not wanting to touch him. "Thank you, Officer."

"You're not rid of me quite yet, Ms. Gray. I'm to wait and collect your clothes."

Casey looked down at her blood-stained outfit. She'd just bought it the day before. She'd never wear it again. She never wanted to *see* it again.

"Sure," she said. "Come on in."

The guard was one Casey hadn't seen before, a young, impossibly good-looking blond thing, probably a college student making money by moonlighting as a security guard. She showed him her ID and signed in. Officer Gomez had only to nod, and he was through.

Casey led Gomez across the empty lobby—not even Jack was there this time—to her apartment, and he waited in the living room while she changed. She brought everything out, including her underclothes and her shoes, and put it in a bag.

"Nice view you've got here." Gomez stood at the window, gazing down at the pool, which shimmered in the dim light. Several apartments in the other two buildings had lights on, but most were dark.

Casey stared at Gomez's back with a knot in her stomach. If she didn't know better, it really could be Reuben standing there. The height, the build, the coloring, the accent. "Here you go." She held out the bag, then dropped it to her side.

Gomez left the window and crossed to her. He hesitated after taking the bag. "You're sure you'll be all right?"

Casey stared into his dark eyes, wanting him to fold her into his arms, to whisper in her ear that everything was going to be fine. Wanting him to take care of her. To be Reuben.

"I'm fine. Thank you, Officer Gomez."

"Manny," he said. "You can call me Manny."

She took a shuddering breath. Calling him by his first name would help absolutely nothing. It made him…even more real. Like a man, in addition to being a cop.

"We'll be typing up your statement," Gomez said. "And then we'll need you to sign it. But I know Detective Binns wants you to get some rest first."

Rest. Right.

"We'll be in touch." He touched his finger to his forehead and left.

Casey closed the door behind him, and leaned against it.

Coming to Florida was a bad idea, after all. A very, *very* bad idea.

Chapter Twelve

Forty-five minutes later, close to six, Casey went downstairs, having used that time to sit at her little dining table and stare into space. Already a crowd had formed in the hallway by the aerobics door, stopped from entering by the crime scene tape. The hum of curiosity cut off as Casey approached.

"I'm sorry." Casey felt like she'd been apologizing for the past six hours. "We won't be having class this morning."

"Why? What happened?" A chorus of voices assaulted her, and she winced at the volume.

"I'm afraid there was…" What should she say? Telling them Andrea had been assaulted could cause mass panic. But anything else would be a lie. "I'm afraid your classmate, Andrea Parker, died over the night."

Several of the women gasped, and one immediately burst into tears. They peppered Casey with questions, but she held up her hand. "Andrea was in the locker room, so the police need to finish their investigation here before we can use it again."

"But why were the police here?" someone asked. "Was she *murdered*?"

Casey took a deep breath through her nose and let it out in a slow exhale. "They don't know what exactly happened yet. That's why they need the room."

"But—"

Casey held up her hand. "I don't have anything else to tell you. I'm sorry."

"What about Krystal?" someone said. "Where's she?"

"The last I knew she was at the hospital. She'll be back soon."

"Was she hurt, too?"

"No. She went to be with Andrea."

There was an uncomfortable silence.

"Too bad *she* didn't die," someone muttered, but when Casey tried to see who'd said it, there was no way to tell. All of the women looked everywhere but at Casey, making the entire group seem guilty.

"Well, she's alive," Casey said, her voice hard. "And I would think you'd want *all* of your classmates to stay that way. Now go back to your apartments, or wherever. We'll be in touch when classes can start again." She spun on her heel and marched away, back up the stairs to her own place. She slammed the door and stood in the middle of the room, unsure what to do with herself.

"Can't blame them," Death said from the sofa. "The woman does sort of suck all of the attention out of a room. You experienced it yourself, at the hospital."

"But I didn't wish her *dead*."

"Not like you wish for yourself, anyway."

Casey turned away and stomped to her bedroom, where she discarded her old shoes and dropped backward onto the bed, putting her arm over her eyes. "Good grief, it's like high school all over again. Let's all hate the pretty girl instead of focusing on our own screwed up lives."

"Hmm," Death said. "What if Andrea *wasn't* the one who was supposed to die?"

Casey lifted up her arm. "What?"

"You just said it. Everybody hates Krystal, and they looked a lot alike. Andrea and Krystal, I mean. Same hair color, skin color, basic size. It was just the...well, you know...that was a bit different." Death sketched an hourglass shape in the air.

"I thought it *was* Krystal lying there in the shower. It wasn't until I moved her hair and saw Andrea's face that I realized it wasn't."

"So even you think Krystal deserves killing more than Andrea."

"I didn't say that! I just thought if anyone would be attacked, it would be Krystal. Jealous women. Boyfriends. Who knows? How many people said things about her yesterday, and they hardly even know me? Sissy. Laurie. Even Del. Krystal was hard to ignore, and Andrea had that chummy feeling, rather than the…" She waved her hand.

"Sex goddess-y feeling?"

"Exactly." Casey dropped her arm back over her face.

"You do realize you have personal training in less than an hour, right?"

Casey groaned. "I have to sleep."

"Go ahead. I'll wake you when it's time."

"You won't let me oversleep?"

"I promise."

Fifty minutes later, Casey felt a cold breeze on her face.

"Rise and shine," Death said, grinning from an inch away.

Casey shut her eyes again. "A little space, please."

"What, no thank you? No appreciation for getting you going?"

"Fine. Thank you. Did you make coffee?"

"You know I can't do that."

Casey eased herself up, her head fuzzy. "I don't know if I'm going to make it."

"Two sessions, then you can come up for another nap during the time you would be teaching aerobics."

Casey chugged a Gatorade and put on her shoes. "If I faint, don't think I'm dead and carry me away."

"But I thought you wanted to come over."

"I do. I just want to actually be dead when I do it."

Casey grabbed her personal training schedule and stumbled down the steps to the weight room, where she purposely did not look to see if there was an obvious spot where the missing weight—the one that had killed Andrea—should be resting. She couldn't keep her eyes from the entire area, however, and the first person she saw was the tall, dark woman from the lobby and pool. She lay on a bench, pumping a massive amount of iron. Sweat rolled from her face, and muscles bulged in her shoulders and arms. Casey caught her eye in the mirror and was about to walk over when a young man stepped in front of her.

"Dylan," he said, tossing a towel over his shoulder. He appeared to be in his early twenties, and couldn't hide the smirk from his face. "*You're* the trainer?"

"That's me. Daisy. I know I look like hell, but I had a bad night."

He went suddenly serious. "I heard. You found Andrea?"

"Yes. Did you know her?"

"Sure. Know her friend better, though."

Casey wanted to smack the smug look from his face, but figured that probably wasn't the best way to start their training. "Come on. Let's begin at the cardio equipment. How about you hop on the treadmill?"

"I like the elliptical better."

"We'll get to that later. You can tell me about your present routine while you're warming up."

With no further argument, he stepped onto the machine and began walking. Casey took another look toward the free weights. The woman was gone. Disappointed, Casey turned her attention back to Dylan, and they got lost in the talk of goals and repetitions and exercises. After five minutes of warm-up, she led him to the free weights. It took only a little time for her to assess his fitness and make some changes to his routine. In-between sets she tried to sound casual as she asked him questions.

"So, how long did you know Andrea?"

He swiped his towel over his head. "I don't know. Six months or so. That's when I moved here. But like I said, I didn't really know her all that well. Just from hanging around Krystal." He got back on the bench and Casey stood over him, her hands out to spot the weights, should he falter doing his presses.

"What do you know about her? Boyfriends? Family? Anything?"

Dylan grunted as he lifted the bar. "She's from the west coast somewhere. Washington, maybe?"

"I think Sissy said Oregon."

"Yeah. That sounds right." He pushed the bar up again, veins popping out on his neck.

"Ever see her hang out with anybody?"

"Just Krystal. No regular guys. You know, Krystal's really the one to ask about Andrea."

Except right now she hated Casey's guts. "You still dating Krystal?"

Dylan let out a laugh as he strained to lift the bar upward. "You don't *date* Krystal."

"What do you mean?"

"You have the privilege of going out with her when she says yes. If she likes what happens, you might get to do it again. But you have to expect she'll be doing it with other guys in-between."

"Doing what, exactly? Sex?"

He grimaced, and set the bar on the stand. He swung his legs so he was sitting on the bench, and ran his towel around his neck. "Could be. But it could also be that you're spending way too much money buying her jewelry. Or taking her rock climbing. Or doing whatever else she's convinced you to do."

"She's got power," Casey said.

Dylan gestured to the heavy weights he'd just used. "You think these are hard work? Nothing compared to Krystal." He shrugged, stretching his back. "But she's worth it."

The door opened and an older man came into the room. He scanned the area, and caught Casey's eye. She held up a finger to say she'd be right with him. "Okay, Dylan, cardio of your choice."

"Elliptical," they said together.

"At least twenty minutes."

"I usually go thirty."

"Good. Check in with me before you head out, okay?"

He held up a fist, and she studied it for a second before bumping it with her own.

"You're okay," Dylan said.

"Gee, thanks."

He grinned, and headed toward his machine.

Casey watched him go, shook her head, and went to meet her next client.

"From the cradle to the grave," Death said.

She gave Death a startled glance. Death wore a weight belt, gloves, shorts, and a muscle shirt, along with a nice pair of Chuck Taylors. "What are you talking about?"

"Dylan. He's a mere babe, and your next guy, not so much."

Death was right. Her next client was eighty-two, and rather than talk about Andrea—and certainly not Krystal, for fear of a heart attack—Casey spent all of her energy trying to keep him from doing more than he should. She felt a surge of sympathy toward Richie, the fitness instructor two before her. If he hadn't stayed firm with people like her present client, it was no wonder people were getting injured. By the time her guy was on the recumbent bike Casey thought she was going to collapse from the strain.

"I'm outta here." Dylan stood beside her, sweaty and so very young. "You know, you don't look so good."

Casey raised her eyebrows. "In what way?"

"In a way like you might keel over. Need help getting up to your room?" He grinned and waggled his eyebrows.

Casey laughed. "I think I can make it. Thanks."

"Another time, then."

"Oh, will there be a time I'm not old enough to be your mother?"

"You're not."

"Baby-sitter, then."

He studied her. "I guess you are. But who cares these days? Anyway, it's all over Cougarville in the Flamingo."

"Really? You have older women after you?"

"All the time, baby. And let me tell you, older women—as long as they're not *too* old—can teach a boy like me a few tricks."

Casey shook her head, trying not to laugh again. "You're awful."

"But sexy."

"Get out of here."

He dodged the towel she threw at him, then picked it up and tossed it back. "See you in a couple days, hottie." He sauntered away, chuckling.

"Now that boy needs a real woman." Death stared after Dylan.

"Well, it's not going to be me."

"No, you'd rather have that pretty Officer Gomez who brought us back last night."

Casey went hot. "I'd rather have nobody."

"Oh, come on. Reuben might be dead, but like it or not, you're still here, with all your female parts working. I thought Eric taught you that a couple weeks ago. I seem to remember some sweating, and some clothes coming off."

Casey hastily threw her towel in the laundry bin and said hello to the woman who stood beside the shelves of clean linen, folding and stacking. What was her name? Rosa? Rosa's nose was red, and her eyes bloodshot. Casey stopped. She didn't know enough Spanish to have a meaningful conversation, but she hated to just walk by a grieving woman.

"Andrea?" she said quietly.

Rosa let go with a sob, and pressed her hand over her mouth.

"I'm sorry," Casey said. "She was your friend? *Amiga?*"

Rosa nodded. "Yes. She was…nice lady."

"Yes," Casey said. "*Sí.*" She patted Rosa's arm, and continued into the hallway. The crime scene tape was still draped across the doorway of the aerobics room, although she could see no sign of activity inside. A couple of women in workout clothes lingered in the hallway, trying to see through the glass in the door, but Sissy was not among them.

"Is it true?" A middle-aged woman in clothes too tight for her extra padding grabbed Casey's arm.

Casey extricated herself from the woman's claws. "Depends what you heard."

"That a crazy man broke in and attacked some women last night. That one of them died, and the rest are still in the hospital." Her chin quivered, and the rest of the group pushed forward, waiting for Casey's answer.

"One person was assaulted, and died. Andrea Parker. No one else was hurt, and no one else is in the hospital."

"But that friend of hers isn't here. Krystal. And we haven't seen Sissy. And *you* were at the hospital."

The mixture of eagerness and curiosity on the woman's face made Casey's stomach turn. This woman wasn't so much worried about safety as she was about landing a juicy scandal. "Krystal and Sissy are probably both still in bed. It was a late night. All of us were at the hospital, but just because of Andrea. None of the rest of us were with her when it happened."

She said all that as fact, but she didn't really know that, did she? Krystal had *said* she'd left Andrea alone, but what if she hadn't? What if she was there when the person broke in? What if she'd had something to *do* with it?

Casey shook her head. That was just stupid. Krystal wouldn't have hurt her friend. And the cameras would have caught two people on tape in the hallway if she'd been there, instead of just the one blurred image. Unless that one person was Krystal.

Casey wasn't seeing it.

The women were asking her something else now, the gossipy woman's fingernails again digging into Casey's arm. Casey shrugged off the woman's hand when she realized what they were asking.

"Of course I didn't do it," Casey said. "And the cops know that."

"But *how* do they know?" the fat woman said, her chins flapping. "They don't know everything. You could be working for…for the mafia."

"What? And Andrea was connected to them?"

"You never know anymore, with all these Cubans coming over, and illegal aliens, and communists—"

"Andrea wasn't Cuban."

"But she could've *known* some Cubans."

"*Everybody* in this part of Florida knows Cubans." Casey took a deep breath, praying she wouldn't kill this woman without being aware of what she was doing in her sleep-deprived state. "I don't know when classes will resume, ladies. We'll be in touch, okay?"

"All classes are canceled for today." Maria Mendez, the administrative assistant, strode toward the door with a sign. It said simply, "All classes canceled," along with the date. "As soon as the police are finished with the room we can get back to our regular schedule. Probably tomorrow."

"But I need my workout," the pudgy woman said.

"So go run around the block. Or maybe walk. You've got legs."

Casey was surprised at the tone of Maria's voice, but the women responded to the sound of authority, and stopped asking questions. They sniffled and fidgeted, gradually moving away.

"You okay?" Casey asked Maria when the women were out of earshot.

"What do you think?" Maria's eyes looked just the slightest bit wild, and her usually perfect hair was lopsided. "It was my key. *My key* was used to get to Andrea. How will I ever be okay?"

"If it hadn't been yours, they would've found another. It's not your fault."

"Easy for you to say." She hiccupped, then closed her eyes briefly. "I'm sorry. I know you found her. That wouldn't have been easy at all."

"No. It wasn't."

"And half the residents think you did it."

"I know. Do you think so?"

Maria shrugged. "How do I know? You could be anybody. A killer. A thief. Or even a woman who was in the wrong place at a very wrong time. The cops say it wasn't you."

"Do you believe them?"

"When do I ever believe cops?"

With that, she turned and walked away.

When she was gone, Casey realized there was still one person left in the hallway. Laurie, the other fitness teacher, sat with her back against the wall, knees pulled up to her chest. Her face was white, and she stared at the carpet.

Casey squatted next to her. "Laurie?"

She took a shuddering breath. "So Andrea's really dead."

"Yes."

Laurie's mouth worked, and she turned her head to look back down the hallway. "Do they know who did it? Did she tell the cops?"

"No, she didn't." She'd used her last breaths to tell them Casey hadn't done it. While Casey was grateful for that, she wished Andrea would have named her assailant. But perhaps she didn't because she didn't know who it was. Had she even seen the face of her killer? Or had she been surprised? Or was her brain too addled by that point to even remember what had happened? She'd told Casey she wasn't able to run. Was that because she was in the confined area of the shower, or because she'd been hit so hard she was unable to move? When Casey had found her, she was lying face down on the tile. That would make sense if the person got her from behind.

Laurie gave a big shiver, and pressed her face against her knees.

"Laurie," Casey said, "were you and Andrea close?"

Laurie gave a little sob. "No. I only knew her from classes. She was younger than me. She had her own friends. Her own life. So much ahead of her. It had nothing to do with me. None of it did." She took another shuddering breath. "She didn't deserve to die. Not like that."

"Of course not. No one does."

Laurie sniffed harshly, and slowly turned her head toward Casey, resting her cheek on her knees. A strange little smile fluttered on her lips, and her eyes looked almost manic for just a moment before she blinked and her eyes dimmed again. "No one does. That's right. Of course." She pushed herself up, leaning against the wall for support. "I'll just...I'll just go."

"Let me help you."

She flapped her hand at Casey. "No, no, I'm fine. I'll be fine. You go on. You do…whatever you need to do." She walked to the elevator and punched the button continually until the doors opened, and she got on.

"Now that was just creepy." Death stood beside Casey in a light yellow uniform, complete with rubber gloves. An embroidered patch on the breast pocket said, *Eternally Clean. For that Spotless Finish.* The name under the logo read, *Enma Daiou.* "Did you see the way she turned her head and looked at you? It was like *The Exorcist* all over again, except she's a lot older. And her head didn't spin around."

"It *was* weird, like she was trying to convince herself Andrea shouldn't have died. Or at least that they weren't friends. I'm thinking there's more to their relationship than we know."

"So Andrea's death really *didn't* have anything to do with Krystal, after all?"

Casey shrugged. "Andrea was a strong woman on her own. Krystal couldn't have overshadowed everything. Could she?"

"But if what you're saying is true, then Andrea had her own darker secrets. If Laurie wanted her dead."

"She didn't actually *say* that. She just protested a little too much that she and Andrea had nothing to do with each other. It could just be she's sad she wasn't better friends with her. Almost like she wished she had been. Or at least that she would have been young like her, and moving in her circles."

"Which means we should find out exactly what went on—or didn't go on—between them."

"Right." Casey sagged against the wall. "But right now I need another power nap. I'm going to my room."

"And miss all the fun?"

"What fun?"

"As we speak, the cops are on their way to take another look."

"Then I'll let them do their job."

"You don't want to watch?"

"I've already seen it, L'Ankou. I don't want to see it again." In fact, the mere idea of going back into the locker room with

Andrea's blood still on the shower floor made her queasy. "You stay if you want. I'm going to bed."

"Don't forget to set your alarm. You have more personal training in an hour."

"Yes, *mother*."

The elevator clunked, signaling the arrival of the police.

Casey ducked into the service stairwell and trudged up to her apartment.

Chapter Thirteen

Casey did, in the end, forget to set her alarm, and woke up only because someone was banging on her door. She rolled out of bed and stumbled to her living room, her right leg asleep from the awkward position she'd lain in.

"I thought you might be here." It was Sissy. Her nose was red, and her eyes swollen, which seemed to have become the uniform look around the building. She wore a subdued maroon pantsuit and clasped a well-used handkerchief in her hands.

Casey rubbed her eyes, not really awake. "What is it?"

"It's two-o'clock."

"Two—" Casey shot a look at the clock. "I'm missing water aerobics." She turned to get her swimsuit, but Sissy grabbed her arm.

"I told the class all sessions would be canceled today, even though the pool is open."

"I missed some personal training appointments, too." Casey groaned and sagged onto a chair. "I'm sorry. First day on the job and I'm letting you down."

"No, no." Sissy shut the door and sat down across the table from Casey. "I should be apologizing to you. You came here and got dragged into something awful that had nothing to do with you." She pierced Casey with a look. "Right?"

Casey closed her eyes, trying to make sense of what Sissy was saying. "Right *what*?"

"She wants to know if you had anything to do with Andrea's death, or know anything about it." Death sat on the sofa in an outfit the same color as Sissy's, with the addition of a jaunty hat. "She doesn't want to admit she might've made a mistake hiring you, but she doesn't completely trust you, either."

Casey snapped her head toward Sissy. "I had nothing to do with Andrea's murder. You can ask the detective. She's already ruled me out."

"I know she has. But some of our residents are inquiring. You show up, and immediately one of our people is dead. It's my duty to check in with you."

Casey felt sick. "I understand they might be wondering. But tell them to ask the cops if they doubt me. The police can prove it wasn't me."

"Can they prove you don't know anything about it? That you weren't a part of it at *all*?"

"A part of— Look. I'm sorry you don't trust me. I'm sorry I didn't have references." She was, in fact, sorry she'd ever even considered coming to Florida, let alone the Flamingo. "But I knew none of these people before coming here, or anyone associated with them. And I don't know anything about who it could have been last night. I certainly didn't see them, or I would have said something by now." She rubbed her forehead. "Believe me, I would leave right now if it would make everyone feel better, but there's no way the cops will let me go before they're done investigating."

"Because they still think you did it?"

"No! Because I'm the one who found Andrea. Remember? I tried to save her?"

Sissy looked down at the handkerchief she was twisting in her hands. "I know. I know you tried." She wiped her nose. "It's just...I've made some bad decisions. I want people to know that this time the bad things didn't happen because I hired you."

Casey reached across the table and laid her hand on Sissy's. "It wasn't me. You can stop worrying about that."

"Just…be careful, okay? Some of them are angry. They're sending a petition around to have you kicked out."

"Who is?"

She hesitated. "Krystal."

"I knew she was trouble," Death sighed, "from the moment I first saw her luscious bod."

"She's in shock," Casey said. "She just lost her best friend."

"Still," Sissy said. "It's awful."

"It's a way for her to deal with her grief." Not a good way, or productive, but Casey really couldn't blame her. "Are many people signing it?"

"That's the thing. They aren't. Those who took your classes yesterday don't believe you would've done it, and those who didn't meet you won't sign it without knowing more. I mean, sure, she's gotten a few dozen signatures, but those are mostly from the retirees who live in the other two buildings and wouldn't set foot in an exercise class to save their lives. They just want a scandal. It's why they moved to Florida, really, besides the beach and the eternal summer."

"Not eternal," Death said. "Poor choice of words. *Perpetual* summer. That would be better."

"So what about the rest of the day?" Casey said. "Do I stay holed up in here?"

"It's up to you. It might be good to show your face around a bit, so people see you have nothing to feel guilty about. If they know your face, they can't just blame some anonymous person. But…" She hesitated.

"What?"

"I don't want to put you in danger. What if…*someone* comes after you?"

"Would Krystal do that?"

"There's no telling. She's never gone after anyone before—physically, that is. I mean, she has *physically*, but not *violently*. I mean…Oh! I'm saying this all wrong."

Death snorted. "She's saying Krystal might *bed* you, but probably won't *kill* you."

"I think I understand."

"Good," Sissy and Death both said.

Sissy got up and pushed her chair in. "I suppose I need to get some things done. Andrea's family is flying in from Oregon. They can't take her…her body away, of course, until the investigation is done, but they feel they should be here, and they'll be packing up her apartment."

"Of course." Casey walked Sissy to the door. "Have you canceled my personal training sessions for the afternoon?"

"Oh!" Sissy's hand flew to her mouth. "I forgot about that. I had Maria put a note on the aerobics door, but not on the one to the weight room. I'll have her do it right now."

"No, actually, I would like to keep the appointments. Can I do that?"

"To show your face around?"

"Partly. And to give me something else to think about." There was no way she'd be able to go back to sleep now.

"Well, that's fine, I guess. Just…watch out for yourself, okay?"

"Okay. Thanks, Sissy." Casey shut the door behind her.

"So I'm not sure what all that was," Death said. "Accusation or warning?"

"Both." Casey stood in the mouth of the hallway leading back to her bedroom. "She doesn't really think I did it, but she's feeling anxious because she made those bad hiring decisions in the past. She doesn't want to get blamed for a resident's death. Especially since she was letting Andrea use the exercise rooms after hours."

"But she also doesn't want *you* getting blamed for something you didn't do."

"Or getting hurt. I appreciate that."

"If she knew your record with thugs, she might not worry so much."

Casey shook her head. "Do you *remember* what my face looked like a week ago?"

"Oh. Right. I was going to call you Hamburger Face, but you were in such a bad mood I decided not to. Where are you going?"

"To take a shower."

"Before your appointments? Won't you just get all smelly again?"

"They're the ones who will be doing the sweating. Not me. And until I shower I'll still feel like I have Andrea's blood on me."

"I don't see any. You changed your clothes, didn't you?"

"Yeah, but I still feel dirty. It's not a good feeling."

"Right. You want to be clean when you face everybody who's after you."

"Thanks. That's very reassuring."

"I do my best."

Casey went into the bathroom and shut the door.

And locked it.

Chapter Fourteen

Casey's afternoon appointments were with two older residents—one man and one woman. Neither one seemed as interested in working out as they were in Casey and the events of the past sixteen hours, but Casey pushed on, refusing to talk about anything but fitness and exercise routines. She wasn't sure if she helped or hindered her own cause by not telling them what they wanted to know, but she would have felt sleazy if she'd used the sensationalism to secure her own reputation.

By the time four-thirty came around, she had to get out of the building. She pulled on a warm-up suit and headed downtown.

"Where are we going?" Death wore a Hawaiian shirt, Bermuda shorts, sandals, and sunglasses. All that was missing from the whole persona was a camera on a string.

"You know you're not supposed to wear socks with sandals. It makes you look like a clueless tourist."

"Of course I know that. If I look like a clueless tourist I'll fit in. No one will think twice."

"You mean that one-hundredth of a percent of people who actually see you. If it's that many."

"Every person matters, Casey. You know that. Anyway, you didn't answer my question."

"Two places. First, I need to stop by the police department to sign my statement—"

"And see Gomez."

"—and then I'm going to the mall. I need a phone."

Death gave a little clap. "Get one of those new ones, with the big touch screen and the full keyboard."

"I'll get whatever's cheapest."

"Spoilsport."

Death was disappointed to find that Gomez was not at the police station, having gone home for some sleep. Binns was also gone, so Casey reviewed and signed her statement with another officer, and was out of there in twenty minutes.

At the mall, Casey found the little booth with the phones, signed up for a two-year plan, and bought the smallest phone available. It looked like a square, but the top swiveled to make it into a rectangle.

"Good grief," Death said. "Are you a junior high girl? Why go for the smallest one?"

"It has a full keyboard. I thought that was what you wanted."

"Yes, but look at it. It's about as big as a matchbox."

"Which is great. Why do I need anything bigger?"

"Oh, forget it. You're never going to fit in with the ways of the world."

They meandered through the mall, Death pausing at every window to *ooh* and *aah* over the displays. Casey kept walking, making Death jog every so often to keep up. The only store she spent any time in was the bookstore, where she picked out a book on new yoga techniques. Death was pushing for her to get the book on tantric massage, but she refused.

"Who am I going to perform tantric massage on? No one. So what's the point of spending the money?"

"I don't know. Cops get very stressed out. I'm sure an officer could use a good massage after a hard day's work."

"I don't think Detective Binns will be asking me over to rub her shoulders."

"Not Binns. *Gomez.*"

Casey walked faster. "Will you get off it? I'm not doing anything with Officer Gomez."

"Your loss, I'd say."

"He's probably married, anyway, and wouldn't have anything to do with me, even if I wasn't involved in an investigation. Most of the good ones are."

"He's completely single. And hetero. I *checked*."

Not what Casey wanted to hear.

By the time they got back to the Flamingo, Casey's stomach was growling. She was moving toward the stairs, head down, when she heard someone calling her name. Or *Daisy's* name.

Jack beckoned her over to the bar, where he was counting money from the cash register. When she approached he shoved it all back in and shut the drawer. "Hey. You okay? I heard about last night." He searched her face, his own a picture of concern.

"Just tired. Trying not to think about anything."

"Can't blame you. Can I help somehow?"

She stifled a yawn. "Can you take a nap for me?"

"Not that I don't want to, but..." He gave a sad smile.

Casey perched on a stool. "Did you know her?"

"Andrea? Sure. A little, anyway. She'd come here some evenings, mostly weekends. Hang out with her friend Krystal and whatever guys were lucky enough to sit with them."

"From what I hear of Krystal, it would have been a different guy every night. Was Andrea the same?"

"The same as Krystal?" He laughed. "Hardly. I mean, she didn't have a regular guy she hung out with, but where Krystal would take them upstairs with her on a regular basis, Andrea always left them at the elevator."

Exactly as Casey had figured it. "Did you ever see anything to indicate people didn't like Andrea?"

Jack shook his head. "Never. Some guys, I think, might have liked to get to know her better, but she really gave off the vibe of not being interested. You ask me, I think she had someone already, maybe back home in Oregon, maybe not, but she just seemed...I don't know...*taken*."

"You know anybody who might have wanted more with her, and felt snubbed?"

"I'm not sure about snubbed, but there were a number I could name."

"Del?" The guy from the weight room.

Jack grinned. "He was one of them. He might have gotten farther than most—I'm pretty sure he took her out once or twice. But I don't think he took it too hard. It's not like other women wouldn't want a well-built guy who can cook."

Casey laughed, then choked it off. Del could cook. *And he was planning on cooking for her that evening.* She'd completely spaced it, with all that had happened. And maybe he wasn't even up for it, with Andrea dying. She wasn't sure she was up for eating anything, let alone high-fat, rich foods. But she should check in with him, either way. If nothing else, he might need somebody to talk to.

She jumped off the stool. "Gotta go."

Jack raised his eyebrows. "So soon?"

"I forgot Del was going to cook for me tonight, if he still wants to."

"He got to you quick, didn't he? Don't blame him." He waved her off. "Go on, then. Enjoy."

Casey was standing in front of her closet, trying to decide what one wears to a homemade gourmet meal the day after someone dies violently, when a knock came on her door.

"Company!" Death said.

"I'm not deaf."

Casey opened the door. Del hunched there, a basket in his hands. His eyes were rimmed with red, and his nose looked like it had been blown more than is good for anyone. Again, the standard look around the Flamingo that day. Andrea had affected more people than she probably realized.

Once again, Casey found herself looking at the clock and feeling inadequate. "Oh, Del, I'm sorry. I was going to come up as soon as I got changed. I'm running a little behind."

He straightened, and plastered a smile on his face. "Figured you would be, so I brought it to you!"

"I don't know, Del, after what's happened today, I'm not sure I—"

Del's face fell.

"Let him in, silly," Death said. "You're hurting the poor man's feelings." Casey glanced at Death with surprise. Death was now wearing a copy of Jack's bartending uniform—dress slacks and a button-down shirt, rolled up to the elbows. A nametag on the breast pocket read *Old Father Time.*

"I'm sorry," Casey said to Del. "Never mind." She stepped to the side, and Del walked past, leaving a delicious smell in his wake. He set the basket on the kitchen counter. "If you'll set the table for two—"

"Oh, make it three," Death said. "Please make it three."

"—I'll take care of the food."

"Of course."

"We'll need soup bowls, salad plates, dinner plates, and dessert plates. For silverware, we'll need soupspoons, salad forks, the usual knife-fork-spoons, and dessert forks. As for drinks, we'll need water glasses and wine goblets. I brought linen napkins."

Casey stared at him. "I have two settings of plastic dishes, cereal bowls, water glasses, and two sets of knife-fork-spoons."

Del smiled, more real this time. "That will work just fine."

Casey set the table with her meager dishes—Death whining all the while at not being included—then sat back and watched as Del went to work. He emptied his basket, fussed around arranging things and putting on some last minute touches, then turned to her. "Ready?"

"Sure." Casey was surprised at how hungry she was. With the horror of the night, she'd managed to forget to eat all day, and now that she smelled food, she was famished.

Del flapped open a square of bright red fabric and laid it over Casey's lap. After setting his own napkin by his plate, he brought over a pan and ladled some orange soup into Casey's cereal bowl, and then his own. The delicious scent wafted up across Casey's face, and she breathed it in. Death moaned, practically doing a face plant in the food. Casey waved Death away.

"I know," Del said. "It's hot."

"Oh, no, it's not that, I just—" She stopped, realizing there was nothing she could say that wouldn't make her look like a raving lunatic. "It looks amazing."

He took the pan back to the kitchen before sitting across from Casey. "*Bon appétit.*"

Casey dipped her spoon in the soup and sipped at it. Her taste buds exploded. "Oh, wow. What is this? It's incredible!"

Death whimpered.

"Butternut Squash Soup," Del said. "A comfort food. One of my favorites."

"Mine, too. Now, anyway."

Casey didn't talk anymore as she finished it up, and was sad when she hit the bottom of the bowl. She scraped up every last bit, then looked up to find Del grinning at her. "What? Oh, sorry. I guess I was hungrier than I thought."

"Yeah, way to go Miss Manners," Death grumbled.

Del kept grinning. "No problem. It's nice to see my cooking so appreciated."

"Um, speaking of that…" Casey held out her bowl. "Is there more?"

"There is, but you want to leave room for what's coming next."

"Oh, I've got plenty of room."

He laughed and got up, returning with the pan. He ladled more into her bowl, and this time she tried to eat in a more dignified fashion. When she was done, she sat back. "Delicious. Thank you."

Del finished his own soup, then rose to clear the dishes. Casey got up, too, but he waved her back down. "You sit. This is my thing. Just relax."

He took away the bowls, then returned to get her dinner plate. When he came back, the plate was filled with an artistic vision—the colors and shapes and smells combined to form a masterpiece. After he sat down with his own plate, Casey said, "So what is this amazing stuff?"

"For your main course you have Ballotine of Chicken, which consists of a breast stuffed and rolled with spinach and leeks with a brandy mustard cream sauce. On the side you have Mushroom Hazelnut Salad, with sautéed Shiitake mushrooms, as well as twice-baked potatoes, with sour cream and cheese. The rolls—" he jumped up and returned with a small basket "—are my special recipe with whole wheat pastry flour and yams."

Death passed out on the couch with a gurgle, and disappeared.

"Is there a special order for eating them?"

"Yes. In whatever order you want."

Casey slathered a roll with whipped honey butter, and savored every mouthful of the feast. Del talked more this course, about his work at the insurance company, his family in Tennessee, and how he liked to go parasailing in the warmer weather. Casey just listened and ate, every now and then offering a "Wow," or a "Really?" but spending most of her energy enjoying the food.

When her plate was clean and she'd eaten her third roll, she sat back and stretched. "I'm going to need to do at least three extra workouts to make up for this."

Del nodded. "Why do you think I spend so much time in the weight room? Life's too short to not eat well." Immediately, he went red, and rested his fork on his plate. "I'm sorry. I didn't mean...I was going to avoid saying anything..." He closed his eyes and took a deep breath.

"It's okay, Del. Really. You've been...this has been great."

He opened his eyes, and she saw the pain in them. "I've tried not to let myself think about it since I heard."

Thus the incredible meal. It had to have kept him busy.

"When did you hear?"

"Lunchtime. A couple of my co-workers live here, too, and they got the news."

"I'm sorry." She remembered Jack's theories, and the way Del had watched Andrea down at the swimming pool. "Did you know Andrea well?"

"No, not really. I would've liked to know her better." He ducked his head, then got up to clear the table.

So Jack was right.

This time Casey did help with the dishes. "Do you know Krystal?"

Del rinsed a plate in the sink. "No. Lots of other guys do, at least as much as they want to, if you know what I mean. Andrea was harder to figure out."

"I can see that. Krystal's pretty much an open book."

"That's one way to put it." He grimaced. "Sorry. Women like her just aren't my type."

"But Andrea was?"

"I wasn't sure. But she seemed like it." He stacked the dishes and turned around, drying his hands on a towel. "I had her up for a meal one time, soon after she moved in at the beginning of the year. She said she enjoyed it, but it didn't seem to make her want to do anything more. I mean, on later days. When I asked her out again she said she was busy, and I never got up the nerve to try a third time. I think she must've found someone else." He was a full red now, and he wouldn't make eye contact with Casey.

"I liked her, too," Casey said, "from the little I saw of her. She seemed smart, and nice."

They fell silent, until Del snapped his head up. "Ready for dessert?"

"Dessert?" Casey considered it. "Of course. I've got a place reserved right here—" she pointed to the top left portion of her stomach "—for dessert."

"Great. Why don't you have a seat again, and I'll bring it out."

Casey could hear him washing the plates, and after a few minutes he carried in a beautiful round cake.

"Coffee Tortoni," he said. "I wasn't sure if you were a coffee drinker or not, so I figured I'd just make the dessert itself the coffee."

"Perfect."

It *was* perfect. Light and cold and delicious.

Del just picked at his, and Casey didn't want to ask if he was full, or if his appetite had disappeared once they'd begun talking about Andrea. From the look on his face, she figured it was grief holding him back.

When they were finished, they washed up the dishes together, and re-packed his basket.

"Would it be offensive to your cooking if I offered you some hot tea?" Casey asked.

"Not at all. I'd enjoy that."

Casey heated up two mugs of water in the microwave, and they took their tea onto the balcony, where they sat and looked over the courtyard.

"Did you see the petition?" Casey asked, after a while.

"The one about getting you kicked out?"

"That would be the one."

"I didn't see it, but I heard about it. Stupid."

"You don't think I hurt Andrea? I'm new. No one knows me. Sissy's made bad choices in the past."

Del took a sip of his tea. "I think if you'd done it, you'd be long gone. You'd change your name, and we'd never see or hear from you again. No, you're the one person who I completely believe *didn't* do it."

"Other than yourself."

He looked at her in surprise. "Well, obviously."

"So there are two of us."

They sat there a few minutes longer, and when they'd finished their tea, they set the cups on the little table. Del reached over, his hand open. Casey looked at him for a moment, then put her hand in his.

And they sat together and watched the sun go down.

Chapter Fifteen

Del stayed until the sun had completely set and he was nodding off. Casey woke him and saw him out, then stood in the middle of her living room, not even remotely sleepy. The napping she'd done during the day had completely screwed her up, and now she had no idea what to do. She turned on the television, but didn't really care about dancing with washed-up stars, or wiping out on a large wet obstacle course, or the next crime on whichever version of *Law & Order* it was, so she turned it off. She sat down with her new yoga book, but wasn't really in the mood. She paced. She cleaned. She sorted laundry.

"So I hope your dinner was good. You know, that scrumptious food you so thoughtlessly ate in front of me." Death was back, in the red housecoat, smoking a huge cigar.

"Put that out."

"Oh, come on. It's not real smoke."

Casey stared at the glowing end until Death sighed and stuck it in a pocket.

"The cops are gone," Death said, "along with the crime scene tape."

"Have they cleaned the locker room?"

"It's sparkling. Like it never happened."

Casey glanced at the clock. A little after ten. "The fitness rooms are technically still open until midnight."

"Are you thinking what I'm thinking?"

"I hope not, because I never can guess what goes on in that head of yours."

"I'm *thinking* this would be a good time for you to look around down there."

Casey made a face. "So we are thinking the same thing, which is scary."

"Come on. Let's see what we can find."

The aerobics room was dark, and just as quiet as it had been the night before. Casey shivered.

"It's okay," Death said. "There's nobody here."

"In either locker room?"

"Or even the weight room. It's like people are freaked out and want to stay away."

"Isn't it usually the opposite? People want to get an eyeful of the murder scene?"

"Guess they got that earlier. The cops and cleaning crew were done a few hours ago, while you were stuffing your face. Folks had a chance after that to look around. I guess since there was nothing to see they didn't spend much time gawking."

Casey left the light off in the aerobics room, not wanting to advertise her presence in case curious people came by. She went into the locker room and stood just inside the door. Here, she did turn on the light, since no one could see her from the outside.

Death had spoken correctly. The room was sparkling.

"Was it the regular cleaning crew who did this?"

"Yup. Sissy didn't want to spend the money on the special crime scene ones. Couldn't blame her, really, since it was just the one shower stall that had, well, *stuff* in it."

"So there would be nothing left for me to investigate."

"Not on the surfaces. But that's the cops' territory, anyway. It's not like you're going to go around collecting fingerprints."

"True. But I can look in my office."

"For what?"

"Who knows?"

Casey let herself into the training room. "Did the cops go through here, too?"

"I'm sure they did. The men's locker room was barred from the outside all day. They figure the killer escaped that way, so he might've left something behind."

"He?"

"Just being grammatically correct. I'm willing to suspect a 'she' just as easily."

"Oh, no." Casey stared at the shelves of hand weights. She'd forgotten about them, and had assumed the weight that had killed Andrea had come from the weight room across the hall. But it was here, in her office, that there was an empty space where a ten pound weight should be.

"Closer to hand," Death said. "It makes more sense than if the killer went all the way over to the weight room."

Casey sagged into her chair. "It does. It just makes it more real, knowing that whoever did it was in here right before it happened."

Death was squatting by the shelves. "Lots of fingerprint dust. You're going to have to clean all of these before you use them"

"I never want to use them. I never want to *touch* them." Casey turned on the computer and opened the door to the men's locker room while it booted up. The room was a mirror image of the women's, except not as sparkly. Apparently the cleaning crew wasn't given the order to sanitize it to within an inch of its life. Casey walked through to the door that led out to the hallway. "Anyone around yet?"

"Not even a mouse."

Casey peeked into the hall, and found herself face to face with the weight room door, as she'd expected. The weight room, which was *not* missing any weights. The hallway, as Death had said, was empty and silent. The security camera hung in the corner, and she went to stand under it, scrutinizing the lens. It looked completely clear of Vaseline, and was probably a new part altogether. She winced, realizing she was giving the security team a nice close-up of her face. Time to go away.

Back in her office, the computer was ready.

Death hitched a hip on the side of the examination table. "What are you looking for on there?"

"Don't know. I guess I just need to get familiar with what's here, first." She explored the desktop, finding old class and training schedules, purchase orders, and individual records of injury care and relief. The Internet was serviced by high-speed wireless, but the search engine's cache had been completely emptied.

"Guess Brandon didn't want us knowing what he was looking at," Death said.

"Or someone *else* didn't want us knowing."

"True."

There wasn't a whole lot left to search through, so Casey moved on to the desk itself. There was the usual office-type detritus in the top drawer—paper clips, Post-It notes, rubber bands—a few almost completely-used-up rolls of athletic tape, and some Band-Aids. The second drawer held paper and not much else, and the third drawer, the one big enough to hold files, was locked.

Casey leaned back and looked around. "See a key anywhere?"

"That top drawer, probably."

But it wasn't there. Casey got up and opened the wall cupboard. The shelves were filled with first aid equipment, towels, and empty water bottles. But no key.

"Curiouser and curiouser," Death said.

Casey went back to the desk and felt around the bottom of the top drawer, in case the key had been taped there, but it was smooth. There was no rug to hide anything under, and the only thing on the wall was a mirrored medicine chest that held only ibuprofen, Ben-Gay, and a box of tampons. The whirlpool was empty of both water and keys.

"You can just kick the drawer open," Death said. "You've done that before."

"And about killed my foot."

"Okay, so a letter opener."

"That doesn't work in real life, although it looks like somebody did try. There are scratch marks all over the lock."

Death swooped down for a better look. "Hmm. You positive no one got in?"

"If so, he was able to lock it after himself."

"Or herself."

Casey jiggled the drawer one more time before giving up. She'd have to ask Sissy if she knew what had happened to the key, because if the drawer was locked, that could mean there was worthwhile stuff inside it. Which wouldn't really make sense, because why would Brandon leave anything valuable behind?

A loud bang sounded in the men's locker room. Casey jumped, then glared at Death. "Thanks for the heads up."

"I'll see who it is." Death was gone, then back in an instant. "It's your infant loverboy from personal training earlier today."

"Dylan?"

"And he's not alone."

"Weight training friend?"

Death laughed. "Hardly."

Casey waited for details, but they weren't forthcoming. "*Well?*" she finally said.

"You're not going to *liiiiiike* it." Death's voice had gone all sing-songy.

"Will you just tell me?"

Death smirked, and walked around the room, hips swaying.

"Oh, no. He's got a *girl* in there?"

"And not just any old girl." Death looked at her meaningfully. "This one's hotter than hot."

"It's *Krystal?*"

"*Ding, ding.* You win a new car!"

"I don't want a new car. I want people to use locker rooms for…locker room stuff."

Death patted her shoulder. "You really have lived a sheltered life, haven't you? Have you not seen *Bull Durham?*"

"But Andrea just died *today*. And her best friend is doing *that?*"

"Need I remind you once again of your little assignation in the back of the theater just two weeks ago?"

"No. And it wasn't an assignation. It was...*panic*."

"Um-hmm."

"And Reuben hadn't died that day."

"Right."

"And Krystal wasn't married to Andrea."

Another loud bang, like something hitting lockers, practically made the walls shake. Death giggled and pushed through the door, leaving Casey with only a back and legs to look at.

"Peeping Tom." Casey threw a pencil at Death's rear, but it went right through and hit the door.

"Uh-oh," Death said, and pulled out of the wall.

"What?"

The doorknob rattled, and something thumped against the door itself. She could hear the mumble of voices, and the sound of a key in the lock.

"Oh, no," Casey said. "They're not coming in—"

The door flew open, and Dylan and Krystal practically fell into the room, clothes half off, hands and mouths all over the place.

Casey sent a panicked glance toward Death, who was having a grand time.

Casey took a deep breath and put on her teacher voice. "Okay, people! Freeze!"

Dylan and Krystal jerked apart, showing Casey more than she ever wanted to see, so she grabbed a couple of towels and threw them at the couple. Krystal caught one and held it up to her chest. Dylan let his fall, and hastily zipped up his pants. His upper body told the story of his workouts, and Casey couldn't help but appreciate the view.

"What are you doing in here?" Krystal screeched.

"Well," Casey said, "last time I heard, this was my office."

"Not for long."

"Oh, I don't know. From what Sissy told me this afternoon your petition wasn't really catching on."

Krystal's eyes sparked. "*Sissy*. What does she know?" She grabbed Dylan's arm. "Come on. Let's go somewhere with a little more *class*."

"Like one of their condos, perhaps?" Death snickered. "Or somewhere a little more private, like the lobby?"

"Wait." Dylan looked at Casey. "What petition?"

"Ask your girlfriend here."

"She's not my—"

"I'm not his—"

Casey held up her hand. "Whatever she is. Ask her about the petition."

He turned to Krystal, and she pointed at Casey. "That...that *woman* killed Andrea!"

Dylan blinked. "Really?"

"Yes, *really*. Why else do you think she came to the Flamingo? She knows about fighting, and is stronger than any of us, and—"

"You know about fighting?" Dylan looked at Casey.

Casey shrugged. "I taught the women a self-defense class last night. Maybe that's what she's referring to."

"Don't talk about me like I'm not here," Krystal spat. "I *saw* you."

"You saw me what?"

"Doing some kind of martial arts workout last night. Late. Just before you 'found' Andrea."

"You were on the fitness floor right then? I wonder if Detective Binns knows that." And if that was the noise Casey had heard, rather than the door in the locker room. That would make more sense, time-wise.

Krystal inhaled sharply. "Of course she knows. She has the security footage. She could see me plain as day. I'd just gone down to check on Andrea, but figured since you were there, Andrea would be safe."

"Right. And you know, Binns could also see *me* on the security footage. *And knows I didn't do it.*"

Krystal's mouth went up and down before clamping shut. "You can say whatever you like. I know you killed Andrea, and I'm going to prove it."

"By making up evidence? Because that's what you're going to have to do."

"Don't worry. I'll find something. And you'll be sorry you ever came to Florida."

"Believe me, I already am."

Krystal spun around and stalked out of the office, back through the men's locker room. The office door stayed wide open behind her.

"Sorry about that," Dylan said.

"Not your fault."

"Well, I mean about barging in on you and…well…"

"Yeah, that *is* your fault. You'd better get after her or your date's going to be over."

Dylan shook his head. "It wasn't a date. She just…she was stalking through the lobby, all mad about something, and ordered me to follow her. I haven't gone out with her for almost three weeks. How could I say no?"

How about by saying the word? N. O. "Whatever it was, date or not, you'd better hustle if you want to catch her."

"She's long gone already. Tonight is way over." A thoughtful look came over his face. "But maybe if I send her flowers tomorrow she'll consider seeing me again." He turned toward the door.

"Sure. You do that. Send her flowers. But you know what might up your chances even more?"

He hesitated in the doorway. "You got ideas, I'm listening."

"Sign her little petition to have me kicked out. That should gain you some brownie points."

"Yeah, but then I'd feel bad."

"Because you don't think I did it?"

"Because I like you."

"I'm not going to bed with you Dylan."

He grinned. "Not *yet*."

"Get out of here."

He laughed, and closed the door behind him.

"Krystal was down here watching me," Casey said. "Right before I found Andrea. What was she doing here? And where did she go?"

Death looked thoughtful. "Came back to check on Andrea, like she said? Forgot something she left behind?"

"I wonder. I'll have to check with Binns to make sure she knows Krystal was here. And to see if maybe I'd heard Krystal in the hallway instead of someone in here."

Casey turned out the light and headed back into the women's locker room. She paused at the shower stall where she'd found Andrea. "I wish I'd been just a few minutes earlier, L'Ankou. I could've…" She raised her hands toward the curtain, then let them drop.

"You don't know that, hon. A few minutes earlier and it might've been you getting killed, too."

"Maybe so. Maybe I used up all my luck the last couple of weeks in Ohio and Kansas. All those cuts and bruises were just foreplay."

"Well, you've been wanting to go home with me. I suppose this could have been your chance."

Casey pictured the blood on the floor, and the fear Andrea must have felt as she lay on the cold tile, her attacker standing above her, beating her, ripping her skin, crushing her insides.

"It could have been my chance," she finally said. "But I don't think I want a chance like that."

Chapter Sixteen

Someone had been in Casey's apartment. She could feel it. She held out her arm, as if she could stop Death from entering.

"Nothing's out of place," Death said after a quick sweep of the rooms.

"You're sure?" Casey immediately ran to the air conditioning vent where she'd hidden her duffel bag. The vent itself looked undisturbed, and a quick check of her stash convinced her it hadn't been found. But just the idea that someone *could* have found her ID—that someone was even looking in her apartment—turned her cold. She rubbed her arms, trying to rid herself of goosebumps. "What do you think the person wanted?"

"Whatever you've gotten hidden there. Proof you aren't who you say you are. Proof that you killed Andrea."

Casey strode through the rest of the apartment, her unease growing. Nothing was damaged or stolen. But things were just a little off. Her toothpaste at a different part of the sink, a drawer that wasn't quite closed.

"You going to tell the cops?"

Casey sank onto her bed. "I tell the cops, I'm going to have them digging into things that aren't relevant to Andrea's death. I'd have to hide my duffel bag somewhere else, and they might get a little too curious about where I came from, and why I don't have a history."

"So you're stuck."

"Completely."

A doorbell tone sounded in Casey's pocket, and she yanked out her phone. Who would be calling her? She hadn't told anyone her number.

It was the phone company, texting her to suggest she back up her contact list.

Death snickered. "Like you have any contacts to back up."

"I will. Someday. Maybe."

"Right." She looked at her phone, longing to punch in Ricky's number and hear his voice.

"Go ahead," Death said. "What could it hurt? He won't know this number."

"Is your head full of rocks? As soon as I call him this number will be stored in his phone."

"So? You can ask him not to tell anyone. He can put it in his phone under an alias."

"And then if I lose my phone, or someone just *glances* at it, they'll get his number and my new identity is blown. You know, sometimes I think you're brain really isn't up to the task."

"Fine. You want to be alone and miserable? You got it." And Death was gone.

Casey clutched the phone, fighting the urge to call her brother. Her mother. Her lawyer, Don. Finally, she shoved the phone under her mattress, where she wouldn't hear if the phone company called to suggest anything else.

She was able to grab a few hours of dream-filled sleep before her alarm went off at five-thirty. She rolled out of bed, thought about and decided against breakfast—she wasn't even close to hungry, after Del's gourmet spread the night before—and was down in the aerobics room before anyone else arrived. By the time women began trickling in she had picked out music and set up her cordless mic. The group was quieter today than it had been the last time, but that gradually changed as people arrived. The class was also a lot smaller than it had been two days before, and Casey figured a lot of them weren't sure how to act. Do they go against Krystal and attend class? Or do they take another look at Casey for themselves before they made a decision? Casey knew they were talking about Andrea, and about the fact that Casey had found her during her first day on the job, and she could sense the surreptitious glances sent her way. She stood quietly at the front of the room, trying to look both innocent and confident.

Casey waited for Krystal to make a grand appearance, waving around her petition and her outrage, but by start time, she still hadn't shown. In a way, Casey was disappointed. It might've cleared the air to have a confrontation in front of the group. Instead, Casey would just have to go on as if she were free of both guilt and suspicion.

The women followed her instructions faithfully, and at the end of the hour were less hesitant to look her in the eye. A few of them even thanked her, and said they'd look forward to class the next morning. None of them stayed to chat, and none of them went anywhere close to the locker room door.

Casey toweled off and headed over to the weight room for her personal training appointments. Both were again young men, neither as charismatic nor suggestive as Dylan, which might have been more proper, but wasn't much fun. Neither showed any interest in the whole Andrea scandal. They just wanted to do their workouts and get back to their world of banking, which is all they talked about when they chose to open their mouths. And which reminded Casey that Andrea had worked at a bank, along with Krystal, and who knew how many other Flamingo residents. Casey wasn't convinced she wanted to open a bank account, since she would probably be headed out of town as soon as the investigation closed, but it might be interesting to see where Andrea had worked, and who she worked with.

She stuck the second client on the treadmill for his twenty-minute workout and ran down to the office, hoping Maria would be in. She wasn't, but Sissy spied Casey from her office door. "Can I help you with something, Daisy? Didn't she find you?"

"Who?"

"Detective Binns. I sent her up to the weight room."

"Must have just missed her. I'll go back up in a minute. But I'm wondering where the key might be for the desk in the training room. The lower drawer is locked, and I'd like to use it."

"It's not in the top desk drawer?"

"I looked everywhere in the office, and I can't find it."

Sissy frowned. "I haven't seen it. When Maria gets back I'll ask her, okay?"

"Thanks." Casey ran back up the stairs and found Detective Binns waiting by the water cooler. Unfortunately, Officer Gomez was also with her, making Casey's insides turn to jelly. Casey told herself not to be ridiculous, and greeted them. "What can I do for you? I already stopped by and signed my statement."

"Yes, thank you." Binns smiled. "You got a few minutes?"

Casey glanced at the clock. "Let me tell my client, and we can head back to my office."

Casey gave her guy a few last instructions, then led Binns and Gomez out of the weight room. "You'll have to go in that way," Casey said to Gomez, pointing at the Men's locker room door. "Don't want to surprise anybody who might be changing in the ladies room."

Gomez blushed lightly. "Yes, ma'am."

Binns followed Casey through the other way, and met Gomez at the second office door.

"You getting settled in here, then?" Binns asked, looking around the room. She pulled up a seat, and Casey sat in her desk chair. Gomez leaned against the examination table, notebook out and ready. Casey couldn't help but notice that he looked like he spent his fair share of time in the gym, the way his shirt stretched across his chest.

"Actually," Casey said, trying to focus, "I've hardly hung out in here. I'm not planning on getting too comfortable."

"Yes, we heard about the petition. But from what Mrs. Williams says, it's not gathering a whole lot of support."

"We'll see. But I can't imagine you really came to talk about that."

"No." Binns crossed her legs and sat back, like she was getting ready to stay a while. "I want your impressions of some of the people here."

"Mine? I hardly know them."

"Exactly. Sometimes first impressions are better than long acquaintance when it comes to figuring out a crime."

Casey didn't like it. Who was she to be talking about these people? What could two day's interaction really tell her? The last thing she wanted was to send the cops after an innocent person who just happened to give Casey the wrong impression. Actually, no. The *last* thing she wanted was for Andrea's killer to get away with it. She'd have to help. "Okay, I can try, I guess. Who are you interested in?"

"Let's go ahead and start with Ms. Patterson."

"Who?"

"Krystal, Andrea's friend."

"Oh. Well, you know her basic thing. She's all about reeling in the men."

"We figured that out pretty quickly."

Gomez made a quiet sound of disgust.

"But now I think about it," Casey said, "I can't help but assume it's not all real."

"She's had surgery?"

"No, I don't mean that. I have no idea if her body's all real or not. I mean the whole sex goddess persona. She and Andrea were friends. Good friends, from the little I saw. They were very easy with each other, and Andrea wasn't afraid to scold Krystal when she made suggestive comments."

"Why would that make you think the sex thing is an act?"

"Not *entirely* an act. I mean..." She had a sudden vision of Krystal and Dylan stumbling into her office the night before. "Krystal and Andrea joked about it. It just felt like...like Krystal didn't take it very seriously. And the two of them did speak some about work, and how they felt the women were still kept under the men's thumbs there. So they did have serious issues going on, too, especially with guys."

Binns glanced at Gomez. "We have looked at the bank, of course, but maybe we need to look at that angle a little more." Back to Casey. "And this petition against you?"

"I don't know. Her way of dealing with grief, I guess. I'm a likely target."

"True. Okay, moving on."

"Real quick, first," Casey said. "Krystal says she saw me in the aerobics room that night before I found Andrea. You saw her on the security footage near the time of Andrea's murder?"

"Yes. First of all, she exited the women's locker room a little after midnight, only minutes before the gloved hand smeared Vaseline on the other camera's lens. Then, about an hour later, just after you appeared on the tape, she came up the service stairs, looked in the aerobics room and at her watch, and went back the way she came."

So the door latch Casey heard was probably Krystal, going back into the service stairs. It was just coincidence that it made Casey look in the locker room.

Binns was still talking. "Ms. Patterson showed no signs of blood on her clothes. Her hair, however, was rather a mess, and her shirt was on inside-out." She raised her eyebrow. "Any ideas how that happened?"

Casey gave a short laugh and glanced at Gomez, who was looking at the floor, his arms crossed tightly across his chest. "I think you can probably figure that out."

"Any suggestions about who the other person might have been?"

Casey thought immediately of Dylan, but from what he'd said it had been at least three weeks since he'd had a "date" with Krystal. At least until the night before, when they'd come crashing into the training room. "Seriously? How many men are there in the Flamingo?"

Binns nodded. "Speaking of that, it's pretty obvious that Ms. Patterson is a man magnet. Any chance Ms. Parker had her eye on someone, and Ms. Patterson got in the picture?"

"I really wouldn't know. And it seems like that would make Krystal the target, rather than Andrea, doesn't it?"

"Unless the man wasn't willing to give up Andrea and take on Krystal. Do you know of any men who were interested in Ms. Parker?"

An image of Del's red-rimmed eyes flashed across Casey's mind. "Del. He lives here."

"Last name?"

"Don't know. But he did cook me dinner last night, and it was amazing."

Gomez looked up at that.

Binns was interested, too. "He's a chef?"

"In his heart. During the day he works for an insurance company."

"And he was after Ms. Parker?"

"I wouldn't put it that way. He was interested in her, but it sound like his interest wasn't exactly returned."

"Hmm." Again, Binns glanced at Gomez.

"I don't mean I think he did it," Casey said quickly. "In fact, I don't think that at all. He's one of the good guys. And I would be *really* surprised if he were interested in Krystal."

"We'll check him out."

Casey felt sick. She didn't want to get a nice man like Del in trouble, and cause him more pain than he was already in. "Who else are you wondering about?"

"How about administration? Mrs. Williams?"

"Sissy?" Casey wanted to laugh. "I think of her as the fruit basket. She's cheerful and colorful and joyful. At least, she was until yesterday."

"Do you think she had anything against Ms. Parker?"

"Not that she told me. I know she's not crazy about Krystal, but then, a lot of people aren't. I've heard negative comments about Krystal from multiple people, not just Sissy."

"Such as?"

"You mean the people? Laurie Kilmer. She helps out with fitness classes. And women from my sessions. More people than I can count, actually."

"And you've only been here a couple of days."

"I hate to say it, but it would've made much more sense if Krystal were the one I'd found in the shower."

"At this point, yes. But back to Mrs. Williams. You don't think she'd have it in her to hurt anyone?"

Casey considered this. Sissy was a woman with some power here at the Flamingo. She couldn't be *completely* fruity and flaky and still get her job done. "Possibly. But I'm not really seeing it at this point."

"And her assistant?"

"Maria?" Casey was remembering her perception of Maria on her first day. That she thought life at the Flamingo wasn't always beautiful. That she lived on the *other side of town*. That she wasn't happy with the *no children* policy. "I haven't seen her much, but I felt some discontent. Not with Andrea, but with this whole establishment. And…" She hesitated. "With the police."

Binns wasn't surprised. "That's a common feeling among the Hispanic community. Especially the newer immigrants."

Casey forced herself not to look at Gomez. Was he discontent? Did he look at her with disdain? Was he an immigrant?

Not that it mattered.

"Anyone else?" Casey asked.

"You mentioned Laurie. Ms. Kilmer. She has something against Ms. Patterson? Could that have translated over to Ms. Parker?"

"I really don't— What do you know about the fitness instructors who came before me?"

"Nothing. Is there something I *should* know?"

Casey wasn't sure how much of the Flamingo's dirty laundry she should air. But Andrea's death had to take precedent over fraud and broken hearts. "Apparently they weren't all they should've been. Two guys ago was just incompetent. Residents liked him a lot as a person, but he apparently didn't know his stuff when it came to fitness, and Sissy threatened him with a law suit to get him to leave. But the last instructor was worse—he seduced older women in order to get their money. And, actually, I'm not entirely sure it was all older women."

Binns sat quietly for a few moments. "And you think this could have something to do with Ms. Parker's death?"

"I don't know. But there are still bad feelings about him. I have no idea who the women were, although I suspect…" She hesitated.

"Yes?"

"I'm pretty sure Laurie was one of them. I have no proof, but the one time we talked about him she got all flustered. And there was a really uncomfortable discussion before a class that involved Laurie, Krystal, Andrea, and Sissy, about just how much time they'd all spent in Brandon's apartment."

Binns gave a half-smile. "Well, I guess we'll have to look into all of *that*. Not just with Ms. Kilmer, but the others, too." She stared at the far wall for a few moments, then smiled suddenly. "You see, Ms. Gray, that's exactly the sort of thing I was hoping for from you. No one else has seen fit to mention those old instructors."

"Yeah, everybody feels kind of stupid about them. Especially Sissy. She thinks their failures were her fault, although at one point she made it sound like it was the residents' choice to hire those guys."

Binns stood up and held out her hand. "Thank you for being so forthcoming, Ms. Gray."

Casey shook her hand. "You're welcome."

"Perhaps someday you'll be just as forthcoming with your own history."

Casey's stomach flipped. "Haven't you checked it?"

"Oh, yes, we've checked it. We've seen your Florida driver's license, and your old address in Tallahassee. We've seen your vita. What we haven't found is a deep history, or actual people who knew you before two days ago." Binns' eyebrows were slightly raised, and she held onto Casey's hand.

"Yes, well, I've always been an introvert."

"I see."

Finally, Binns let go, and Casey wiped her hand on her pants.

"Okay, Gomez," Binns said. "I'll meet you in the hallway."

Casey glanced at Gomez, only to find he was staring at her, his eyes narrowed.

"Good-bye, Officer," Casey said.

Gomez blinked. "Yes, well, good-bye." He left through the men's locker room door.

Binns turned to go. "We'll be in touch. Oh, I meant to ask, do you have a phone number?"

"Yes." Casey felt her pocket, but the phone wasn't there. Right. It was still under her mattress. "But I just got the phone yesterday, and I don't remember the number. It's up in my room. Can I call you with it? My aerobics class is just about to start."

Binns handed her a card. "Anytime you think of items of interest." She looked like she'd just remembered something.

"What?"

"Ms. Parker's phone. We've been able to identify every number but one, and it's an important one. She called it—or it called her—every day. Sometimes more than once, up until about two weeks ago, when the calls stopped. Any ideas?"

Casey shook her head. "I'd have no way of recognizing a number. I don't even remember what the area code is around here."

"I guess you're right." Binns sighed. "We'll be seeing you." She left, and Casey slumped into her seat.

Why did she get involved in these things? Why?

"Because that's what you do." Death stood in the doorway, this time in baby blue Nike warm-ups, with silver cross-trainers. "Krystal may be a man magnet, but you, my dear, are a magnet for trouble."

"Thanks," Casey said. "That's just what I needed to hear."

"Always at your service. Now, get your butt over here. These exercise fanatics are ready to rip down the door."

Chapter Seventeen

The women had not only set up their own steps, but Casey's as well. This class didn't seem to be afraid of her. In fact, the crowd was even bigger than the last time, with mostly retirement-age women filling the rows. These were the ones who had met her in the hallway the day before, the fat leader defiantly stating that Andrea was probably killed by Cubans. Or the Mafia. Or the Cuban Mafia. The women gazed at her now with no sign of timidity, but with intensity, as if they were trying to read her soul. She thanked them for setting up her step, plugged in some music, and got things going without saying anything beyond the necessary. She turned her back to them and watched in the mirrored wall as they put their minds to exercise instead of scandal.

Sissy was absent. She had attended this class on Casey's first day, but Casey imagined she had a lot to prepare, with Andrea's family coming, and all. She'd be going over paperwork, and talking with the police, and who knew what all legal matters the Flamingo was liable for. Casey didn't want to even think about that.

But as Casey moved and encouraged and sweated, her brain was moving even faster about other things, such as her own predicament, and what had just happened in her office.

Why in the world would Binns come to *her* for information about people she barely knew? Did Binns really believe that first impressions stuff? Or was that just an excuse to study Casey at closer range? She obviously didn't believe Casey was who she said she was. Why else would she have asked those pointed questions about her past? Just the implications of what that could mean made Casey stumble on her step. She righted herself, and forced herself to concentrate on what she was doing.

For a few minutes.

Maybe she should just leave. Throw away Daisy Gray and start over. She hated to do it, for a lot of reasons, but maybe it was the best option.

No.

If she took off now she'd not only have the Ohio cops after her, but the Florida ones, too. At least the Florida ones *said* they didn't suspect her. And she wasn't behind bars yet. She pounded the step as she jumped. Could nothing be easy? Did she not deserve even one week of peace?

Another thought struck her. Was there any way they'd be able to connect her fingerprints from the locker room with the murder of that thug in Ohio? Or her DNA? Oh, God, she hoped not. She couldn't imagine it, but it was within the realm of possibility. She'd bled during that street fight, and knew she'd touched the car that had been sitting there. Had the forensic team been so thorough that her information was just sitting there in storage, waiting for them to connect the dots?

The music changed, and she realized it was time to cool down. She sent the women to their mats for a few minutes of abs work. The women grunted and groaned, and some simply collapsed onto their backs, completely done in.

"This is terrible," one woman moaned. "Brandon never worked us this hard."

Another one giggled. "Sure he did. And he worked some of us just as hard in other ways, too."

A smattering of laughter flew through room. One woman stopped her sit-ups and rested on an elbow, looking across the sea of bodies. "Bernie could tell us about that, couldn't you, Bern?"

Bernie, who apparently was the smallish, darkly-tanned, heavily dyed woman on the far left side of the room, didn't answer, but closed her eyes and counted out loud as she crunched.

"Bernie knows more about Brandon's work out sessions that any of the rest of us." It was the smarmy woman talking now, the big one who had led the group yesterday in the hallway, her eyes flashing with eagerness at the excitement of it all. "I believe some of those sessions were held in Bernie's condo, rather than here in the aerobics room. Weren't they, Bernie?"

The poor woman's dark tan was now a dark red, whether from embarrassment or exercise, or a combination of both, Casey wasn't sure. Her breath was coming in gulps.

"Okay, ladies." Casey clapped her hands. "A little more stretching, then you're good to go."

After the last deep breath holding their arms upward, the women broke formation. Bernie shot out of the room so fast Death made a show of dodging her, arms flailing.

"So, is there anything new about the investigation?"

Nasty Woman, again, peering eagerly at Casey.

Casey turned off the stereo and set her mic in its cubby. "What's your name?"

"Vonnie."

"Well, Vonnie, I'm not part of the investigation, so I wouldn't know."

Vonnie's eyes narrowed. "I saw the cops taking you back to your office."

"To talk. And when I say, 'talk,' that doesn't mean they're the ones doing the talking."

Vonnie's eyes lit up. "So you're a suspect? Or they think you know something? Maybe you know something but don't *realize* it."

"I don't. Know anything, that is." That's all Casey needed. To have someone coming after her because this stupid woman thought she knew more than she should. "So what happened with Bernie and Brandon?"

Vonnie tittered. "It was embarrassing, really. I mean, she's so *old*. And she went after him like he'd actually *want* her."

"But he did spend time with her?"

"Oh, sure. Brandon wasn't one to turn down a willing woman."

"Were there others?"

Vonnie guffawed this time. "Others? How about a dozen others? Brandon wasn't exactly a one-woman man, although he somehow made them all think he was."

Apparently Vonnie wasn't one of them. Not that Casey could blame Brandon. Even a crook would want to stay away from this old windbag.

"Do you know who any of the others were?"

"A few." She looked at Casey slyly. "Why do you want to know?"

Why *did* she want to know? It couldn't have had anything to do with Andrea's death, could it? Unless Brandon and Andrea had hooked up. But she couldn't see it. Del had said Brandon went after the needy types. Andrea didn't strike Casey at all as "needy."

"Never mind. I don't."

"Uh-huh. You just watch you don't go seducing the men here, now. Although who you'd want to go after, I sure wouldn't know. They're either too young, too old, or too gay. And not necessarily just one of those, either."

Casey opened her mouth to object, then saw that Vonnie was smiling. "Right. I'll do my best to keep my hands to myself."

Vonnie laughed out loud. "You do that." She gathered up her towel and water bottle. "And if you're still wondering about Brandon's women…you might want to check out some of the employees, as well as the residents. Seems they weren't immune from his charms, as they'd like you to believe. Bye, now!"

Casey watched her go with a mixture of curiosity and revulsion. Vonnie was a mean gossip, but a spewing fount of information, as well.

"Sometimes I wish I could take them when I want to," Death said, "instead of waiting for Ms. Big up there to decide."

"Yeah, well, that one would be kind of heavy, if her soul matches her form."

"Nah. Once they're gone, they weigh as much as a butterfly. I carried that huge guy from *The Princess Bride* without any trouble at all."

"André the Giant?"

"That's him. He was a wrestler, wasn't he? *Ginormous.* But enough about dead people. Clock's ticking. Next client's up in three minutes."

Casey rolled her neck. "They do keep me hopping, don't they?"

"It's what you wanted, remember?"

She remembered. She'd been afraid she wouldn't have enough to keep her brain occupied, otherwise. She hadn't been counting on one of her new neighbors getting killed her first night on the job.

Her next client was waiting by the water cooler, bouncing on the balls of his feet and glancing around the room at the others already working out. He had to be at least eighty years old, and exuded more energy than Casey's entire last class. He wore short, tight gym shorts and a tank top, exposing more of his skinny limbs than was necessarily attractive, and his head was entirely bald except for one patch of thin gray hair on the very top. Casey loved him immediately.

"You must be Marcus."

He grabbed her hand and shook it vigorously. "Just so you know, I'm on a very strict exercise regime."

"Really? Why don't you hop on the treadmill and tell me all about it."

"Oh, it won't take that long. You see, I started a running program just yesterday, and I've only missed one day so far." He cackled merrily, and slapped his thigh. "Got that off late night TV."

Casey laughed and guided him toward the cardio equipment, glancing toward the free weights, in case the tall woman was back. She wasn't.

"Oh, he's a laugh and a half, this one," Death said from the next treadmill over, where the speed was on the lowest possible setting.

"Well," Casey said to Marcus, "let's see if we can't get you on a better schedule."

"You betcha." Marcus literally hopped on, as Casey had suggested, and turned the speed up to high.

Casey quickly adjusted it. "Let's start out nice and easy, get you warmed up, okay? Now, what kind of exercise have you been doing lately? For real," she added, as she spied the twinkle in his eye.

His shoulders slumped, and he leaned way over toward her, gripping the arms on the machine. "I haven't actually been doing any. But there's a cute lady, see, and I need to do something to get her attention."

"Ah. Someone here?"

He glanced around fervently. "Not in this room, thank goodness. But she lives in my building. The Palm. I *love* her. She'd been seeing someone else for a while, but I think she's free now. Free for *me*."

"Okay. Let's see what we can do to get you ready for her."

Marcus giggled, and pushed his speed button again. Again, Casey reached over and turned it down. "Any kind of exercise you specifically like? Other than sex," she said, when his eyes sparkled dangerously.

"Woman, you're taking all the fun out of it." But he was grinning as he said it.

Casey laughed. "Okay, come on, Marcus, let's go." She got him off the treadmill and over to the machines, where she herded him from place to place, dodging jokes and slaps on the back as he told them. At the end of the half hour, when she placed him on the treadmill, she was exhausted, but entertained. "So when are you going to ask this woman out?"

"Oh, not for a bit. She's really busy these days, you see, with the murder and all."

"Really? Why is that?"

"Because she's in *charge*."

"Of what? The investigation?" Marcus *couldn't* be in love with Detective Binns. She was way more than even he could handle. Besides, she didn't live in the Palm.

"No, silly. Our apartment complex."

"You're in love with *Sissy?*"

Marcus jumped, and smacked his hand over her mouth. "Quiet, now. Don't need to go broadcasting my intentions to the entire world."

"But…" All kinds of objections came to Casey's mind, the main one being that Sissy was entirely too young for Marcus, and putting the two together would be almost too much giddiness to bear.

"Oh, come now," Death said. "You're really going to tell me that this cute, little old man doesn't have what it takes to please Sissy? He's got more going for him than most people I've seen."

Death was right. "Sorry, Marcus. I'll be quiet. And she's a lovely woman. Very…colorful."

Marcus sighed, his eyes drifting toward something in the unseen distance. "She lights up my world."

"But…who was she seeing before? Someone here?"

Marcus' face darkened. "She would never tell me. She was very secretive, and every time I'd ask she'd just say he was wonderful, and he made her feel like a woman, but that their relationship had to be kept a secret so the others wouldn't get jealous." He thumped his chest. "*I* could make her feel like a woman. I'd make her feel so much like a woman she wouldn't know what to do with herself."

"I believe you could." Casey looked at Death, wondering if their minds were again working in tandem. "This other guy, do you know anything else about him?"

Marcus frowned. "He was *young*. Too young for her. She liked to brag about it."

Casey had been afraid of that. "Okay, Marcus, enough about him. From what you say, that's all over. Now we'll get *you* in shape to take her on."

He smiled. "That's what I like to hear."

"Now keep the speed down for today, you hear me? I'll be checking."

He sighed dramatically. "Yes, ma'am."

Casey got him settled, then went to the door to wait for her next client.

And to wonder just how many people knew that Sissy had been one of Brandon's adoring harem.

Chapter Eighteen

Casey got through her next client and class with nothing more out of the ordinary than one of the women passing out during cool down. Turned out she'd been awakened by the emergency vehicles two nights earlier and hadn't been able to sleep well since. Once Casey got her sitting up against the wall, the woman also admitted to not eating anything but cabbage for the past five days, because she needed to lose five pounds by Thursday in order to win a bet with her sister, who lived in Arizona.

Incredible.

Two of the woman's friends promised to get her back to her room and feed her, so Casey let them go.

"No wonder she smelled bad," Death said. "Like sauerkraut, gone bad."

Casey trudged up the stairs to her apartment and crashed onto the sofa. "She's not even fat, that's the stupid thing."

Death grunted. "Fat in the head, maybe."

"Speaking of fat, I'm *still* not hungry after that feast last night."

Death plugged both ears. "Not listening. La, la, la."

Casey forced herself up and into the kitchen, where she made herself a salad. She might not be hungry, but she didn't want to end up on the floor like that dumb woman. She'd just taken a first bite when there was a knock on the door. She sighed heavily and closed her eyes.

"No rest for the suspicious," Death said cheerfully.

Casey looked out the peephole, and was surprised to see Maria standing there. She opened the door.

"I'm sorry to bother you," Maria said, "but Sissy said you were looking for a key to the desk in the office."

"No problem. Come on in." Casey wiped her mouth with a napkin, and made sure she didn't have anything on her hands.

Maria hesitated. "I'm interrupting your lunch."

"It's all right. I'm not really all that hungry."

"I know what you mean. Ever since...well, you know, I haven't been able to eat much."

"So, about the key?"

"Yes, I'm sorry, but we don't seem to have it. Mrs. Williams says you looked all over the office?"

"Yup. Not there."

"And you haven't been able to find it here?"

"In the apartment? No, but then, I hadn't looked. Has anyone?"

Maria's eyes darted around the apartment. "We had the apartment cleaned. And if anyone on staff needed the key and thought it might be here, this apartment has been vacant for a couple of weeks for them to search it. No one's said anything about finding it. I could help you look, if you would like me to."

"No, that's all right. I'm sure it'll show up somewhere."

"If you're certain."

"Thanks."

"Okay. I'll see you later, then." Maria took one more quick look around the room, and left.

As soon as the door was shut, Death jumped up and down. "Oh, she was *so* itching to turn this place upside down."

"But as she said, she had two weeks to come up here and search. She mustn't have found anything before."

"But now you've brought it up again, and she's worried. Which means she was most likely yet *another* of his women, and he has something on her. Maybe financial papers." Death made a face. "This guy's really starting to give me the creeps. I'm surprised I haven't seen him yet. You'd think he'd have died of AIDS or a smackdown ages ago."

Casey agreed. "You know, if Maria was that worried, she would've found a way to open the drawer without a key."

"Someone *did* try, remember? And couldn't get in that way. But if they'd busted the drawer, there would have been some explaining to do."

"Right." Casey looked around. "So where do we start?"

She yanked the cushions off the couch to reveal lint, a button, two quarters, and a pencil. She felt around the sides, but found nothing except dust and a few dried up mini Shredded Wheat squares. "Didn't she say they cleaned this apartment? This is pretty disgusting."

"Under here, too." Death lay on the floor, peering underneath the couch. "Can you see anything?"

Casey tipped up the sofa to see underneath. "Nope. Nothing but dust bunnies, stale pretzels, and a rubber band. And there's nothing taped to the bottom. Let's check the chair." Casey pulled off that cushion, too, but faced only the same sort of trash as in the sofa. The floor below was also clear of anything valuable. Casey put the cushion back and looked around the room. "Okay. Let's think like an unethical, sleazy con man. Where would I hide something?"

"You do realize your salad's going to wilt."

"Let it." Casey went next to the picture on the wall. Nothing behind it or on it, or in-between the picture and the matting. There was also nothing behind the blinds, in the lamp, under the table, or in the cabinets of the kitchen. The bathroom was clean, the bed was free of extras, and the vents, other than her own hiding place, were empty of everything but dust.

"Smoke alarm?" Death said, looking at the bedroom ceiling.

Casey pulled off the cover. And found a key.

Death squealed. "There it is! Let's go!"

Casey glanced at the clock. "Can't now. I've got BODYPUMP in two minutes."

"Oh, these women, needing to be all fit and everything." Death stomped the floor.

"It's what got me this job, don't forget. Without people to exercise, we wouldn't be here. Which I guess would be a *good* thing."

"So I can go back to complaining about the people?"

"No."

"Fine. At least take the key with you, so you can check the drawer after class."

Casey slid the key onto her key ring, stuck her salad in the fridge, and made her way downstairs to the aerobics room. "Do you think the person who was in my apartment last night was looking for the key?"

"Doubtful." Death slid down the railing. "Those two weeks, remember? They had plenty of time to toss the place."

"Which means they really were searching for dirt on *me*."

"Afraid so."

Casey found a full house when she arrived in the aerobics room. She didn't really have a feel for this class yet. The group that had gathered two days earlier had been a much different demographic from the earlier classes, except for Sissy, who had come and given up halfway through. Today looked like the same bunch as before, mostly young women on their lunch breaks. Some of them were monsters, as if they'd been using weights for more than just a one-hour class three times a week. Casey's heart lifted. Here were women who actually cared about fitness, and weren't just there to put in the time and say they exercised. She *liked* it.

"So," one of the women said, stepping in Casey's path. "You the one who found Andrea?"

Casey gazed up at the tall, coffee-skinned woman, and her abs constricted the way they did when she was preparing to fight. It was the woman she'd seen several times before—in the weight room, across the lobby, staring up at her room from the pool. Up close the woman looked even bigger. Casey reminded herself that she was in a yuppie condo, and not a back alley. This was a Flamingo resident, not an opponent in the ring. She took a step back. "That's right."

The woman studied her, checking out her eyes, her physique, and the way her hands hung loose at her sides. "You've been hit recently."

"I thought those scars were gone."

"Nah, I can see it. I've had 'em myself." The woman frowned. "But they're not so recent as two days ago, when Andrea was attacked." The woman nodded, as if she'd made a decision. "My name's Tamille Jackson."

"Hello, Tamille. It's time for class. Are you ready to—"

Tamille slapped at the side of Casey's head, her hand open. "My point." Tamille smiled with one half of her mouth, and came at Casey with her left hand, not giving Casey time to recover from her shock. Casey blocked it easily.

"No points," Tamille said, not taking her eyes from Casey's. She jerked her head at the women surrounding them. "Clear out, ladies."

They backed away so quickly it was like they were pushed out by force.

"Oh, goody," Death said, clapping. "This should be fun."

"What is this?" Casey said. "I don't want to—"

Tamille threw a punch at Casey's mid-section, and Casey blocked it with an upturned forearm. Tamille's hand was a mere inch from Casey's chest. Close enough to scare, but not close enough to do any damage. She was pulling her punches, which meant two things: one—she wasn't trying to hurt Casey, and two—she knew what she was doing. Casey pushed Tamille's fist away and stepped back, studying her opponent. Taller than Casey. Smiling. Bouncing on the balls of her feet. She was coming at Casey with a full frontal attack, which meant she was trained in a different manner from Casey. An offensive fighting style, as opposed to Casey's hapkido, which was mainly a defensive art. Probably a form of karate, one of the most popular martial arts for Americans. The art which had people breaking through layers of bricks or boards. Or people's heads.

Tamille took a step forward, throwing a one-two punch toward Casey's face, right arm, then left. Casey blocked both hits and circled around, snapping her right foot at Tamille's stomach. Tamille spun away, then responded immediately, sending a left-handed roundhouse toward the side of Casey's head.

Casey ducked, then swung her left foot at Tamille's ankle. Casey's foot made contact and Tamille tripped, falling to one knee. She rebounded right back to standing. "Your point," she said.

She came at Casey again, fists up. Casey stood her ground, took her weight on her right leg, and kicked toward Tamille's right hip. Tamille swiveled away, and Casey used the opportunity to get in a quick second kick, just missing Tamille's thigh.

Tamille's face set in more serious lines, and she put her hands up again.

Casey stood back, waiting, hands loose, knees bent. The sounds of the room faded away, until all she could hear was her own breathing, and her heartbeat pulsing in her throat. Tamille's eyes were probing and strong, and Casey's could read the determination there. Tamille came suddenly pushing forward, right jab, left jab, right uppercut, left roundhouse. Casey dodged and weaved, throwing up blocks as necessary, taking backward steps. At Tamille's final swing of the set, Casey ducked again and circled left, coming up with a left snap with her foot. She connected with Tamille's stomach, and Tamille grunted. "Your point."

Casey backed up again, gaining her balance, not taking her eyes from Tamille's. It was a friendly match, at least as friendly as sparring could be, but she could see in the other woman's stance that she wasn't going to give anything away.

Casey waited, wanting Tamille to make the next move. Tamille seemed to be waiting, too, but Casey wasn't bothered. She could wait all day. Until Sissy came and told her to get her butt in gear, anyway.

Tamille didn't want to wait, and came at Casey, punching right-left, and following up with a front kick. Casey backed up so quickly she bumped into one of the other women. She stumbled, and Tamille took advantage, jabbing Casey in the side.

"My point," she said. "Back off, ladies, you're cramping our style."

Two points to two points.

Sparring matches went only to three.

Tamille backed off, that smile tickling her mouth. Casey went over her options. Tamille was too tall for Casey to hit effectively. She would block anything Casey threw at her. Casey had already gotten her with kicks twice, so Tamille would be expecting that again. And Tamille, with her arms and legs way longer than Casey's, had the upper hand when it came to distance.

But one thing Casey had that Tamille didn't? Grappling skills. Probably. Most karate fighters used their arms first, legs second, and never learned the art of grappling.

Hapkido fighters did.

Casey returned Tamille's smile, and Tamille's eyebrows rose a fraction.

Casey took a large step forward, put her weight on her left leg, and kicked toward Tamille's right thigh. Tamille blocked it easily, but Casey followed with a right-footed kick toward Tamille's left thigh, making Tamille block again. Casey circled around quickly and came at Tamille from behind. She grabbed Tamille's left wrist, pulled it back straight, hooked Tamille's ankle with her right foot, and drove her to the ground, knee on Tamille's back, heel of her hand on Tamille's outstretched elbow. Tamille struggled only minimally before tapping the floor.

Casey knelt over Tamille, chest heaving, sweat dripping from her face. She let go of Tamille's arm and stood, still ready. Tamille rolled over, sat up, and held out a hand. "Okay. Your point." Casey took her hand, aware it could be a trap, but Tamille just got up, squeezed Casey's hand, and let go. She put her hands together and bowed, keeping her eyes on Casey. Casey returned the bow.

Tamille gave Casey that same half-smile, and rolled her shoulders. "*Now* I'm ready for class."

One person in the class began clapping slowly. Soon all of the women were clapping and cheering, and smacking Tamille on the back.

None of them came close to Casey, except for one, who picked up the portable mic and held it out. Casey thanked her, and hooked the mouthpiece over her ear.

"What style?" Tamille said, following Casey to the front of the class.

"Hapkido. You're karate?"

She nodded. "Shotokan."

"You have a good teacher."

"My dad started me out. He believed his little girl should be able to protect herself, so he decided to make sure. Now I have a teacher here in Raceda."

"Your father did a thorough job."

Tamille shrugged. "Nobody's ever challenged me outside the ring, so I don't know if it works in the real world."

Casey looked her up and down. "One look at you and they run."

Tamille smiled, a full-on one this time. "That's my problem. It's why I'm still single."

Casey laughed and clapped her hands, focusing on the rest of the class. "Okay, ladies, time for you to stop observing and get to work." She turned the music up loud and worked them hard, barking at them like a drill sergeant. These ladies could take it. They wanted it. They were here for serious, hard work.

Death sat this one out, alternately watching the women and scanning the titles on the spines of the CDs. By the time class was over, Death had gone off somewhere. Casey wasn't complaining.

This class didn't seem to have the same revulsion of the locker room as the earlier classes, and went right in to shower and change.

Tamille came up to Casey, sucking on her water bottle. "What's your schedule this evening?"

"I work till four-thirty, then I'm off until eight."

"Want to do dinner?"

"Sure. Where?"

"There's a Japanese place just down the block. Kyoto's. Meet me there at six?"

"Do I have to eat raw fish?"

Tamille laughed. "I can't see anyone forcing you to."

"Then I'll be there."

"Great. Now I gotta hustle back to work. See you later!"

Casey had to hustle, too, and went into the locker room so she could change into her swimsuit. The women from the class were talking and laughing, and one was even using the shower where Andrea had been found.

Short attention spans? Or an inherent toughness? Casey wasn't sure. She ducked into her office and made sure both doors were locked.

"Try the key!" Death perched on the edge of the desk like a vulture, draping over the side.

Casey knelt beside the drawer and slid in the key. It turned. She opened the drawer.

"What is it?" Death leaned over so far Casey had to scoot to the side so she wouldn't get chilled.

The drawer was empty.

"Oh, man," Death said. "What a letdown."

Casey tried to take the drawer out of the desk, but it wouldn't come all the way out. She felt all around the sides, under the lip of the front, and up on the top. Her neck was just starting to complain about the awkward position when her fingernail snagged something in the very top, front corner.

She pulled it out.

Death groaned. "Another key?"

"Yeah, but look at it. This one belongs in a bank."

"Ah. Safety deposit box."

"I wondered why nobody had just forced this lock. Now we know they probably did, but couldn't find anything. The only other place they could think of, if Brandon had left anything behind, would be in my apartment."

"But they came up empty?"

"I guess. Because they don't have this."

Death clapped. "And we're going to the bank later, right?"

"You got it. As soon as we can after class lets out this afternoon. But now I have to get to work." So Casey slid yet another key onto her key ring, and headed for the pool.

Water aerobics was a different sort of class, comprised of women who never set foot in the regular aerobics room, except perhaps to use the lockers. They cheerfully talked amongst themselves, and followed Casey's directions the best they could. When class was over some of them stayed to swim laps, while others hung out in the shallow end to talk. Casey climbed out of the pool and dried herself off as she walked toward the locker room.

"Daisy?" Laurie was sitting on a chair at the side of the room. Her hair was flat, and her skin blotchy. She clutched the edge of the chair like she would fall off, otherwise.

Casey stopped beside her. "Hey. You doing okay?"

"Not really. Do you have a minute to talk?"

"You can come with me to the locker room. I need to change and get ready for some personal training appointments in fifteen minutes."

Laurie chewed her lip. "I don't...is the locker room...did they clean it up?"

"Yes. The last class used it."

She hugged herself. "I don't think I can go in there yet."

"Okay. Give me a few minutes, and you can meet me in the weight room while I wait for my next client. Will that be all right?"

Laurie nodded.

Casey changed as quickly as she could, and hustled to meet Laurie in the weight room. Laurie wasn't there.

Rosa was back again, folding towels, and smiled at Casey.

"*Ola*," Casey said. "Have you seen Laurie?"

Rosa shook her head, but Casey thought it was because she didn't understand what Casey was asking.

"Laurie?" Casey held her hand up to about Laurie's height, and Laurie's hair length. "Teaches classes?"

Rosa shook her head again.

"Okay. Thanks." Casey looked around at all of the stations in the room, and back out in the hallway. Maria was waiting at the elevator, a stack of papers in her arms.

"You seen Laurie?" Casey asked her.

Maria shook her head. "Not since this morning. I need to talk to her, actually. She's been skipping her classes, and we need to get back on schedule." The elevator came and she got on.

Casey walked around the corner, toward the aerobics room, but Laurie wasn't there. She opened the door "Laurie?" But there was no answer. She knew Laurie wasn't in the locker room, because besides Laurie's aversion to it, Casey had just come from there. Laurie must have decided not to talk with her, after all, or else she was just late. Well, she was going to be *too* late, since it was time for Casey's next appointment. She went back into the weight room.

"You Daisy?" A stick-like girl, mid-teens, stood beside her, one ear plugged with an earbud. She held the other earbud in her hand, with her iPod strapped to her upper arm.

"That's me."

"I'm only doing this because Grandma said I have to, and because…well, never mind."

"Because your Grandma wanted you to see what all the fuss was about over here?"

The girl made a face. "It's all dumb, anyway."

"I agree. So are you down here visiting your grandma, or do you live here?"

The girl rolled her heavily outlined eyes. "Do you really care?"

No. Not really.

Casey got the girl going on the treadmill, and was able to convince her to work half-heartedly on the weight machines, having to pull out an earbud every so often to make sure the girl could hear what she was saying. When she finally delivered the girl to her final cardio, she shook her head and looked around for client number two. He was the exact opposite of the girl in every way—huge, talkative, and determined to do every exercise imaginable. Casey pulled him back to a realistic routine, all the while marveling that a guy with thighs that big could walk around without wearing holes in the legs of his pants.

When four-thirty came she dragged herself up to her apartment, where she drank a Gatorade in about three swallows and took a long, hot shower.

Afterward, Death was standing in the hallway, dressed in a kimono.

Casey took a deep breath. "What are you doing?"

"Coming to Kyoto's. Does this make me look fat?"

"It makes you look *stupid.*"

"I'm getting into the spirit of—"

"You're not invited."

"Of course I am."

"Tamille didn't invite you."

"Only because she couldn't see me. If she could see me, she would definitely have asked me to dinner. That girl and I, we would be like *this*." Death held up crossed fingers.

"Anyway, we're going to the bank first. Don't you think you're a little...overdressed?" Casey went back to her bedroom, where she chose some dark jeans, a light blue shirt, and a pair of sandals she'd picked out at the store. For once, she let her hair fall to her shoulders, instead of putting it back. She was about to leave when she remembered her phone. No point in having one if she left it hidden in her apartment all the time. She reached under her mattress to get it, then keyed in Binns' phone number from her business card. She texted simply, "*Here's my number.*"

There. Now Binns could find her any time, day or night. Just what Casey liked.

Death blinked when Casey went out to the living room. "Wow, who are *you*? I mean, look at you. You combed your hair and everything."

"Will you shut up?" Casey grabbed her purse, yanked open the door, and froze. A shadow fell across the hallway, elongated by the light coming through the window at the end of the hallway. The shadow of a man. And at the end of his arm, the shadow of his hand held something long and thin, that looked exactly like a knife.

Chapter Nineteen

Casey swung into the hallway, grabbed the man's arm, and twisted it back, bending him forward so he would drop what was in his hand.

"Who are you?" Casey said in his ear. "What do you want?"

"Casey," Death said. "Stop. It's—"

"It's me. Dylan. *Ouch.*" Dylan waved his free hand frantically.

Casey let him go and took a quick step back.

Dylan straightened, rubbing his shoulder. "Is that part of our new fitness routine? Because wow, that hurt. A lot."

"Sorry. I'm a little jumpy." Jumpy? Maybe she should say, *completely paranoid.*

He winced, windmilled his arm, and rolled his neck. "Lesson learned. Always stay as far away from you as possible."

"Why were you loitering in my hallway?"

"I was waiting."

"For…?"

"Well, you, actually. I was getting up my nerve to knock on your door."

"Told you he would be jumping your bones sooner or later," Death said. "He needs an older woman to show him the ropes."

"What do you want?"

"Well, I was *going* to ask if I could take you to dinner." He knelt and picked up what he'd been holding. A single rose.

Casey shook her head. He'd brought her a *flower*, and she'd assumed it had been a deadly weapon. She'd misjudged the situation in a whole new way. Now that she took the time to look, she saw also that he was wearing khakis and a dress shirt, and smelled like a fresh dose of cologne. Maybe a whole quart of it.

"Dylan, I don't think Krystal would like it very much if you were wining and dining the enemy."

"Screw Krystal." He blushed. "I mean, forget about her. She's sort of, well, gone off the deep end. She's outside Sissy's office right now, hoping to convince the family that you killed Andrea."

"The family's here already?"

"No. Krystal's just waiting. She wants to get to them first. Maria's trying to make her go away, and even threatened to call security. I only know this because they were making quite a scene when I got home from work. Everybody was sort of all jammed up in the lobby, watching."

"So you thought you'd get me out of the way by taking me out to dinner, in case Krystal got to the Parkers?"

"Well, kind of. They might be crazy enough to believe her." He shifted uneasily. "But I also thought going out might be... fun." He grinned sheepishly, his cheeks and throat going an even deeper pink.

"Aww," Death said. "Look at that puppy dog face."

"It *would* be nice," Casey said. "But I've already got plans."

His face fell. "Really? Who is he?"

"Not a he."

"Then a she?"

"What else would it be?"

"A supernatural?" Death said.

Dylan brightened. "Can I come?"

"No."

He drooped again. "Why not?"

"Because I think Tamille would eat you alive."

He blanched. "That huge Amazon woman? She just about did one time."

"Really? What happened?"

"She..." He looked away. "It was nothing. I was using the weights and she wanted them. No big deal. I just try to stay out of her way, now, so she can't capture me and grind my balls into tiny little pieces."

Casey laughed. "Another time, okay, Dylan? And thanks."

"Tomorrow?"

"What about tomorrow? Our next personal training session?"

"It's Friday. And yeah, we have another session in the morning. But what I *meant* was that in the evening I'll take you to this really nice Cuban restaurant on the other side of town. It's a hole in the wall, but it's authentic. They make killer tamales."

Casey shook her head. "Okay."

He pumped his fist.

"But listen, Dylan. It's just dinner, okay? And I'll pay my own way."

"But—"

"Dinner. Dutch. Or I don't go."

His shoulders slumped. "Fine. I suppose you want to just meet me there, too?"

"You already know where I live, Dylan. Meeting someone at a restaurant is a way to keep them away from home before you know them."

"So we can go together?"

"I'll meet you in the lobby. What time?"

"Do you have to get back for class?"

"Nope. Friday night is off. So I'm all—" She was going to say, 'all yours,' but stopped herself, before she confused the poor boy any further. "I'm free for the evening."

"Great. Six-thirty? Lobby?"

"Sounds good. Thanks." She closed her door behind her. "But now I have to get going."

"To meet Wonder Woman. Can I at least get your phone number, just in case?"

"In case what?"

"I don't know. In case I get tickets to something, and want to switch dinner to a concert."

Casey pulled out her phone, found her number, and gave it to him. After a few seconds, her own phone rang.

"There," Dylan said. "Now you have my number, too."

Great. Now she had a detective and a sex-starved twenty-something in her Contact List. She was moving up in the world.

Casey headed for the staff stairway. "See you tomorrow, Dylan." She left him in the hallway, the rose drooping from his hand.

"You're so hard on the poor kid," Death said. "He's only trying to be nice."

"No, he's trying to get in my pants."

"Well, maybe he thinks that's nice."

Casey laughed. "At least I don't have to worry about that with Tamille."

"That you know of."

"True."

She exited the building through a back door and circled around, not wanting to meet Krystal in the lobby. When she got to the front, there was a taxi letting off a middle-aged couple.

"Andrea's parents," Death said.

Casey slowed, and stopped in the shadow of a palm tree to watch. The woman was leaning over the man, who still sat on the back seat of the taxi. He grabbed the door and pulled himself up, the woman with her hand under his elbow.

"What's wrong with him?" Death said.

"Grief." Casey recognized it. Remembered it. The feeling that you couldn't even stand, couldn't lift your foot to take a step. Couldn't raise your head to look in front of you. Andrea's mother was moving through the grief in a different way. Perhaps just this day. Perhaps tomorrow it would be Andrea's father holding her up.

It had been Ricky who had held Casey up during those first days. Weeks. Months. Her mother had tried, but she'd been so enveloped in her own grief she couldn't do much for Casey. Ricky had been the strong one. The backbone. The steel.

She missed him with a sudden, almost debilitating, ache. What would he have to say about Dylan? Or Gomez? Or this hell she was going through? She fingered her purse, where she'd put her phone. One phone call. The push of a few buttons. That's all it would take. She could be talking to her brother in seconds. Her hand gravitated toward the top of her purse, and her fingers grasped the zipper pull. Eased it back.

"So are we going, or what?" Death said. "The bank's going to close in forty minutes."

Casey jerked her hand away from her purse. "The bank! Right. I'd forgotten all about that." She shivered. She'd been so close to giving it all away.

She made a wide loop around the parking lot and made her way down the sidewalk. Tourists were out in abundance now, window shopping, strolling, checking the menus on placards outside restaurants.

Death whistled, and practically skipped down the street. "See? I keep telling you I'm a good sort to have around, but you never believe me."

Casey looked up the road. "Is that Andrea's bank?"

"It's the only one on this road."

"Must be it, then."

It was, and *Geena the Way Too Energetic Teller* was "more than happy!" to give Casey access to her safety deposit box, and led the way, her ponytail bouncing.

"This is good for you, right?" Death said. "Now you don't have to open an account to have an excuse to be here."

Casey tried not to react to Death's clothes, which were now comprised of a dark suit, patent leather shoes, and a nametag that said, *My name is Thanatos. First Bank of Infinity.*

Casey followed *Geena!* to a small room with a thick bank vault wall, an empty table, and a chair. After the one-key-each, turn-at-the-same-time ritual, the teller set the box on the table, gave Casey instructions to just "let her know when she was finished!" and smacked a sign-in sheet in front of her.

Casey stared at it. Brandon had signed for the box at least a dozen times. Would the teller notice Casey wasn't exactly a Brandon?

"Just sign his name," Death said. "Tell Geena your parents were hoping for a boy, if she asks."

But wasn't it a federal crime or something to impersonate someone at a bank? Casey thought so. But then, could she really be in any more trouble than she already was?

Hardly.

Taking her time, Casey made her signature look as much like Brandon's as she could. The teller gave it one small glance, and trotted out of the room.

"Better make it quick," Death said. "In case the impossible happens and she comes to her senses."

Casey opened the top of the drawer. It was filled with manila folders. She pulled out the first one. It had Sissy's name on it.

Death was behind Casey now, peering over her shoulder. "Anything good?"

"It's Sissy's resume. And newspaper articles about the Flamingo. Photos…"

"Oh, ick, he didn't take the pictures while they were…you know…"

"No." The first shot looked like it had been taken in a business setting, through the glass wall of an office. Sissy sat behind a desk wearing a bright fuchsia suit, and was talking to a man who sat in front of her desk. Outside the office was another desk, with a young woman at a computer. "No, this was from years ago, at some other place. I don't recognize either of the other people, or the office." She put it back and studied the second photo. "This is more recent. There she is, talking to Maria in the outer office downstairs. Why would he keep a picture of that?"

"What's that paper, underneath the photos?"

She pulled it out. "A reference letter, dated nine years ago, to the director of another apartment complex in Georgia." She scanned it. "On second thought, it's not a reference letter. It's a hire-this-woman-at-your-own-risk letter. Seems Sissy took on a few too many 'mistakes' at her old job. Hmm. So this policy of hiring before looking isn't anything new." She picked up the older photo again. "Think this is from that job?"

"Do any of the newspaper articles correspond with it?"

Casey skimmed the first one. "Seems a man she hired—this man? I don't know—ended up embezzling more than half the company's money. Once they looked at him more closely, it seemed some major information was missed when he was hired. He'd been suspected of embezzling in the past. Some people seemed to think Sissy knew about it, and hired him anyway."

"Wonder what was in it for her?"

"Or if she was just gullible." Casey swallowed down the bad taste in her mouth as she thought of Sissy being taken not only by that guy from the past, but Brandon, as well. "Oh, Sissy."

"What's in the other folders?"

Casey picked her way through. "All of them have women's names on them. Krystal. Bernie—that woman from my aerobics class. A bunch of names I don't recognize. Laurie. Even Maria." Casey pulled that one out. The first paper in the stack was a copy of an expired green card, with the name Melina Reynaldo, and an old photo of Maria. Following that were copies of government papers—denied citizenship applications, searches for other family members, even deportation reports citing other people with the last name Reynaldo. All from the last year and a half.

"Oh, no," Casey said.

"Maria's here illegally?" Death *tsked*. "Under an assumed name? She's a naughty girl. And that would explain the second picture in Sissy's folder. Maybe Brandon thought Sissy knew about Maria's illegal status and hired her anyway."

"If this Melina is actually Maria. And even if it is, she's got kids. Who knows if *they're* citizens or not? You can't ask a woman to leave her kids behind while she's deported. She's going to do everything she can to stay." Casey glanced at the clock. "I've got to go. We'll study these more later." She looked around for a bag, but had to settle for shoving the folders sideways into her purse. "No wonder Maria wanted that key. I'm surprised there aren't more women looking for it. I'll have to think about where to stash these so they don't get stolen." Casey shoved the drawer back in its spot and headed to the lobby.

"Another question," Death said. "Why are the folders still here? Why didn't Brandon take them with him?"

"That is strange. And dangerous. But maybe these are just copies and he has the originals with him. Like he left them here for back-up."

"Makes sense. Although if I were Brandon, I would have destroyed the evidence before I got out of town."

"I don't think Brandon believed anyone would ever come after him. They'd be too embarrassed to admit he'd scammed them."

"All done?" Geena the Teller finished with a customer and whirled to face Casey, her smile blinding.

"Yeah. Thanks. Hey, I was wondering, did you know Andrea Parker?"

Geena's smile disappeared. "Of course I did. She was...did *you* know her?"

"I live at the Flamingo."

"Oh. She loved that place." Geena came out from her window and flung her arms around Casey. "Isn't it awful?"

Casey went stiff, but managed to pat Geena on the back until she finally backed off.

"Aw," Death said, giggling. "Just what you like. Close, personal contact."

Casey stepped farther away from the teller. "What about Krystal?"

Geena wrinkled her nose and glanced behind her. No one was close enough to hear, but she still closed the gap between the two of them, pushing Casey against the wall. "I've never been able to figure out why those two were friends. Andrea was so nice, and Krystal is so...*you* know."

"Yes." Casey gave Geena a girl-to-girl smile. "What exactly was Andrea's job here?"

"Loan officer. Mostly for small businesses, but she'd do some personal loans, too."

"And Krystal?"

Geena stepped even closer, her crossed arms touching Casey's. "She's a loan officer too. For big business. But I always get the feeling she doesn't do a whole lot of actual *banking*, if you know what I mean."

Casey knew. "So she's just a show piece?"

"The boss seems to use her that way. Although I'm not sure how much it's just for *show*." She shrugged. "I could be wrong, of course. Maybe she really does know about money and stuff. It's just hard to look past—"

"Geena!" A man came up behind her. He wore a dark gray suit, blue tie, and shiny black shoes, looking almost like Death's fashion twin. His eyes were wary and alert. "Shouldn't you be in your window instead of talking to your friends?"

Geena went pink and swiveled away. "Oh, sorry, sir! This is…" She faltered, her hand waving at Casey. "And this," she said to Casey, "is our bank manager."

"Hmm," Death said. "The plot thickens. Remember how Andrea and Krystal were talking about the 'men at the top?' This guy looks a little too big for his britches."

He looked like a typical businessman, as far as Casey could tell. Clean-shaven, a little taller than Casey, a tiny paunch around the middle. His smile was too white, and his hair too dark for the age he seemed to be.

He set Casey's teeth on edge.

"I'm a new customer," Casey said, holding out her hand. "Geena was telling me about your bank."

The manager shook her hand, his suspicious expression relaxing. His hand was soft, like he wouldn't know manual labor if it hit him on the head. "We have customer service people specifically for that. Can I direct you to one of them?"

"No, thank you. Geena has been very helpful."

"So you've opened an account?"

"We've done what we needed to today." Casey smiled at Geena. "Thank you so much for everything. You've been very helpful."

Geena nodded and scurried back to her window.

"She's a very pleasant girl," Casey said to the manager. "A good asset for your business."

He looked like he'd swallowed an entire orange.

"Casey, darling?" Death said. "Times a-ticking. Somehow—stop me if I'm wrong—I don't think we want to keep Tamille waiting."

Casey thanked the bank manager and headed out. She had to wait, as someone else was coming in the door.

"Del?"

He squinted, moving from the brightness of the afternoon into the darker lobby. "Oh, Daisy." He smiled, his eyes looking a little less tired than they had the day before. "Good to see you."

"So you do your banking here?"

"Sure. It's the closest to the Flamingo. Most of the residents have accounts here. At least those staying long enough to warrant the change from their hometowns. Were you here to open one?" He put a hand to his forehead. "Sorry. That's none of my business."

"I just asked you about your banking," Casey said. "But anyway, I was checking it out. Haven't made a decision yet."

Del's face clouded. "Andrea worked here. She was trying to push through a loan for me, to see if I could start my own business."

"A restaurant?"

"Yes. We were looking at options, but nothing seemed to be working."

"And now?"

"I'll have to start over with someone new, won't I?"

"I guess. Couldn't Krystal help you?"

He opened his mouth, but seemed to think about his words, and changed course. "I don't believe that's her expertise. They'll match me up with someone, I'm sure. So, you going out for dinner?"

"Kyoto's."

"Oh, that's good stuff. You should enjoy it."

"See you back at the Flamingo?"

"I'm sure you will. Goodnight, Daisy."

"Goodnight."

He held the door for her, and disappeared into the bank.

Chapter Twenty

Death was back in the kimono, although this time it had more embroidery, with yellow flowers from top to bottom. Casey hoped she herself was dressed all right. She never knew how to dress for dinner in a new town. But then, she'd never been all that concerned about her attire, and figured there was no reason to start just then.

"So Krystal is window dressing?" Death said as they walked. "While Andrea actually worked for a living?"

"I don't know. But I can't see their differing job descriptions being motives for murder. Hopefully her folder will give us a clue." She watched a taxi go past, filled with young business-types, probably on their way to happy hour somewhere. None of them looked like they had a care in the world.

Death frowned, hesitating at the curb. "Could personal and small business loans be motive for murder?"

"You're kidding, right?" Casey waited for the walk sign and headed across the street. "In this economic climate? People would kill for a minimum wage job, let alone money to keep their mom and pop store going."

Death scurried after her. "Which means *Del* could have a motive. He just told us he was one of Andrea's clients, and she couldn't get his loan through. What if she wasn't really trying to *get* him a loan? What if she turned him down for more than just a date?"

Casey didn't like to think about huge, gentle Del using that strength for violence. But she would be remiss to toss the thought aside.

"Here we are." Death stopped in front of a dark brick storefront. "Kyoto's. Are you supposed to just go in, or wait for her?"

"Don't know." Casey stepped into the foyer and allowed her eyes a little time to adjust to the darkness. Soft, far eastern music surrounded her, and the odor of something delicious drifted past her nose.

"Good evening, miss." A little woman in a kimono like Death's, although this one a midnight blue, was bowing to Casey. "This way, please."

Casey followed the woman to a coat check room, where rows of shoes sat in cubbies.

"You leave shoes, please."

Casey took off her sandals, and the woman offered her a pair of slippers. Casey tried not to make a face.

"Eww," Death said, mirroring Casey's thoughts. "You don't know where those have been."

"We wash each time," the little woman said. "Strong soap. You take."

Casey took the slippers.

"You have reservation?" the woman asked.

"I'm meeting a friend."

"Ah." Her eyes sparkled. "Man friend?"

"No. A woman. She's very…tall."

Recognition lit the woman's eyes. "Yes. Very big. Dark."

"Yes, that's right."

"Follow, please."

The woman led Casey to a small room, cordoned off with paper walls. For the second time that night Casey saw only shadows, which both elongated and enlarged the person within the room. The little woman held aside a beaded curtain, and Casey stepped in. Tamille was already seated on a cushion, sipping a cup of tea and eating fried noodles.

Casey thanked the woman, set her purse in the corner, and pulled another cushion to the low table. Death made do with the floor.

"Sorry," Tamille said. "Couldn't wait."

"That's fine."

Tamille picked up the teapot and filled another cup. "Here. You probably need this."

Casey wrapped her hands around the mug and allowed the steam to wash over her face. The room was decorated with reds and varying sheens of black, with multiple curtains, pillows, and murals. Her slippers were soft, and even without food on the table, the smells floating through the room made her mouth water. "I can see why you like this place."

Tamille finished her tea and set the cup on the table. "It relaxes me. I can't imagine anything loud or fast happening here."

Casey took a deep breath through her nose, and let it out slowly, allowing her tension to slip away.

"You came to Raceda at a bad time," Tamille said.

"I know. Trouble seems to follow me."

"Ah. Those scars we were talking about earlier?"

Casey stirred some sugar into her tea. "Nothing I want to talk about."

"Right. Who wants to talk about their troubles?"

"Do you know about Andrea Parker's?"

"You mean other than that she's dead?"

Death snorted. "I guess you could call that trouble."

"Yes, like what *made* her dead."

"I don't really know anything about her. I'd see her from time to time—as I saw you the past couple of days—but we never had what you'd call a conversation."

"You never attended the early morning aerobics class?"

"I go to my *dojo* in the mornings. I don't usually attend any classes. The only reason I came to the one today was to check you out." She smiled and sipped her tea.

"And what did you think?"

"We're here, aren't we?"

Voices came from outside the room, and Tamille set down her cup and stood, facing the doorway.

"What's going on?" Casey asked, looking at Death.

Death shrugged.

The bead curtain parted and the hostess ushered in a man who was just as little as she, just as Asian, and just as old. He wore a wrap-around shirt and loose pants, a skinny mustache, and a graying ponytail. Tamille bowed and said something to him in another language. The hostess backed out of the room, her head lowered.

"Oh, great," Death said. "If I would've known, I would've brushed up on my Japanese."

Casey knew instinctively who this was, and stood, her palms flat against her hips. When the man turned to her, she gave a little bow. "I apologize for not speaking your language, sensei."

Tamille gave Casey a little smile. "May I introduce my teacher, Sensei Asuhara. Sensei, this is Ms. Daisy Gray." She cleared her throat. "Aerobics instructor."

The man lifted his chin and regarded Casey through dark, steady eyes. Casey willed herself not to fidget, but felt suddenly wanting. All those years she'd studied hapkido, all those medals she'd won, the men she'd beaten…he would know none of that. And he wouldn't care. All he would see was what was before him at that moment. A woman in a strange place, with basically nothing to make her stand out. A vagrant. A poseur. She kept her eyes on his, but stayed slightly bent, out of respect. She wished she could talk with him, to try to explain herself, but Japanese was not something she'd ever studied. She was ashamed.

Asuhara finally blinked, breaking the spell and waving his fingers. "Eh, don't worry about the Japanese. I never was very good at it. My mother *despaired* over me." He smiled brightly, clapping his hands. "I'm starving. Did you order yet, Tami? I've been thinking about tempura all afternoon. "

Death let out a screeching laugh, and Casey's mouth fell open. *This* was Tamille's teacher? No, not Tamille. *Tami.* Casey stifled a chuckle.

Tamille glared at her good-naturedly. "I did order the tempura, sensei. And some inagi and shrimp Ebi. I hope that is acceptable."

"Whatever you want, my girl. Whatever you want. Pour me some tea, will you?"

Casey took a seat on her cushion, trying not to break into laughter. Sensei Asuhara was not exactly what one would expect from a karate master. He was so...*cute*.

Tamille poured his tea, and he dumped four teaspoons of sugar into it. Like he needed more nervous energy.

"So," Asuhara said. "Tami tells me you are quite the fighter." He leaned over and elbowed Casey. "I'd like to see that. Someone beating my Tami? Takes a special person. I've seen multitudes go down under her fists."

Tami scoffed at that. "Multitudes?"

"I do not lie." He turned back to Casey. "You are new here, Tami tells me. Just moved in?"

"That's right."

"Coming from?"

Casey wracked her brain. Where had Daisy last been?

"Tallahassee," Death said.

Right. "Tallahassee."

"And why the move to Raceda? Men troubles? Money troubles? A strong urge for a good tan?"

Tamille watched Casey with amusement. You don't refuse to answer a sensei's questions, even if they are more personal than he should be asking at first meeting.

"I needed a change. Staying in Florida sounded good, and the job at the Flamingo came up."

"Ah." He speared a piece of sushi on a chopstick and stuck it in his mouth.

Casey used his chewing time as a reprieve, to prepare herself for what he might ask next. Who knew, with this guy? He was a live wire. He swallowed, and Casey braced herself.

"And how do you find the Flamingo?"

Casey shot a quick look at Tamille, who innocently picked up a fried noodle and ate it, watching Casey all the while.

"The Flamingo is…challenging."

He laughed. No. Giggled. "That's exactly what Tami says. It's why she stays there, even without anyone to hang out with." He shook his head, giggling some more. "*Challenging*." He tried to spear another piece of shrimp, but his chopstick slipped, and the shrimp flew across the tray, landing on the floor. Tamille picked it up without comment and set it aside, wrapped in a napkin.

Asuhara waved his chopsticks at Casey. "So tell me a story."

"About what?"

"Something at the Flamingo."

"That I find challenging?"

He considered. "No. Something you find disturbing."

Well, that was easy. "A woman was murdered on Tuesday."

"Tami told me all about that, and of course it is very disturbing. But I want to hear about something else."

Casey sat back on her pillow. What could be more disturbing than a murder?

"Oh, please," Death said. "Like there aren't a million things at the Flamingo that make you wonder why God ever made people to begin with."

"Hair dye," Casey said.

"*Hair dye*?" Death shrieked. "You can pick anything you want and you pick *hair dye?*"

"Not…hair dye itself, though, I guess," Casey said. "But what it represents."

Asuhara nodded, as if he'd heard it all before, and gestured for her to go on.

"No one there is what they seem, because they're all dyed, plucked, tanned, whitened, buffed, muscled, or who knows what all. They're squeezed into expensive clothes, or easing the awkwardness with alcohol, or sleeping with everybody who asks, or pretending they're younger than they are. It's like high school all over again, except for then people try to act *older* than they are."

Tamille and Asuhara exchanged a glance.

"What?" Casey said.

"Your response sounds just like the complaints I hear every week from Tami." Asuhara took a sip of tea, and Casey used the opportunity to eat something.

He set down his cup and searched the tray, his chopsticks hovering in the air. "*No one* there is what they seem?"

"Well, I certainly don't know everybody, so I can't say for certain. But just about everyone I've come into contact with. Except Tamille here, maybe." She smiled, and Tamille acknowledged the compliment with a nod. "Oh, and Jack, the bartender. If I had to say, I'd guess he's just who he seems to be, with ordinary clothes and only the hair God gave him. Talking to him after a day with the others is…a relief."

"I see." Asuhara set down his chopsticks. "Tami, dear, will you please go ask for a fork? I'm about to starve to death looking at all this wonderful food."

"Of course, sensei." She rose, gave a little bow, and left the room.

"Now," Asuhara said. "I want you to tell me another story."

"Uh-oh," Death said.

"I want you to tell me *your* story."

Casey stared at Asuhara, whose face suddenly held the seriousness and gravity she would expect from a sensei.

"Quickly, now," he said, "before Tami comes back. Unless, of course, you want her to hear the story, too?"

Casey looked at Death, who shrugged. "It's up to you. Spill or split. I think those are your choices."

"Our friend puts it very succinctly," Asuhara said. "Spill or split evokes just the right spirit."

Casey choked. "You can see…that?"

"*That?*" Death said. "Have a little respect."

Sensei Asuhara rose, and bowed deeply. "You are most welcome in this room, Shinigami. I was not sure, when I first arrived, whether or not you were here for me, but I see now you travel with this lost soul."

Death acknowledged the bow with a slight nod. "I seek to ease her path, sensei, although most often she does not view it that way. Now please, sit."

Asuhara sat back down on his pillow, turning again to Casey. "Please, my dear, explain to me how you come to be in this place, with such an exalted companion."

Again she looked to Death, who nodded gently. "Tell your story, love. Go on."

Casey's chin shook, and she pressed her lips together. "I… lost my family in an accident. I wished to follow them, but Death…won't take me."

"I see. And how long has it been since you have been home, to those others who are left, who know and love you? Parents, perhaps? Siblings? Friends?"

"I don't know. A long time."

He studied her face. "And as you think back on this *long time*, what challenges can you recall?"

A rush of memory flooded Casey's mind—seemingly endless cold nights alone; miles of unfamiliar roads; days turning into weeks, turning into months. But more recently, passion in the back of a theater; Pegasus, scouring the earth to find her; a mobster bleeding onto the street; a good-hearted group of teenagers; the smell of Omar's knit cap; a trucker, dying in her arms; Andrea's blood on her clothes…

She shuddered. "There have been too many challenges to name, sensei."

"I see. And how were you able to overcome these challenges? To go on?"

She gave a small, painful smile. "By following my own advice."

"Which is?"

She closed her eyes and breathed through her nose, acknowledging the exhaustion in her body, in her mind. "To run. To always, forever run."

"There was no other option?"

She pressed her hand against her mouth to stop the trembling. "I guess the other option would have been…to stay." To turn herself in to the cops, to face Eric, to take the blame, to be with

Ricky, to live in her own town, her own house, her own bed. To learn to live without Reuben.

"But of course you had your reasons to act as you did," Asuhara said.

Of course she did. It was all about the pain. The pain of loss. Of living alone. Of realization. Of acceptance. And, ultimately, of moving on. That involved more pain than would be bearable.

Asuhara leaned across the table and cupped her chin in his hand. "And, tell me…" He looked at Death.

"Casey," Death said.

Asuhara's eyes softened. "Tell me, Casey, my dear, if you could, what things about this chapter of your life would you change? If you could go back to just after the accident?"

Casey's chin trembled again, and her eyes filled. "I don't know, sensei. *I don't know* what I would change. If I *should* change it."

The beads in the doorway clacked together, and Tamille swept in, holding a fork as if it were the Olympic torch. She bowed with a flourish, holding it out. "Your silverware, sensei."

He let go of Casey's chin, patting it gently. "Thank you, my dear. That should make things a little easier."

Casey swiped at her face with her napkin, looking down at her lap.

"I'm sorry," Tamille said, the fork dangling from her fingers. "Am I interrupting—"

"Not at all," Asuhara said. "Come in and sit."

Tamille returned to her pillow, and Casey could feel her eyes upon her. Casey forced herself to look up and attempt a smile. She could tell it didn't fool Tamille.

A loud, tinny melody began playing in their small paper room, competing with the ambient Japanese music. Casey looked at the speakers, wondering why the restaurant would do such a thing. Tamille and Asuhara, however, were looking at her.

"Um, you gonna answer that?" Death said.

Casey blinked. "What?"

"Your phone," Tamille said. "At least, that sound is coming from you, so I *assume* it's a phone."

"Oh, I'm sorry." Casey scrabbled in her pocket to pull it out. "I just got this thing. I hadn't even set a ring tone."

The screen of the phone gave a number, but no name, seeing how Casey hadn't actually identified anyone in her contact list yet. The only people who had her number—other than the phone company—were Detective Binns and Dylan, and she had no idea which one this was.

"Excuse me, please." She rose, bowed to Asuhara, and left the room. "Hang on a minute," she said into the phone. The paper walls would hide nothing, and her dinner mates would be able to hear everything she said, not that it would matter with Asuhara anymore. She walked briskly to the front of the restaurant, waggled her phone at the hostess, and went out to the sidewalk.

"Sorry. I'm here."

"Somewhere far eastern, I take it?" It was Binns.

"Kyoto's."

"Ah. I know it well. Any chance you're about finished with dinner?"

"I guess I could be, although we haven't even gotten our main course."

"I'm calling from the Flamingo. Ms. Parker's folks are here, from Oregon, and they would like to speak with you."

Casey sank against the brick wall. They would want her to talk about Andrea's last moments. What she had said. How she'd been. What was Casey supposed to say to them? That their daughter had been gasping for breath? That she hadn't sent them any last messages?

Or else the parents would be watching Casey, looking for signs that she had been the one to end their daughter's life. She wondered if they had already seen Krystal, and been poisoned by her hatred.

Casey sighed. "Do I have to see them?"

"No."

"It's just I'm not sure how helpful it would be."

"I understand. You aren't required to talk with them. They wanted to speak to the person who found her, and I told them

I'd ask. They'll be around for several days, you know, so you'll probably run into them at some point. But you might want to just get it over with."

Casey looked up at the sky, which was beginning to show signs of the night to come. The blue was now tinged with orange, and the clouds stood out in stark relief. A seagull sat on the branch of a palm tree, its head cocked to the side as it eyed her.

"All right," Casey said. "I'll be there soon."

"You could wait until dinner is over. They're not going anywhere."

"What's the point? I don't have an appetite now, anyway." She hesitated. "Are you going to be there?"

"I'm not going anywhere. Gomez and I will protect you."

Gomez. Great. The way Casey's brain addled when he was around, Binns would end up protecting Gomez from *her*.

Casey hung up the phone without saying anything else.

Back in the room, she grabbed her purse and made her apologies to the sensei and Tamille. "The police need me back at the Flamingo."

Death crooked an eyebrow, obviously wondering if she was stretching the truth.

"Of course," Asuhara said. "Then you must go." He rose and met her at the door, taking her hands in his. "Go, with the strength of a sensei. And of those who travel with you." He bowed, his hands warm on hers.

Casey bowed back, then nodded at Tamille. "I'll see you later?"

"Count on it."

Asuhara let go of her hands and focused his eyes just over Casey's shoulder, where Death stood. "Until we meet again."

"I will look forward to that day," Death said. "But I hope, for your sake, that it will not be for some time."

Asuhara bowed again, and Death swept through the beaded curtain, moving it ever so slightly, as if a draft had caught the strands.

Chapter Twenty-one

"You all right?" Death still wore the kimono, but had replaced the slippers with sneakers, since Casey was in a hurry to get back to the Flamingo. Casey herself was glad to be in her regular shoes, but still felt off-balance from the way Asuhara had read her. It was like he'd known she was hiding something. Like he'd known *her*. Behind his giggle and his bad Japanese he truly was a sensei, testing everything she thought she'd learned since Reuben and Omar's deaths. Asking those questions her own Master had put to her so many times before, before Omar, before her marriage, before she'd even met Reuben. He'd asked them about hapkido. About life. About *living*. What were the challenges? How did you overcome them? What were your options? And perhaps, most importantly, what would you change if you had to do it again?

Oh, so many things.

Death jogged ahead and stopped in the sidewalk, hands up. "Um, I know you're a bit freaked out and all about what just happened—"

Casey walked around. "I'm not freaked out."

"Okay. Are you at least impressed that Asuhara saw me? And thought I was, well, something to be respected? Unlike some people I know?"

"Oh, L'Ankou, I respect you. I don't always *like* you, but that's different."

Death jumped ahead and blocked the sidewalk this time, arms out. "How could you not like me? I'm so *fun*."

Casey didn't respond.

"Fine. Do you at least love me for my mind?"

Casey waited silently until Death got out of the way, and she could walk again.

"Well, you will after this. I've been thinking—"

"Scary."

"—about the night of the murder. Something's not right."

Casey gave a short laugh. "A lot of things aren't right. Andrea's *dead*."

"No, listen, it's about the security."

Casey perked up. "Okay. I'm listening."

"Okay. Obviously the security at the Flamingo isn't the best, but they should have known if a non-resident entered the building. Especially at that time of night. There wouldn't be a lot of people going by the front desk or clogging up the video feed. You with me so far? *But...* someone had messed with the camera in the hallway. The killer is unrecognizable."

"So?"

"The murderer knew about the camera, but didn't have the ability, or the opportunity, to actually *disable* it. There would have been security there all the time, watching the monitors."

"So it was a security guy who killed her?"

"No." Death put on a patient voice. "I'm saying security would have noticed someone messing with the camera lens. If they didn't see the person smearing it, they would have at least seen that the lens was blurry. Unless..."

"L'Ankou, I'm tired. Just tell me."

"Unless the guard was *distracted*. It took only a few seconds to mess up the lens, and only a moment for the killer to enter the hallway and get into the locker room door."

"So you're saying what? There was a second person?" Casey went suddenly hot, then cold. "There was an *accomplice*?" Casey's heart felt like it was lodged in her throat. Because who better to distract a lonely security guard than Andrea's supposed best friend? It should have been unthinkable—that a woman would sell out her best friend—but what kind of woman were they talking about? A woman who, by all accounts, had few scruples about what she did in her dating life, and was going to do just that the day after Andrea's death, not twenty feet from where she had lain dying. Unless, of course, Krystal and Dylan had been planning on moving right through Casey's office into the women's locker room. Then they would've been practically on the spot of Andrea's death.

Which was way too creepy for Casey to think about. Too creepy to believe.

"But why would Krystal do something that awful? If she hated Andrea, why didn't she just kill her herself? Or, maybe, you know, *talk* to her about whatever the problem was? They were supposedly friends, after all."

"We really don't know anything about Krystal, do we?" Death said. "Other than the fact that she likes men."

"Does more than *like* them." Casey stepped around a man and his German Shepherd, who was examining the post of a mailbox.

The dog spun suddenly around, sniffing at Death's legs, and Death did a little two-step to avoid it. "Well, the top reasons for murder are money, sex, and…something else."

"Revenge."

"Right. So, anyway, sex is right at the top, and Krystal is all about that. If I looked up the definition of sex, it would claim her as its top example, right along with a photo. Hmm. That would be a way to sell more dictionaries, wouldn't it? Except everything's on-line these days, and who's going to buy an on-line dictionary?"

"What else do we know about Krystal?"

"Not much, except she works at the bank, and we didn't find out a whole lot there. At least nothing surprising. Andrea was good at the actual banking, and Krystal…isn't. Maybe Andrea's folks will know something more substantial about her work."

"I doubt it. Andrea was, what? Twenty-five? And she lived in the opposite corner of the country from her parents. They probably knew she worked at a bank, but more than that…I can't really see it."

"Maybe she was one of those kids who text their parents ten times a day with every little problem."

"No. She was way too self-sufficient for that. I could tell that right off. She was out on her own, for real."

"Running from something? Or someone? Maybe even her parents?"

"She didn't seem like a runner. She was sure of herself. And content."

Death laughed. "You talk like you knew her for years. What makes you think she was so happy?"

"I didn't say she was *happy*. I said she was content. There's a huge difference."

"Like you would know. You're neither."

"But I remember what they both felt like. It wasn't so long ago I've forgotten."

The Flamingo reared up in front of them, in all its pinkness, and Casey's step faltered. "Oh, L'Ankou, I don't want to talk to these people. I don't want to talk about their dead daughter. What do I have to say to them? How can I possibly help them in any way? I have nothing to offer them."

"Binns said you don't have to talk with them."

"I know. But if it's not now, it will be sometime in the next few days, when I have less control over it." She let out a sound of frustration, anger, and hopelessness. It was all so pointless. "So I guess I'm getting it over with now. All right?"

"I guess."

Casey walked toward the front of the building, but hesitated again.

Death sighed. "What now?"

Casey held up her hand. She could see someone at the base of one of the palm trees, hiding behind the bushes. There. Peeking around, then ducking back. The encroaching darkness cast shadows along the ground, and among the foliage, so Casey couldn't get a good feel for who was waiting for her. Whoever it was obviously didn't want to be seen.

"Should we cross to the other side of the street?" Death said.

"How would we get to our building, then? No. We're going head on."

Casey pulled her confidence out of reserve, rolled her shoulders and cracked her neck, and approached the tree with caution. The person didn't look out again, and the average passerby would never know someone was there. Casey left her purse behind a bush, then walked straight, as if she were going to pass the tree. She spun around the trunk, pressing her forearm against the person's throat and slamming her against the bark. Casey leaned forward, surprised. "Laurie?"

Laurie gagged, her wind cut off by Casey's arm. Her hair was even wilder than it had been by the pool that afternoon, and her eyes shone wide and glassy. Casey released her, and she stumbled to the side, putting her hands to her neck.

"Sorry," Casey said. "I didn't know it was you."

Laurie blinked several times and cleared her throat, her eyes darting from side to side.

Casey looked around, but didn't see anyone else. "Were you waiting for me?"

"Yes, I... The guard saw you...I just wanted...never mind." She turned to go.

"No, wait. Please. I won't touch you again." Casey held up her hands, as if in surrender.

Laurie fidgeted, then stepped a little farther back into the trees, gesturing for Casey to follow.

"Careful," Death said.

"I'm always careful."

Laurie frowned. "Me, too. At least I used to be."

Casey couldn't believe the mess of a woman Laurie had become. "What do you want, Laurie? I was waiting for you in the weight room earlier and you didn't show up."

"I'm sorry. I wanted to. I just...couldn't. Not right then. Maria was at the elevator and she...she was looking for me all day, wanting me to teach. I just can't yet." She glanced around, and shrank back into the foliage even more.

"Laurie, what is going on? Who are you afraid of?"

"I'm not afraid."

Death laughed. "Could've fooled me. Look at her, cowering in the greenery."

"Laurie," Casey said gently, "you're hiding in *bushes*."

Laurie sank to the ground, her back against a tree. She muffled a sob behind her hand. "Andrea's family is in there."

"Yes, I'm supposed to be meeting with them."

Laurie winced. "What are you going to tell them?"

"I assume they want to know about when I found her."

"That's all?"

"I don't know anything else. What else would I say? Look, Laurie, is there something I should know? Something you want to tell me?"

Laurie shook her head, still not looking up. "I don't want to tell you anything."

"Oh, great," Death said. "Com*plete* waste of time. And I think a bug just dropped down my collar."

"Then why am I back here with you?" Casey said, trying to be more patient than Death.

"Because I want you to know Andrea's death is *not* my fault. And it's not *his* fault, either. He never meant to hurt anybody. He just wanted to make people *happy*."

"Brandon, I assume she's talking about," Death said. "He wanted to make people happy by screwing them and stealing their money? Tell me where the 'happy' is in that equation."

"Why would anyone blame you?" Casey said. "Why would you hurt Andrea?" Casey took a deep breath, and took a chance. "Look, Laurie. I know you were involved with Brandon, okay?"

Laurie inhaled sharply.

"And I know it ended badly. All of his relationships seemed to have ended badly. If he was involved with Andrea, that ended, too. Probably badly."

"He wasn't with her. He *wasn't*! I would have known it!"

Casey was confused. "So if you were that sure, why would anyone think you'd hurt Andrea?"

Death laughed. "You think she's going to confess out here in this mini jungle?"

"I *wouldn't* hurt her," Laurie said. "That's what I'm telling you. People just *think* I did." She sniffled. "But I never would have hurt her! Never!" This last was said in a wail, so loud that Death recoiled, and Casey grimaced, thinking of how peaceful it had been back a week ago in that smelly boxcar, with the drunk singing about bottles of beer. No one was dead. No one wanted anything from her. She'd just been uncomfortable and tired and hungry and injured and annoyed. Other than that, it had been heaven.

"Look," Laurie said, lowering her voice. "I was jealous of her, okay? She was young, and pretty, and I was convinced she was with Brandon. She seemed so content. So unworried about all of the men and problems and frustrations the rest of us had. Just the fact that she could be friends with Krystal—well, that tells you something, doesn't it? That she thought she didn't have to compete? I finally couldn't take it anymore. I confronted her. I asked her why she had to pick Brandon, out of all the men in the building, and she assured me I didn't need to worry about her taking him away from me." Laurie rubbed her eyes. "And then…then she said she was sorry. That she knew it must be hard being in love with him when so many women wanted the same thing."

She looked at her hands. "I hated her for that. That she would be *sorry* for me. That she obviously thought I didn't have a chance. I was too old, or too ugly, or too *something*." She sniffed loudly. "I was so *hurt*. I'm sure someone knew. Someone heard. And now they think I killed her."

Casey took a deep breath and let it out. "Laurie, no one has said anything to me about you killing Andrea." That was, by all accounts, true. Binns had *talked* about Laurie, but hadn't actually said she *suspected* her.

"Really?" Laurie peeked up at her.

"Really. I don't think anyone is after you for it. Look, can I help get you inside? Maybe walk you to your apartment?"

"What? No, I'm fine. You…you go on. They're waiting."

"But—"

"I'm *fine*." Laurie got up, dusted herself off, and held out her arms. "See? Good as new." And she skittered off, out the front of the trees and away on the sidewalk.

Casey stared after her. "Wow, that is one messed up woman."

"She's sad."

"But about what, exactly? On the one hand she's sad Andrea's dead, on the other, she's still angry with her."

"She's sad about everything." Death walked out of the trees and waited for Casey to retrieve her purse and follow. "She feels guilty about Andrea's death, she's devastated that Brandon is gone, and she's absolutely *crushed* because she knows he never would have chosen her out of all the women here."

Casey shook her head. "I guess I can see all those things. But maybe it's really just that she has a screw loose."

"Well, granted, there are probably several clanking around in there, but they're probably because of all the guy trouble."

Casey took a deep breath, held it, and let it out. "Well, I really don't know what to think. Is she a crazy killer or just a pathetic, dumped woman?"

Death held out an arm toward the front door of the Flamingo, indicating that Casey should go first. "I think we both know the answer to that."

"Pathetic and dumped?"

"I really think so."

"Yeah," Casey said sadly, walking away from the trees. "I think so, too."

Chapter Twenty-two

The security guard was the same one as when Casey had returned from the hospital with Gomez two nights before. The young, good-looking one. He recognized her this time, and waved her in. Gomez was there, too, waiting in the lobby under one of the palm trees.

Casey's heart leapt, and she reached out, as if to steady herself on Death's arm.

"Steady there, girl. Just a handsome guy who looks like your dead husband. Cuban, though. Not Mexican."

As if that made any difference in the way Casey's body responded to him. It wasn't like her feelings knew anything about nationality. Or even what would be helpful.

Jack, straightening up the tables in the bar, saw her before Gomez did. "Hey, Casey. You all right?"

She must have looked awful. Everyone kept asking her that.

"I'm fine. Just...I have to go talk with Andrea's parents."

"Sure. I saw them come in. Poor folks."

Behind Jack, Casey could see Gomez taking notice of her and walking her way. She looked back at Jack's kind face for strength. "You'll be out here later?"

"Till twelve-thirty or so. Just like last night."

Gomez reached them. "They're waiting for you in Mrs. Williams' office, Ms. Gray." His forehead wrinkled. "You okay?"

"Just what I asked her," Jack said. "You'll take care of her?"

"Sure. I got her."

"Hey," Casey said. "I'm right here. And I'm fine. Where's Binns?"

"She had to leave," Gomez said. "Asked me to tell you she'll call tomorrow."

Great. "Thanks, Jack. See you later."

"I'll be here."

Casey stepped away from Gomez and walked briskly toward Sissy's office, not wanting to receive anything from the policeman, including his compassionate expression, the scent of his cologne, or even the movement of air around him. Just that brief interaction had made her feel all giddy, and that wasn't what she needed heading into this conversation.

The light was on in Maria's office, and Sissy's door was open. Casey could see Sissy's hands resting on her desk, and two sets of feet on the opposite side of the doorway—one in women's low-heeled boots, and one in loafers. Casey shuddered.

"Deep breath," Death said. "It's just old people."

"Old people who just lost their daughter," Casey muttered.

"Excuse me?" Gomez leaned toward her.

Casey jerked away. "Nothing."

"Ah, here she is." Sissy got up and pulled Casey into the room. She wore the same maroon outfit she'd had on earlier, but her make-up had been freshly done, and her expression was all blank and businesslike. "Mr. and Mrs. Parker, this is Daisy Gray, our fitness instructor. She was friends with your daughter."

Casey stared at her. *Friends*?

"I'm sure she'd be glad to tell you about Andrea and what she'd been doing here in Florida."

Sissy gave Casey a bright smile, as fake as they come. Casey swiveled her eyes sideways to look at Death, who was perched on the back of Mr. Parker's chair, watching Casey with raised eyebrows. The Parkers themselves weren't really looking at anything. Mr. Parker had slouched so far down he seemed to be sinking into the chair, his eyes level with Sissy's desktop. Mrs. Parker sat ramrod straight, her eyes aimed straight across the top of Sissy's desk, even with the aerial photo of the complex. Neither one had acknowledged Casey's arrival. She wondered if they were even really present in the room.

"Excuse me." Officer Gomez stood in the doorway. "If you're not needing me anymore, I'll be off."

"Oh, yes, we're fine, officer," Sissy gushed. "*Thank* you *so* much."

He looked at Casey.

Yes, she needed him, but not in any way that would be appropriate. "I'll be fine. Thank you."

He gave her a gentle smile, and left.

"Go ahead," Sissy urged Casey. "Tell the Parkers all about their daughter."

"Um..." Casey really, *really* wasn't up for this. Confusing senseis, sexy police officers, crazy women hiding in the palm trees, being expected to talk about a woman she'd only known a few hours... "I actually only got to know Andrea—"

Sissy cleared her throat loudly. "Ms. Gray is going to be modest, no doubt, Mr. and Mrs. Parker. Andrea was a member of Ms. Gray's aerobics classes, and one of her best students." She fluttered her eyelashes at Casey, but Casey could see steel underneath the falseness. "She showed a lot of stability there, and at work, where she never missed a day."

Was it possible Sissy would know this? Casey couldn't imagine how. It's not like anyone took attendance at fitness classes. And Sissy certainly wasn't checking off little boxes to make sure everybody got to work on time.

Sissy opened her eyes wide and gave Casey a frightening stare.

"Andrea was a...regular class member," Casey said. It wasn't a lie. In the one day Casey had been there, Andrea had actually attended *two* sessions. Three if you counted the impromptu self-defense lesson. "She was very fit, and enjoyed the time with the other women."

The Parkers didn't move. They didn't even act like they knew anyone had been talking. It was a kind of existence Casey recognized. Just as when she'd seen them exit the taxi, she could feel their grief, and their utter, complete exhaustion.

"Sissy," she said quietly. "They don't want to hear this right now."

Sissy slumped, the forced brightness evaporating in a heartbeat. She leaned against her desk and rubbed her forehead. "I know. What I don't know is what to *do* with them."

Casey traveled back to the days after her family's accident, those first hours when she'd had no idea how exactly her life had changed, unable to bring herself to the present because of the battering pain that would find her. "Do you have access to Andrea's apartment?"

"Yes. The police have already been through it."

"Then I suggest you put them there, and try talking to them tomorrow. They're exhausted. They're in shock. They need somewhere to…to just be quiet."

Sissy chewed on her lip. "Okay. Okay, we'll do that." She sidestepped to the door. "Maria!"

Maria appeared in the opening, much to Casey's surprise. She hadn't seen her when she'd passed through there. Casey sent a questioning glance toward Death, who shrugged. "Maybe she was hiding? She's apparently gotten good at that. Just like some other people I know. Fake names. Illegal ID. You know the drill."

"We're going to put the Parkers in Andrea's place," Sissy said to Maria. "Can we get clean sheets on the bed?"

"Of course. The cops took the old ones, but I'm sure there's another set. Give me a couple minutes."

Sissy nodded and stepped back into the room, facing the Parkers. "We're going to get you to bed now, okay?"

No response. Sissy looked helplessly at Casey.

"Go ahead," Death said. "You're good with damaged folks."

Casey ground her teeth, but knelt in front of the Parkers. She put a hand first on Mrs. Parker's knee, and then on her husband's. Casey waited until the warmth from her hand seeped through the fabric of their pants, and they realized something had changed. Slowly, with small jerks, their heads turned toward her.

"We're going to take you to Andrea's apartment now," Casey said. "You can get some sleep."

Without a word, Andrea's mother stood, and looped her purse over her arm. She stood there, unmoving, watching Casey for further instructions. Casey turned to Mr. Parker, peering up into his face. "Time to move, Mr. Parker."

His eye twitched, and he pushed himself up, using the arms of the chair to get first into an upright sitting position, then finally into a standing one. Mrs. Parker clutched his right elbow, and Casey took his left.

Casey and the Parkers followed Sissy to the elevator, where the Up button glowed. Casey left them there for a few moments while she ran back to the office to grab their bags. Everyone was silent as they went up. Maria met them at Andrea's door, which had several signs taped onto it, saying, "We'll miss you," or bearing the image of an angel.

A tissue-wrapped bouquet of flowers leaned against the door-jamb, and Maria scooped it up. "I've already brought in several of these. Most don't even have names."

Casey seated the Parkers in the living room, Mrs. Parker on the couch, her husband on an easy chair. The room was fragrant with flowers, which decorated Andrea's table and windowsills, and even the floor, a testament to how much she was appreciated at the Flamingo. There had been floral arrangements at Reuben and Omar's funeral, too. The blooms had ended up back at Casey's house, because there was nowhere else to go with them. The funeral home didn't want them. The church had taken one for the front of the sanctuary the next Sunday morning, but they had no need of twenty. So Casey's home was filled with flowers. So many Casey had thought she would faint from the overwhelming odor.

She remembered another time, one of the many occasions she'd visited the place where the accident had happened, where Reuben and Omar had died in a ball of flaming gas. The scorched and muddied grass had healed, so Casey could see no sign of the horror that had happened there. A spray of wildflowers had grown up, small purple ones with pointy grayish-green foliage. She had wept at the sight of that beauty, spread over the spot where her own life had ended, along with her family's.

What would happen if she were to die? If she were here in Florida, so far from her home, with no one to even know her real name? Who would visit her? Who would come, bringing flowers to her grave?

Sissy plucked Casey's sleeve. She seemed at a loss for words, so Casey shook herself back to the present and squatted in front of the Parkers, who seemed to be aging right in front of her. "We'll see you tomorrow, okay? Do you need help getting to bed?" She put her hand on Mrs. Parker's arm, and the older woman jumped.

"No, we'll be fine. He'll…he'll help me."

Casey really didn't want to say that her husband seemed worse off than she, but figured once they were alone, the two of them might be able to get themselves moving. She squeezed Mrs. Parker's hand and stood.

It wasn't until Sissy and Maria were in the hallway and Casey was closing the door that Andrea's mother looked up. "Excuse me?"

Casey paused. "Yes, Mrs. Parker? Can I get you something?"

"I was just wondering…do you know when he's going to get here?"

Casey glanced at Death, who shrugged.

Maria looked uncertain, as well. "Who, Mrs. Parker?"

"Why, him, of course. You know." She looked back and forth between Casey and Maria. "Andrea's fiancé."

Casey's mouth dropped, and Death did a little dance. "Hee, hee, the plot thickens."

Sissy stood in the hallway, frozen. Casey leaned toward her and whispered, "Andrea was *engaged*?"

Sissy shook her head. "I didn't…I never heard anything about it before. And she…she…" She slumped, her face falling. "It's all so *horrible*!"

"Oh, boy," Death said. "Here come the waterworks."

Sissy's eyes filled and overflowed. She put her hands to her mouth. "I'm sorry. I'm sorry." She gulped once, loudly, and rushed away.

Casey watched her go. If Sissy was that upset, it could only mean one thing. Well two things. Either she was upset that she as the building manager hadn't known this good news about a resident, or—more likely—she suspected that Andrea was engaged to a man Sissy thought was hers.

This Brandon fellow had a lot to answer for these days—women were crying all over the place. He'd only been gone a couple of weeks and all hell was breaking loose. Assuming he was the one Andrea had been "engaged" to, she was dead, Laurie and Sissy were complete disasters, and who knew how many others there were, weeping into their pillows. She'd seen the one—Bernie—in her class today. And if there were that many, it only made sense there would be more. Casey wished she could have a few minutes alone with this Brandon person.

She at least needed to see a picture of the guy, so she'd know what all the fuss was about.

Casey stepped back into the room, brushing past Maria, who stood in the doorway, silent and frowning. Casey went to the Parkers. "Did you know her fiancé? What was his name?"

Mr. Parker looked blankly at the floor, and Mrs. Parker lifted her hands slightly off of her knees. "We'd never met him, and she only talked about 'him.' She promised to bring him home at Christmas, but said things were a little tricky, so they were keeping it quiet until then. But she seemed so happy, until…" Her mouth twitched, and she looked at her hands.

"Until what?"

"Until just a couple weeks ago. She sounded tired, like she wasn't sleeping. And she stopped talking about…about *him*."

Casey glanced at Maria, who had gone pale, as if she'd had a shock. She was no help at all. But Casey was remembering Binns' words about Andrea's phone. The unidentified phone number had stopped two weeks before. Right when Andrea stopped talking to her parents about 'him.' Right when Brandon left the Flamingo. "May I look around a little bit, to see if I can find his information?"

Mrs. Parker waved weakly. "Whatever you want."

"I really don't think we should snoop around." Maria's voice was firm, but Casey wasn't about to let the opportunity pass her by. The police had obviously been through everything, but it was certainly possible they missed something.

Casey made a quick sweep through the apartment. Andrea had only a few family photos—one in the living room, and a couple pinned to the refrigerator with magnets. There were no pictures that could possibly be of her and a fiancé. Casey went through the desk in the corner of the living room, in case Andrea had kept an address book, but if there had been one, the police must have taken it. The same with any computer she might have owned. There were a few letters, but they all were from back home in Oregon, from her parents.

Andrea liked a variety of magazines, which lay on the coffee table, from *Cosmo* to *Newsweek* to financial rags, all bought off the rack, and she had several novels stacked on the end table by the sofa, dog-eared and bookmarked with scraps of paper. The kitchen held only food and the things necessary to make and eat it, and the bathroom brought no surprises.

Casey peeked out at the living room, but the Parkers hadn't moved.

"We really should go." Maria had come further into the apartment now, and indicated the open door.

Casey went into Andrea's bedroom. The bed was all done up in clean sheets, and clothes were piled neatly in a laundry basket. The closet held clothes, too, as well as shoes and a suitcase. The trash can had been emptied—probably by the cops—and there was no journal on or in the bedside table. Casey felt between the mattress and the box springs, and looked under the bed.

"Ms. Gray." Maria stood in the doorway of the bedroom.

"Yeah, I'm done." Casey followed her out to the living room and perched on a chair beside Andrea's mother. "I can't find his information right now, Mrs. Parker. We'll continue looking and see if we can find him for you, okay?"

Mrs. Parker gave her a wobbly smile. "Thank you, dear. Thank you."

Casey and Maria said goodnight and stepped into the hall, closing the door.

"So you didn't know about this engagement?" Casey asked.

Maria's mouth compressed into a thin line. "Andrea never showed a public preference for any one man. She hung out with different men, you know, just like..." She waved her hands.

"Like Krystal."

Casey started down the hall, but Maria seemed rooted to her spot. "I don't mean I think she was *like* Krystal. She just gave the impression of being unattached. It's impossible for anyone to keep track of all the residents. And it's not like it's my job to do that, or Sissy's. The people who live here can have whatever life they choose, as long as it doesn't disrupt *other* people's lives." She marched down the hallway, pushed the elevator button, and closed her eyes.

Casey wanted to close her eyes, too. Already it had been a long day, and she still had two classes to teach. Maybe this teaching-for-fifteen-hours schedule wasn't such a good idea, after all. Even women with tragic pasts and no real desire to live needed a break now and then.

The elevator came and they got on, Death standing close to Maria and studying her. Casey punched the button for her floor, and Maria for the ground level.

"She's freaking about something," Death said. "This whole thing about Andrea having a fiancé is big stuff. It's driving her crazy."

Casey could see that Death was right. Maria's hands were clenched into fists, and any hint of pinkness had been leached from her face.

"Going home now?" Casey asked, hoping conversation might keep Maria from fainting.

Maria whipped her head around. "I'm sorry?"

"Home? You going there?"

"Oh. Yes. Finally. I've been gone since six this morning. My kids are going to think I don't live there anymore."

"Who watches them while you're gone?"

Guilt flitted across Maria's face. "My mother, sometimes. Rosa. A friend."

"No dad, I take it," Death said.

"None of my business," Casey said.

Maria gave a little wave. "Oh, that's all right. It's a natural question."

Casey took a deep breath. She really *was* tired. The elevator stopped, and she got off. "Hope you can get some rest."

"Thanks. You, too."

"That woman will get no sleep tonight," Death said when the elevator had gone. "She's going to spend the night trying to figure out who Andrea was marrying. And wondering if it was that blackmailing Brandon." They went into Casey's apartment, and Death collapsed onto the sofa. "We're finding lots of reasons why people would have wanted to kill Brandon. But he's not the one who's dead."

"If Andrea was engaged to him, she might have known a lot of his secrets. She could have known about Sissy's last job, and Maria's illegal status. And who knows what more secrets we'll find in those files when we look at them."

"No time now, chica. You've got to be down in your class two minutes ago."

Casey rushed to change her clothes—again. She was going to have to do laundry every other day, if this schedule kept up.

The kickboxing class was sparse that evening, missing all of the women Casey knew. Laurie, obviously, was in no shape for exercising, let alone being in public, and Sissy was down for the count, having run off crying. Krystal hadn't been lurking, waiting to pounce, and Casey hoped she would stay away.

Casey apologized to the class for being late, then put herself on autopilot through that session, as well as through abs, which had only two women in it. The pair skittered out as soon as Casey turned off the music.

"Nine-thirty," Death said, stretching. "The night is young."

"For you, maybe. For me it's a crotchety old lady."

Death gasped. "Your twin!"

"Oh, shut up. Besides, I want another look at these folders."

Death didn't argue with that, and left Casey to find her own way upstairs.

Chapter Twenty-three

"So who all we got?" Death had been remarkably patient as Casey took yet another shower and pulled on Reuben's T-shirt. Death wore flannel pajamas and bunny slippers. They sat together in the middle of Casey's living room, her purse emptied.

Casey set aside Sissy and Maria's folders, and picked up the next one. "Looks like Bernie really did sign over most of her money. Or a lot of it, anyway. I don't know how much she started with. Here are the accounts where Brandon stashed it."

Death whistled. "That's a lotta dough, baby."

"And here are several other folders with the same kind of stuff. Our dear psycho Laurie is one of them. He got every penny. From what I see here, she's living at the Flamingo out of the charity of Sissy's heart."

"Doing classes for free?"

"That would make sense. She's paying her way by teaching, and Sissy might feel some sisterhood with her over the whole getting-screwed-by-Brandon thing. Although I've seen Sissy treat Laurie with more disdain than charity." Casey shook her head. "Wherever Brandon is, assuming he can access these accounts, he is sitting more than pretty."

"Mexico," Death said.

"You think?"

"How should I know? I'm guessing. And look here. A list of the older women who put him in their wills. I can't imagine he's really going to come around to collect, do you? I'm sure he preferred the straight cash exchange, but couldn't quite bring himself to romance the over-eighties."

Casey picked up the next folder. "Ah, our lovely Krystal. Let's see what we have on you."

"Nude photos?" Death asked hopefully.

"Don't see any, which isn't surprising. It would be hard for Brandon to blackmail Krystal over sex, when she makes no secret about her lifestyle. In fact, she advertises it." Casey remembered that first day, with Andrea telling Krystal to watch what she was saying, or people would think she was a slut, too.

"So what is that?" Death pointed at the one photo in the folder. It was a five by seven school picture of a little girl. She was smiling with two missing upper teeth, and her shoulder length blonde hair had been tied back with a ribbon. "Is that Krystal as a child?"

"I don't think so." Casey picked up the photo to reveal the single sheet underneath. A birth certificate. The name of the baby was Adrienne Noelle. The space for the birth father's name was blank. The line for the birth mother read, Krystal Patterson.

Even Death was speechless. For a moment. "Krystal is a *mother*?"

"In the biological sense, maybe. I don't see her mothering anyone around here. There aren't any kids at the Flamingo."

"Think she's hiding one?"

"Not in this building. But if this is in Brandon's secret black-mail stash, then yes, Krystal is definitely hiding that she has a daughter."

Death studied the picture. "I can see Krystal in her, now that I know."

"Yup. Those eyes. And the hair. Think you can track her down?"

"You know I can't. Not unless she's dead, or maybe if I pick up an immediate family member. But she's nowhere on my radar at this point."

Casey leaned back against the sofa. "Again, this all comes back to Brandon, not Andrea. We may be uncovering crime here, but not the crime we're investigating."

"It's like you said before. If Andrea was engaged to this guy, she knew his secrets."

"But he's not *here*. If she was engaged to him, where is he?"

"He's only been gone a couple of weeks. It's not like he's been gone *forever*."

Casey went quiet.

"Uh-oh," Death said. "I know that look. You got an idea."

"Not one I like."

"Even better."

"You saw Andrea's apartment, right? There was nothing personal there, other than family stuff. No other photos, no mail. The magazines were ones she'd picked up at the store—so no address labels. How long did Del say she's been here? Six months?"

"That was Dylan. And he said he'd *known* her six months, since *he* got here."

"Oh, I remember. Del said he'd asked her out soon after she'd moved in the beginning of the year. So January, maybe. Not sure that would work."

"What are you thinking? Spill."

"Well, what if she was in this with Brandon? She obviously hadn't made her apartment a home. There was nothing there she couldn't leave behind. Nothing of sentimental value—at least that I saw. She and Brandon could have been fleecing the gullible folks, always ready to take off. But I really can't see it. I just didn't get…criminal vibes from her."

"Criminal vibes. What, are you psychic now?"

"You know what I mean. You can just tell about some people. She had such a good feel about her."

"Yeah, for that less than a day you knew her." Death frowned, brow wrinkling, then smiled. "You're wrong."

"She really was a crook?"

"No, she really *wasn't*. You're wrong about her and *Brandon*."

"How do you know?"

"Because she knew Richie. Remember? That first day, she told you he was a sweetheart, but he just didn't fit here."

"So?"

"How would she know there would even *be* an instructor job here for Brandon? It's not like those jobs are always popping up, as you know from your search last week. And the job was filled already, by Richie."

"She and Brandon could've done their research. Found a place where the instructor was a loser, and then Andrea gives Sissy a recommendation to hire Brandon when Richie's gone."

"No. Too convoluted. It wouldn't work. I think you just have to admit it. She was not a con artist."

"Well, good. I hope you're right." She closed her eyes.

"Um, Casey?"

Casey jerked her head up. "What?"

"You fell asleep just then. I think you might want to go to bed, or you'll get a crick in your neck."

"So thoughtful of you."

"Actually, I just hate having you fall asleep in the middle of me talking."

Casey stacked the folders and shoved them into the vent, with her other things.

Death watched. "You do realize you're completely screwing up the ventilation in this apartment?"

"I'm not here enough to care."

"True."

Casey stumbled to her bedroom and crawled under the covers. Her eyes opened halfway. "Wasn't I supposed to go somewhere? Or meet somebody? I think I promised..."

She fell asleep before Death could even answer.

Chapter Twenty-four

"Wakey, wakey!" Death stood beside Casey's bed in a velour sweat suit the color of egg yolks.

"Oh, my *God*," Casey said. "What are you *wearing*?"

Death looked down. "Don't like it? It was all the rage in the seventies."

"Well, get it out of this century! Argh!" Casey rolled out the other side of the bed. When she turned around, Death wore modern red and white warm-ups, with dark blue accents.

"Better?"

"Much."

"And?"

"And what?"

"*Thank you for waking me up in time for my class.*"

"Oh. Yeah. That." Casey used the bathroom, then went to the kitchen for some yogurt.

"You'll fit right in with the Land of the Dead class today," Death said. "You look like hell."

"Thank you. So very much."

Death beamed.

Casey put on some clothes and tromped down the service stairs to the aerobics room.

"Uh-oh," Death said.

Krystal sat alone on the floor by the door. Casey stopped outside the stairwell, and Krystal looked up.

"Wow," Death said. "And here I thought *you* looked bad."

Krystal did look terrible, like she hadn't slept or eaten in a week. She had bags under her eyes, and her hair draped in greasy strands against her face and shoulders. Even her voluptuous body lay hidden underneath wrinkled clothes and despair.

Casey prepared herself, waiting to see what kind of attack she would need to defend against—verbal or physical. She wasn't worried about the physical damage this depressing Krystal could do, but Casey needed to be careful not to hurt the other woman if she came at her.

Krystal lurched to her feet. "Daisy. Daisy, I'm sorry. I'm sorry. I…" Her face crumpled, and tears leaked out of her eyes and down her cheeks. She stumbled forward, hands outstretched, snot running from her nose.

"Now that is *really* not attractive," Death said.

Casey had to agree, and stepped out of the way of the weeping woman. Krystal kept moving, ending up against the wall, where she rested her forehead, her hands spread out above her like she was surrendering to the police. Casey felt like giving the cops a call to take advantage of the moment, but Krystal hadn't actually done anything illegal. Just malicious. And probably out of grief.

"I'm sorry," Krystal mumbled. "I was just…I'm just…" Slowly, she turned to rest her back against the stairwell door. "I can't believe she's *gone. Ooooooh.*"

"Again with the wailing," Death said, hands over ears. "I'm outta here." Death disappeared, walking right through the wall into the aerobics room.

Voices drifted around the corner from the public stairs, and Casey stepped closer to Krystal, to hide her from view. "Krystal, have you slept at all?"

Krystal sniffed, and wiped her nose with her sleeve. "Yes."

"In the past two days?"

"Oh. Well, I'm not sure about that."

Casey pulled out her phone and glanced at the clock. "Okay. I've got a few minutes. Come on." Casey pulled Krystal into the service stairwell. "What floor do you live on?"

"What?"

"Your apartment. What floor?"

"Same as Andrea."

So, the fourth. "Let's go."

Krystal squinted up the stairs. "Up there?"

"Move."

Casey propelled Krystal up three flights of stairs, having to prod her at every landing. When they reached the fourth floor, Casey dug through Krystal's pockets to find her key. There was nothing to indicate which door it opened.

Krystal gripped the jamb of the stairwell door. "It's all my fault."

"No, it's not."

"It is. I should have been there with her, instead of…"

Casey waited. "Instead of where, Krystal?"

Her face crumpled. "Instead of in the guard room."

Casey sucked in a breath. So she and Death were *right*. "What were you doing in the guard room?"

Krystal's eyes widened. "Have you *seen* the night guard? He's so…*hot*."

"So you decided on a whim to go down and seduce the guard?" Casey couldn't believe it was a coincidence.

"No. He sent me a note."

"A note?"

She gave a wavery smile. "It was so sweet. He said he loved me, that I was so beautiful…"

"And?"

"And that I should come down to be with him that night. Around midnight, he said. No one would know. No one would find out." She frowned. "He was surprised when I showed up. Like he didn't think I'd really come. But we had…a good time."

So Krystal *had* distracted the guard. But if she was telling the truth, she'd been invited to visit him. A coincidence? Or trickery? Not a trick of the guard's. He wouldn't need to distract *himself* from seeing the monitor. Whatever it was, at least Krystal hadn't betrayed her best friend on purpose.

Even if she was a skank.

"I went back to check on Andrea afterward," Krystal said. "I saw you in the aerobics room, so I figured she was gone."

Casey peered down the hallway at the look-alike doors. Andrea's door was closed, and the strip at the bottom was dark. Casey hoped the Parkers had been able to fall asleep. "Which door is yours, Krystal?"

Krystal swayed on her feet.

"Which one!" Casey barked.

Krystal staggered ahead and stopped at Andrea's door, leaning her head against it. "This one. This one's mine."

Casey pulled her away. "No, that's Andrea's. "

Krystal's breath hitched, and she looked at the door with confusion, touching one of the "missing you" cards. She spun around and pointed at the door directly across from Andrea's. "Then it's that one."

Casey used the key and swung the door open. Krystal stood unmoving in the hallway, and Casey yanked her into an apartment with the exact same layout as Casey's, and as Andrea's, for that matter. The curtains were closed, but with the light from the hallway, Casey could see food lying on the table, and a few days' worth of newspapers scattered over the floor just inside the door. Other than that, what she could see looked neat, like no one had been in it for a few days. Casey made a quick check of the entire apartment, to be sure there weren't any stalkers or anything, and it was no surprise there weren't piles of dirty laundry, or even wet towels on the floor. Krystal obviously hadn't changed for quite some time, as she was still wearing the same clothes she'd had on when she and Dylan made their impromptu appearance in Casey's office the other night.

Casey strode to the living room window and flung open the curtain. The beginnings of a sunrise lightened the sky, but not enough to illuminate the room, so Casey turned on all the lights she could find. The first thing she noticed was another stack of papers spread over the sofa. They'd been ripped in half. Casey picked up one fragment, and saw that it was the petition Krystal had been circulating to get Casey fired.

Casey shook her head. "At least she's come to her senses about *that*." She dropped the paper back onto the pile. "Okay, Krystal. Shower." She pushed Krystal down the hallway to the bathroom and started the water. "Strip."

Krystal's face screwed up with confusion.

"Oh, good lord, do I have to do everything?" Casey gripped the hem of Krystal's shirt and yanked it over her head.

"Now *this* I want to see." Death suddenly appeared on the toilet tank, feet on the closed lid.

"Oh, for heaven's sake," Casey said. "Give the woman some privacy."

"Like you're giving her, you mean?"

"She's not exactly in her sex goddess state right now, so I don't know what you're even here for."

"A few days of bad hygiene and grief doesn't change anatomy, my friend."

"I'm not your friend." Casey concentrated on getting the rest of Krystal's clothes off, trying not to smell the ripeness of her damp skin.

"I'm sorry about going into your room," Krystal said.

"What?"

"The other night." She leaned close and whispered. "I went in to see if I could find out your *secrets*." She frowned. "You didn't have any."

Casey glanced at Death, but spoke to Krystal. "Was this just before you and Dylan came crashing into my office?"

"Dylan." Krystal giggled. "Yes, I saw him just after...I was mad I couldn't find anything good in your condo. He was...he's so *cute*." She got so distracted she almost fell over.

Casey kept her upright, glad to have the mystery solved of who'd snuck into her room. "Okay, Patterson, the water's fine. Get in."

Krystal looked at the shower curtain, and Casey swept it aside. "In." She grabbed Krystal's elbow and helped her step over the side of the tub before shutting the curtain. She found a towel under the sink, and gestured for Death to get off the toilet so she could set the towel on the lid. "Come get me if she faints or drowns or anything, okay?"

"What am I, your servant?"

"Yes."

Death's eyebrows rose.

Casey sighed. "Please?"

"Well, since you asked so nicely."

Casey locked the apartment door behind her and ran down the stairs, getting to class just as the clock hit six.

"Okay, ladies! Let's wake up!"

She blasted some loud music and put the class through the paces, until some of them had to stop, hands on their knees. Casey figured she'd better ease up, and spent the last twenty minutes on body shaping and abs. By the time seven rolled around, half of the women lay flat on their backs, staring at the ceiling.

"See you tomorrow. " Casey jogged out of the room and back up the stairs to Krystal's place. She used Krystal's key to get in, only to find Death sitting on the couch with a nametag that said, *SuperNanny: Behave or Die*. The torn petition pages lay spread out on the couch, where Casey had left them.

"So I've been looking at the signatures I can see," Death said. "I don't recognize any of these names."

"Where's Krystal?"

"In bed. She got out of the shower after about twenty minutes, wrapped herself in a towel, and collapsed on top of her quilt."

Casey went back to the bedroom. It was exactly as Death had said. Casey figured she should let Krystal sleep, but couldn't see letting her lie there in a wet towel. She found a fluffy pink robe in the closet, rolled Krystal out of the towel, and covered her with the robe. Her hair was still wet, but there was nothing Casey could do about that, except put a dry towel under her head.

Casey went back to the living room and swiped up the torn petition pages, dropping onto the couch beside Death.

"See?" Death said. "All strangers."

"That we know of. I'm not anywhere close to knowing the names of all the people in my classes."

"But you know your personal training folks. And a few others."

"Right." Casey scanned the names, and saw that Death was right. Nobody she actually knew by name was on the list. A small but welcome development.

Casey jumped up.

Death jumped up, too. "What is it?"

"Krystal's daughter that we saw in the folder. Have you seen any evidence of her?"

"Not in plain view."

Casey took a quick look through Krystal's desk, kitchen drawers, and bedroom, not worried about waking the snoring occupant. There were no photos, birth certificates, or anything that would say Krystal had had a baby.

"Not a crumb," she said, back in the living room.

"She doesn't want anything to do with a kid," Death said. "It's obvious. She wants to have fun and land a rich husband."

"How do you know?"

"Come on, Casey. It's what women like her do. You don't hear her advertising her motherhood, do you? Guys like Dylan wouldn't come anywhere near her if they knew she had a child. They'd be scared to death. Not that her having a child would really kill them."

"*Good* men wouldn't be scared off by a child."

"*Good* men don't get involved with women like Krystal. At least, not the side of her she shows everyone. But maybe there's another side. Think about it. She must've been in her teens when she had the baby. A teen who was nowhere *near* mature enough to raise a child. She's not mature enough *now*."

"I guess."

"So now she's distanced herself from her daughter to give the girl a chance at a traditional family. The girl looked happy in that photo, didn't she?"

She did. Happy and healthy. "Oh, no." Casey looked at the clock on Krystal's wall. "I gotta go. I'm late for Dylan."

Death smiled. "He'll wait. He wants you *bad*."

Casey ran back downstairs, got what she needed from her office, and jogged into the weight room.

Dylan *was* waiting, and slumped with obvious relief when she appeared. He twisted his towel in his hands. "I thought you were going to stand me up after…well, I was afraid I scared you off last night."

"It takes more than a guy asking me out to scare me off, Dylan. Sorry I'm late. Why don't you jump on the treadmill."

"That's it?"

She looked up from the clipboard she'd grabbed in her office. "What else were you expecting?"

"Aw, come on," Death said from the closest exercise machine. "Look at the poor kid. He's smitten. You're hurting his feelings."

Casey propelled Dylan over to the cardio machines. "Dylan, I have another client in forty minutes. I want to get your workout in."

"But—"

"I'm not mad at you, okay? I promise."

He straddled the treadmill, his feet on the sides. "I'm not worried about you being *mad* at me. I want to…Oh, forget it." He punched the Go button and began running.

Casey closed her eyes and rubbed her temples. What was this thing with her and younger men? First Eric, in Ohio, although he wasn't nearly the baby this one was, and she somehow thought his sexual experience—and morals, perhaps—were a bit more traditional.

"Oh, *no!*" Dylan yanked the safety clip from the machine, and the tread jerked to a stop. Dylan's water bottle, phone, and keys dropped to the floor with a clatter, and skidded away.

Casey's head snapped up to see Dylan staring with terror at something behind her. She spun around, ready to defend him. Then held back a laugh. It was Tamille.

"Hey," Casey said, relaxing.

"Hey, yourself. Everything turn out okay last night, then?"

"Sure. Thanks for understanding. I hope Sensei Asuhara wasn't too upset that I left early."

"Nah. He's not exactly the uptight type, as you could probably tell."

"He wasn't what I was expecting, that's for sure."

Dylan made a little whimpering sound and stayed behind Casey, his fingers clutching her upper arms so tightly she thought her circulation might cease.

She looked at her watch, then over her shoulder at him. "You done already?"

"I'm plenty warm."

"I'd say you're plenty *hot*," Tamille said, looking him up and down.

Dylan groaned, and from what Casey could see, it was almost certainly from fear.

"Tamille," she said, jerking her thumb over her shoulder, "this is Dylan. Dylan, Tamille."

Dylan attempted a smile, but it looked more like someone was stepping on his toes.

"You Daisy's little plaything?" Tamille reached over and pinched his biceps before nodding appreciatively. "Not so little, I guess."

Dylan gave a timid laugh. "No, I'm…I'm…"

"He's my client," Casey said. "Personal training."

"Mmm-hmm. Well, when you get tired of her, Dylan, honey, you come find me, you hear?"

Dylan swallowed so loudly Casey could hear it.

"Come on, *Tami*," Casey said. "You're scaring the poor guy."

"Me? You're the one he should be scared of. Or doesn't he realize that?"

"I haven't told him yet."

Tamille narrowed her eyes as she studied Dylan's face. "Hey, haven't I seen you down in the bar, or somewhere? I know your face."

"Oh, I doubt it was in the bar," Dylan said, forcing a laugh. "It was up here, probably. I mean, I know your face, too."

"He said you scared him off the weights one time," Casey said.

"Oh. Sorry. I don't know why people think I'm so terrifying." Tamille bared her teeth in what Casey was sure was supposed to be a smile. It looked more like a tiger ready to pounce. Or devour her young.

"Um, shouldn't we get going with my workout?" Dylan still gripped Casey's arms. "You said you wanted to make sure to get it all in."

Tamille crossed her arms. "You trying to get rid of me?"

Dylan made a choking sound. "No. No, not at all. You're welcome to…to…"

Tamille slapped him on the shoulder, and he recoiled, his fingers digging even deeper into Casey's shoulders. Casey pulled him down off the treadmill. "Come on, Dylan. Let's get back to work. See you later, Tamille."

Tamille gave Dylan one more head to toe gander, and sauntered away. Dylan released his death grip once Tamille was out of sight. He'd gone all sweaty, and was way whiter than a young man in the prime of his life should be.

"Whoa, Dylan," Casey said. "What is *up* with you?"

"She scares the *crap* out of me."

"But why? It can't just be because she didn't want to share the weight room."

His mouth twitched. "You really want to know?"

"I wouldn't have asked, otherwise."

He glanced over his shoulder to make sure Tamille was gone. "I didn't tell the cops. I know I probably should have, but I didn't really think it mattered, or that it was relevant."

"*Dylan…*"

"She *did* see me down in the bar. A few weeks ago."

"So?"

He ducked his head. "I was with…Krystal. Krystal, Andrea, and another guy."

"Who was the guy?"

"Curtis Somebody. He was from out of town, visiting folks in the Palm. Their grandson or something. Huge guy, I think he might've been a football player in his former life, but now he's in something boring, like estate planning. Or maybe real estate. Or I guess it could've been—"

"Dylan!"

"Sorry. But he was pretty cool. Tall, dark dude, with a gold earring and brands on his arms. The four of us were sitting around in the bar, just talking, you know? And Tamille comes up, out of nowhere. It's kind of dark down there in the evenings, and she just sort of loomed up, like a ghost or something out of some spooky movie, or maybe a Stephen King nov—" Casey made a move toward him, and he hurried on. "And she went off, saying how other women would like a chance at the new guy, so maybe *some people* should share him for the evening."

"Had he been here long?"

"Several days, I guess. I'd seen him talking to Krystal and Andrea other nights at the bar. I had a few beers with him, too. Nice guy, really."

"And Tamille's little speech was enough to put the fear of God into you for life?"

"Oh, geez, no. It was what happened later."

"And what was that?"

Dylan swallowed. "We were walking the girls—*women*, sorry—to the elevator when Tamille showed up again. She brushed past me and Curtis and got right up in her face, pinning her against the wall. 'You leave him alone,' she said. 'You leave him alone, or you're going to answer to me.' And she stared at her a few seconds, before she spun around and left. I thought I was going to pee my pants."

Casey gave a little laugh. "Were there other women around to cheer?"

"Cheer? Why would they?"

"Dylan, I know you like Krystal, or you lust after her, anyway. Lots of men do. But you've got to know women feel just the opposite. If there were any around, I'm sure they were all wishing *they* would've been the one to give her the ultimatum."

"But she wasn't talking to Krystal," Dylan said.

"What?"

"Krystal was with *me* that night. We went back up to her apartment and—" He blushed. "*Andrea* was the one with Curtis. Tamille backed *Andrea* up against the wall and threatened her. Right there in front of God and me and everybody."

Chapter Twenty-five

"But I *like* Tamille." Casey took a gulp of water and slammed her cup on the table. She'd finished her session with Dylan, promised him she would offer protection from Tamille if need be, taken care of her other clients and classes, and moved robotically from one thing to the next, completely stunned by what Dylan had told her.

"Lots of people like killers," Death said. "It's the way the world works. Nice people—or even people like Tamille—can get pushed to murder by the strangest things."

"I don't believe it. I just don't."

Neither Sissy nor Laurie showed up in class, and the Parkers hadn't yet made an appearance. Casey was itching to ask them more about Andrea's supposed fiancé, but she knew she needed to give them their space. If they were sleeping, she didn't want to be the one to wake them up.

Now, on her lunch hour, she struggled about what to do with the landmine Dylan had dropped in her lap. She probably should tell Detective Binns and get Tamille on Binns' radar, even if a threat made in the heat of the moment didn't prove later violence. But should she take the word of an overly-dramatic young man who wasn't exactly the best when it came to judging women?

"Why didn't he say anything *before*?" she whined.

Death took a seat at the table. "He was terrified. Tamille has that effect on people, you know. You might be just as accomplished as she—maybe more so, seeing how you beat her the other day—but you just don't have the...you know..." Death waved a hand.

"The tall, Amazonian, I-could-eat-you-as-soon-as-kill-you thing?"

"Exactly."

"So Dylan didn't tell Binns he thinks Tamille is a killer because he was afraid—"

"—she'd kill him. You got it."

Casey lay her head on the table. "Why? *Why* do I get involved in these things?"

"Bad karma?"

She rolled her head back and forth on the wood, then got up and went to the kitchen, where she stared into her refrigerator. She grabbed a rotisserie chicken she'd bought, cut off some slices, and made a sandwich. "There's got to be something in Andrea's room to prove she was engaged to Brandon. If she really was. No woman has a fiancé and doesn't have at least one thing in her apartment that's his.

"Unless she was hiding the relationship."

"Even then." She drummed her fingers on the counter. "I wonder if Binns knows about it."

"Call her. You can at least tell her about *that*."

Casey wiped off her hands and grabbed her phone.

"This is Binns."

"It's Daisy Gray."

"Oh. Sorry I had to run out before you got there last night. You spoke to the Parkers?"

"Yes, and they told us Andrea was engaged."

Silence on the line. "Name?"

"Don't know. Her parents didn't even know his name. But they're expecting him to come around now they're here."

"They're going to be disappointed, aren't they?"

"I think so. You haven't heard anything about this, I take it?"

"Not a peep. Thanks for passing it on. Anything else?"

Casey hesitated.

"What is it, Ms. Gray?"

"Nothing. Not now, anyway. I need more information."

"About what?"

"Gotta go." Casey hung up.

The phone began ringing immediately. Casey could see from the display that it was Binns.

"You can't give a cop that kind of stuff and hang up," Death said.

"But I can't rat out someone who hasn't had a chance to tell me the truth."

"So you're going to ask Tamille."

"She deserves that much, at least."

"Why?"

"Because she's like me."

"A woman with a fake name and a tragic past, with law enforcement on her tail?"

"No. She's…you saw her take me on. She's a fighter."

"And you're a fighter, too? The woman who's always asking me to take her to the other side? Who's always turning tail and running?"

"I've stopped asking you, haven't I?"

"For five whole days. That's convincing. You wanna place a bet on how long it is till the next time you come to me crying, saying life's not worth living?"

But Casey wasn't listening anymore. She was thinking about Tamille. "Do we know where Tamille works?"

"I don't."

"Let's find out." Casey took a few last bites of sandwich and ran down to the office, stopping suddenly at the sight of the lobby bar.

Death stopped, too. "What?"

"Now I remember. I was supposed to come down and talk to Jack last night. I completely forgot."

"Makes sense. The one normal person here is bound to get ignored."

Casey groaned. "I hope he didn't wait long."

"He doesn't seem the type. When you didn't show he probably figured something came up, and went to bed."

"I don't want him to think I stood him up on purpose. Do you think it hurt his feelings?"

"You're mean to *me*, and *I* don't take it personally."

"But I *want* to get rid of *you*."

Death sniffed and turned away.

Maria was at her desk, looking only marginally more rested than she had the night before, but was at least back to her unwrinkled clothes and perfect hair.

"Tamille," Casey said. "Where does she work?"

Maria regarded her coolly. "I can't give out that information. It's *personal*. We don't give out personal information."

"Oh, please. You don't think I can find out on my own?"

"If you could, would you be in here?"

"Not if I could find it *quickly*. I have a class in thirty-five minutes. Come on, Maria. Please?"

Maria pinched her lips together, but her forehead relaxed. "Fine. She works down at the marina. The one just down the street. Bayside."

"I've seen it. I turn right out the front door?"

"That's it."

"Thank you!" Casey called this last over her shoulder as she trotted toward the street.

"Daisy?" Del sat at one of the tables in the lobby, eating a gourmet sandwich on a paper wrapper. His face was open and happy, and he looked like he was going to keep talking.

"Hey, Del. Can I catch you later? I need to run out quick before my next class."

"Sure. Go. I'll tell you about it later."

"About what?"

He grinned. "I thought you didn't have time."

"I do if you spit it out. Not the sandwich. The good news."

"How do you know it's good?"

"Because you're lit up like the beach in July."

He laughed. "I got my loan."

"Really? You can open your restaurant?"

"The new guy at the bank pushed it through. We're closing next week."

She high-fived him. "That's *awesome*, Del. Congrats."

"I hope you'll be one of my first customers."

"You know I will." If she was still living in Florida. "I can't wait. But now I gotta go. I'm sorry."

"No problem. But I'm going to be using you for a guinea pig as I get my menu ready!"

Casey gave him the thumbs up and continued out the front door to the sidewalk.

"You know what this means, don't you?" Death now wore tight baby blue shorts, a tank top, and running shoes, and was having no trouble keeping up with Casey while running backward in front of her.

"Rich food?"

"No, dummy. Are you forgetting something?"

"If I am, I'm sure you'll tell me."

"Del said the *new officer* pushed the loan through. Apparently Andrea wasn't making it happen for him. Otherwise, why could it happen this quickly after she's gone?"

Casey stuttered to a stop. "Oh, crap."

"Or something more profane."

Casey let out a breath, then started running again. She didn't want it to be Del. She *didn't*.

The masts of the boats in the marina poked up behind the buildings, and as she turned the corner she was again swept breathless with the wealth spread out before her. Dock upon dock lay lined with boats, some small, others loaded with everything a sailor could want. Deeply tanned, shirtless men, young and old, were dotted here and there on the decks, with fewer women alongside them. The smaller boats bobbed gently in the water, while the larger ones sat unmoving, the water lapping against the smooth white hulls.

Casey searched for Tamille. "Where do you think we'll find her?"

"Wrangling some huge boat into submission. Or carrying one on her shoulders."

Casey headed toward the front door of the main building. "I bet she runs the whole place. Can you imagine anyone actually being her boss?" She pushed open the front door, and a bell jangled.

A young man at a desk acknowledged her. Like the ones outside, he was tanned, and his hair had been bleached a white blond. "Help you?"

"I'm looking for Tamille."

He jerked his head toward a door at the back. "Out in the garage."

"Thanks." Casey followed his directions to the huge building. Gigantic roll-up doors revealed two boats on skids, in various stages of repair. A couple of men in gray coveralls were hunkered down beside the first one, in a heavy discussion about something they kept jabbing their fingers at. Another coveralled man stood to the side, talking with a couple in clean, non-boating and non-mechanic clothes. The couple kept shooting anxious glances toward the boat being discussed by the two mechanics, so Casey figured they were the owners.

Casey didn't see Tamille.

Casey walked past the first boat toward the second. She could see booted feet on the other side, and when she got there, she saw they belonged to Tamille. Casey didn't know why she was surprised Tamille wasn't in a suit and heels. Tamille in coveralls, with grease on her face, just made sense.

"Hey," Tamille said. "What are you doing here?"

"Checking to see if you're coming to class."

Tamille barked a laugh. "Not today. Got to get this baby finished and back on the water." She put down the putty knife she was holding. "But somehow I don't think that's why you're really here."

Casey looked over her shoulder at the other people in the garage, and took a step closer to Tamille. "I need to ask you something."

"Uh-oh. Sounds serious."

"It is. It's about Andrea." Casey didn't expect trouble from Tamille, but still she took a cleansing breath and balanced herself as unobtrusively as she could. "You know that kid you met in the weight room this morning?"

"The cutie? Sure. He was terrified."

"Do you know why?"

"Because I'm terrifying?"

Casey couldn't stop her grin. "Well, that's true. But…do you remember a few weeks ago when there was a guy visiting? His name was Curtis, Dylan said. He was hanging out with Andrea in the bar."

Tamille's face cleared. "I *knew* I recognized that kid. He was with them, wasn't he? When I gave them the old Dutch Uncle talk."

"You remember?"

"Of course. Curtis' grandma came to me. She feels some kind of kinship with me because there's so few of us in the development with the same skin tone. Understand? She was worried, because she heard Curtis was hooking up with Krystal. She asked me to make sure he didn't get involved with…I think she called her the Whore of Babylon, or some other Biblical reference."

"He wasn't with her."

"I know that *now*. But I was already into my whole give 'em hell routine before I realized he was with the other chick, and then it was too late to stop."

The tension in Casey's neck released. "So the message you gave Andrea was actually for Krystal."

"Obviously. Andrea may have been pretty, but she wasn't one to chew them up and spit them out. Not like her good buddy, who wants to get you kicked out of the Flamingo."

"Not anymore." She held up her hand. "Sorry. Dylan told me the story, and I—"

"—thought I was capable of killing Andrea over some dude I didn't even know? Thanks so much." Tamille's mouth compressed into a thin line, and she looked away.

"No, actually, I thought you *weren't*. That's why I wanted to talk to you. Didn't want the idea to fester, when I knew it was ridiculous."

Tamille hesitated, then gave one short, quick nod. "You're right." She held out a fist, and Casey bumped it. "The funny thing? Andrea told me later she wasn't even interested in Curtis. She had someone else, she said, and was just hanging out."

"Do you know who it was she was talking about?"

"Nah. It's not like we were buddies or anything. She just said it in passing in the lobby. How about dinner tonight? I know a great seafood place."

Casey opened her mouth to agree, but Death, who suddenly appeared on top of the boat in sunglasses, a visor, and Bermuda shorts, waved frantically. "Dylan, remember? You promised he could take you out."

"Right," Casey said.

Tamille blinked. "What?"

"I forgot I already made plans. Rain check?"

"Sure."

"And now I have to run back for class in—" Casey checked her phone. "Ten minutes."

Tamille picked up her putty knife. "Then you better get a move on, girl."

"I'm moving. See you later."

Casey was at the mouth of the garage when Tamille called her name.

"Thanks, Daisy. I appreciate that you came to me."

"No problem. Now I'll see if I can convince Dylan you're not a psycho killer."

Tamille smiled. "I think you'd be better off convincing him to stay away from Krystal."

Of course, she was right.

Chapter Twenty-six

Neither Laurie nor Sissy showed up for class. Sissy was probably dealing with the Parkers, and Laurie was most likely hiding under a rock somewhere. Casey did have the pleasure of seeing the gossipy Vonnie, however, and pulled her aside after class.

Vonnie took a deep draught from her water bottle and patted her face with her towel. "What is it?"

Casey hated talking to the woman, but knew she would be a fount of information, true or false. Casey would just have to take a shower later. "Who was Andrea seeing?"

Vonnie shrugged. "It was hard to keep track, with Krystal having guys around all the time."

"I don't think so."

Vonnie gave a sly smile. "What's it worth to you?"

Casey stepped closer to Vonnie, looking deep into her eyes. "I found Andrea bleeding to death on the floor of that locker room three days ago. Her parents are here, wondering how their beautiful daughter could have been murdered. Her friends are falling to pieces. I am very, *very* motivated to find out what happened. That's what it's worth to me. Do you understand?"

Vonnie gave a high, forced laugh. "Of course. I understand."

"So who was Andrea seeing?"

Vonnie glanced around the empty room.

"There's no one here to hear you," Casey said. *Or to save you.*

Vonnie swallowed. "I don't know. No one really talked about Andrea. It really was all about Krystal."

"You've got *nothing*?"

"She would be in the bar sometimes, mostly with Krystal and various guys. But nobody regular. Nobody who seemed to mean anything."

She was sweating again, and this time is wasn't from exercise.

"What about Brandon?"

A shifty look stole across Vonnie's face. "That would make sense, wouldn't it? She wouldn't want anyone else to know. And then she dumped him, and he came back and *killed* her." She inhaled abruptly and slapped her hand over her mouth. "It's too perfect!"

"It's all in your head."

"I don't think so."

Casey decided Vonnie really was telling all she knew—along with a bunch of speculation. "If you hear anything that has to do with actual *facts*, let me know."

"Of course I will." Vonnie was backing away now, a smile plastered on her face. When she saw she was close to the door, she spun and scurried out.

"Yuck," Death said.

"And it wasn't even helpful."

"Except to confirm what we already know."

"Which is?"

"That if Andrea was seeing somebody exclusively, it was a secret."

Casey went through the locker room to her office, where she gestured for Death to turn around before she changed into her swimsuit. "So did she meet Brandon here? After he got the job, and after he'd begun scamming the residents?"

"She must have."

"But how could she *stomach* that? Not only seeing him hurt other people, but knowing he was *sleeping* with them?"

"Maybe she couldn't. Maybe that's what the final straw was. Why he left." Death was getting excited. "Maybe Andrea finally realized he wasn't going to stop, and ratted him out to Sissy."

"But Sissy already knew, because he was blackmailing her, remember, besides other things?"

"Then she ratted him out to the other women who were giving him money and putting him in their wills."

"That would make more sense. Her parents said she stopped talking about the guy a couple weeks ago, just in time for Brandon to leave. So now he's back, getting his revenge?" Casey thought about it. "It's possible, I guess. He'd know the security procedures of the building. He might even still have keys."

"Or…" Death held up a finger. "One of his ladies discovered Andrea was the reason he's gone. And she was pissed."

"Or they thought Andrea was in on the scam." Casey considered that scenario, as she had before, and shook her head. "But think who the women are. Sissy. Bernie. Laurie. A bunch of older women who showered him with money. Could any of them really do that much damage to another woman? Especially a young, strong one like Andrea?"

"Laurie is the other fitness instructor here, remember. When she's not freaking out and talking like a crazy person, she's probably got it in her. And Sissy and Bernie both take classes, so they're at least somewhat in shape. Besides, Andrea was most likely attacked from behind or by someone she knew. Or both. She could've been turning on the shower, talking to someone, and *bam*! You can do a lot of damage if the other person doesn't suspect anything." Death stole a glance back at Casey. "You could've done me in just now, and I wouldn't have been able to respond."

"Not with my luck. What about Maria? She might not have been one of Brandon's 'women,' but she had a reason to be afraid because of her citizenship problems. If she thought Andrea was in cahoots with him, she could have assumed that now that Brandon is gone Andrea would tell her secret, and get her deported." Casey grabbed a towel from the cupboard and went back out through the locker room, toward the pool. "Too many possibilities."

Death followed. "I think you're ignoring the obvious."

Casey couldn't talk, because there were women in the room, changing.

"Tamille has the strength. It would've taken her two seconds to do that kind of hurtin'."

Casey shook her head.

"I know. You trust her. Think she's like you. Just remember, dearie, that just a couple of weeks ago you yourself put down a bad guy, and he ain't getting' back up."

Casey pushed out into the empty hallway. "I just don't believe it. There's no motive. I think Tamille's telling the truth that she went to the bar to talk to Krystal, not Andrea. I guess we could ask the guy's grandma."

"Nah. I'm just playing devil's advocate. If Tamille really was going to beat the crap out of somebody, she wouldn't do it when their back was turned."

Casey went to slap Death on the shoulder, but stopped in time. "Now you're getting it."

The pool room was hotter than the day before, and Casey grew lightheaded as she padded across the cement. She sat on the bottom row of the bleachers and took a deep breath.

"Thought I might find you here." It was Binns, followed by—of course—the gorgeous Officer Gomez.

"Told you," Death said. "You were naughty."

Casey held her towel up in front of her swimsuit, feeling exposed in front of Gomez. "Hey. What's up?"

"You're holding out on me." Binns stayed standing, looking down at Casey. Gomez checked out the rest of the room.

"I'm not," Casey said. "I thought I might have learned something this morning, but I was wrong."

"You want to share what that was and let me decide?"

No, she really didn't. But Binns wasn't going to let it drop. Casey tried to think of something else she could share that wouldn't compromise someone. Maria was in the country illegally. Bernie had given away most of her money. Sissy was being blackmailed *and* having an affair with the unscrupulous Brandon, who was possibly engaged to Andrea, and she'd had a bad end at her old job that was documented on letterhead. Laurie was going just a bit off the deep end.

There. That might be good.

"Have you seen Laurie Kilmer lately?"

"No. Should I have?"

"She accosted me last night outside the Flamingo."

Gomez swung around, his eyes searching Casey's face, and her bare shoulders. Casey went suddenly hot, but managed a little smile. "I'm fine. Really. I saw her coming. But something's not right there. She says she was jealous of Andrea being involved with Brandon, the last fitness instructor, but also says Andrea assured her it wasn't true. I'm not convinced she's handling it all very well."

"So you think that's who Andrea was engaged to?"

"Probably. But I don't have anything concrete on that."

"We'll check it out. But why didn't you just tell me about Ms. Kilmer this morning?"

"Didn't want to make something out of nothing. I haven't seen her today, though, and I'm wondering what's become of her."

"What about Ms. Patterson? Has she been after you today?"

"I'm not worried about her anymore. At least as far as my own well-being." She told Binns and Gomez what had happened that morning.

"That's a big turnaround," Binns said.

"Grief," Casey said. "It does weird things." She glanced at Gomez, who colored slightly and looked away. "On another subject, have you checked out the banking angle?"

"In what way?"

"People Andrea may have been working with. Loans she didn't approve."

"We have someone working on it. Nothing jumps out at us, but sometimes what seems small to the rest of us is a mountain to somebody else."

Like Del.

"Did you have someone in particular in mind?"

Casey kept her face neutral. "No. I just thought it might be a good place to check, and I certainly don't have the authority to be asking."

"So you recognize that? That's interesting." Binns gave her a blank look. "Don't worry. We've got it under control." She waved a hand toward the pool and the women gathering there. "Class waiting for you?"

"It is time."

"We'll let you go, then. But Ms. Gray, next time just tell me what you're thinking. I'm not going to rush off and arrest people without cause."

"Sure. Of course."

"Come on, Gomez." Binns clicked across the concrete in her sensible pumps. Gomez hesitated, meeting Casey's eyes for one last look before following the detective.

"Oh, he's caving." Death's hands rubbed together. "He'll be ripe for the picking, soon."

"I'm not harvesting anything," Casey said from behind her towel. "And I'm certainly not going after a *cop*. Okay, class!" She clapped her hands. "Ready to get started?"

The class was fun, and the women ended with a splashing contest, ultimately ganging up on Casey and giving her a good dousing. When they'd dispersed, giggling, Casey pushed herself out of the pool.

She was getting water out of her ear with her towel when she felt a presence at her elbow. It was Sissy. "The Parkers want to talk to you some more."

"Why?"

"They won't say. They'll only tell me they have something they need to ask you."

"I have personal training in twenty minutes."

"Then you can just tell the Parkers it has to be quick."

Casey let out a big breath. "All right. Are they in her apartment?"

"They haven't left it all day."

"I'll change and go up."

"Thank you, Daisy."

Casey got into dry clothes and went up to the fourth floor. She knocked on Andrea's door, which had yet another bundle of flowers leaning against it. And then she knocked again. No response. She picked up the flowers and opened the door.

"Hello? Mr. and Mrs. Parker?"

It was dark in the apartment, just like Krystal's had been that morning. Casey pushed the door open far enough she could see Andrea's parents sitting in the living room, her mom on the sofa, her dad in the easy chair. Casey wondered if they'd moved at all since she'd left them, because it looked like they were still wearing the same clothes as the day before. She stepped in and turned on the light. Mrs. Parker swiveled toward her, squinting.

Casey set the flowers on the table. "It's me. Daisy Gray. You wanted to see me?"

Andrea's mom regarded Casey with confusion, and then her face cleared. "Oh, yes. Please, come in."

Casey shut the door and went to sit beside Mrs. Parker. "How can I help you?"

"They're telling us we can't take Andrea home. They won't let us have her."

"The police have to finish their investigation first. Once they're satisfied they have everything, they'll release her."

"But we want to go home. We want to take her *home*." Her voice was quiet and thin.

"I know. They're doing everything they can."

Mrs. Parker sagged back into the sofa. Mr. Parker hadn't yet moved.

Casey cleared her throat. "Have you remembered her fiancé's name yet?"

Mrs. Parker shook her head slowly. "He should come. He should be here, shouldn't he?"

If there was a 'he,' he definitely should.

Casey patted Mrs. Parker's knee, then got up and went back to Andrea's bedroom. Where would Andrea keep something with his name? And why was it hidden? She was beginning to think the whole fiancé thing was just a story for her parents benefit. Casey looked again in the closet, under the bed, and between the mattress and the box springs. She flicked on the bedside lamp and opened the drawer of the nightstand. Nothing but an old devotional book and an extra box of tissues. She slid the drawer shut and hesitated, studying the top of the stand. A fine layer of dust covered the exposed wood, but on the side closest to the bed lay a line which appeared less dusty. The bare spot was about five inches across. Like a photo frame. Casey let out a breath. If there had been a photo by her bed, and now it was gone, that said something. Something big. There were still pictures of Andrea's family in the apartment, so there couldn't be a secret there. The missing photo had to be of her mystery man.

She went back out to the living room, took the family photo off the wall, and showed it to Andrea's mother. "All family?"

"Yes. That's David and me, of course, and Andrea's brothers, and…and Andrea."

Casey hung the photo back up and went to the kitchen. The refrigerator held the same pictures as the night before, which all showed family members.

Back in the living room, she took one last look between the magazines, and under the books. *The books.* She checked the bookmark in the top one. A receipt from the grocery store. The next book had a folded tissue. Casey picked up the third one, a paperback romance. She pulled out the scrap paper. It was a handwritten note.

My love,
You are an angel for understanding. Give it just a few more weeks, and it will be your turn. She is so grateful, and I don't want to leave her before things are taken care of. I'll be in touch.
With all my love,
Richie

Chapter Twenty-seven

Casey went cold. *Richie?* Andrea was involved with *Richie?* The "sweetheart" instructor who hadn't known anything about his job? Who couldn't show his face anywhere near or Sissy would take him to court? Not Brandon, the stud con-man? But Richie had been gone for…she didn't know exactly *how* long he'd been gone. Casey looked up, hoping to see Death to compare reactions, but Death was—for once—nowhere to be seen.

Casey's fingers shook. Everything she'd been told about Richie was that he had taken off, *never to be heard from again.* That if he did show up, Sissy would have him thrown in jail, or would take him to court, or whatever.

A few more weeks, he said in the note. A few weeks from when? From when he disappeared? From much, much later, when everyone else thought he'd disappeared for good?

And then she remembered, the one time she'd talked to Andrea about the previous instructors. She had said, "Richie *is* a sweetheart." Not was. Is. Casey hadn't picked up on it at the time, but now it stuck out like Death at a baby shower.

Casey smoothed the note out on her leg. "Mrs. Parker, does the name Richie mean anything to you?"

Mrs. Parker's face remained impassive. "No." She brightened. "Is that Andrea's fiancé?"

"I don't know. I just…I found this note." She held it out.

Mrs. Parker read it, her brow furrowing. "What does he mean? Once *what* is taken care of?"

"I don't know. May I keep the note?"

Mrs. Parker absently handed it back over, the spark disappearing from her eyes.

Casey stood. "I need to talk to someone. I'll be in touch, okay? Are you all right here? Do you need anything?"

She got no response, and left them to their silence. She ran down to her apartment and waited for Death to join her, so she could share what she'd just found. But Death didn't come. When she couldn't wait any longer, Casey jogged down the service stairs to the weight room, where she met her personal training client. It was one of the older men she'd had on Wednesday, and she basically just stood by, making sure he didn't drop a weight on his head.

She couldn't believe what she'd found. Andrea had been involved with *Richie*? What did that mean? Why would that get her killed? Maybe it didn't. Maybe someone else was under the same false impression Casey had been—that Andrea had been involved with Brandon.

But why would anybody think that in the first place?

Casey put her guy on the treadmill, and got her next client started. Again, an older woman who didn't take a lot of thought. As soon as her time was over, Casey hustled down to the reception area, hoping to catch Maria. She was still there, with a young woman who was signing papers. Sissy's door was closed, but light showed at its base. Casey hung back, and saw Jack getting the bar area ready for the night's happy hour.

She walked over. "Sorry about last night."

He looked up. "Hey. No problem. I figured you were exhausted after these past few days, and hit the sack early. Was I right?"

"Exactly."

He picked up a glass and looked at her expectantly.

"No, thanks. I'm waiting to talk to Maria."

"Anything I can help you with?"

Casey thought for a moment, then pulled the note out of her pocket and shoved it across the bar. "What do you think of this?"

He read the note. "Who was this to?"

"Want to take a guess?"

His eyebrows rose. "Andrea?"

She nodded. "I just found out she was engaged. I thought it was to Brandon, but it seems I was wrong."

"Andrea and Brandon?" Jack let out a sharp laugh. "No way."

"How come?"

"Because she was smart. And a good person. She saw through him from the first."

"As did you."

"Of course."

Casey frowned. "Then why didn't you do something about it?"

"What was I going to do?"

"I don't know. Tell somebody."

"And who was I going to tell, exactly? The manager of the condo, who just happened to be sleeping with him, and makes all of the hiring decisions? I would've been the one without a job, not him."

Casey winced. "Did everyone know?"

"About Sissy and Brandon? I don't know about *everyone*, but let's just say it wasn't as big a secret as she thought."

"How old was he?"

"Twenties. Late twenties, maybe, but still just twenties."

Casey shuddered. "What is *wrong* with the people here?"

"The same thing that's wrong with people everywhere. They want to be loved."

"You call that love? Going after men young enough to be your sons? Or seducing women twice your age just to get their money?"

"I don't, no. But most people just want *someone*. Look around you, Daisy. Who are you surrounded by? Single people. I know they advertise this place as a home for singles and young professional couples, but all the couples I know of—married ones, anyway—are out in the other two buildings, all retirement age and beyond. The Flamingo?" He held out his arms. "It's filled with people who just want something better than what they have. Than what they are. Everyone wants to be younger, fitter, richer, sexier. No one's happy with just…being themselves."

"Just like high school," Casey said, repeating the words she' said to Sensei Asuhara.

Jack nodded. "Only worse. Because these people are old enough to know better. You wouldn't believe the things I see…" He grabbed his cloth and began polishing the shiny metal area on his side of the counter.

"What about things you *saw?*"

He looked up.

"Who did you see Brandon with? Anyone other than Sissy?"

"I never saw him with her. And beyond that, he was pretty discreet, if you can believe it."

"Afraid of all the women he was screwing," Casey said.

Jack laughed. "As he should've been. It's a wonder…" He stopped and shook his head.

"What is?"

"I was going to say it's a wonder *he's* not dead."

He looked like he wasn't done talking, so Casey waited. He picked up a lemon and began cutting it into wedges. "There was one woman who really bothered me."

"She was after you?"

"No, I mean it bothered me to see her with Brandon."

"And who was that?"

He finished that lemon and grabbed another one. "The other fitness instructor."

"Laurie?"

He cut the lemon in half with a *whack*. "She could be so pretty. She's fit, she energetic, she's nice with the residents—older ones, especially. I always wished…" He shook his head.

"What, Jack?"

"When I saw her with Brandon, the way she fawned over him, and they way he treated her like she was just a plaything… it made me want to spike his drink."

"And did you?"

His seriousness broke, and he laughed. "Just in my fantasies."

A movement by the office caught Casey's eye, and she saw the woman in Maria's office accepting keys and grabbing a suitcase. She came out of the office and turned left, toward the elevator.

Casey slid off the stool. "So did you ever tell her?"

"Who?"

"Laurie. Did you ever tell her you think she's pretty?"

"You crazy? Look at me. Do I seem like the kind of guy she'd want?"

Casey smiled. "Good-looking, energetic, nice with residents...sounds like a good combination to me."

His face clouded. "Yeah, but you're not like the other women here, are you? You really are who you claim to be."

Casey gave a small laugh. "Oh, Jack. I wouldn't be so sure about that."

He put down his knife and looked Casey right in the face. "Are you just pretending to be my friend? Or to care about Andrea? Or to be disgusted with the toxic atmosphere this place can produce?"

"No."

"Then I don't care about anything else. You know what's important."

"Do I?"

"Look in your heart, Daisy Gray. See what's important there. That's who you are. Not blond hair or tan skin or white teeth. Your wishes. Your desires. Your honor. Look in your heart and tell me none of that's there."

"And if I told you that everything you see in front of you is a façade? That I'm nothing like you think I am?"

Jack smiled. "Then I'd say you're a liar. And I'd be right. Now, weren't you needing to talk to Maria? Looks like she's free."

He tossed the lemon in the air, caught it, and moved down the bar, turning his back on Casey, the big, fat liar.

Chapter Twenty-eight

Casey wandered over to the office, trying to remember what she'd even come down there for. She took the seat the woman had just occupied. It was still warm. Maria looked tired, but was definitely back to her business-like self. Her nail polish wasn't even chipped.

She glanced up. "Can I help you, Ms. Gray?"

"Um, new resident?"

"Yes. All the way from Iowa. Very sweet and...innocent."

"Good for her." She hesitated, still trying to get back to her thinking before the conversation with Jack.

Maria waited. "Ms. Gray?"

Oh. Right. "I was wondering if you could help me with a timeline."

"Timeline?"

"Yes, the fitness guy before me. Brandon Greer. Exactly how long was he here?"

Maria frowned. "Why do you need to know this?"

"It's not a secret, is it? I could ask the residents, but I don't think you'd want that."

Maria's jaw clenched. "No, we wouldn't."

"So?"

Maria pulled up a calendar on her computer, tapping the keys with her fingernails. "He arrived the beginning of June, and left two weeks before you got here."

"So basically, three months."

"That was long enough." Her face and voice were both hard.

"And the guy before him? Richie Miller, was it?"

Maria's jaw tightened again. "Yes. He was here a little longer. He came…" She clicked back several months. "In November of last year."

"So he was here six months?"

"Seven." Maria clasped her hands together on her desk. "Ms. Gray, why is this important?"

"I don't really know. Look, I heard from various people that Brandon was…unethical. That he was a cheat and a blackmailer. What can you tell me about that?"

Maria went white, then glanced at Sissy's door and lowered her voice. "He hurt several women…in different ways. Mrs. Williams wanted to stop him before he hurt any more."

Maria and Sissy included, although Casey didn't say it. "Did you ever hear anything about Andrea being one of his victims? Or lovers?"

Maria's eyebrows went up. "No. Never."

"What about Andrea and Richie?"

Maria went red now. "She was not involved with him, either. What are you suggesting, Ms. Gray?"

"You're sure about Richie? You sound very certain."

"I never saw anything that would have led me to believe Richie was involved with Andrea Parker when he was here."

So they'd hid it well. At least from the administration. "What about other women? Did he have any favorites?"

"This is not something I am free to discuss, Ms. Gray. Maybe you should wait until Mrs. Williams can talk to you."

"Fine. I'll wait. But while I'm waiting, do you have any photos of Richie? Or Brandon, for that matter."

"Why would I?"

"I don't know. Employee file, community activities…"

Maria turned to her computer and typed. "Here. This is Brandon." She swiveled the monitor so Casey could see the photo, which was taken in a weight room—not the Flamingo's.

He stood sideways, smiling and holding a huge barbell, his biceps bulging more than seemed natural.

Casey wrinkled her nose. What a letdown. He was huge, yeah, but with one of those wrestler necks that sort of merged his head with his shoulders in a weird, alien-like way. He was both young and blond, which would be selling points, but his nose was weirdly small, and his eyes a bit too close together. You'd think if he was so attractive to all those ladies he would be a lot better looking. "I guess it was his personality?" Casey said.

Maria sniffed. "He did have an…aura. If you like that sort of thing."

"How about Richie? Any photos of him?"

Maria looked uncertain.

"From when he applied, maybe?"

Maria swiveled the monitor back her way and typed for a bit, paging up and down. "Here." She glanced again at Sissy's door, and kept her hand on the monitor, like she was ready to spin it back around at a moment's notice.

Casey smiled. Now this guy was more like it. She was surprised the women hadn't gone for him. He looked as nice as they'd all said, with sandy brown hair and an easy smile. He wasn't nearly the size of Brandon, but Casey thought he looked better. More like a normal person. "Now *he's* cute," Casey said. "Much more worth getting to know, don't you think?"

Maria sniffed again. Was she allergic to these photos? She turned the monitor back toward herself again and clicked out of the picture.

"From what I hear, Sissy pretty much told him if she ever saw him again she'd slap a lawsuit on him."

Maria's nostrils flared. "Yes, that's correct."

"Was he really that bad?"

Maria rested her elbow on the desk and kneaded her forehead. "I think he bit off more than he could chew here, but that he was really a good person at heart. Many of the things that happened were not his fault, but Mrs. Williams needed someone to blame, and he was convenient. It's much easier to fire someone who's only been with you a little while than to lose residents who bring in money."

"Yes. That's what I thought. Everyone else seemed to really like him. Andrea included. I really wonder if there wasn't more to him than people realized. *You* seem to realize it. Were you and Richie close?"

Maria jerked her elbow off the desk. "I have to go. It's the beginning of the weekend, and I need to get home. You can let yourself into Mrs. Williams' office when she's ready."

"Oh. Of course. That's no problem."

Maria yanked her purse out of her desk, dropped it, picked it up, and grabbed her jacket, buttoning it wrong and re-doing it. "Goodnight, Ms. Gray."

"Goodnight, Maria."

Casey watched her go, startled at her sudden departure. As soon as she'd gone, Sissy's door opened. She came out holding some papers, and jumped when she saw Casey.

Casey smiled. "Sorry to startle you."

Sissy fanned herself. "Don't mind me. I just wanted… Where's Maria?"

"She left. Said she was headed home for the weekend."

Sissy frowned. "It's not even five yet."

"I think I made her nervous, sitting here."

"Yes, I can see that. She doesn't like to be watched over."

"Who does?"

"Speaking of watching over, did you go up to see the Parkers?"

"Yes. They're wondering when they can take Andrea's body home."

Sissy's face fell. "What did you tell them?"

"I don't know why they were asking me. But I said when the cops were ready for them to take her, they could."

"You don't know more specifically than that?"

"How would I?"

"Well, you seem to be chummy with the cops."

"I'm not."

"But you *want* to be," Death said.

Casey spun around, heart in her throat.

Death was in the other chair, one leg flung over the arm, back to wearing the cop uniform. "Or were you just flushed from the heat in the pool room the last time Gomez came around?"

"Everything okay, Daisy?" Sissy stood frozen, one arm extended over Maria's desk as she held the papers.

"Yes, I'm fine. And I'm not involved with any cops."

Death chuckled.

"They only talk to me because I'm the one who found Andrea. Really."

Sissy took a step back toward her office. "Of course. Um, I have some more things to do. I'll be in here." She backed into her office and shut the door.

"Where have you *been?*" Casey growled at Death.

"What? Now you want me around? You really need to make up your mind."

"Things have been *happening*." She told Death about the note from Richie.

"I don't understand how that could involve *me*," Death said.

"It doesn't. Not everything is about—Oh. Right. Andrea's dead. But here, you might be interested in these." Maria had left in such a rush she'd forgotten to turn off the computer. Casey went around the desk and clicked around until she found Richie's picture again. "That's Richie Miller. Isn't he cute? He and Andrea would have made an adorable couple."

"Adorable. But why are you showing me?"

"Because I thought you'd be interested to see who came before me. Let's see if I can..." She searched some more. "Here he is. This is Brandon Greer. What do you think? Kind of disappointing, isn't he?"

But Death didn't answer. Instead, Death went pale and made a choking sound.

Casey looked from Death to Brandon's picture, and back again. "What's wrong?"

"*Who* is that?"

"Brandon. You know, the guy right before me. The black-mailing Don Juan."

"It can't be."

Casey stopped breathing for a moment. "You mean you *know* this guy? You've seen him…before?"

Death swallowed. "His name is not Brandon Greer. This guy's name is Wayne Pritchfield. He died last night in an apartment a couple towns over from here. He'd been stabbed to death with a kitchen knife."

A cold chill ran down Casey's spine, and she shivered. "Brandon Greer is *dead*?"

"No, Wayne Pritchfield is. Murdered."

"Do you know who killed him?"

"Nope. Didn't ask. He wasn't real talkative at the time."

A noise came from Sissy's office, and Casey clicked away from Brandon's—or *Wayne's* — photo. She jumped up and practically ran to the service stairs. She flew into her apartment and right to the bathroom, where she stood over the toilet for a few moments, afraid she was going to throw up. Nothing happened, except she got covered in cold, clammy sweat.

"Wow, you look nasty."

Casey slammed the door in Death's face, and when Death's face poked through the door, she threw a bar of soap at it. Death retreated.

Casey stood under a hot shower until she stopped shaking, then washed her hair twice and scrubbed her body, as if she'd been sullied somehow. Brandon Greer was dead. Murdered. That changed everything. No wonder the folders were still in the bank. He'd still been around, all along. No one had known it, apparently. They'd thought he'd cut all ties, but he must have had other reasons to remain silent. Now he didn't have a choice. He'd be silent now because he was *dead*.

She had to tell Binns.

She turned off the shower, wrapped up in a towel, and went out to the living room to get her phone. She got Binns' voice mail.

"Call me," Casey said. "It's urgent."

Casey scrabbled through the desk and found an old phone book. She dialed the police department.

"Raceda Police."

"Detective Binns, please."

"She's not available right now, may I take a message?"

"How about Officer Gomez?"

"You should have his number, anyway," Death said. "For when you get that yearning in the middle of the night."

"He is also out of the building."

Casey ground her teeth. "Have Detective Binns call Daisy Gray, please. It's important, about the murder at the Flamingo."

"Of course. I'll get her the message right away."

Casey hung up and stood, still dripping, in her living room.

"Um, you might want to put on some clothes," Death said.

Casey dried herself off, yanked on some jeans and a blouse, and brushed her hair. "Good enough?"

"Hope so, 'cause Dylan's just about here."

"What?"

"Your date, remember?"

A knock came from the door. Casey strode to it and swung it open. Dylan stood there, with an entire bouquet of roses this time.

"What are you doing here?" Casey said.

"Um, dinner, remember?"

"Yes, and we're meeting in the lobby at six-thirty."

"I couldn't remember. And I couldn't find my phone to call and ask."

"Didn't you ever pick it up in the gym this morning, after Tamille scared you half to death?"

"Oh. Duh. I couldn't think of where I'd left it. All that terror must have erased my memory."

Casey shook her head. "Well, come in, then. I'm almost ready, anyway."

Casey went to put on some shoes, making sure she had her phone for when Binns called back. When she got back to the living room, Dylan was looking out her window. "Nice view."

"Would be nicer if I actually saw the ocean, but then these wouldn't be the cheap seats."

"I have a view of downtown from my place, which isn't all that exciting, believe me. I'd much rather see the pool and palm trees."

Casey stood beside him and looked down at the pool, where people had already begun the weekend. A couple dozen people were in the water or lounging around it, with a waiter going in-between tables, taking orders.

"So, Dylan, you were here when Brandon got the fitness job, right?"

"Sure."

"Did you hear anything about where he came from? Or where he went when he left?"

"Nah. He wasn't exactly a guy's guy, you know. The most I saw of him was if he happened to be in the weight room when I was, or down in the bar. I never really talked to him."

"And Krystal never said anything about him?"

He looked at her sideways. "You mean like whether or not they were, you know, doing it?"

"Could be. Or anything else about him."

"All I got from her about Brandon was that she hated his guts. She thought he was a creep. She wasn't even going to aerobics those last few weeks he was here. Said it wasn't worth it to have to breathe the same air as him every day."

Casey stared down at the pool, not seeing it. Who all hated him? Or loved him? Or maybe both? Sissy. Shelly. Bernie. Maria. Krystal. All of the other women listed on those folders. Had one of them killed him? And then killed Andrea because she thought she was involved with him? Would any of them have the strength to take on a guy as huge as he'd been?

"Have you heard any rumors about where he went?"

"Oh, there are all kinds of rumors. Which ones do you want to hear? That he went to work for Arnold Schwarzenegger? That

Flowers for Her Grave 245

he's living in Guadalupe with his gay lover? Or that he got put up in an apartment by his Sugar Mama, working his glutes and waiting for her to die so he can inherit her fortune?"

"Do any of them seem likely?"

Dylan grinned. "All of them, actually."

Casey could have believed any of them, too, before she'd learned he was lying in the morgue with a toe tag that said, "Wayne Pritchfield." Now the theory that stuck out was the Sugar Mama one, seeing how he'd died in an apartment close to Raceda. Had one of his jilted ladies or blackmail victims found him, and brought an end to his greedy polygamy?

"So," Dylan said. "I'm pretty hungry."

Casey wasn't. But what else was she to do? Binns could get in touch with her wherever she was. And being in the Flamingo was giving her the willies. "Okay. Let's go."

After a quick and unfruitful stop in the gym to check for Dylan's phone, he led her to his car, a dark green Toyota Corolla.

"Too far to walk?" Casey asked.

"It's on the other side of town. We *could* walk, but it would take forever, and I'm so hungry…"

Casey got in the car.

"Oh, this is so exciting!" Death's head was suddenly between Casey and Dylan, arms over the backs of the seats. "Your first date in such a long time!"

"It's not a date," Casey said.

Dylan sighed so heavily Death's head wavered. "I know. You've already made that perfectly clear."

Whoops.

Death fell into the backseat, laughing.

Casey rolled her eyes. "Dylan, don't give me the whole injured little boy thing. It was only two nights ago you and Krystal barged into my office, clothes flying."

He went red. "I know. I'm sorry. I'm…" He gripped the steering wheel so hard Casey was afraid he was going to snap it.

"Forget it. Tell me about this restaurant."

He gave a shaky smile, and relaxed his hands. "It's Cuban. They make a great shrimp enchilada."

"Bet it's not as good as Del's."

"Who?"

"Big guy in the weight room. He's going to be a chef." Which made her stomach knot, because who knew if that was only because he had made sure Andrea was no longer his loan officer?

She just couldn't believe that.

But Del would certainly have the strength to kill a guy like Brandon. The only question was...would he have *reason* to? He'd said he was making good money at the insurance company. Why wasn't that enough to be seed money for a loan, or at least to satisfy Andrea that he was a good loan candidate? Was Brandon was blackmailing him, too, and taking his money? Or maybe Del had a history Andrea couldn't ignore, and Brandon couldn't resist? But there wasn't a folder with his name on it. It seemed like Brandon only targeted women.

When they got to the restaurant Casey and Dylan had to wait only a few minutes for an empty table, then squeezed their way through the packed little room to the far corner. Casey took the side against the wall, looking out toward the door.

"Told you it was a hole in the wall," Dylan said, grinning.

"Yeah." Death stood behind Dylan with crossed arms. "No room for a third."

The waiter brought a basket of warm, freshly fried tortilla chips, and Casey smiled at Death, who could smell them, but not eat them. She found that once they were in front of her, she actually was hungry, and dug right in.

"Dylan," she said around a mouthful. "You know Tamille?"

He choked on a chip, and grabbed his water glass. When he'd recovered, he set down the glass and took another chip, like nothing had happened. "Uh, yeah."

"I talked to her. She promised not to devour you."

He blinked several times. "Really?"

"Really. You're safe. Even if I'm not around to protect you."

He made a show of wiping his forehead with his napkin. "Whew. I will sleep better tonight."

Casey laughed.

She had shoved another whole chip, complete with a large dollop of salsa, into her mouth when Death gave her a brief wave and disappeared in a puff of mist. She had just enough time to wonder what had happened before her phone rang in her pocket. She grabbed it, expecting Binns, but was surprised at what she saw on the display.

"Dylan," she said with her mouth full. "You're calling me."

He lit up. "Someone found my phone!"

She swallowed. "Hello?"

A stream of hysterical Spanish assaulted her ears, a mixture of wailing and screaming. She held the phone away, her head ringing. "Do you know Spanish?"

Dylan shook his head. "French all through high school. Japanese in college."

"Really? Japanese?"

"It makes sense, business-wise."

The voice was still shrieking. Casey waved down her waiter and thrust the phone at him. "Can you tell me what this person is saying, please?"

He made a face at the noise, then took the phone and held it gingerly at his ear. He looked shocked at first, then spoke something that must have been calming, because Casey could no longer hear the waves of distress. The waiter's face went completely serious, his dark brows lowering over his eyes.

"She says there is a house that has been…things have been damaged."

"What? Who is it?"

"She says her name is Rosa. She's afraid. The people from the house are missing."

Rosa? From the Flamingo?

"Has she called 911?"

He went back onto the phone, patting the air as if he were consoling the caller. He turned to Casey. "She wants you to come."

Casey looked at Dylan, who sat with his mouth open. "I'm sorry, Dylan."

"It's okay. Let's go."

"I don't know if—"

"I'm not sending you off to face some home invasion by yourself."

Casey asked the waiter to get an address. He scribbled it on his order pad and ripped it off, also handing her phone, which was still on.

"Thank you," Casey said. "*Gracias.*"

He nodded, and Casey and Dylan ran out the door.

Chapter Twenty-Nine

They clambered into Dylan's car.

"Address?" Dylan said.

She gave it to him.

"That's on this side of town, which makes sense, since she's speaking Spanish. I think that road is..." His voice trailed off as he concentrated on pulling out into traffic.

"We're coming," Casey said into the phone. "We're coming, okay?"

Dylan turned around a corner at high speed and skidded to a stop at the curb in front of a small stucco house with rust-colored shutters. "We're there."

"Already?" Casey jumped out of the car.

Dylan ran around beside her.

"You stay here," Casey said.

"But you need me to—"

"Dylan," Casey said. "You are young and strong. But if anyone will need protecting, it's you. It will be better if you just stay out here, okay?"

"Daisy—"

"*Stay.*"

His shoulders slumped, but he nodded.

Casey moved briskly up the walk, listening and watching for any movement. "Hello?"

No response.

She detoured off the path and stood sideways by one of the front windows, tilting just far enough she could peek in. Everything looked dark and quiet. She went back to the front door and tried the knob. It turned easily, and she pushed the door open with her foot. "Hello?"

Again, nothing. She stepped into the front room, which was filled with sofas and chairs and the usual living room furniture. Books and papers lay scattered across the floor, but the furniture was all still lined up, as if nothing violent had happened. Casey could see no one hiding there. "Hello? It's me. Daisy. You called me."

A rush of Spanish filled the air, and Rosa, the maid from the Flamingo, barged around the corner. She grabbed Casey's arm and babbled in Spanish, the words crashing over Casey like whitewater. Rosa was sobbing and talking, and flinging her free hand in the air.

"Shhh." Casey put her hand on Rosa's shoulder and ducked her head to look the woman in the eye. "Quiet, now, Rosa. Quiet. Shush now."

Rosa hiccupped and sniffed, and buried her face in her hands.

"Are you here alone?"

Rosa looked up, her face red and sweaty.

"Just you?" Casey said, pointing at Rosa. "*Una?*"

"*Si.*" Rosa hiccupped again. "*Si.*"

Casey set Rosa on one of the living room chairs and gestured for her to stay. She stood still, listening. No sound came that would say anyone else was still around. No creaking. No breathing. She held up her palm to Rosa again, and walked carefully toward the back of the house.

To the right was a kitchen. A few drawers hung open, and plastic baggies lay in disarray on the counter, surrounded by crumbs and a partial head of lettuce. The sink was filled with dirty dishes and an empty milk jug. No people.

To the left, down the hallway, were four doors. The first on the right was a small bedroom. From the furniture and bedspreads on the two twin beds it looked like children slept there.

Dresser drawers were flung open, with socks and shirts hanging over the fronts, and piles of clothes lay haphazardly on the floor. Pillows and sheets had been stripped from the mattresses, and a lone shoe huddled in the middle of the purple rug. The closet door was open, the light inside still on. Clothes on the rack were interspersed with bare hangers, and several shirts had been dumped onto the carpet.

The second door was a bathroom. Casey paused to listen again, and when she heard nothing, she slowly pushed the door all the way open. Nothing moved, so she flipped on the light and looked in the closet and behind the shower curtain. No one there. Just half-filled shampoo bottles, and damp towels on the floor. An empty toothbrush holder lay on its side on the counter, and all that was left of any toothpaste was a dried blue glob in the sink.

Casey was beginning to think this was not a burglary. It was a family leaving in a mad rush.

She turned to go back to the hallway and tripped on Rosa, who stood at her elbow, lower lip clamped in her teeth. Casey stopped her natural inclination to attack, and took a deep calming breath. "It's okay, Rosa. Come on."

Once in the hallway, Rosa kept behind Casey. The door to the last room on the right was half shut, and someone moved toward her. Casey dropped into a defensive stance, arms up, but realized with a start she was preparing to fight herself. The outside of the door held a full-length mirror. She stood back up, shaking out her arms.

Rosa nudged her toward the door.

"I'm going, I'm going." Casey shuffled forward, and shoved the door open with her shoe.

Again, this was a bedroom, and again, it was in disarray. Women's clothes spilled from a Rubbermaid storage container, which lay toppled over, its lid standing crookedly against the wall, as if it had been flung there with no thought as to its position. The ceiling fan turned in slow circles, the pull-chain clicking at each revolution. The curtains were pulled tight. The bed was unmade, any blankets and pillows gone, leaving only wrinkled sheets, partially pulled off the mattress.

"Nobody here. One more room." Casey gently pushed Rosa to the side and faced the last door in the hallway. It was closed. Casey directed Rosa to stand against the wall, out of the way of the door. Casey stood between the two doorways, flattened against the adjoining wall. She reached forward, turned the doorknob, and flung the door open.

Nothing moved.

Casey inched forward, then bent and forward-rolled into the room, avoiding any kick or punch that may have been struck at abdomen or head level. She snapped up into a ready crouch position, but there was no one to defend against. The room was as empty as the others. She stood, surveying the mess. This time, however, it was men's clothes that were draped over the unmade bed and carpet.

"Oh, my God."

Casey spun around. Dylan stood in the doorway.

"What?" Casey said.

Dylan's forehead was all crumpled, like he couldn't believe what he was seeing. "That sweatshirt."

Casey looked where he was pointing, at a purple and gold University of Washington hoodie.

"What about it?"

"I've only known one person who's had that."

"Dylan, Washington is a huge school. *Thousands* of people have that sweatshirt."

"I know, but that's *Washington*. This is Florida. I've never seen another one here."

"Okay. So you know the sweatshirt. Why is it a big deal?"

"Because why would it be here? He's been gone for months."

Casey took a deep breath, trying to keep her patience. "Dylan, whose sweatshirt is it?"

"The old instructor from the Flamingo."

Casey's mouth fell open. "Which one?"

"Two before you. The nice guy who knew nothing about exercise. His name was Richie Miller."

Chapter Thirty

"*Richie?*" Casey's head spun. "What is Richie's sweatshirt doing here? Whose house is this? Rosa, *su casa?*"

Rosa shook her head. "No, no. Maria."

"Maria?" Casey looked at Dylan. "Why is Richie's sweatshirt in *Maria's* house? And where's Maria?"

Dylan shrugged. "I don't know. Maybe he left it behind and Maria grabbed it out of lost and found because she liked it."

No. Maria was not the kind of woman to wear a man's sweatshirt, or to give away lost and found items. She wore tailored business suits and completely put-together *female* clothes. The kind that were in the *other* bedroom.

Casey took a deep breath and looked around, her suspicions growing stronger. This was definitely not a home invasion. This was a panicked woman taking her family and running. Something must have made her believe her illegal status was about to be discovered. But why would Richie be running with her? If, indeed, it *was* Richie.

"Rosa, who lived here with Maria?"

Rosa blinked at her without comprehension.

Casey slowed it down. "Maria's children? *Ninas?*"

"*Si. Dos.*" She held up two fingers.

"Anyone else? Just *tres* people?"

She brightened. "No, no. *Quatro.*"

Casey glanced at Dylan, who looked just as curious as she. "Who?" she asked Rosa. "Who made it *quatro*? A man?" Casey held up the sweatshirt.

Rosa nodded. "*Sí.*"

"Was his name Richie?"

Rosa nodded, then froze, her hand going over her mouth. She then gushed forth with another slew of desperate Spanish.

Casey tried to take it in. Richie was living here. With Maria. And writing notes to Andrea about how "she" was so grateful and it would only take "a few more weeks."

Whatever it meant, this connected Maria to Andrea in a way that was impossible to dispute.

Casey took out her phone and dialed Binns, praying she'd answer this time.

"This is Binns."

"Where have you been?"

"Ms. Gray?"

"Listen. I have a lot to tell you, but first, I've discovered something you need to see."

She told her the address, and ten minutes later Casey and Dylan were leaning on the Corolla out front when Binns and Gomez pulled up. Casey had put Rosa in the back seat, with the door open, where she alternately cried and stared into space.

Binns and Gomez parked behind Dylan's car. Binns got out, eying the house, their little group, and the neighborhood. Gomez came to stand directly in front of Casey, looking down at her.

Casey kept her eyes on Binns, trying to ignore Gomez's presence, until Binns had finished her visual inspection and come to stand beside her.

"Tell me," Binns said.

Casey inched back from Gomez, explained Rosa's phone call about what she'd thought was a burglary, and pointed out Rosa herself, who was in one of her staring into space moments. Casey went on to describe the discovery of Richie's sweatshirt, and Rosa's admittance that he'd been living at the house, which belonged to Maria Mendez.

"That's all I can get from her, though," Casey said. "She'll only speak in Spanish, and I'm not fluent enough to catch much."

Binns jerked her chin, and Gomez knelt beside Rosa. His voice was low and comforting, rising and falling with Spanish cadences. Rosa let out a sob, then began talking again, in halting spurts. Casey wanted to lay her hand on Gomez' broad back, to steal some of that comfort for herself, to feel the vibration of his voice.

Binns waved her hand under Casey's nose. "Hey. Gray. Any idea why Rosa called you?"

"She used Dylan's phone."

"What?"

Dylan gave a half smile. "I lost my phone in the gym today. She must have picked it up. She works there."

"And she knows me," Casey said. "At least, by name. I might have been the only one in his contact list she would feel comfortable calling."

"About a burglary."

"What she *thought* was a burglary."

"And you came over here and went *inside*. Don't you know you're not supposed to do that? Don't you watch TV?"

"No. Anyway, I wanted to be sure Rosa wasn't in danger, that there wasn't someone still in the house with her. I didn't touch anything with my hands except the shower curtain and the bathroom closet door. Oh, and the front doorknob and the bathroom light switch. Dylan came in, too, but I don't think he touched anything."

Dylan shook his head. "Nope."

Binns frowned. "Fine. Nothing we can do about it anymore."

A police cruiser drove up and parked at an angle, effectively cutting off any chance Dylan's car had of getting out of its spot. Binns stalked away and gave some instructions to the responding officers. She pointed her finger at Casey. "Do. Not. Move." She went into the house with the uniformed cops, and returned several minutes later. "So. What do you think?"

"I think Maria hightailed it out of town, and took her kids with her."

"And this Richie person who supposedly lived here with her?"

"He must've gone with them."

Binns sucked on her teeth and stared at the house.

"You were here before," Casey said. "The night of Andrea's murder. Did you see a man?"

"I didn't come myself. We sent patrol officers to check it out. They woke her up from a sound sleep, and there was no mention of a man."

"How would they know for sure she'd been sleeping? She could've been acting."

"Her car was cold. She hadn't used it."

"What about taxis?"

"We checked those, just to cover our bases. No one admitted to picking her up or dropping her off."

"So someone at the Flamingo would have needed to help her, if she was the one who killed Andrea."

Binns breathed through her nose, and out again. "You're making a huge leap between Ms. Mendez's leaving and Ms. Parker's murder."

"Of course. Aren't you?"

"Other than the fact that Ms. Mendez works at the Flamingo, and Ms. Parker lived there, I've got no evidence of anything tying them together. For all I know, Ms. Mendez left on a whirlwind vacation to Disney World, and we have no business being here at all."

Whoops.

"Let me fill you in on a couple of things I've discovered."

Binns' expression was dangerous. "You've been holding out on me again?"

"Not on purpose. I mean, I haven't seen you…Anyway, I found a note today in Andrea's apartment—which your officers already went through and cleared, remember?" Casey felt her pocket before remembering she'd changed pants, and the note was back in her room. "It was to Andrea from Richie."

"*This* Richie? *Ms. Mendez's* Richie?"

"Yes. The same Richie who was the fitness instructor at the Flamingo two people before me."

A light dawned in Binns' eyes. "And what did this note say?"

"That Andrea was an angel for understanding, and she should give him a few weeks and he'd be back for her. He wanted to hold on a little longer, until he worked something out."

"Worked what out?"

"Well, that's something else you should probably know. Maria Mendez's name is actually Melina Reynaldo. Her green card expired over a year ago, and she hasn't been able to get it renewed."

Binns opened her mouth, looked at Gomez, then back at Casey. "And you know this how?"

"I found a stash of folders with secrets about people at the Flamingo."

"What?" Dylan exploded, reminding them all that he was still there. "Richie was blackmailing people?"

"No, not Richie. Brandon."

"Wait a minute." Binns' forehead wrinkled. "This Brandon guy was the next fitness instructor, the one just before you, right? I checked him out. He got fired, but Mrs. Williams wouldn't tell me anything except she had to let him go."

"He was blackmailing Maria," Casey said.

"Only her?"

"No. Several other women, as well. Or else he made women romantic promises, and they put him in their wills."

"I can believe that, "Dylan said. "Women were all over him."

Binns' eyes were steely. "Why are you just now telling me this?"

"I'm sorry. I only found the folders yesterday. I forgot. But what I *really* need to tell you I just found out this evening. I tried to call you, and left a message at the police department, and on your voice mail."

Binns frowned and pulled out her phone. "Sorry. I didn't see it. What is it?"

Casey swallowed and glanced at Dylan. He raised his eyebrows. "What?"

"Brandon Greer," Casey said to Binns. "The guy who was blackmailing people? His name was actually Wayne Pritchfield. Nobody's heard from him since he left the Flamingo. He was killed last night."

Binns jerked her head, like a fly had landed on her face. "He was *what?*"

"*Killed?*" Dylan grabbed Casey's arm to steady himself.

"Murdered. Somewhere close, but I don't know what town. Stabbed to death with a kitchen knife."

Binns blinked. "I think I heard about that. It was in Birmingham. They haven't found the killer."

"Birmingham, Alabama?" Dylan said.

"No, Florida. It's about thirty miles down the road." Binns pinned Casey with a stare. "That was *this* guy? How do you know this?"

Oh, boy. How to explain without bringing Death into it all. "I saw his picture on Maria's computer and recognized him. From the news."

"Really."

"It's true." Sort of.

"So how does that connect to this?" Binns waved at Maria's house. "And Andrea's death?"

"I don't know. Maybe it doesn't."

"Of course it does." Binns sounded exasperated. "Two murders involving people from the Flamingo? They have to be connected."

Casey's head hurt. "Okay. How about this? First, Maria is blackmailed by Brandon. He's going to turn her in to the INS unless she pays him, or has sex with him, or who knows what? Before he leaves, he tells her that even though Richie is living with her, she shouldn't get her hopes up about a future with him, because he and Andrea are secretly engaged."

"And how does he know this?"

"How does he know anything? He's good at snooping, and getting information out of people. Anyway, she tells Richie she's found out about Andrea. Richie decides to stay with Maria, and tells Maria he and Andrea are finished."

"What makes you think that?"

"Two weeks ago Andrea stopped telling her parents about her fiancé. Made it sound like it was over. And the phone number, remember? It was probably Richie's, and he stopped calling once Maria found out."

"But that was *two weeks ago*," Binns said. "If Maria found out about Andrea that long ago, why did she wait so long to kill her? And she wouldn't have a reason, anyway. In your theory, Richie stays with Maria."

"Maybe Richie just this week decided he wasn't willing to give Andrea up? I don't know. Maybe he'd chosen, after all, to go back to Andrea, and leave Maria in the lurch. She went berserk. It makes sense. It was Maria's key, after all, that let the killer into the building after hours. She would have access to the locker rooms, and would know Andrea and Krystal often worked out late at night. She could have faked the note to Krystal, so Krystal would make a surprise visit to the guard. It would be easy for her to sneak up, kill Andrea, and leave without being seen. She probably ran right to Andrea's room after killing her to steal the photo of Richie and anything else of his she might find there."

"And what note to Krystal was this she supposedly faked?" Binns' voice was hard.

Casey winced. "Sorry. Krystal told me about it today. The hot young guard wrote and asked her to come down at midnight to…um…*see* him. That's when she left Andrea alone on the fitness floor."

Binns' jaw worked, and she spent some time staring at the sidewalk before returning her attention to Casey. "Okay. All of the circumstantial evidence supports the idea of Ms. Mendez killing Ms. Parker, because of Ms. Mendez's familiarity with the building and her involvement with Richie, but what about the transportation angle? If she really didn't use her car, she would have needed another way to get home. There was no chance she could have walked here, or even ridden a bike, in the time between you calling the cops and us dispatching a cruiser."

"One of the Flamingo vehicles?" Casey said. "They have trucks. And a Gator."

Binns shook her head. "Nothing unfamiliar was seen here that night. Unless she parked blocks away, and then she would've gotten here too late."

"Maybe she hitched a ride," Gomez said. "That wouldn't be hard. Lots of immigrants live on this side of town, and work on that side. She could have easily found someone she knew to bring her home."

Casey looked at the neighboring houses. All dark, even with all the commotion in the street. "Somehow I don't think you'll get anyone to come forward."

Binns shook her head wearily. "Same old story. But we'll try."

Casey considered the state of the inside of Maria's house, and wondered what had precipitated Maria's sudden departure. Had it been something Casey had said? Had she made Maria nervous asking about Richie earlier that evening? Probably. Sissy had said just moments afterward that everyone considered Casey in league with the cops. Casey had been there, asking Maria very pointed questions about Richie, and about Brandon. She had to admit it, if only to herself. She had most likely driven Maria—and her family, and probably Richie—away. "Maria's gone for good, isn't she? Everything's a mess in there, like she left in a hurry."

"Looks that way. Something got her spooked, and she took off. We'll put out a call for her, now that I know about her illegal status and the possibility she killed Ms. Parker and the guy in Birmingham. We'll hope she hasn't made it too far yet."

Dylan shook his head. "I don't get it. If Richie left the Flamingo in May, why take the chance and stay in Raceda when he knew what Sissy would do if she found out? And if he really was involved with Andrea, why was he keeping that a secret and living at Maria's house? It makes no sense."

"I have a theory," Casey said.

Everyone looked at her.

"When Richie was first working at the Flamingo he got to know Maria. Maria trusted him, and told him her green card has expired. From everything I've heard, Richie is a nice guy, and would do anything for anybody."

"Super nice," Dylan said. "Even to guys."

"The note to Andrea was asking her to be patient. I'm guessing Richie had promised Maria he would help her with her citizenship, maybe even by marrying her and getting her a green card, I don't know. But after he'd already promised to help Maria, Andrea moved into the building, and he fell in love with her. He didn't want to break his promise to Maria, so he stayed with her while she worked at getting her citizenship."

Binns didn't look convinced. "He was still going to marry her, even after falling in love with Andrea?"

Casey shook her head. "I don't think so. You saw the bedrooms. They were obviously sleeping separately."

"That could've been a show for the kids."

"I don't think so. I think the marriage was all just paperwork. At least on his side. But maybe it wasn't to her, and when she found out about him and Andrea she freaked out because it meant their green card wedding was off."

Binns looked hard at the house, thinking. "Right. When Maria found out about Andrea she wouldn't necessarily have been angry about him having a girlfriend, at least from a romantic perspective. But she would have been losing her way to stay in the States if he married Andrea instead of her."

"What I don't understand," Casey said, "is why Richie took off with her now. How could he *possibly* want to stay with the woman who killed Andrea?"

"Unless she has him believing she didn't do it. Or unless she's killed him, too."

Casey shivered, realizing that Death was gone. Was Death off delivering Richie to the next life?

"Who knows?" Binns said. "Love—or sex, anyway—can make people do the strangest things, and threats to your family's life are just as bad, if not worse. We'll find her, and once we do, we'll have a lot of questions to ask about Ms. Parker *and* the guy in Birmingham."

"But why did Maria kill Brandon? Or Wayne. Or whatever his name is?" Dylan asked. "I mean, I know he'd been blackmailing her, but he's gone. How did she even know where he *was?*"

"He might have still been blackmailing her," Casey said. "Once Andrea was dead Maria probably figured her future was secure with Richie. He would marry her and they would be set. Maybe she set up a time to pay off Brandon, but really went to try to change his mind. And when he wouldn't…"

"She killed him." Dylan's voice was hoarse.

Casey shrugged. "Brandon could still prove the marriage was done just for a green card, especially since he knew about Richie and Andrea's engagement. That's as good as sending both Maria *and* Richie to jail. Maria wouldn't leave her kids parentless, so she did what she had to do to keep her family safe."

Dylan's face went a shade paler, and he sat hard on the curb, his head between his knees. Casey patted his hair.

"Now, you two," Binns said. "Back home. We'll talk tomorrow. Tonight I need to take care of things here, and get in touch with law enforcement in Birmingham. If Ms. Mendez killed both of these people, we'll want to work together. I'll send someone over in a little while to pick up Mr. Greer's folders, Ms. Gray. *Do not go anywhere.*"

"Can I have my phone?" Dylan asked.

"We'll return it to you as soon as we can."

"How about my car?"

"Gomez," Binns said. "Transfer Ms. Rosa to our car, please, and back up so they can get out."

Gomez said something to Rosa, and helped her out of that car and back toward his. He hesitated beside Casey. "You going to be okay? You need me to take you back?"

"I'll be fine. Dylan will drive me."

Gomez looked over at Dylan, who stood a little straighter and puffed out his chest. Each man regarded the other with calculating eyes.

"Oh, good grief," Casey said. "Dylan, let's go."

Her voice snapped the spell, and Gomez continued leading Rosa toward the unmarked car. With a pang, Casey watched how gently he guided her. Just as Reuben would have done.

"So we're going?" Dylan stood by the driver's side door.

Casey returned her attention to the house. Until earlier that day, Maria, her kids, and Richie had made a sort of family there. Now Maria had most likely killed two people, possibly three, and she and her kids were gone. On the run. Fugitives. Who knew what would happen to them tomorrow?

Casey opened the passenger door of Dylan's car, and got in.

Chapter Thirty-one

Neither one of them said a word all the way to the Flamingo. Dylan's hands again gripped the steering wheel like it was going to fly off, if he let it. Casey felt drained, and sank way low in her seat, watching dully as the streetlights drifted past.

It all was too sad. Finally, a couple who really did love each other. They wanted to do the right thing by Maria. Then they wanted to get married. No wonder Andrea's apartment looked like a stop on the way to somewhere else. She was just waiting for Maria's papers to go through, and she and Richie could go somewhere else. Somewhere he wasn't in danger of being taken to court if Sissy saw him.

It made her so, so tired. And felt so, so wrong.

"We're here," Dylan said, bringing the car to a stop.

Casey undid her seatbelt.

"So that cop," Dylan said, his hands squeaking as he squeezed the steering wheel. "He likes you."

Casey gave a little laugh. "Just because he was concerned for my welfare doesn't mean he *likes* me. And what are we? Fourth graders?"

Casey got out of the car and stretched, putting her hands on her waist and letting her head drop forward.

"So that wasn't pretty." Death stood beside Casey, leaning against Del's motorcycle in the next spot. For once Death wore the traditional outfit—a long, black robe with an over-sized hood. The head of a scythe peeked over Death's right shoulder, strapped on with a black leather belt.

Casey was shaken, and whispered, "Where have you been? It wasn't Richie was it?"

"Nope. Haiti. They've had such terrible luck lately. Earthquakes. Cholera. Hurricanes. Today it was the ground shifting under a road and causing a bridge to buckle. Dozens of people, smashed like very fragile bugs."

Casey shuddered, and Dylan put his arm around her shoulder. "Want to go in?"

"Actually, I think I'll walk on the beach for a bit."

"By yourself?"

"Doesn't matter. You can come, if you want. You probably need to clear your head, too."

She allowed Dylan to take her hand, and they walked around the Flamingo toward the beach. The sound of the ocean was drowned out by the music around the pool, and conversation and laughter floated across the air. When they drew even with the pool, Dylan hesitated.

Casey stopped, looking at the lights and people with smiling faces. "You want to stay here?"

Dylan shrugged, obviously embarrassed. "It's just so…*opposite* of what we've been thinking about. Of this whole week, with Andrea getting killed, and now Brandon."

"Sure." Casey let go of his hand. "Go on. In fact, I see someone you might want to get to know. See that woman sitting off by herself? She's new. Just signed a lease today."

Dylan saw her. "You don't mind?"

"No." She really didn't.

"Okay. I'll be around, though, all right? Come find me later."

"I will if I need to."

She watched as he headed toward the pool, his stride growing stronger the further he got from her.

"Superficial," Death muttered.

"Just young. And he's got an excuse—you missed everything from the past couple of hours. Come on, and I'll tell you about it."

Casey and Death walked past the palm trees to the private beach as she talked. Several couples had the same idea of semi-privacy, either strolling along the edge of the water or lying on blankets.

"So it looks like Maria killed both Brandon and Andrea, and has now taken off with Andrea's man?" Death took a deep breath and blew at the water, causing a wave to crash onto the shore, tinged with ice.

"You said Haiti wasn't pretty. This isn't, either. And I'm having a hard time believing it all. It seems so…complicated. Did Maria know about Andrea, or not? Was Richie going to marry her now? And why did Maria wait so long to kill Andrea after she knew about her? I have all these theories, but none of them really works."

Death conjured up a stone and threw it into the sea. "Remember back on your first day, when Maria stood here and said how un-beautiful things could be? We had no idea what she was really talking about, or how ugly it was going to become for her. For everyone close to her."

Casey stood for several minutes, listening to the waves, trying to erase the movie in her head of Maria pummeling Andrea to death, and stabbing Brandon. Something about the whole scenario was still eluding her. But perhaps that didn't matter anymore. Binns was on the case. She turned back toward the building. "I've had enough. Let's go."

At the pool, Casey spied Del overseeing a table of food. He wore a tall, white chef's hat, and a smile a mile wide. Casey was glad he could start his restaurant free of guilt. She saw other people, too. Vonnie, the gossip, surrounded by a group of women, all talking loudly, each hoping to be heard over the others. Bernie, the older woman who had been one of Brandon's conquests, leaning a little too close to a younger man. Marcus, Casey's Energizer Bunny client, handing a drink with an umbrella to Sissy, who sat on a high stool by a little round table. Sissy caught Casey's eye and held up the drink, as in a toast. Casey didn't respond. It was all too weird. All of these people, back to normal, with Andrea dead less than a week, Brandon gone forever, and Maria's life basically over. But then, none of them even knew about that.

Casey looked a little further and found Tamille with a small cluster of people along the side of the pool, their feet dangling in the water. Casey was going to walk right past, but Tamille spotted her. "Hey, girl! Come have a drink!"

"No, thanks. I'm headed up. I'm exhausted."

"Want some company?"

"No, I'm good, thanks. Enjoy yourself."

Casey continued on into the building. The lobby bar was much more subdued than the pool area, but there were people in small groups, talking quietly over drinks. Jack leaned on the bar, talking to a woman on a stool. Casey smiled when she saw who it was, and walked over. "Hey, you two."

Jack smiled. "Hey, yourself."

Laurie turned and smiled at her. Casey wouldn't say she looked like a new woman, but she was a far cry from the crazed lunatic in the bushes the night before.

Jack held up a glass. "Want a drink?"

"No, thanks. I'm headed upstairs. It's been a long, long week."

Laurie almost met Casey's eyes, but not quite. "I'm sorry about…everything."

"Yeah. Me, too. You've had a rough time, haven't you?"

Laurie's lips twitched, and she sent a quick glance toward Jack before looking back at Casey. "I'm hoping things are about to get better."

"Yes. I hope so, too."

Jack winked at Casey. "I told Laurie here I much prefer talking to women my own age. Those young things don't have enough between their ears to keep me interested. If all someone has to offer is a pretty outside, they're not worth the time it takes to learn more than their name. Someone with some miles under her belt, now, is *much* more interesting." He shot an admiring look at Laurie. "Laurie here has the potential to keep my attention for quite some time."

Laurie blushed prettily, her eyes meeting Jack's.

Jack tore his eyes from hers and nodded toward the other side of the room. "Thought that might interest you, Daisy."

In a darkened corner, Krystal sat with Andrea's parents on a sofa. What looked like a photo album lay open on Mrs. Parker's lap, and Krystal leaned over, pointing at something. Her arm was on the older woman's shoulders, and Mr. Parker looked at the book with the closest Casey had seen him to having animation.

"You know what that's about?"

Jack shook his head. "No idea. None of my business, anyway, is it?"

"Of course not." Casey yawned widely, and covered it with her hand. "Sorry."

"Go get some rest, Daisy. We'll see you tomorrow."

"Right."

Laurie touched her arm. "And maybe we can have that talk about water aerobics sometime?"

Casey smiled. "I'd like that."

She left the two talking, and headed toward the elevator. Krystal looked up as Casey passed, and waved her over. "Thank you."

"For what?"

"This morning. Taking care of me. For forgiving my behavior this week."

"You're welcome."

"And thank you from us, too." Mrs. Parker regarded Casey with watery eyes.

Casey nodded. "You looking at pictures of Andrea?"

"One of her albums." Krystal sat back so Casey could see the pages. Photos of Andrea. Laughing. Smiling. Arms around friends. In the pool. At work.

With Richie.

"So she really was involved with him."

Krystal sniffed. "He's a great guy. Terrible aerobics teacher, but super person. He and Andrea were so perfect for each other. I don't know what he's going to do now."

Casey figured she knew. He would run far away with Maria and her kids, where no one could find them. But one thing still bugged her. She leaned toward Krystal, speaking quietly. "I know about Maria."

Krystal's mouth dropped.

"But I was wondering—did Maria know about Andrea?"

"Of course. She helped get them together in the first place."

That made so much more sense. Maria was older than Richie—not that that seemed to matter here at the Flamingo— and seemed so put together. Casey just couldn't imagine she really had romantic notions about someone like Richie, who seemed so young and inexperienced. "But Richie and Andrea's being engaged—didn't that get in the way of Maria getting citizenship?"

"Of course not. They'd promised her they would stick around until she was set."

"But he couldn't marry her anymore, if he was going to marry Andrea."

Krystal let out a surprised laugh. "He was going to marry *Maria?*"

"Well, wasn't he? I thought that was the best way of securing her place in the US."

"That was never in the plan. Really. Even Richie, with all his good intentions, wasn't going to marry a woman for a green card."

"So what was the plan?"

"He was an advocate. Look, he may not be a fitness guru, but he's got a way with people. He spent hours with the INS, trying to figure out just what Maria needed to be secure."

"So if the whole love triangle thing wasn't a problem, why didn't Andrea go live with them? Why stay here and pretend the whole relationship didn't exist?"

"I asked them the same thing. But as I said, they weren't going to leave without knowing Maria and the kids would be okay, and who knew how long that would take? As long as they were here, it only made sense for Andrea to keep her job. Richie obviously wasn't working, so they needed the money. If Andrea would have moved out, but still worked at the bank, people from here would have seen her, and that could have led them back to Richie, and we know what trouble that would have caused."

"With Sissy."

"Right. The old witch."

Ouch. "But Richie stopped calling Andrea two weeks ago. Why would he do that if Maria knew about her?"

"So the cops identified his number, huh?" Krystal smiled grimly. "Yeah. Someone else identified it, too, and made threats to tell the cops. Or at least tell Sissy."

"Brandon."

Krystal frowned. "Asshole. He just couldn't let anyone do anything good. As one of his final gifts, he assured Maria he'd be keeping tabs on her. If she stopped paying him off, he would go to the authorities. And he would let Sissy know where she could find Richie. He thought he was so smart."

"So Richie really was a good guy."

"Yeah. The best. And Andrea was an even better woman."

Then why on earth would Maria kill Andrea? Brandon, she could see, but to murder a woman who only wanted what was best for Maria and her family? The whole thing felt so wrong.

"So who's that?" Casey pointed at a picture on the far page that showed Andrea with a little girl.

"Oh, her." Krystal shifted in her seat, not saying anything.

Casey recognized the child, and leaned down to talk quietly into Krystal's ear. "She's yours, isn't she?"

Krystal jerked her head up. "What?"

"It's okay. I won't tell anybody."

Krystal's eyes watered. "We only saw her the one time. Andrea helped me find her. We visited, but that was it. It's over. She's happy where she is."

"But she's a secret, isn't she?"

Krystal's lips trembled. "For now, yes. She was…that was a hard time for me."

"I understand." Casey stood back up. "And now I'm going to say goodnight."

"You're not going to tell them we found Andrea's murderer?" Death hovered over the photo album, looking at the photos upside-down. "And that it's the woman who has now set off with Andrea's fiancé?"

Casey shook her head. The Parkers were already back in their own world, looking at photos of their daughter, and the last thing Casey needed was to have them or Krystal freaking out in the lobby. Informing the family was the cops' job, anyway. She'd let Binns and Gomez have that privilege. She turned away, but Krystal grabbed her wrist.

"You'll keep my secret?"

"No one will hear it from me. And Krystal...no one's going to hear it from Brandon, either. You're safe from him."

"Safe?"

Casey was glad to see surprise in Krystal's eyes. Even though Casey was certain Maria had killed him, she was relieved to have confirmation that Krystal was innocent.

"Brandon's...dead."

"*What*? How?"

"Look up the news from last night, about the single man in Birmingham, Florida, who was stabbed to death. But for now, just know your secret is safe."

Krystal's eyes filled, whether with relief or sadness, Casey wasn't sure. "Thank you. *Thank* you, Daisy."

Casey slid her arm from Krystal's grasp and walked toward the stairs.

"Those are three miserable people right there," Death said. "Glad I don't have to hang out with them."

"Right. I'm so much more uplifting and cheerful."

Casey trudged up the service stairs toward her room, thinking of all of the people at the pool, and in the bar. All of the people in this community who were connecting, interacting with each other, even if it was like high school, all over again. She wanted only to get inside her apartment, turn out all the lights, and climb under her covers.

And call her brother.

Oh, Ricky. Why does this have to be so hard?

She went into her apartment, stripped off her clothes, and crawled into bed. And couldn't sleep.

"What's the problem?" Death sat propped up against the headboard on the opposite side of the bed.

"It just feels so wrong. Richie and Andrea were trying to help. Trying to make sure Maria and her children were safe. How did it turn out so badly? What made Maria turn on them?"

"Life isn't all tied up neatly, I'm afraid." Death sounded tired. "It's a mystery to me why the Big Kahuna chose to let people run free in the first place. It would have been so much *simpler* to just tell them what to do. No war. No starvation. No oppression."

"No cars being built badly so they explode on impact."

Death sighed heavily. "My job would be very different, I suppose. Every death would be expected. Old age. Surrounded by loved ones, in the home. Plenty of time to make amends, show love, clean out the attic. All nice and neat." Death paused. "But then, the world would be overrun with people. Kind of like the whole thing about prey and predator in the wild. When the predator population decreases, the prey increases, and they end up starving to death, or being forced out of their territory because there are too many critters."

"So people are like wild animals?"

"Well, yes, in a lot of ways. But you have a few things most animals don't."

"And what are those?"

"Opposable thumbs. Literacy. Compassion."

"Compassion." Casey sat up and rolled out of bed.

"What did I say?"

"I told Krystal that Brandon is no longer a threat, but I haven't let others know."

"They'll find out soon enough."

"But I have the ability to tell them *now*."

"Okay, okay. If it means we'll get some sleep later."

Casey pulled her clothes back on and went out to the vent to grab Brandon's files. "Let's make some deliveries."

"Binns is going to be mad if you don't give her those folders."

"Let her."

Together she and Death were able to find most of the women listed on the files. Only a few of them were home, and while Casey wasn't exactly received with warmth—they were embarrassed at being conned, after all—she could see the relief in their eyes. She gave each of them Detective Binns' contact information, telling them that while she wasn't sure they could get a return of any of their money, they could give it a shot. This approach was better than giving Binns the information. The women could make their own choice this way. The ones who weren't home would return to a file shoved under their door, with a note saying they were free. Casey hoped this would be enough to ease their minds.

"Only one left." Casey held up Sissy's file. "I'd kind of like to give her this in person."

"She was out at the pool being courted by Marcus, remember?"

"Hmm. I hate to interrupt if he's getting somewhere."

"But it might make her a little more receptive to know her problems with Brandon are a thing of the past. At least financially. Maybe not heart-wise. But we can't do anything about that."

"You're right. Let's just have a peek and see if she's still there."

Casey and Death walked back toward the Flamingo from the Pelican, where they'd made their last drop off. Sissy was not in sight at the pool, and neither was Marcus.

"Well," Death said. "The man does quick work."

"They probably just went somewhere quieter to talk."

"Whatever you want to think."

"I know what I *don't* want to think, and that's about them going off to do something else." Casey shuddered. "I've had enough close up viewing of that this week."

"So what now?"

"I really don't feel like going back to the Palm and figuring out where she lives. Let's check her office."

It was after midnight now, but the bar was still hopping. Open till two on the weekends. Krystal and Andrea's parents were gone, but Laurie still sat at the end of the bar. Jack filled some orders, then sauntered back to talk with her. Casey couldn't help but feel just a little proud they seemed to be hitting it off.

"Office is dark," Death said.

"Let's see where we could leave it."

Her key got her into the receptionist's area—where Maria would never return—but not into Sissy's office.

"Well, I guess shoving it under the door will have to do. I really don't want to keep this until morning."

"Go for it."

Casey squeezed the pack under the door, using a ruler from Maria's desk to make sure it was all the way under. "There." She brushed her hands against each other. "Mission accomplished."

"*Now* can we go to bed?"

"Either that or pack."

"We're leaving?"

"On a jet plane."

"Really?"

"No, not really. But that's how the song goes. *I'm leaving*—"

"*—on a jet plane.* I know, I know. I'm the one who's good at these things. Not you. That's why you have to use such an old reference."

"Goodnight. Go away. See you tomorrow."

Death clapped. "Is that an invitation?"

"No." Casey tromped up the service stairs to her room—*sans* Death, thank goodness—and unlocked the door. She stepped into the entryway, slid her shoes off, and turned to flip on the light.

"Freeze!" someone yelled.

Casey did. She held her arms out in front of her, hoping whoever was there would hesitate before shooting her. At least that's what she assumed they were going to do. Usually the command to *freeze* was given when the person was holding a gun.

"Take three steps back." It was a woman's voice, shaking and low.

Casey considered the distance to the still-open door. Could she make it out before bullets ripped into her back? She was at least five feet from the hallway. Plenty of space for someone to shoot her. The woman wouldn't even have to have good aim, not at that distance. *Run*, Casey told herself. She turned her head slowly, trying to see what was going on behind her.

"I said freeze! And take three steps back!"

Kind of contradictory, but Casey was in no position to argue. She stepped back, hoping the woman's nervousness wouldn't cause her to pull the trigger without meaning to.

Casey tripped, steadying herself on her table. The table's chair was upended, its leg in Casey's way, and the entryway rug had been crumpled and tossed to the side. Casey took the last two steps, ending up at the front of the living room, even farther from the door and freedom.

"Now, turn around, nice and slow, hands up."

Casey turned, and as she did, she saw that her apartment had been torn apart, reminiscent of Maria's house, only far worse. The furniture was overturned, the curtains ripped off their hangers, and silverware and broken plates littered the little she could see of the kitchen. Casey's eyes flicked to her hidey-hole vent. The cover still lay unmolested against the wall.

Her eyes finally landed on Sissy, who stood in the middle of the living room, pointing a gun at Casey.

Sissy? But she was with Marcus, being charmed by his love and enthusiasm.

Wasn't she?

Casey held her hands out in front of her. "It's okay, Sissy. It's all right."

"No, Daisy. It's not." Her hand shook.

"Sissy. Let's talk a little bit."

"I'm done talking! Move over here!" She jerked the gun toward the overturned couch, and Casey picked her way slowly across the floor, over and around chairs and kitchen utensils. She should run. Take off. Like she'd told her class. But she couldn't, not with Sissy holding a gun four feet from her face. And not with Casey's things—her ID, Omar's hat, her other treasures—held hostage. Not with the high likelihood that Sissy would bring attention here to this place, and Casey's true identity would be discovered. And not when Casey could bring down this woman with a few well-aimed strikes.

"What do you want?" Sissy screeched.

Casey was confused. "Nothing. I don't want anything."

Sissy's face darkened. "Oh, sure. That's what your little stunt with the folders tells me. Oh, yes, the women called me. I suppose my folder is tucked under my apartment door, too?"

"Actually, I put it in your office."

"Of course. The women said you'd been around. They all sounded so happy that you were there, handing the information back, saying we're all free. Photos. Newspaper articles. Bank accounts. Until tomorrow. Who are you going to tell then, Daisy? How soon will you be making your demands? Why can't you people just leave us alone? First…" She swallowed loudly. "First Brandon. Now you. Can't a woman just start over? Do it right the second time?"

"Sissy, I gave the folders back so you could destroy them. I'm not going to use them *against* you."

Sissy's face crumpled, her gun hand dropping slowly toward the floor. Casey made sure she had her balance and took a step closer, getting in range to grab Sissy's arm. Sissy swung her hand up, the gun barely missing Casey face. Casey stumbled backward, tripped over a pillow, and fell.

"You're just like him, aren't you? You could let it go, allow me to move on, but you won't. You want to drain me dry. Why? Why can't you just let me be?"

Casey scooted back, crab-like, until she was at her balcony door. Maybe this hadn't been such a good idea to stay instead of bolting out the door. She was tired. Tired of thinking, and tired of tragedy. And now she was tired and *trapped*. If she could just get the sliding door open, she could roll out. She'd seen that first day how she could swing to a neighboring balcony, and escape. There was no way Sissy could follow, in her state, and it would be much harder to shoot a target swinging from one balcony to another. Casey reached up toward the handle of the door, remembering too late the dowel rod in the sliding track which would keep the door from opening.

"Don't move!" Sissy screamed. "Please…please don't move." She sobbed and lurched forward, the gun just out of Casey's reach. "Where are your copies? I couldn't find them when Brandon lived here, either—where do you people hide your dirty, awful papers?"

"Sissy, I swear, I'm not blackmailing you. I don't have my own copy. I gave you the only one."

"But I thought I'd *already* destroyed the only one. And then you come at me with another." She shuddered. "I'm sure *she* knew where it was. But she wouldn't tell me, either." Her eyes were wild. "So I made sure she couldn't tell anyone anymore. She couldn't be in it with him. Not for one more day."

Casey's breath hitched. "Who are you talking about, Sissy?"

"Andrea, of course, the little slut. Taking my man. Taking Brandon. My sweet Brandon."

"But Brandon was *blackmailing* you."

"No, not once he got to know me. He gave me what he had on me. Told me to burn it. And I *did*. *She* must have had another copy. But now it's too late to know. I should have waited."

"Sissy. What did you do to Andrea? Did you…are *you* the one who killed her?"

Of *course* Maria hadn't done it. That solution had felt wrong all along. Richie and Andrea had promised to *help* her. And Maria had gotten Richie and Andrea together in the first place. Richie loved *Andrea*. It wasn't a love triangle. It was a triangle of *friends*.

Maria hadn't killed Andrea.

The cops were chasing after an innocent woman.

A tear rolled down Sissy's cheek. "Andrea took my *man*."

Sissy's gun hand again sank toward the floor as she cried. Casey slowly tipped up onto her feet, into a squat position. "Sissy, you did all that planning to get Andrea? The security cameras, and Maria's key?"

The gun rose again. "That was all easy. Maria keeps an extra key in her desk, and our security isn't exactly high tech. I just wanted to talk to Andrea. To tell her Brandon was mine. That he wasn't going to blackmail me anymore, so she should forget him."

Casey balanced on the balls of her feet, ready to spring up at the first opportunity. "So you lured Krystal away from the aerobics room. You sent her a fake note from the guard."

"I knew she couldn't ignore an opportunity to screw somebody, especially that hot little number." Sissy's eyes went unfocused, as if she were thinking of Krystal, and what she and the guard might have gotten up to. Her hand dropped a fraction, and Casey lunged forward. She grabbed Sissy's wrist, lowered her head, and rammed Sissy in the gut with her shoulder, sending her back several steps, like she was sacking a quarterback.

Sissy screamed, clawing Casey in the back of the neck. Casey reared up and headbutted Sissy in the chin. Blood spurted from Sissy's lip, spraying into Casey's eyes. Casey jerked her head away, and Sissy twisted the gun toward Casey. Casey tried to gain some traction, but slid on a sofa cushion and fell backward. Sissy threw herself on top of her, howling. Casey raised her foot just in time to catch Sissy's ribs on her way down, and Sissy jerked hard sending the gun clattering to the floor. Sissy lunged for the gun while Casey reached down and yanked out the dowel rod that braced the balcony door. Sissy swung the gun toward her, and Casey smacked her with the rod, hitting her wrist and sending the gun flying backward, into the entryway.

Sissy scrambled toward the gun, beating Casey there, and raised it, aiming at Casey's heart. Casey froze.

"I didn't mean to kill her," Sissy sobbed. "I didn't *want* to kill her. I just…" She wiped her nose with her sleeve. "I just wanted to scare her. To get her to leave him alone! Leave my Brandon *alone!*"

Casey eyed Sissy and the gun. There was no way she could reach Sissy before she got a shot off. No way Casey could reach down and pick up anything to throw, or dodge behind something that could protect her. Nothing there would stop a bullet. There was a good chance Sissy would miss, if she did shoot, but then the bullet might go right out the window, hitting someone down at the pool.

Casey decided to just stay still and talk, hoping she could find an opening to strike. "So what made you go after Andrea that night?"

Sissy blinked away tears. Casey couldn't help but think Sissy's bright blue outfit had the opposite of its usual effect. Instead of making Sissy look like a fresh, vibrant blueberry, she looked old and pale. Tired. Washed out.

"That day," Sissy said. "Before class. They were talking about who had spent time in this apartment. I wasn't surprised about Laurie, of course, I knew she was in love with Brandon. I wasn't surprised about Krystal, either. She screws anything that moves. But Andrea? Why was Krystal trying to cover up the fact that Andrea knew this apartment? It could only be...it could only be because Andrea was in love with Brandon, too." She sobbed. "And then to find out later that she was *engaged* to him!"

Her gun hand shook so much Casey was ready to hit the ground. If only she could get a step closer she could disarm her.

"I just wanted to talk to her," Sissy said. "I was sure if I told her he and I were in love she would back off. She was always so nice. But she kept lying. Saying she wasn't involved with him. Saying she didn't even *like* him. That she hadn't seen or heard anything from him since he'd left. Why did she lie to me? Why?"

"Sissy, about that engagement—"

"She wouldn't listen to me. She turned her *back* on me, saying I needed to get a hold of myself, and she would talk to me when I was calmer. The nerve! I left her and sat in the office—your office, I mean. I tried to calm down, but I just got madder and madder."

She looked mad now, and not just in the angry sense. Casey was ready to move closer when Sissy blinked and focused on her again. "So I grabbed one of those weights by the desk, and went back. She was in the shower area then. Her back was still turned. I was going to talk some more, but I was *so angry*. So I hit her. I hit her, and hit her, and hit her." She chopped with the gun, as if she were demonstrating. "Until she was just lying there. Staring up at me. Just staring."

Her eyes flicked up to Casey's, and she steadied the gun. "I didn't mean to do it. I didn't. All I wanted was for Brandon to love *me* and not her. And I realized then that he would. She wouldn't be in the way anymore. So I told him…he couldn't have her. She was dead. He had to come back to me."

Casey's breath hitched. "You told Brandon Andrea was dead?"

"He needed to know so he could move on. Back to me."

"You knew where Brandon *was*?"

"Of course I knew," Sissy said. "I put him there."

It suddenly all made sense. Dylan's theory about a Sugar Mama. It was true. And the Mama was Sissy.

"Sissy. When did you tell him this?"

Her lips trembled. "Yesterday."

Oh, God. Yesterday. The day he died. "You told him you killed her?"

"Of course not. Just that she was dead."

"And what did he say?"

"He said he wasn't engaged to her. *He* wouldn't tell me the truth, either. Even then, even after she was dead. All that time I'd been worried about him wanting Krystal, and I had no idea it was Andrea. The one woman here I *liked*. And neither of them would tell me the truth."

"Sissy, they weren't—"

"I was there, at his apartment, cooking him supper. *Cooking* for him. And he told me he would be staying only long enough to get his things together, his papers, his money, and then he would be *gone*."

"Without you."

"Of *course* without me!" Her eyes shone. "I was making dinner for him, in the apartment *I* was paying for, and he told me I was nothing to him. *Nothing*." Her grip tightened on the gun, her knuckles white. "He came into the kitchen, and I ..." She gasped, tears choking her.

"You stabbed him, didn't you?"

"Just once, at first, just a little. And then again. And again. He was so surprised. Blood went everywhere. All over the counter, and the food, and my...my clothes. He begged me to help him. To save him. But it was too late. Too late." She took a shuddering breath.

"I'm sorry, Sissy. I'm so sorry. Can you put the gun down now?"

She swept it up, pointing it straight at Casey again. "And now you know. But you knew already, didn't you? That's why you want to continue his work. Blackmail me some more. Because that's what people like you do."

"Sissy, I do not want to blackmail you. I was bringing you the folder so you could get *rid* of it."

She was crying in earnest now. Tears streamed down her face. "It doesn't matter. Not anymore. Brandon doesn't love me. He never loved me. He loves *her*. He loves her." She dissolved into sobs, keeping the gun trained on Casey.

"Sissy. Sissy, listen. Listen!"

Sissy hiccupped, the gun wavering dangerously.

Casey put her hands out, as if that could protect her if the gun went off. "Sissy, they were telling you the truth."

Her forehead wrinkled. "About what?"

"About not being engaged."

Her grip tightened on the gun. "But I heard her parents say it. They said she was engaged. That two weeks ago something happened and she stopped speaking about him. Two weeks ago Brandon left."

"Yes, I know. But Andrea wasn't engaged to him. She was engaged to *Richie*."

Sissy's face went blank, and then paled so quickly she looked like she was going to faint. "Richie? The little…but I told him he couldn't come anywhere near here, or I would sue him for everything. He was so…"

"He was a scapegoat. When people got injured you had to have someone to blame, didn't you, Sissy? He may have been unqualified, but he wasn't malicious. He only wanted to do good."

"But I'd hired him. If people looked too closely…Andrea was engaged to *him*? Not my Brandon?"

Still on about *her* Brandon. Even after she'd killed him.

"But that means Brandon was telling me the truth. He wasn't going to marry her. He must have loved me! He loves me, after all!" Her face lit up, and she looked over Casey's shoulder, out toward the ocean, and the pool.

Casey leapt forward, her hand swinging up to push Sissy's gun hand away, but Sissy saw her, and her finger was tightening on the trigger, and—

"Hi-yah!" A flattened hand arced through the air, chopping Sissy at the base of her neck. Sissy gave a startled grunt, and collapsed, dropping the gun. Tamille stood in the entryway, hands on her hips, like a superhero. All that was missing was the cape.

Several moments passed before Casey was able to speak. "Tamille?"

Tamille showed all of those shiny white teeth and nudged the unconscious Sissy with her toe. "Good thing I decided to ignore your plea for solitude, isn't it?"

Casey slumped onto the bottom of the overturned easy chair. "Company does have its good points."

Tamille looked at the woman lying at her feet. "Want to explain?"

"Huh-uh."

"Didn't think so. But I do suppose this is something for the cops?"

"Most definitely."

Tamille smiled again and pulled out her phone. "So how about I go ahead and call them?"

"You do that. But do you mind calling from the hallway? I have something I need to take care of."

Tamille looked around at the destroyed furniture and shrugged. "Whatever. Just don't do anything more to Sissy. She should be out until long after the police get here."

"I won't hurt her. I promise."

Tamille went out into the hallway, but didn't close the door. Casey hoped she wouldn't see what she was about to do.

"What is going on here?" Death suddenly stood just inside the balcony door. "Did I miss all the excitement *again*? And what is Sissy doing here?"

"Long story short—she killed Andrea and Brandon."

Death about choked. "Seriously?"

Casey took off the air conditioning vent cover and pulled out Maria's folder, the only one that was left.

"You're getting those ready to give to the cops *now*?"

Casey held up the file. "You know how we all figured Maria was the killer, and sent the cops off chasing her?"

"Yeah."

"Like I just told you—she didn't do it."

"Right. So?"

"Think about it. She's out there, on the run from the cops—or the INS, anyway—trying to keep her kids safe, as well as this man who just lost his fiancée and thinks he will get taken to court if he shows up anywhere near here. He can't even mourn her properly."

"What does that have to do with her papers?"

Casey shook her head. "You don't get it, do you? What's the difference between her and me?"

"You're actually a citizen? She's got two kids? She has a friend? She's not intimately acquainted with *moi*?"

"Okay. So there are differences. But we're both..." She worked to form the word. "Fugitives. We're wanted by the law. We have no place to call home. No...no stability."

"So what are you going to do?"

"I'm going to give her a head start."

Casey pulled everything out of the folder, from the expired green card to the failed citizenship applications to the attempts to bring over Maria's family, ripped the papers into tiny little pieces, and flushed them down the toilet.

Chapter Thirty-two

"At least Sissy didn't break the skin," Tamille said. "Who knows what diseases she's carrying with the kind of company she kept."

They were in Casey's office. Casey sat on the examination table, while Tamille doused the shallow claw marks on the back of her neck with antiseptic, just in case. Binns sat with one hip on the desk, Gomez leaned against the whirlpool, and Death stood just inside the door. The room was packed.

"So I guess we were all wrong about Maria," Binns said.

"Way wrong." Casey waved Tamille away so she could pull the shoulder of her shirt back up and not feel so exposed in front of Gomez. "But even now I can't believe how it turned out. All of it about a guy who really wasn't worth it."

"Oh, what a tangled web a blackmailing, unethical scamp weaves," Death said.

Casey sighed heavily, feeling exhaustion from her head to her toes.

"You going to be okay, Daisy?" Gomez' voice was gentle, and Casey wasn't the only woman to look at him with interest. He colored slightly, and stood a little straighter. "What? I can't be concerned?"

Binns gave her head a little shake. "Thank you for all you did, Ms. Gray. And you, Ms. Jackson."

Casey nodded, and Tamille held out her fist for Binns to bump it. Binns looked at it for a moment, and left Tamille hanging. "Now we need to follow Mrs. Williams to the station. It's going to be a long night."

"One final thing." Casey slid off the table and grabbed a paper from the desk. "While you were taking care of things earlier, I wrote out my statement. Will this be enough?"

Binns looked it over. "You've signed it. Dated it."

"And got the signatures of two witnesses." Tamille had signed it, and had threatened Dylan into it, as well. Even though Casey had promised him Tamille wouldn't kill him and throw his body in a ditch, he was still scared of her. Rightfully so.

"All the details are here?"

"Everything I could remember."

Binns nodded. "I'll go over it. I may need some things clarified, but this is a good start."

Casey hoped it was more than that, since it would be all Binns would ever get.

"And the blackmail folders?"

"I gave them back to the women they belonged to."

Binns stared at her.

"I figured the guy's dead, what else is there to do?"

"Ms. Gray, it is not your place to—"

"I gave them all your contact information, okay? Told them that if they want to try to get their assets back they could call you. They can't press charges anymore, right? Not with him dead?"

Binns took a deep breath through her nose and let it out slowly. "You're right. But we'll need to talk more about this. Another time."

"All right."

Binns' phone rang, and she looked at the screen. "I've gotta take this." She held out her hand, and Casey shook it. "We'll be in touch. Binns here." She turned away and walked out of the room, right through Death. She shivered visibly, but kept walking.

Tamille looked at Gomez, who was staring at Casey. "Well," Tamille said to Casey, "I'll see you later."

Casey's throat constricted for more than the fact that she would probably never see her again. "Where are you going? Why are you leaving?"

"It's late, and I've gotta be up early for a session at the *dojo*. Besides, I think you have something else you need to do." Tamille smirked. "Don't stay up too late now."

"But—"

"Officer Gomez, it's been a pleasure."

He was like a deer in the headlights, with wider eyes.

Tamille scooted out of the room, instinctively skirting Death.

Casey looked at Death in a panic, and Death grinned. "He's all yours, honeybun. Don't overanalyze the situation, okay? Just...let it be."

And Death was gone.

Casey and Gomez stared at each other for several very long seconds.

"I guess I'll be going, then," Gomez said.

"Yes, of course."

Neither of them moved.

"Binns will need me."

"Sure."

Gomez took a step toward her, and then he was kissing her, his lips soft and warm, so gentle, so sweet. Casey slid her hands up his chest to the back of his neck. His arms went around her waist, pulling her closer, his chest solid against her trembling. Casey ran her fingers into his hair, pulling his head closer, until she thought she couldn't breathe. Couldn't stand anymore. His lips, his warmth, his strength.

And then they parted, his arms releasing her as her hands slid back down his chest and away.

"Goodnight, Daisy Gray," he said.

"Goodnight, Officer Gomez."

He searched her eyes with his own, then turned and walked away. Even after he had disappeared, and the door to the men's locker room had clicked quietly shut, Casey stood, watching the way he had gone.

"Good-bye, Manny," she whispered.

And she went upstairs to retrieve her bag from the vent.

Chapter Thirty-three

"Don Westbrook."

"Don? It's Casey."

"Oh, thank *God* you called. Where have you *been*?"

"Don, what is it?"

"Casey…it's Ricky."

Oh, God. Death nowhere to be found. Nowhere near, making smart comments. Where was Death?

Where was Death?

"Ricky's in trouble, Casey."

No time to consider. No time to even think.

"I'll be there, Don. Tell him to hold on. Tell him…tell him I'm coming home."

To receive a free catalog of Poisoned Pen Press titles, please contact us in one of the following ways:

Phone: 1-800-421-3976
Facsimile: 1-480-949-1707
Email: info@poisonedpenpress.com
Website: www.poisonedpenpress.com

Poisoned Pen Press
6962 E. First Ave. Ste. 103
Scottsdale, AZ 85251